DECEITFUL TRUTHS

The Caspian Wine Suspense Thriller Series

Maggie Thom

QUADESSENCE PRESS

First Edition: Published 2017

Revised Edition: 2025

Published by: Quadessence Press

Editing: P. Terrell (P.I.S.C.E.S)

Cover Design: GMT Books

Images: DepositPhotos & Canva

ISBN: 978-0-9917272-6-1

Paperback

Read to Escape... Escape to Read...

To the stories that refused easy answers...

Chapter 1

SHE OPENED HER EYES. Or at least she thought she had, that was her intent... but everything was black. Maybe it was still dark out. She tried again, and this time there was a fuzzy blur... a shadow... a stray bit of light... and a voice... but as quickly as it all came, it disappeared.

Sometime later, she became aware of sounds and sensations. Everything was still dark. She had no sense of who or where she was. There was a feeling of being but not of knowing anything else. It was just blank. Something brushed over her body that was light and delicate. She recoiled inside, pulling back, trying to shrink more into the deep, dark hole that seemed to be her companion. Fear wrapped her in its cloak like a living, breathing monster, capturing her in a net she felt unable to escape.

A very distant part of her brain screamed at her to get the hell away... to move... to do something... but it was so far away, so faint. Desperation clawed at her, but she couldn't grasp what it was telling her to do or why it was there. The panic, which had been so remote a moment ago, was suddenly all there was. The harder she fought it, the more she plunged down the dark well. There was no sensation of self; no meaning of who she was. There was a heaviness pressing her down, keeping her immobile, but beyond that gloomy little hole, there were only slivers of something sinister.

She made a sound—or at least she thought it came from her—but when she couldn't repeat it; she wasn't sure. Something moved, maybe even touched her. There was a tiny sense of pain, but then it receded, taking the anxiousness with it... then there was nothing.

Sounds filtered into her little world.

"Now... do it."

"She's..."

Only snippets of their words drifted into her consciousness. She wanted to ask what the two men were talking about? Who they were talking about? And where was she? Who was she?

She wanted to call out but remembered the last time she'd attempted a sound, everything had disappeared. It was better to keep quiet. She waited. Gradually, things started to become clearer.

She was lying spread-eagled on a bed; at least that was her assumption as underneath her was something soft and cushiony. Cool air brushed over her skin. It was the first time she actually knew she was naked. Her first instinct was to cover herself, but when she tried to lift her arms, they felt pinned. Weighted. They wouldn't move. Everything felt fastened down, although she couldn't feel any restraints. Her entire being felt heavy, lethargic.

Everything was a blur. Had she gotten drunk? Passed out? As hard as she tried to remember, anything that might have had any meaning seemed to dance at the far edges of the darkness surrounding her.

There was a sound. It was soft and unidentifiable. And gone. Focusing on her hearing, she waited patiently, searching for anything that would thrust her out of this fog.

This time, words.

"...leave..."

"Why... seen her..."

"Go."

"... just... pregnant." *Who?* Taking a chance that this time she'd be able to see, she opened her eyes. There were shadows, but then something moved into her line of vision. It was a shape—no, a blob, a blurry thing. She tried hard to focus, but everything was whitish-gray, meshing together in various shades. What was real? What wasn't?

More came into focus. It was a body... a big shape... a man? The strain of looking was too much. Her heavy eyelids closed.

There was a prick of something in her hip. It hurt, but the words wouldn't come, so she was unable to tell him. There was an odd sensation of something cold... sterile... entering her body... It wasn't natural. It shouldn't have been happening. Her mind limply gave her a command: to fight. But she felt locked in place, unable to move.

What was happening to her? The only thought that seemed to be getting through was to run, but it didn't matter what she tried to do; nothing happened. Her body felt separate from her; no longer under her control.

"Ssssh. It's okay. It's okay. You're not alone. Casp... 2011 814 CW. Got that?"

Whether that's what the man really said to her, she wasn't sure, but she held onto the kindness with which those words were spoken, as her world went dark once more.

****

"So?"

"So, it's done."

"Good. Good. This time it had better be a boy."

"You have a son."

"He's gay."

"He's eight."

"He's gay."

"You have several daughters."

"Not the same. I need a son. There will be no question about what role my heir will get to play in this world. Old school still trumps modern times. An heir is always male. Don't worry. I won't make the same mistake twice. The child will be with his mother until he's two, and then he's mine. I'll raise him and teach him. He'll know right from wrong. And he will right all the wrongs that have been done against me."

The doctor gathered his belongings and strode to the door.

"If you're successful this time, this should be our last meeting, Doctor. I should have a healthy baby boy by spring."

The doctor left without a word.

****

Vancouver Sun, June 25, 2012

Doctor Simon Bretton, a well-respected and dedicated obstetrician/gynecologist, died in a freak accident yester day...

CHAPTER 2

"BOBBIE? IT'S TARIN."

"Tarin? Oh, my god. Where are you? How'd you find me?" That soon gave way to sobs.

"Oh Bobbie. I've missed you." Tarin fought hard to keep her emotions in check. It had been easy to locate her friend, thanks to social media. She'd wanted to reach out for a long time but hadn't been sure how she'd be received. It hadn't mattered that they'd been best friends as kids and as teenagers; sometimes things couldn't be forgotten... or forgiven. If she hadn't been desperate, she probably wouldn't have contacted Bobbie. But Tarin needed her and had no one else to turn to.

It made her the worst friend. Her shoulders sagged wearily at the thought of calling someone whom she hadn't seen in almost twelve years to ask for her help. It meant asking so much of her friend but sharing very little with her. Not that she could tell Bobbie much anyway, because there was still so much she didn't know herself.

Pushing away her depressing thoughts, she pulled her attention back to her friend and her rapid-fire questions.

"Where are you now? I've thought of you so often, wondering what happened to you. What have you been up to? How's your father? You're still working for him? He doesn't know you called me though, right? I'm still in Toronto. Well, in that general area. God, I've missed you. I've wanted to call you so many times but, well, you—"

"I know, and I missed you too. I wasn't sure whether you'd want to talk to me." She could clearly picture her beautiful, big brown eyes that had always made her feel so warm and welcome.

"Oh, Tarin."

It sounded as if she was trying to muffle some sounds. "Bobbie?"

"Where are you now?"

She bit her lip. "Hey, I'm coming out eas—uh, out there and was wondering if you knew of a place I could rent? A two-bedroom would be great."

"Uh, where exactly do you want to live? I'm sure there is something in Forrest Hill, Bloorwest Village—"

"Nope, too ritzy. I want something low-key, nice, and with cheap rent. Well, you know, something reasonable for a good, quiet neighborhood."

"Oh? Really? What's going on? Your dad will have a fit when he finds out."

"I don't intend for him to find out."

"Things finally blew up between you. I figured this would happen one day. I knew you'd blow a gasket when you found out. In fact, I can't believe you're talking—"

"What are you talking about?"

There was a moment of complete silence. "Well.. . nothing... I mean... I'm sorry to hear about your dad's problems."

Tarin was certain she'd changed the subject, but she sure had gotten her attention. "What problems?"

"His business is being audited. He's spitting mad about it."

"You keep in touch with him?"

There was a bit of hesitation before Bobbie answered, "Uh... no. He was ranting in the newspaper about your family, especially your grandfather."

"Oh that. I think the threat of audits happen in big business, right?" Though she had no idea what Bobbie was talking about, she'd check the news for stories about his business. At one time, she'd read everything there was to know about C-Lite Hotels. She'd planned on being in charge of them one day, but that had all died a quiet death.

"I don't know. Anyway, I'll see what I can find for you. Nothing is really cheap, but Richmond Hill and Pickering are probably your best bet. Is there any place in particul ar...?"

"Just some place I can rent. Affordable."

"Uh... I have a house in Vaughn with a basement suite that's going to be available soon. Would that work? At least for starters?"

"That would be great. I need it by the end of the week, though."

"No problem. I'll make sure it's ready by tomorrow."

"If it's going to cause—"

"It's not. Don't worry, softy; the person moving out will be fine. Glad to see some things haven't changed. I've so missed you."

"Thank you. Me too."

"I guess, well, I figured when your dad yanked you from school and refused to let me see you that you—"

"Let's not go through all that old stuff. So, how are you doing?"

"Good. Life is good. Nothing to complain about, as my grandmother would say. You never met her, did you? She passed away a few years ago. I still miss her. She was quick as a whip at ninety-three."

"No, I never met her. She sounds nice. How's your mom?"

"Oh, good. She's Mom. Doesn't change. Busy. Still trying to look eighteen at fifty-eight. Still dating men half her age and flipping through them like underwear."

Tarin burst out laughing. "I'm sorry. I shouldn't find that funny..." Her mom's need to look years younger was why Bobbie had always been a little heavier than she needed to be, and at only five foot two, it hadn't taken much for her to appear overweight.

"Don't worry, I'm not offended. I've about had it with cleaning up her messes. Anyway, forget about her. How about you? What are you up to? Did you ever find your moth—sorry; forget it."

"My mom? No, but I'm still looking." She didn't bother sharing that she had checked into adoption and government agencies on the off chance that someone might be looking for her.

"Do you really think she's alive? Your dad said—"

"He said she died when I was born, but it wouldn't be the first lie he's told me. Forget it. It's dumb, I know." Tarin grabbed a strand of long hair and tugged on it. It was odd talking with someone with whom she'd once shared every secret but now felt as if she couldn't—and she didn't know why. "I'm, uh, changing careers. I'm looking at... some data entry. Should be a good challenge for me, you know me and computers."

"Isn't that the truth? Remember in school, I had to hack into your English exam to change the mark and give you the one you deserved."

"I do." Bobbie had always been there for her. "I'm leaving the day after tomorrow. I'm going to rent a car in Montreal and drive out—"

"So you're in Montreal. It's six to maybe an eight-hour drive—depending on how you drive. It'll give us plenty of time to catch up."

"I can't—"

"You can, and I will."

Tarin chuckled along with Bobbie. It had always been that way between them. Bobbie always got her way. "Okay. But I need a car seat for a two-year-old."

"Awesome. You have a child? Boy or girl?"

"Boy."

"Does your dad know?"

"Uh—no and I want it to stay that way."

"When he finds out—he always wanted a son."

"I know. He just can't find out. Not right now."

She didn't ask any more questions, but Tarin knew that she would, eventually. For now, it was enough to know she was okay with it. Time dropped away, and they were two teenagers at boarding school experiencing true friendship. The lack of contact hadn't changed the bond they had.

"Remember Anna and Stacy?"

"Oh, my God. Those two tormented me every day. I know it was that witch Stacy who put gum in my hair."

"Yeah, I think so too, but putting those frogs in her boots was priceless."

They reminisced about many of the silly things they had done. It felt good, especially since she hadn't thought about any of it since the day she'd left twelve years before.

"So what are you doing now?" Tarin asked.

"Oh, nothing much. Mom keeps me busy."

"Did you ever get married?"

"No. Well... there are some things you need to know, but I'll share all that when you get here. I don't want to bore you with my news. So, what's new with you? I guess that was a stupid question. Obviously, something or you wouldn't be coming out here on the sly with a young child."

"Uh, yeah. A few things happening in my life, too. I guess we have a bit to catch up on."

"It's been a while. Almost half of our lives have been apart."

"I hadn't thought of it like that."

They talked for a few more minutes, but it had become somewhat strained as the years apart started to show. Tarin really didn't care to share what was going on in her life, and she had the feeling Bobbie was holding back too. After she hung up, she wondered why she hadn't told her the truth about her career or where she lived. Or why she'd felt the need to fly into Montreal, when it would have made more sense to fly straight to Toronto. From the moment she'd made the decision to leave, a niggling voice cautioned her to be careful and to keep her true plans quiet, at least until she knew who she could trust.

Setting down her phone, the tears she'd been holding back poured down her face. Silently, she watched her son dance like his favorite cartoon characters were doing on television. He was grinning from ear to ear. It warmed her heart to see him so happy. Maybe he could teach her about having fun.

CHAPTER 3

"HEY, HOW ARE WE doing with that ad to hire a new tech assistant?"

"Just fine there, boss. Hyuh. Hyuh," Graham said.

"Oh man, who knew when we went into business together, I'd have to deal with the Bugs Bunny troop, well, at least Goofy." Guy shook his head.

"Well, one of us has to stay sane; the other one's getting hitched."

"Happily getting married."

"Yeah, I don't know if those two words go together." He laughed outright when Guy flipped him the bird. "All right, I'll quit ribbing you. I really am happy for you. Bailey's a hell of a catch. Not sure she got the same deal."

He grinned at Guy's response. Figuring he'd bugged him enough, he got back to business. "We have a few applicants but nothing very exciting. I haven't checked in a couple of days, been busy going back through that ingenious tax fraud scam we looked into a year or so ago."

"Do the cops have enough to charge him?"

"Yes and no. He'd been doing taxes for the past eight years in this little out-of-the-way town, a place small enough that everyone was thrilled to have him plus close enough to other towns to draw in a large customer base. And it was far enough north to tap into a region with high-income people that needed income tax expertise. So when this guy came along and greatly reduced their tax liabilities, no one looked too closely at how he was doing it. He had a huge client base. They figured he made about four million, although they've only been able to track about three and a half. Not bad pay." Graham showed Guy his report.

"Christ. He was doing their taxes, filing them on time but then claiming he'd received a government notice that they owed a bit more because of some new law or some such thing. He skewed the tax laws just enough for each client, and he always had the cheques sent to himself. When he'd cut them a cheque, he'd of course take about ten percent. Crazy. Do the cops need more evidence to tie him to it?"

"Yeah. He was selective in the ones he embezzled—obviously the ones who knew little about tax law. Reminds me of someone else. You?"

"Yeah, it sounds like something my dear old Uncle Geoff would have been involved in if he wasn't dead. Anyway, let's not go there. Let's get to work, see what we find."

Graham opened the website for Knights Associates. Then he logged into another, more secure site to check out new requests. They worked closely with the police, other government agencies and sometimes a business or two. They primarily investigated cyber fraud but also cases of abuse, prostitution, or child pornography, and truth be told, almost any illegal activity involving the internet was likely to involve them.

"Holy cow. We have twenty-seven new requests in the last hour. Doesn't that seem odd to you? It's been a year since we started the website, Knight Safe, for financial fraud research, but we didn't get a single hit until after Christmas. Now we go from four to ten a month to this. In the last six months, there have been at least fifteen times that we've had more than a few requests at once. Most I've deleted because we don't have time to take more on. But something is really off about this."

Guy sat at his computer and quickly logged in. "Are these even genuine companies?"

"I don't know. I haven't had time to even look at them all. Some are obviously garbage, and some I've dumped because they just don't seem like a good fit. As you can see, we have over a thousand that need to be explored, down from nearly two thousand. With the legitimate requests we get from our five biggest contracts, I've been swamped on this thing." Graham scanned the list quickly. "How are they getting our contact information? My spidy sense is tingling."

"Mine too. The question is what are we going to do about it?"

The two worked for the next couple of hours, going through the massive amount of messages. Guy worked on checking out the companies—verifying a website, a contact person named—and then he sent emails asking for additional information. Graham worked on those lacking a company name and website, sending back an email requesting more details. They'd done this before but rarely received a response. They were hoping this might at least determine whether they were legitimate requests or phishing. Nothing had shown up so far, though. Graham spent a bit of time trying to trace some of the emails back to where they originated from.

Knights Computers constituted their downstairs business. Clients could drop off, call or contact the business through their website for computer work—removing viruses, trojans and malware, updating computers and doing general repairs. It was very different from their real bread and butter, Knights Associates, but very few knew about its existence upstairs except for an elite group that used them regularly. And now they had Knight Safe, strictly an online business. Even the employees downstairs didn't know half of what Guy and Graham really did on the second floor. Every day they monitored important information, a risk they had both agreed on, but it wasn't something they did lightly. But sometimes, people wanted them off doing useless stuff. Hackers were relentless.

"Okay, whoever has gotten our email address is good. I can't find any valid IP addresses."

"You mean there's another Graham-computer-genius running around out there?"

"Sadly, it would seem so. I don't like it. It's probably some pimply-faced little bugger raised on computers."

"I'd say just like you, but I know for a fact you have an amazing mom."

"Yeah, not her fault I'm a geek."

"Well, according to the last three women you dated, they all seemed to think you were pretty cute. You and your shaggy, provocative look."

Both men looked up as soon as they heard Bailey's voice.

"Why, thank you, ma'am." Graham grinned as he looked at her and then at the locked outer door. There was no question of trusting her. She had a key and was welcome to use it any time; he just wished he'd heard her come in.

She smiled as Guy grabbed her in a bear hug. "I've learned a thing or two since hanging out with you guys." Guy and Bailey started kissing.

"Shoo, lovebirds. I have work to do. Some of us aren't sleeping with the boss, so we have to jump at the crack of a whip."

Bailey laughed.

"How's Grandma?"

"Exhausting. That woman has more stamina than a tank, but she's tired. She tried again to talk me into taking over the winery. I don't think I could do what she does."

Graham leaned back in his chair. "Any ideas about who could take over the CEO position? It sounds as though she's ready to step down."

"No, but I've put some feelers out. I think we need to add it to our list of things to do. We need to find someone soon. She's looking haggard but won't slow down. She's so concerned that someone will find out family secrets, especially how evil her brother, Geoffrey, had really been and all he'd done to others, to her and to the company." Bailey pressed her fingers to her lips.

"Thank goodness he's dead. That son of a bitch really did a number on her and on..." Guy and Bailey's eyes met.

There was a long silence. Graham knew they were all remembering what he'd done to Bailey as well.

"Let's not get into it today. If each of us can look for an appropriate CEO for Caspian Winery, we'll find someone suitable. We'll do the background checks and run the people through interrogation," Graham said in a stern, deep voice.

Guy and Bailey burst out laughing.

"Okay. Now you've hurt my feelings. I can be tough. Okay, well maybe I'll leave the thumbscrew interviews to the two of you. I'll do the background checks. Now git." He waved them away as he went to the front office to pour a cup of coffee and grab a couple of muffins.

Guy and Bailey left for lunch, promising to bring him back a sandwich. They were smiling and holding hands and finally looked happy, unstressed, and ready to move forward. They'd sure been through enough. Guy had told him it had taken a year before Bailey stopped having nightmares thanks to what Uncle Geoff had done to her. Kidnapping her with the intent of killing her would have messed up anyone. He was glad Guy and Bailey had each other and had reached the point where they were going to get married—not something in *his* cards, but he was happy for them.

Needing a distraction, Graham sat down at his computer, which had logged off automatically after one minute of inactivity. He logged back on and, after tracking a couple of his current cases, he opened one sent by Detmier, a PI they sometimes worked with. A mother swore her child was a genius and had hacked her computer.

Graham had been working on cybercrimes for several years. After he and Guy left the police force, they'd fallen back on private detective work, and Knights Associates had been born. Graham worked at tracking criminals on the internet, and Guy did the private investigative work. Knights Computers, the division that repaired computers, had really come about to hide what they did at Knights Associates.

In the beginning, Knights Associates had taken on pretty much anything, but only from a limited resource pool. Once they'd started making connections and getting a reputation as being one of the best, the requests had started coming in from high-end clients—government, police and other private investigators. They decided to limit their clientele; five contracts had kept them busy. But then they'd come across a company victimized by identity theft, which had lost a lot of money. Afterward, they'd realized that if they hadn't helped the little company, it probably would have folded. It made them realize that a lot of companies were probably in the same situation. So they'd developed Knight Safe. They hadn't needed more business but had seen the need and were curious as to the demand. They hadn't advertised the service, which is what made all the incoming requests even more fishy—especially since most of them never responded once they'd reached out to get more information. And some were so unbelievable.

Kind of like the situation he was currently looking through. It intrigued him, since he'd never had to catch such a young thief—but what made it so interesting was how creative people were in what they sent in. Usually, they went after people who were laundering money, living a double life. His thoughts immediately went to Bailey, as well. Thirty years after a baby was kidnapped, they had been expected to find her. And the kicker was their client had been Guy's step-grandmother, Dorothea Lindell—not someone you declined. It was precisely the case that made him reluctant to discard some requests as crazy.

A computer alert reminded him he had other work to do, and he'd allowed himself to be distracted by non-critical emails that weren't top priority. All the incoming requests frustrated him to no end. He was sure some punk had hacked their system and was sending fake situations to chase. What ticked him off was that he didn't know how the bugger had done it.

Graham slammed his fist onto his desk. Someone was screwing with them, and it was driving him nuts. It wasn't as though they could ignore all the cybercrime requests, but who had time to read them all and get any work done? What they needed was someone to go through the emails and figure out what was legit. Then he could spend some time figuring out what was really going on, catch the twerp and get some of their crimes solved.

He certainly hoped some better applications came in for the Tech Assistant position.

CHAPTER 4

TARIN STARED LONG AND hard at her monitor. Did she or didn't she? It hadn't been in her plans to find a job immediately, but this was too perfect. She'd been trying to figure a way in and this was it. Her gaze was immediately drawn to the beautiful strawberry-blonde-haired boy who had become her life. Sitting in the corner of her office, he was busy vrooming his car up and down a racetrack. It was for him that she was doing this. She looked at her portfolio, checking it over again. Then she reviewed all the background information she'd scattered throughout the internet. Facebook users expected closer relationships, so she'd chosen Twitter for its rapid-fire information instead. Over the months, she'd tweeted and scattered business information. While her website boasted of her computer expertise, if someone tried to contact her, they received an automated message stating she was so swamped she couldn't take any more business and referred them to another computer company.

Even though it was mostly false, it was enough for several individuals to have asked for her expert advice. At first, it had felt great to have people seeking her out for her knowledge, even if she didn't do anything for them, but it hadn't taken long before she felt cheapened—a fraud taking advantage of people. It would have filled her father with pride, but it was not who she was. She learned to tamp down those feelings and continue on because the façade she created was so important. Her future depended on it. She'd also placed a couple of archive stories she'd written in the *Edmonton Journal* and the *Vancouver Sun*. No one ever checked them to determine their legitimacy.

If anyone cared to look deeper, she had enough information trickling back to her childhood to satisfy any snooper. Everything seemed in order. Her trembling fingers lingered over the key that would change her life—or at least she hoped it would. The thought of finally learning something about a blank period in her life caused her breathing to become shallow and choppy.

Before she could even acknowledge it though, the slightest of sounds set her heart to pounding. It alerted her to what was coming. Her index finger punched downward with the speed of light. In a heartbeat, her resume was gone, and she had changed her circumstances. She hoped. Closing that out, she looked over her emails. There was one she had flagged from the month before. It had been the kick in the butt she'd needed to stop putting this off; an email that meant someone else might have answers to the week she'd lost three years before.

'Left naked and alone. No memory.'

It resembled her story so much; it hurt to think that someone else had been through the same experience. Sadly, the person wasn't ready to share more, but she hoped she would soon.

It was crystal clear that if she was going to find answers, she had to go east to Ontario. If the blank piece of paper with nothing but a logo and a code that had been stuck to her back meant anything, then it had to be the key to her lost memory. With one last hopeful glance that she was doing the right thing, she closed out her email and clicked on the icon for the website she always kept open just in case.

"What are you doing?"

A shudder shook her insides as he wrapped his arms around her, his hands automatically groping her breasts. She grabbed them and tried to push them away. "Not in front of Chance."

But he would not be deterred. Stephen squeezed harder. "Why? He's going to have to learn, eventually."

"He's only two." Gritting her teeth, she quit responding. Eventually he let go, but only to slide his palms down the sides of her body.

"I'm looking at dresses. I think I found—"

He straightened, pulling away. "I told you, I already bought your dress. It'll be here tomorrow."

"Mommy. Mommy. Look, a spida."

"Geez. I thought I told you he was not to bring any more bugs into my apartment. I'm going to have to fumigate the damn place," Stephen huffed. He grabbed the offending daddy- longlegs, dropped it on the floor and stepped on it with his loafers.

"Noooo."

"Clean it up," he said before leaving.

Tarin scooped up her son, turning his head away from what Stephen had done. She placed her hand on her son's tummy. "Your tiny friend is fine. Remember our song. The itsy-bitsy spider climbed up the waterspout." Her fingers slowly crawled up his tummy. He sniffled a bit. "Down came the rain and washed the spider out. Out came the sun and dried up all the rain. The itsy-bitsy spider climbed up the spout again." As she was singing, she slowly rolled her chair over to where Stephen had left the dead daddy-longlegs and, with a slight grimace, she wiped it up with her foot. Her son finally quieted down and was snuggled against her.

"The spida, Mommy."

"Ssshhh. It's okay, love. Look. He got up and went home."

His perfect blue little eyes looked down in wonder at the spot she pointed to and then back at her. His grin was more than enough payment for the little white lie. He grabbed her cheeks and gave her a big sloppy kiss. Tears instantly flooded her eyes as she hugged him tight, but he was ready to be put down. He started squirming. Reluctantly, she stood him on his feet, gave him a quick kiss and let him go. Her arms felt lost and empty without him, but he'd already moved on. He looked for his little friend, but when he couldn't find the Daddy Longlegs, he went back to his toys in the corner, and was soon playing as though nothing bad had happened. She prayed he would forget all of this.

She listened to make sure Stephen wasn't lurking before clicking back onto the website she'd designed. At first, it had been a place where women like her, women unhappy in their marriages, could vent; but it had morphed into so much more.

Stephen never had a clue. He hadn't wanted to know what she did with her time, before or during their marriage. They'd met at one of her father's hotels; he'd assumed she was a guest, not an employee. It had been flattering to have someone interested in her, not for what she did or who she was but for her. Though her own feelings hadn't progressed past mild interest, he'd been very attentive. Her lips stretched taut in a self-deprecating smile. It had been the first sign of trouble, a scandal involving her—when she'd leapt into his arms, his bed, and his life. She'd done it without any doubts, expecting that he would protect her from the big, wicked world, like her father always had.

She dropped her head into her hand, realizing she'd gone from trying to please her dad to pleasing another man, while both thought they had the right to dictate how she lived her life. And she had allowed it. Pulling herself together with a promise not to be sucked into self-pity, she read through the forum to see if there had been any new comments, or if there were new women reaching out to share their stories. It had been several days since she'd checked. Stephen had been a lot more attentive lately. It just reinforced that what she was doing was right, but it also made her wonder if he knew she was up to something.

Praying it wasn't the case, she logged in and sifted through the new member requests. Anyone could become a member; all they had to do was leave their name and email. They would have access to basic information on a site that looked like it was full of information for women trying to stand on their own. Those who wanted to share their deeper story, the one of abuse, abduction, prostitution or whatever their lot in life had been, had to share much more. And they had to be invited. They had to be willing to tell their story, even if just to Tarin; the reasons they were joining and what they hoped to get out of the group. This was all done privately through emails back and forth with her. Once she believed they were legitimate, she'd accept them into the inner circle, where her plan was to have women open up and share and find ways to heal their lives.

It had taken a while for the first person to do so, but then it had opened the gates with several asking to join the inner circle. They wanted to tell their stories to others who would understand what had happened to them. Not all were ready to open up to everyone, but all of them had shared with her. One had really touched her. They'd been emailing back and forth.

'I've never known anything but abuse. It's the story of my life.' LJ

'I'm sorry to hear that, LJ. I too have had more than my share, but I'm making changes. I hope you do too.' Tarin

'I've made some bad decisions, but I'm trying to change that.' LJ

Frowning, she sifted through the higher than usual number of emails. There were a few new comments that questioned the legitimacy of the website, and some had her wondering what they were talking about. Flipping through her site, it dawned on her, she hadn't installed an effective firewall and spam filter, as someone had posted sex pictures and videos. They were very crude and terribly brutal to the women who trusted her. The scenes made her ill. She quickly deleted them, but the damage had been done. There were several very nasty comments left for her. She wrote a statement on the homepage and responded to every angry reaction. Then she tried to backtrack to find out who might have put up the insulting media. Whoever had done it was very good. They'd obviously used a proxy, so she had no way of finding their IP address.

Initially, the site was to have been a safe place for women who were sick of their marriages and simply wanted to vent, but Tarin had soon realized there were a lot of women in abusive situations who had no one to turn to. Hearing their stories made her realize hers wasn't so bad. The site soon became a haven for those who had been or were being abused, raped, violated or were just dissatisfied with life. Most had never been reported, nor had they ever been talked about with another living soul, which was what she hoped to change for her and for them.

Often, she went on her gut instinct about whether someone was ready to enter the inner circle. The one thing she'd promised herself was that she wouldn't perform background checks unless she had a hunch something was off. She really wanted to help the women heal. A moment of guilt stopped her from what she was doing. She wanted to help these women. They had been through something awful. To be alone and not to have anyone who understood just compounded the issue. But the truth was she had an ulterior motive. Her hope was that someone could shed light on what had happened to her three years before.

Seven days of her life were gone, but she had no idea what had happened.

She glanced at her son. Her top priority was to keep him safe.

Stephen was tall, blonde and sexy as hell. He'd been so charming in the beginning—flowers, gifts, diamonds—whatever he'd thought she needed or deserved. He'd had the swagger, the smile, the charm and beneath it all she'd discovered he was as plastic as a Ken doll. For over a year, he'd tried everything to get her to go out with him. Finally, she'd given in. It had been so flattering to have someone pamper her. He'd been so attentive and nice. Then, her life had changed. After the lost week she couldn't recall, she'd been more frightened than she'd wanted to admit. She'd needed a change quickly, and he'd been her answer. He'd been thrilled when she finally said yes to his proposal; only she'd gone from one nightmare to another.

Now almost two and a half years later, he was a reminder of her old world. The one she had really wanted to leave behind—the wealth, the greed—everything centered on money and the cold pursuit of power.

She'd thought by landing Stephen, the son of the owner of Welton, a huge international oilfield company, she'd redeemed herself in her father's eyes.

The joke had been on her. He hadn't taken her call to hear about her upcoming wedding. Nor had he returned it. Not then. Not when she'd been in trouble.

From a young age, she'd seen her father's disdain for family in the way he'd treated his own father, her grandfather. She'd never met him but was sickened by the ruthless way in which her father had tried to ruin him. She'd never understood why he hated his own father so much. The media always portrayed him as a good, kind person, so different from the man she'd never been allowed to call dad. One day, she hoped to meet her grandfather and find out for herself—but that was assuming he'd want to meet her. Or maybe her father hadn't really fallen far from the tree and had learned all he knew at his knee.

Her wedding ring's enormous diamond flashed in the afternoon sunshine that filtered through her window. It was as though it had winked at her, telling her the joke was on her. In truth, her dad's ignoring her had been a blessing. If he'd have approved of her marriage, she might never have found the guts to plan to leave Stephen.

In the beginning, Chance had taken all her energy, her attention. He'd been a miracle, not one she understood but one for whom she took full responsibility—and one she promised to love and protect. That reminded her it was time to put in an appearance and put away Chance's scattered toys before it became an issue. Since her son was sitting quietly in the corner, she decided to briefly step away.

A quick look around revealed an apartment that was sparkling clean, devoid of any indication of a child lived there. Except for a few toys in her office and the ones in the living room she hadn't had time to put away, there was really no sign of life in this house. There were no fingerprints, no colors other than black, chrome and clear glass, definitely no life. Some people saw it as classy and sophisticated, but she saw it for what it really was: shallow and all show. Just like her husband.

She wanted out and out now. The reality of what she had been doing to herself and to Chance made her shudder, though she worked hard to make sure it didn't show on the outside.

As she entered the living room, Stephen came out of the kitchen. "Did you get my suit pressed?"

"Yes, it's hanging in the closet, still in the plastic."

"Good. Make sure my shoes are polished."

"Why don't you do it yourself?"

"What? Did you say something?"

"I'm sorry. I'm exhausted."

"My promotion party is at the end of next week. Get some sleep before then. Be ready by 5:00 p.m. on that Friday."

"Right, you want me to get into my hot slinky number and sit quietly by the door awaiting your arrival?"

"No, I'll be home before that."

He leered at her. She turned away, pretending ignorance.

"I got you a new Ruby Jane necklace that will look stunning with the hot black number." His eyes crawled down over her physique as though she were his masterpiece. "You will be perfect. Men will drool."

Oh yes, let's be the envy of every male there.

He started walking across the room toward her. She was trying to think of distracting distraction for his one-track mind when he resolved it for her.

"Ouch, Jesus. What did I tell you about his damn toys?" He kicked viciously, sending the castle and walls the two of them had spent all afternoon building flying in all directions.

"Steve!" That barely got her a glance as he marched across the living room to sit in his leather and chrome chair. Usually, he'd have reminded her he preferred to be called Stephen.

She looked at Chance, who had come up behind her and was clinging to the back of her leg. His eyes were full of tears, and his bottom lip was sticking out. The pain that zapped through her heart dropped her to her knees. She gathered him to her, picked him up and went down the hallway to his bedroom.

"Oh, baby. I'm so sorry."

"Mad."

"Oh honey. He's—" *a jerk*. Not something she could tell a two-year-old. "Not your fault."

"Sorry, Mommy."

That was it. The tears flowed like a river bursting free of a dam. She hugged her son tight to her chest, not wanting him to see her cry, but when she felt his little body convulse with sobs as well, he'd seen through her masquerade. She worked hard to stem her emotions; her son was already carrying too much guilt for someone so young. He snuggled against her. His tiny arms held her with a strangling grip that served to remind her all the more how fragile her beautiful boy was. She felt so connected and so loved in that moment. He was strong, her boy.

It was time for her to do right by him. She held him with tenderness, but there was an underlying desperation that one day he could be ripped from her arms, gone forever. Her heart felt as though it was being crushed by the weight of her mistakes; the things she'd ignored for too long. Her body convulsed as nothing was going to stop the tidal wave of emotion. At some point, she must have fallen asleep, for the next thing she was aware of she was being shaken awake.

"Are you coming to bed?"

She blinked a few times as she looked into those blue eyes that had first sucked her in. Revulsion was all she felt now.

"No, I'm fine here."

"I want you in our bed. Now."

She wanted to scream in defiance but knew he'd take it out on Chance. "Give me a minute."

"Don't make me come back here."

She waited until he'd left before gently untangling herself from her son. She pulled his snuggly, soft bear blanket over him, gently kissing his forehead. "A few more nights, baby, and that's it. I promise you," she whispered.

She'd learned so much the hard way. A snob would have looked like a social butterfly next to her husband. She had made some stupid mistakes, but he'd been a colossal one. He'd been so easy in the beginning to hang out with; to lean on. He was someone she was familiar with, stoic, professional, focused on his career, really only needing her to praise him and serve as eye candy, which she'd done and then some.

Slowly trudging down the hall, the dread of what she was doing crawled over her like molasses that was sucking her into the depths of a big vat. At their bedroom, she hesitated before entering but knew that wouldn't prevent anything. Knowing this had to be the performance of her life, she squared her shoulders, tossed her braid over her shoulder and focused on when they'd first met, when he'd first meant something to her.

Stripping off her clothes, she crawled into bed. His body was so still that she prayed it meant he was sound asleep. A few seconds later, her prayers weren't being answered. With no foreplay, he jammed himself between her legs. She grunted in pain, but other than that she didn't move, didn't make a sound. When he was done, she felt bruised and battered and dirtier than if she'd been beaten and dropped in a mud hole.

"Oh, God. That was awesome. Thanks." He rolled over and was soon snoring like an old, misfiring vacuum cleaner.

For several minutes she lay there shivering, her fists clenched, her mind blank. Slowly, she climbed out and went down the hall to the guest bathroom. She turned the shower on hot and scrubbed her body until it was raw.

Never again. Never again.

CHAPTER 5

TARIN HAD NEVER BEEN so glad to see 5:00 a.m. Stephen was out the door almost to the second the clock struck that hour. Just like every morning, off to the gym, shower and then to the office. Not that she cared, but on this day she was more than grateful. The minute she heard the door close and lock, she flew out of bed. She pulled out her suitcase and quickly stuffed in the clothes she wanted. The closet full of long, flowing dresses made her pause; was there any way she could sell those and get some money? It seemed wrong to leave them, not because she'd ever wear them again but because she didn't want him to have the satisfaction of having them.

The long, plastic-covered gown she hadn't yet seen hung on the corner of the door. Grabbing it, she laid it on the bed and slowly stripped off the protection. She gasped as it was unveiled. The material was exquisite. It would feel like delicate rose petals brushing over her body, but what grabbed her attention was the plunging neckline, front and back. If she were to guess, her belly button would be bare in front and damn near the crack of her butt in back. She held it up. Light was visible through it. It was almost see-through.

"That bas—" She couldn't believe it. It was similar to what he liked her to wear when they went out—slinky, tight. This one, though, was a lot more revealing and daring, something she would never wear. She wondered if he really had that promotion or if this was how he thought he'd get it.

In the drawer beside the bed was a pair of scissors, and she stared at them long and hard, unable to believe what she was contemplating. She opened and closed them a few times, finding that she liked the sharp, slicing sound they made. Picking up the dress, she carefully separated the scissor blades and inserted them in the plunging neckline and cut downwards. Starting at the bottom, she randomly attacked it, slicing upwards to different heights. It wasn't until a chunk of it flew past her head that she realized what she was doing and what she had done.

Her eyes opened wide as she stared in horror at the shreds of material that looked like unwoven threads hanging there. Setting what was left on the blazing red silk comforter she hated, she plunged the scissors through all of it: the dress remains, the comforter, the eight hundred thread count bed sheets and the memory-foam-movement-isolation bed.

She blinked a few times as she looked at what she'd done. Her shoulders sagged in defeat. She had given in to her basic urge—anger. Something she'd been suppressing for too long. Her father's disappointment immediately came to mind. If he'd been a witness to her display of emotions, he wouldn't have been able to look her in the face because she'd lowered herself.

Slapping her palms to her cheeks, she pressed hard to force the memories and the guilt to recede. She'd never be able to please the man who'd fathered her, one of the reasons she was in this predicament. She turned her back on the mess. It truly made her sick to think she'd acted that way. And it scared her that she'd lost control. Realizing with a start that time was of the essence, she pushed it away.

On her dresser were three ornately carved jewellery boxes, each loaded with whatever baubles Stephen felt she should wear that week. Grabbing each one, she dumped them into a leather duffel bag. She thought about all the others, the more expensive ones he had locked in the safe. They were worth more, but she'd never opened the locked compartment and wasn't sure what kind of security measures he might have employed. What she had taken already should bring at least forty thousand dollars—or so she hoped. She was planning to pay cash for everything, at least for a while.

Fifteen minutes later, she was sure she'd taken all that would help her get some quick money. She was about to close her suitcase when she looked at the closet again. All the clothes she was leaving were worth thousands, if not hundreds of thousands. She hated to leave them for Stephen, as he saw them as trophies. Without her in them though, they might not hold the same appeal. She had no use for them, so left them behind.Zipping up her bags, she hauled them to the front door before taking a last dash to her office. Quickly, she logged onto her computer. It might be several days before she could log back on. Her future was a mystery. After checking her website and her emails and dealing with a few things, she was tempted to hack Stephen's account but the few times she had, there hadn't been anything much in there, other than some love letters from his girlfriend, the one he didn't think she knew about.

He was arrogant enough that he thought he was untouchable. She really didn't know the man she'd married; a fact she'd discovered almost from the moment she said her vows. As soon as the ring was on her finger, he'd hustled her out the door to a swanky hotel for a twenty-four-hour marathon of sex. When he'd finally let her get up, he'd thrown out her wardrobe and bought her a brand new one. It hadn't mattered whether she'd liked it.

He'd changed from a sweet, attentive guy to a demanding, self-centered man. A very dirty one. He'd been selling some of his father's company secrets. Discovering that had been a shock, but Chance had taken up all her time. He'd become her world. At least until Stephen felt threatened and started dictating those moments with her son.

That had been the deciding factor. She had to get out.

A sense of urgency came over her. He'd left an hour before, but what if he came back? What if he'd forgotten something? It had never happened before, but it could. She was not going to take the chance that it would be that day when he decided to take time off. Running to her son's room, she gathered everything—toys, stuffed animals, pictures—that had meaning to him, along with some clothes and stuffed them in a suitcase. She leaned down over him, kissing him on the forehead before she awakened him.

Chance's eyes opened, full of sleepy wonder. His small arms reached for her as a smile touched his lips. This was the best part of her day. Her heart swelled as she picked him up and hugged him.

"Okay bud. We've got a big, fun day ahead of us. I need you to get dressed, and then we're going on an adventure."

As only children can, he went from barely being awake to fired up and ready to play. She swung him into the air. He giggled. The sound was so refreshing and filled her with so much joy; it reminded her of what was really important. His coming into this world might not have been under the best of circumstances, but she wouldn't give him up for anything. She would protect him with her life, which, ironically, was what it felt like. She didn't know if Stephen would make an issue of finding him; she couldn't see why he would, as he'd never shown an ounce of love or compassion for Chance. In fact, he'd barely even acknowledged him. Something she wanted to make sure continued. Stephen was not the man she wanted to influence her son. The thought of Chance turning out like Stephen made her shudder.

Why had he married her? He could have had anyone. Something told her, somehow he'd known who she really was, a daughter of a hotel magnate.

Chance wiggled, snapping her back to the present. She got him cleaned up, gave him his favorite toy, and was walking to the kitchen with him when her cell phone chimed. Fear crawled up her spine and wrapped around her neck, making swallowing almost impossible.

"Again, Mommy."

She had no idea what he was asking of her. She smiled at him, set him down, distracting him with the stuffed car he was carrying.

It's okay. It's okay. It's okay.

Finally able to take a deep breath, with shaking fingers she picked up her cell phone from the charger by the front door beside her bag. With a quick stab, she opened her text messages.

Not home tonight; something came up at work. Back tomorrow night. Buff my shoes again. I want them to shine as bright as you.

Almost gagging, she let her head drop back and stared at the ceiling. The weight of those simple words almost sent her to do his bidding, but it didn't take long for her to come to her senses. She'd just shined the stupid things. Yet it surprised her how quickly she had been about to jump at his command.Blowing out a calming breath. It meant she had another day to put distance between them before he discovered she was gone.

CHAPTER 6

DECIDING IT WAS WAY past time to get moving, Tarin playfully wrestled Chance into his clothes and then into his spring jacket and hat. His grin was infectious and something she sorely needed. She smiled back. He gave her a zerbert kiss. It was a moment like this one that made her wonder if she'd done the right thing by not letting her father know he had a grandson. It might bring a light to his eyes, laughter to his soul and life to his days, things she'd never seen in him but she still had hope. But she couldn't tell him. If he knew the trouble she was now in, he'd help her, but she wasn't sure at what price. It wasn't something she was willing to risk.

One last look around the immaculate glass and chrome apartment, skimming over a place that was as emotionally stale as the man she'd allowed herself to be hitched to. It had been yet another colossal mistake.

This whole situation made her momentarily ill, but she steeled her spine; she was made of tougher stock. Raised under her father's firm hand and because of her solitary life, she'd learned to take care of herself from a young age. When he'd tired of her, he'd sent her off to boarding school with only weekend visits home. He'd been so proud of his little offspring robot. They'd parted ways a few years before, and she wasn't about to mend that rift. For the first time in her life, she felt as though she was on the cusp of living her own life and doing what she wanted to do. A basement suite sounded like the perfect place to start. But then, living on the street would have been preferable to living with Stephen or her father's rules.

Grabbing her large suitcase and pulling out the handle, she stacked as many other bags as she could on top. It worked fine as long as she was standing still, but as soon as she moved, they toppled over. That meant she was going to have to make two trips.

Unloading, she hauled as much as she could and headed into the hallway after checking to make sure no one was there. She grabbed Chance's free hand, noting his other one was hugging his big green rabbit.

The elevator trip to the garage was uneventful, but it didn't ease her nerves or stop the feeling that someone was watching her. Once the doors opened, she walked quickly across the underground parkade, her heels clicking loudly, making her wince at the noise. Once at Stephen's Mercedes, she stuffed all she'd hauled down into the trunk and was closing the lid when the guard walked by.

"Mrs. Roth. How are you today?"

"Tarin, please. I'm good, Dale, and you?" During one of their many chats, he'd told her he'd been a guard there for over ten years. He was a bit of a gruff old guy, but he'd taken a liking to her. The one time he'd seen her with a bruise on forehead, he'd told her that he was pretty sure a cupboard door hadn't done it. It had actually been the truth, but she wasn't sure it hadn't been deliberate on Stephen's part. Since then, Dale had checked on her regularly and hinted many times that if she ever needed a place for a short getaway, he had the best one for her. He meant with him and his wife.

"Good. Good. The missus wants me to go on a cruise, but I'm not sure I have the legs to be at sea for a week. I prefer solid ground under my feet. She's trying to get me into retirement mode. I'll be done in a couple of months."

She laughed. "Oh, but it'll be fun. You probably stop at a lot of islands and get off the ship, right?"

"Yes, but we have to get to those islands first." He smiled. "Anyway, can I help you? I saw you were hauling a lot of things. If there's more, I'd be more than happy to help you bring it down."

Though she tried hard not to react, she felt the color drain out of her face, and she was certain from his look of concern that he noticed.

"Are you all right?"

"Yeah. Yeah. I have a few things to do. Thanks, but I... uh... don't need help. I'm good. But thanks."

"Hungry. Hungry," Chance, hiding behind her leg, chanted softly but loud enough for her to hear.

"I know, love. We have to get a few more things and then we'll go out for breakfast, okay?"

"Now, Mommy. Now."

"How did his birthday turn out?"

Tarin smiled. Dale had bought him a present each birthday since he'd been born. She wondered who'd be there to give him a present when he turned three. "He loved it. Thank you so much for the car; he barely puts it down. He plays with it all the time." She didn't know how to tell him his gift was the only one that hadn't come from her. Stephen hadn't wanted any other kids over. Not that she knew any.

"Mommyyyyy."

"Want me to watch him for a few minutes while you go back up?"

Instant panic gripped her. "Uh, no. No, thanks, though. I can manage."

She had no idea what he saw in her face or in her eyes, but he held her gaze for a long time. She refused to look away.

"No problem. I'm not supposed to be down here anyway. I've been in Mrs. Brown's apartment looking for that damn cat again. You have a good day. And take care." He was halfway across the parking lot before she could move.

"Wait. Dale?"

He looked at her over his shoulder.

"Do you still volunteer at that place, Suit the Men?" It was a charity that gave men who couldn't afford it nice suits so they could interview for good jobs.

"Yes, we're busy trying to get thirty suits right now. Well, actually we need closer to two hundred, but thirty will do for now."

"Maybe you can help me then."

An hour later, with a banana and a juice for Chance and having cleaned out her closet and half of Stephen's, they loaded them into Dale's van.

"If anyone should question you, show them this. I..." Not knowing what to say, she handed him a note, hugged him, loaded Chance up and climbed in behind the wheel. She checked her purse for the tenth time to make sure the cash she'd withdrawn from the bank a little every day that week was still there. The fear of Stephen finding it had kept her on her toes. Hiding it in Chance's stuffed gorilla had been the answer. Stephen had never gone near the toys.

She would be fine for a while. The jewelry would provide more money once she found a few places to pawn them. If she managed it right, she'd have a job right away. Pulling into Calgary International Airport later that morning, she parked in the farthest corner she could find and then unloaded the trunk. She got them checked in and while waiting; she got Chance a juice to drink and a cracker to munch on. With him busy, she checked her phone for messages. There were no texts. She released a huge sigh of relief because that meant Stephen still had no clue. There were a few emails, which she checked. The third one was the one she had been hoping for. She had an interview in a couple of days. It was going to be a crazy rush, but she confirmed she'd be there.

After they were settled on the plane, she thought about how crazy her life had become. Bobbie, her friend since first grade, was going to pick her up in Montreal and then drive her to Toronto. She wasn't accustomed to asking for help from anyone, especially when they had to go out of their way to help her. Bobbie had a big heart, although she kept it hidden under a tough exterior. She wondered what Bobbie would do to Stephen if she ever shared with her how he had mistreated her. Bobbie had been there through every damn stupid thing she'd done as a kid and had still been her friend.

She hoped she hadn't made a mistake in including Bobbie in her plans. The idea that her friend could be hurt because of this situation slammed into her like a freight train. She must be insane to follow through with this plan. It reminded her when she was sixteen and had been accused of doing something she hadn't done, so she'd come up with a plan to fix it—only that had made things worse and it had lost her Bobbie's friendship for a very long time.

Am I doing the same thing again?

Though there were never any guarantees, she had to believe this was going to change her life for the better. The thought of what Stephen might do was something that kept playing out in the back of her mind. It was part of the reason she'd decided to travel across the country and get far away from him. But that was only part of it. The real one was because of a piece of paper, one that contained Caspian Winery letterhead. Why would someone keep her locked up, drugged up, whatever else they had done to her and then give her a code and leave her a logo? It didn't make sense. What she did know was that Caspian Winery was the only connection she had to that missing period of time. She'd read everything she could find about them, but nothing explained a connection to her. The letterhead was the only clue she had, and she had to pursue it. She had to find out who had played this sick game with her and why. It was key to Chance's future and her own.

She pressed her palms together and placed her index fingers against her lips. She'd never been religious, but that didn't stop her from praying for something better. If she played it right, she'd have a new life.

One, she hoped both she and Chance would survive.

CHAPTER 7

"HOW ARE THINGS COMING with that acquisition?"

"All sewed up, Mr. J. The paperwork is on its way. You're now the proud owner of Reynolds Wines."

"Good. Good. Glad to hear it. I take it there weren't too many problems convincing them to sell?"

Cal smiled as he sat across from Mr. J, the man who had changed his life and for whom he'd do anything... and did. Not that he ever shared the details with his boss. That had been the unspoken agreement between them since the day he'd taken him off the streets and into his home. "No more than usual. Had to get a little tough to let them know we were serious, and they were going to be handsomely paid for their lowly business."

"So we paid market price?"

"No. Not even close. They were convinced they were getting all they were going to, and it was in their best interest to sell. Their only concern was the staff."

"For now, we need to get someone new in there because we're changing how they do business. Get Williams to perform a business analysis and hire someone to manage it. I want him to keep a close eye on it over the next six months. I want profits doubled in that time."

"Got it, boss. I'll have him find someone ruthless who also knows the wine business."

"Excellent. And I want it renamed. I want my name on that place. We'll be selling that wine at all our hotels. It's rather small, but at least a start. Now, did you look into the one that neighbors it?"

"I've started some things in motion but wanted to get this deal done before I moved forward."

"All right. Let me know once you've had a chance to—you know what, give me the name of the other owner. I'll call myself. I'll handle the negotiations, and if there are any problems, you handle the convincing. Good job, Cal." Mr. J turned his attention to his tablet.

Cal knew that meant it was time for him to leave. He stood but didn't move toward the door. "I know this probably isn't any of my business, but I know how to make the audit go away."

He glanced up, shook his head. "Right now, this requires a little bit of the old-school quid pro quo. I've got it." His attention immediately dropped back to his screen.

Silently, Cal made his way out of the expansive office, his heels clicking on the marble flooring. It still gave him a thrill. That sound was the echo of money, something he was getting very accustomed to. It also made him smile that a lot of tactics used in business weren't all that different from those he'd learned on the streets. He could get away with a lot more in a suit, though, than he had in blue jeans. He brushed an imaginary piece of lint off his jacket, giving him an excuse to feel the expensive material that reminded him of power and the new life he'd created for himself.

Thoughts of the new winery he'd acquired for his boss made him grin. It was jobs like that where he was of real value. He was thankful Mr. J hadn't asked him for details of what he had done to convince the people to sell. He'd had to be a little underhanded to persuade the family to sell their century-old winery.

As he entered the elevator, his thoughts drifted to the other problem he was monitoring. Soon he would inform his boss, the father figure he'd never had, what was really going on. He'd be angry; so before Cal told him what had been occurring over the last few years, he had to figure out a way to deflect it from himself. The fallout could destroy the relationship he'd worked so hard to build up, and all because of her. He thought he'd finally solved the problem of Tarin, but it appeared she was heading back to Ontario. Too close for comfort. It was only a matter of time before she started asking questions and wanting answers. There was no way she was going to screw up all that he'd built.

If she vanished, that would solve everything. He pressed his thumb into his right temple in an attempt to ease the pounding pulsing through his skull. It was time to find out her plans.

CHAPTER 8

'*YOU BITCH. I DON'T know where you've gone or what you
think you're doing, but good riddance.*'

Tarin shuddered as she thought about the four texts
Stephen had sent her. He'd obviously arrived home and
found her message—the dress with the scissors sticking
out of it and a lot of her possessions gone. Never mind
most of his suits. He'd sent her several nasty messages that
she felt compelled to read. Part of her, perhaps, needed to
know he was simply blowing hot air and had no plans to
come after her. Thankfully, it looked as though he wasn't
going to waste his time or energy looking for her.

"More, Mommy." Chance's request for more water-
melon brought her back to the present. His face was drip-
ping with juice while he triumphantly held a squished
piece in his hand. She gave him a new one. He proceeded
immediately to suck on it.

"Thank you, Bobbie; that was great. You've obviously learned a thing or two about cooking since school."
Tarin sat back and patted a stomach filled with shrimp
shish kabobs, crab cakes, puff pastries, vegetable salad and
lemon meringue pie. Maybe she shouldn't feel so relaxed,
but for the first time in a long time she didn't feel like
she had to sit up straight or scan the area for kids' toys to
make sure they were out of the way. The last few days had
been a whirlwind of packing, flying, driving and trying to
settle into Bobbie's basement. It felt so good to be lazing
in the backyard as though she had no cares in the world.
Bobbie had been gracious and so far hadn't asked too

many questions about Stephen. All Tarin had told her was that he'd cheated on her. Bobbie had been ready to take him out at the knees. It made Tarin smile.

"Well, thank you. I got Mom's chef to teach me. I was tired of mac and cheese, brown beans, toast." They were sitting in Bobbie's backyard under a huge umbrella that kept the midday sun off them.

"Well, you did awesome."

"Bobbie? Where are you?"

Bobbie jumped to her feet and disappeared into the house. Tarin looked at Kim, Bobbie's teenage daughter.

She shrugged but made no move to follow. "Grandma."

Tarin's eyes trailed toward the house. She was a little perplexed by both of their attitudes. She was tempted to follow Bobbie, but she'd never gotten along with Mrs. Benson; and she didn't want her to see her in case she was still in contact with her father.

"Tarin, it's so good to see you."

"Uh, hi, Mrs. Benson," she said politely, while cringing inside. Her friend's mom was dressed in a short, flaming red cocktail dress that seemed more suited to a Friday night outfit for someone half her age than a midweek morning one. Although Tarin knew she shouldn't judge, since that had been most of her clothing when living with Stephen. She'd have to ask Bobbie who the man in her mom's life was.

"Okay, so what do you have planned for this afternoon?"

"Go to the water park," Kim said to her mother's groan.

"I'll pass. Sitting in the scorching sun with noisy kids all around? Forget it. I'll go home and sit by the pool," Mrs. Benson air-kissed Kim. "Besides, I'm going to test drive a new Mercedes this afternoon."

"No, you're not Mom."

"Don't talk to me like I'm two, Bobbie. I am."

"You're not buying it."

"I never said I was. I'm just taking a convertible for a spin."

"Do not, Mom." Bobbie glared at her, but she seemed oblivious to it.

She turned to Tarin. "Nice to see you. It's been so long. I'll tell your father you're looking great. And his grandson is adorable."

Tarin's eyes widened as her head snapped around to Bobbie, whose horrified look met hers. "I'd rather you didn't. And I'd rather he didn't know I was here yet."

"Oh. Is something wrong?" She waved her heavily ringed fingers in the air.

"It's okay. I'll talk to her. She only talks to your dad when she wants—" Bobbie's eyes widened. Looking like a street urchin in her sweats, she grabbed her slender, glammed-up mom and directed her firmly off to the side of the patio. The two had their heads together, and it was obvious the words were rather heated. Bobbie's face was puffed up and red as if ready to explode, but it was the surreptitious glances her way that concerned her. She focused on Chance, not wishing to reveal that she could see the anger and could hear some of their words.

Kim started stacking the dishes. Tarin jumped to her feet to help, thankful for something to do. "I'll do that. You keep an eye on Chance." The huge smile that was bestowed on her son was thanks enough.

"Is everything okay there?" Tarin nodded in the direction of Bobbie and her mom as she stacked dishes.

"Mom and Grandma? Oh yeah. They fight a lot, but it's usually because Grandma wants to buy something she can't afford. My guess is she'll be driving that car by the end of the week."

"Oh, and how will she do that?"

"Mom says that's why she has a string of men and there's always at least one with a guilt-ridden conscience."

Surprised, Tarin looked at Kim.

She laughed. "Mom's nicer definition of the guys in Grandma's life. The other is—"

"That's okay, Kim, I don't need to know about your grandmother's boyfriends. I'm sorry that's caused some problems between the two. I guess that's why your mom doesn't date much?"

"Probably. Mom gets so mad at Grandma, and the way she dates the young and the old. It's kind of funny, but she sure gets some nice things. I wonder if she'll let me drive her Mercedes?"

Tarin carried the dishes into the house. Kim and Chance followed her. "You know you don't need a guy to buy that for you, right? If you get the right education and a good job or start your own business, you could buy it yourself one day."

"You sound like Mom. She's always telling me, 'don't turn out like Grandma—work hard, save your money.'"

The sliding of the patio door alerted her to Bobbie's return. She quickly finished cleaning up their meal.

"Okay, I guess we're ready. Do you have a bathing suit and trunks for Chance?" Bobbie said as she approached them, her face red and her eyes still snapping with anger, although she modulated her voice to a gentler, softer tone.

"I have some shorts I can wear, and he has some he can put on. We'll play in the kiddies' pool. So no worries." Tarin smiled. She wanted to hug her friend, but there was something in Bobbie's expression that kept her at arm's length.

"Do you mind if we stop at the cemetery on the way, to leave some flowers on my grandmother's grave and my sister, Tammy's? I've been meaning to take Kim, but one thing or another has gotten in the way." Bobbie pulled Tarin aside. "I'm sorry about Mom. She almost never comes over. Well, unless she wants money. I'm—"

"It's okay. Forget it. One of these days, I'm going to have to deal with Dad. And yes, let's visit your grandmother and your sister's gravesites."

Thirty minutes later, they were walking through Mount Pleasant Cemetery, one of the oldest ones in the Toronto area. Tarin read the names on the tombstones as they passed by. Bobbie laid a beautiful bouquet of roses on her grandmother's grave. As she watched, it dawned on her that she had no idea where her mother was buried. She had to have a tombstone somewhere, didn't she?

She got a chill up her back and an eerie feeling they were being watched. Her head snapped around as she scanned the graveyard. Nothing looked out of the ordinary. It was a gorgeous sunny day. There were a few other people paying respects, but none were looking her way or seemed the least bit interested in her. She watched for a moment before she put it off to cemetery nerves. Chance picked up a three-leaf clover, thrusting it at her. She got down to his level and helped him explore but couldn't shake the uneasy feeling she had. Finally, she attributed it to all she'd been through the last few days and the fear that Stephen or her father would find her. She wasn't sure which bothered her more. Being only an hour away from her dad was a bit unsettling. Or that he might know she was there.

Later that day after they'd arrived home, she put an exhausted and freshly bathed boy to bed. He'd had so much fun splashing and giggling and running; all things he wasn't accustomed to. Gently kissing her son, she tiptoed from the room, feeling tired but overjoyed at seeing him so happy. He seemed like any normal boy who hadn't been through a lot of ups and downs in his young life.

She needed to do some research. Wondering if she should use her laptop, she decided she couldn't take the chance. She wouldn't put it past Stephen to have installed a tracking device on it and since she was still unsettled from the cemetery, she decided not to push her luck. He didn't know about Bobbie, and he wouldn't know she was looking for someone who'd been dead for twenty-nine years, so she asked Bobbie if she could use her laptop.

Having never looked for someone's gravesite before, she had no clue where to start. Two hours later, she had learned a lot about cemeteries and interment but still did not know how to find her mom. Tarin wanted to go onto her own website but didn't want to open that door. She didn't want others she hadn't invited to know about it.

Bobbie was probably as good or better on a computer than she was, and although she loved having her friend back, something was stopping Tarin from sharing too much.

She started to type in her mom's name, only to realize she wasn't sure what it was. Tara Louise is what came to mind, but when she searched that name, along with Madsen, her dad's last name, nothing showed up. In fact, she couldn't find anyone with the name Tara Louise who had lived in Ontario. Frustrated, she slapped the kitchen table she was using as her desk.

"You could ask your dad, you know?"

She slapped her hand to her chest. "Jesus, Bobbie. You scared the heck out of me."

"Cool. But so you know, if you want to vent, then slam your fist onto the surface." She did just that. "Okay, your turn."

Tarin laughed a little uncomfortably. "I'm fine."

"Come on. You are so repressed, girl. You need to let go of some of that anger."

"I'm not mad."

Bobbie looked at her with a raised eyebrow.

Tarin tapped her fist on the table.

Bobbie burst out laughing. "Well, it wasn't much, but I'll take it."

She smiled, feeling better. "I should have been able to find something about my mom, right?"

"You'd think. But you could save yourself a lot of time by asking your father."

"I know. Just not yet. I don't understand; shouldn't my mom's name, Tara Louise, show up somewhere?"

"Where's your birth certificate? It'll have her information and maybe help with tracking her down."

"I don't have it."

"Hey, no problem, you can apply for a new one."

"Right." She didn't bother to tell her that her father had it. He'd always had it. In fact, she'd never seen it. When she'd applied for her driver's license, he'd sent one of his flunkies with her to 'protect' her and to hand over her birth certificate for the licensing office to get the information they needed. They'd handed it back, and he'd taken it. Then when she'd gone for her passport, her dad had obtained all the paperwork for her to fill out and then had sent another flunky with her to apply. He always claimed he did it so she wouldn't have to worry about the small stuff. She could focus on her job, and he'd keep track of everything else. It hadn't been such a big deal then, but now she was seeing how big of a deal it really was.

What had he been trying to hide?

She decided to check out how to apply for a new birth certificate.

It seemed easy enough if she had all the information. No matter how much she tried, she couldn't shake the question—was her mother dead? Or alive?

CHAPTER 9

"GOOD MORNING, DOROTHEA. SORRY to bother you."

Dorothea looked up from the ledgers for Caspian Winery. Everything in her business was computerized, but she was still old school and preferred everything to be on paper. For a long time, she'd had her accountant make a computer copy, and a handwritten copy. It had taken her a long time to trust that what went into an electronic device would not get lost. Her staff had been annoyed. The redundancy was time-consuming, but she hadn't been ready to believe electronics were safe. She still wasn't sure, but she'd eased up a bit. She'd leave it for her successor to embrace the computer era... whoever that might be.

"Good morning, Tom. What can I do for you? Has something happened since our Monday meeting?"

The tall, slender man took off his hat and held it as he stood there. "No, well, I mean yes. But it's not about me. Although I'm sure Oliver will try to convince you of that."

Dorothea rested her elbows on her desk and clasped her hands firmly in front of her.

"Do you mind telling me what you're talking about?" She didn't want to hear it and didn't have time to play referee between the two again, but it looked as though she was going to be doing that anyway.

"Well, it appears that we have bad wine—"

Oliver came sailing through the door. "Dorothea, excuse me for barging—what are you doing here?"

"He was telling me something about some bad wine?"

"What did you do, stand outside my door eavesdropping? And then—"

"I wasn't eavesdropping. I was passing the office when I heard you talking with someone about one of our bottles tasting like vinegar."

Dorothea gasped. "What are you talking about?"

"So, you heard part of the conversation and had to run to the boss with what you think you know."

"Well, I'm not going to be blamed for it," Tom said.

"Neither am I, but I think that new ice wine we started making was a mistake."

"Of course you'd think that. You haven't done anything different in fifteen years."

"Gentlemen, can you please tell me what's going on?" Dorothea got to her feet, placed her knuckles on her desk and leaned forward, but neither man was paying her any attention. She stacked all the papers in front of her and slid them into the top drawer. All things breakable had long since been removed from her desk.

"This is not my responsibility."

"Well, it's not mine either. I just grow the grapes."

"Stop!" Dorothea knew he was talking about his suggestion a year before that Tom look into using Riesling grapes so they could make ice wines, which were becoming quite popular. They were always quibbling about something. Tom didn't like Oliver and felt he was overpaid, prissy in his suit and ties and should keep his nose out of the growing end of the business and do his job, which was to distribute the wine. Sadly, it was almost word for word what Geoff, her second-in-command, had said. Some days, she felt like throwing both men into the sandbox and see what happened. Or maybe throw them in with five-year-olds so they could learn something. On that issue, she had sided with Oliver but had made it clear that he was to bring any ideas to her first and she'd share what she deemed was appropriate. She'd done the same with Tom, who had frequently made suggestions to Oliver on how he could improve shipping and distribution.

They were both territorial and, thanks to her brother, Geoff, adversarial in their dealings with each other. He'd played them, like he'd played so many, convincing each of them the other was out to destroy them. And there had been incidents she'd thought were manager oversights only later to learn Geoff had orchestrated it all. Oliver seemed to have come around, but Tom was still grumbling. She'd spent some time with each of them and thought she'd made headway, but one little incident later and they were fighting like toddlers. As if she didn't have enough to do with trying to save the business that her brother had darn near driven into the ground.

"How would you know? You've only been here for three."

"Because you're a typical guy in a business suit."

Dorothea reached behind her and picked up her cane. She lifted it in front of her, only then realizing she'd picked up the one that her granddaughter Bailey and fiancé Guy had given her. It was beautifully crafted with intricate designs by a native elder. She felt very touched by it. Although it would never be used for its intended purpose—walking—she still enjoyed it. Setting it back, she lifted the one she'd meant to pick up. It was made of the polished ash wood. The doctor had recommended she get one to help her with walking. She, however, had found a much better and more effective use for it.

"What does that even mean?"

"It means—"

Lifting it high, she brought the cane down hard atop the shiny wood desk. Both men froze. They had been standing nose to nose, hands clenched, and cheeks mottled with anger, but now they both slowly turned to face Dorothea.

"Glad I've got your attention. Sit down. I'll ask the questions and tell you who is to answer. Got it?" She sank slowly back into her chair, feeling a bit drained. "Oliver, since you took the call, what is this about bad wine?"

"I got a call from Don Wilson. He's the manager of the Sunrise Villa Resort on the outskirts of Toronto, with its twin resort in northern Ontario. Anyway, he called to say that one of the bottles from their last shipment was bad. Thankfully he called us, because he could have called the Liquor Control Board of Ontario (LCBO), since they control wine distribution in this province. We could have had a disaster on our hands."

"What do you mean, bad?"

He closed his eyes briefly before meeting her gaze. "Vinegar. He said it tasted like vinegar. I haven't gotten all the information, except it was one of our new ice wines." He turned to glare at Tom. "We send all our wine to the LCBO's warehouse, and they ship it from there. To check the shipment, I'll have to call them."

"How many cases were bottled?"

"Thankfully, it's one of our newer brands, so we only made two hundred cases."

"Has anyone else complained?"

"No. But to check all of those—"

"Don't. Do we have any left here?"

"Yes, almost half."

"Okay. Run a quality check on one bottle from each of twenty to thirty random cases. Let me know the results immediately."

Dorothea had learned the wine industry as a young girl, but it was she and Jonathon, her now-deceased husband, who had worked hard to make the winery what it was. But there was one thing she hated, and that was waste. And to discover what had gone wrong, there was going to be a lot of waste.

"What are you going to tell the LCBO? They keep track of the number of bottles of wine made."

"Internal quality control audit; it's quite standard." She wrote a couple of things on her notepad. "Get Mr. Wilson to open twenty—"

"He did. The rest are good, but because he opened them to check them, I told him we'll send out a new shipment tomorrow—only it's supposed to go through LCBO."

"Ship it and let me handle the LCBO. There'll be hell to pay, but let me deal with it. Add in an extra case of our Bordeaux for Mr. Wilson. Ask him to please keep this to himself but be discreet about how you say it. I want that bottle back. I hope he didn't throw it out?" Oliver shook his head. "Actually, all of them, the empty as well as the full ones. Today. "

"There is nothing wrong with that wine or the grapes. Besides, if something tastes bad, it needs to be addressed with Martin, our winemaker."

"Yeah, but—"

"No. This stops now. I'm bringing in a mediator to sit down with the two of you. I'm not going to let this continue. You'll learn to get along." She didn't have to threaten dismissal; she could tell by their expressions that they understood the implications. She shouldn't be wasting her time on their squabbles, especially as busy as she'd been putting out all the other fires Geoff had lit. And she just didn't have the energy to deal with it anymore.

Perhaps it was her knuckles rapping on the desk or her frown, but both excused themselves politely and left.

She was about to pick up the phone when her direct line rang. Frowning more deeply, she glanced at the caller identification. She sighed heavily; James Madsen wanted to talk to her... again. She'd already told him no, so she ignored it, letting it go to voicemail.

She made several calls. "Graham. Is Guy there? He's not answering his cell."

"No, he's not. He should be back in about fifteen—"

"I need to meet with you both. I'll be there in ninety minutes." She hung up and called her driver. This was no small deal. In the almost hundred years Caspian Winery had been in business, not once had the wine tasted like vinegar. There had been some poor years that weren't worthy of their award-winning wines, but never had they ever shipped out anything but the best. Something didn't feel right about this. She reminded herself that they'd managed to get through some other bad times. This too would pass.

A dull ache in her left shoulder grabbed her attention. She pressed her hand over the area. Hopefully this, too, would pass. She took a few deep, calming breaths. The pain reminded her she had seriously considered stepping down. The problem was who would replace her as CEO. She couldn't very well have resigned her position before then as she'd had to clean up all of Geoff's messes. Someone else could have tracked all that he'd done—the embezzling, the fraud, the lies and the fake companies—but the embarrassment for her family had kept her in a central position. The media had already spread vicious rumors about her relatives, so she had done everything she could to stop the gossip.

The guilt was still front and center when she considered all her brother had done—killed several prostitutes, stolen from their own company, Caspian Winery, kidnapped her granddaughter as a baby and then tried to kill her as an adult. It was still so unbelievable what he'd pulled off. She'd forgiven him for a lot of what he'd done to her—the stabbing, the abuse—but not for what he'd done to her family nor to the business. It had taken two years to straighten out his mess—the fake vineyards they'd supposedly purchased, the excessive bank account under a fictitious name—though they'd found another one recently, so she wasn't sure they were done looking at the misdirecting of funds.The list kept getting longer and longer. The only thing that made it slightly bearable was that he had paid the ultimate price with his life. It made her sad. She missed the boy she'd so adored, but not the man he'd become. If he were still alive, he'd be doing something else to make her life hell. And for that, she could not forgive him.

The latest argument between the managers reminded her she hadn't succeeded in fixing everything Geoff had messed up. Her shoulders drooped more than usual as she felt years of exhaustion wearing her down. She'd had enough. The thought of dealing with this latest issue, which could literally shut their doors if it went public, made her shudder.

Now that Guy and Bailey were getting married, maybe she'd have a great-grandchild to spoil soon. She could only hope. But if she kept up her current pace with this job, this company, it might just put her in the ground... and soon.

Her daughter, son-in-law, granddaughter and soon-to-be grandson-in-law had all made it clear they did not want to run Caspian Winery. And thanks to Geoff, she couldn't even groom one of her managers for the position, as the others would leave in a heartbeat, having the proof they needed she was treating them equitably. It would cause an internal war, and she couldn't afford to lose any of her managers' expertise. She didn't have the strength or the desire to hire and train another.

Who was there to take over for her? Yes, she could sell; the offer was there for her to take, but that was more painful than the sword her brother had stabbed her with fifty years before. She reached for the phone and dialed a number from her distant memory. It was time to call in a long overdue favor.

CHAPTER 10

GRAHAM SCANNED HIS NOTES for the eight cases on which he was currently working. He set aside the first three, even though he still had a lot to do on them. For the next two, he typed up his summary of what he'd found, with all the proof from the internet and any footage or evidence Guy had found in his preliminary investigations. He sent those off to the contact; two of them, he and Guy, had worked on around the clock. They had wanted to get some of their priority cases done so they had time to spend on the additional work coming in and figure out who was screwing with them. Guy did the surveillance, and Graham hacked their systems and tracked them online.

One case was rather odd—a woman was trying to prove her son was trying to kill her so he could steal her dog, to which she'd left her entire eighty-million-dollar fortune. They had it all set up and should be running the sting soon. The other one was a husband who was stealing from his wife, and his wife was stealing from her job. It was strange but not out of the ordinary among the situations they investigated. But there was something they were missing. Graham was sure of it, and he and Guy needed time to discuss it.

The last one was Caspian Winery. It had only been a minor incident—one bottle of bad wine but Dorothea had been very upset and was adamant that they look into it. In almost one hundred years, a vinegar-tasting wine had never been shipped. Either someone at the winery was going to be fired for incompetence or it had been done deliberately. Either way, Dorothea wanted some answers now. So, he'd spent almost forty-eight hours straight, minus a few catnaps, to get further ahead on all the assignments and perform some research on Caspian Winery staff, the Liquor Control Board of Ontario—which was no easy feat—the shippers and the resort staff. It had taken a lot of time. And he had but a few answers for her. The bottle just seemed to appear. From all they'd been able to find out thus far, no other spoiled bottles of wine had shown up anywhere.

Caspian had tested 200 bottles to ensure they contained quality wine. No other bad-tasting wine had been found. And he and Guy had done their own test. They'd gone to over twenty liquor stores and bought a bottle from each to test it. The five they had tested had been fine ice wine. A little too fine and a little too hard on the head. He pressed his hand gingerly to his forehead to ease the gentle throbbing. It has seemed like a good idea at the time.

He scrubbed his hand down his face, groaning at the bristles he encountered. A jaw-splitting yawn, complete with tears, threatened to send him off to sleep immediately. A quick glance at his cell phone told him he had been at this for too long. Add the wine in there, and he wasn't sure how he'd made it past five hours. Searching through all of Caspian Winery's employees and trying to find the little bugger who might have hacked their system was keeping him busy. It didn't shock him that he'd been searching for so long; he'd done it plenty of times before. What did surprise him though, were the twenty text messages and ten calls he'd missed. Somehow he'd inadvertently muted his phone. Several were from Guy. Nothing too serious, just that he hadn't found any answers, either.

Graham laughed, only to groan when the noise was too much for his headache. He pressed his hands to his head trying to stem the wine hangover. They were the worst.

He moved a few things on his desk, eventually uncovering the office phone, only to discover the receiver was off the hook. That's what the buzzing noise he'd heard at some point but had chosen to ignore, mainly because he'd thought it was from the alcohol he'd been indulging in. If there had been anything really serious, Guy would have shown up at the office.

Graham was about to listen to the messages when there was a knock on the outer office door. His head snapped up before he pulled up his schedule. The visitor was presumably the first of two interviews for their new tech assistant position.

Guy had obviously left the downstairs door unlocked, probably because he knew Graham would forget the interviews.

Crap!

"Just a minute." He did not know whether the person could hear him.

Swearing profusely, he stretched his eyes wide and then tried to blink away the tiredness. When that didn't work, he stepped into the bathroom tucked in the corner, just down the hall from the reception area of their offices. He splashed cold water on his face, soaked his head, combed his hair straight back, and pulled on some clean clothes he kept at the office. Going to the coffee pot he downed half a cup of coffee on his way to the door. Pasting on a genial smile, he unlocked and pulled open the door, only to discover there was no-one there. He stepped into the hallway in time to see a blonde-haired woman's head disappearing from view.

"Excuse me? Are you Tarin?" He was thankful he'd put her name in his scheduler because he couldn't remember a thing from her resume. He hoped he'd filed it somewhere where he could quickly find it.

The woman turned slowly. Her hazel eyes were arresting, and he couldn't help but notice she was gorgeous—not that she was playing that card. She was dressed very conservatively in a dark blue pantsuit, wore no makeup, and had her hair slicked back as though it was wet.

He felt like the kid in grammar school on the receiving end of a teacher's glare. Without a word, she turned and continued down a few more steps before hesitating. She glanced back at him. Her face wore a look of resolve but also one of determination.

"I am. And you?"

"Graham. Owner of Knights Associates."

Her eyebrows shot upward as her eyes drifted over him before settling on his face. There was a wariness in her gaze.

He felt the need to defend himself. "Look, it's been a long day—" A quick glance at his watch let him know how stupid that comment was. It was only 9:00 a.m. Without another word, he returned to his office and headed straight for the coffee, downing another cup. His stomach clenched, protesting the inadequate feedings over the last few days. Searching the cupboard, he discovered there were no snacks, and he was totally out of caffeine. Leaning over the end of the counter, he filled his cup with water from the dispenser.

"Hmm-hmm."

He spun around so fast that he sloshed the last bit of his drink over the edges of his mug. The woman looked almost as startled as he felt. The lowered eyebrows and pursed lips—like she was staring at a weirdo she couldn't trust—were his undoing. It was like the response many gave the homeless guy, Bill, before they walked away from him in disgust. There was so much more to him than people saw. Graham hated people who looked and judged.

On impulse, he hunched his body forward, and arched his back, leaving his left arm swinging down toward the ground, with his right one tucked against his ribs. To top it off, he twisted his face into as ugly a look as he could.

Her appalled look at his Hunchback of Notre Dame impression made him laugh. He straightened up.

"This was a mistake." She stepped back, not taking her eyes off him.

He moved toward her but couldn't mistake the fear in her eyes or the rigidity of her body. He stopped, flipping up his hands. "I'm really not as bad as I look. I've had a long night. Well, actually make that a few days. Sorry for the joke. I have a little off-kilter sense of humor."

He moved back to the coffee machine and refilled his cup before taking a drink. "This job isn't easy. If you're successful, you'll have regular hours, if you're lucky. I don't keep regular hours. When I have a project, I work pretty much until it's done. Still want to be interviewed?"

Her gaze never wavered from him. She watched him. Deciphered him. Was still very wary of him. It bothered him that she appeared to wonder if she could trust him. She placed her hand on her neck as though wanting to grasp something. After a few swipes, she dropped her hand. It reminded him of his sister and her habit of tugging on her long hair. Had this woman recently cut hers?

"Look, I'm sorry I'm not at my best, but this is who I am. I won't apologize for that. But by George, I think I've found a winner," he said in his best English accent. He took another drink of water.

She cleared her throat. "Can I have one of those?"

Her voice, coming from not far behind him, jolted him, letting him know how tired he was. He hadn't heard her move. "Uh, yeah, sure."

He grabbed a mug and poured her some water. He had her sit behind the desk in the outer office, the reception area as Bailey called it. To him, it was his workout space, which he now realized would have to change. He pulled up a folding chair and sat across the desk from her.

"All right, can you tell me a bit about yourself?"

"I've worked with computers most of my life. I don't have a degree or any formal training. All that I've learned is self-taught or from having apprenticed with some of the best programmers there are. I have a few as my references. I'm good at research, finding and getting rid of trojans, malware, ransomware, viruses. You name it, and I've dealt with it."

"What interested you in applying here?"

There was the slightest hesitation before she answered. Her evasive eyes suggested he would not get a complete answer.

"I've been working for myself for about two-and-a-half years, so it's been a while since I worked for someone else." She glanced down. "I moved out here to help a... friend. I don't have time to establish my company in a new market, so I need a job. This seemed perfect. I know computers." Her gaze was strong and defiant as it met his.

Graham asked her several more questions. One thing he hated was listening to people tell him all they knew when what he needed was for them to show him what they could do.

"If you want to start the laptop in front of you, it's only in sleep mode. I've given you several tasks to do. You've got twenty minutes. Let me know when you're done. I'll be in my office. Just knock."

She nodded and immediately got to work, barely giving him any notice as he walked into his office, closing the door behind him. It felt as though he'd barely had time to sit when both the timer on his watch and the alarm on his computer sounded and she knocked at his door. If anyone had asked him, he would have sworn he'd been wide awake, but the shock of her knuckles rapping against the wood had him jerking so hard he almost toppled over backward in his chair. Only by flailing out his arms and snagging the windowsill behind him, did he prevent that from happening.Wide-eyed, it took a moment for it to sink in what was happening. The office looked the same as usual—a cot in the corner, papers all over Guy's desk, none on his, a dartboard on the far wall, his ten-speed bike tucked in the corner, a treadmill, a Bowflex machine and a few other odds and ends. When none of that caught his attention, his gaze flew to the door and the woman who was patiently knocking again. He was thankful she couldn't see him.

He scrubbed his hands down his face, pried open his eyes and wearily got to his feet. He strolled to the door and opened it.

"I'm finished. Can I show you what I've done?"

"You know what, leave it. Let me go through it. If I need to, I'll call you. I have all your contact information?"

She glanced away before taking a deep breath and then looking him in the eye. Hers were the most arresting color he'd ever seen—brown with flecks of amber scattered throughout. Mesmerizing.

"I have a new phone number and email address." She quickly scribbled down her new information and handed it to him.

"Thank you, Tarin. Once I'm done with the interviews, I'll let you know our decision. We're looking to hire someone who can start right away."

She nodded at his questioning look. "I'm available tomorrow, if you need me."

"Great. Good to know, because frankly, we needed someone yesterday. I'll be in touch either way. Thanks for coming in." He shook her offered hand and walked out with her, locking up the office as he followed her down the long single flight of stairs. The slump of her shoulders told him how disappointed she was. There was no question she sounded good, but he'd have to spend some time going through her responses on the computer to see.

The actual issue he was having was that there was something about her, but he couldn't put his finger on it. Not that she was lying, but she was very careful with her answers, like she wanted to make sure she didn't say too much. It bugged the heck out of him. As they stepped outside, the cool wind whipped around him, and the freshness of it slapped him like a cold splash to the face. He closed his eyes and let it do its magic. Exhaustion was a gritty burn, numbing his brain and depleting his energy.

"Thank you."

His eyes snapped open to stare at the beautiful, blonde-haired woman he'd completely forgotten about. That had never happened to him before. He still had another interview to do before he could crash, which he intended to do for about fourteen hours. He nodded and then looked around. There were several people travers- ing the street, headed to wherever their busy schedules were taking them, but none looked as though they were searching for a certain place. Sure that his next interview hadn't arrived, he turned back to the hazel eyes that were studying him, with a bit of a perplexed frown. Another day, he'd have made a joke.

"Look, I know this is rather... would you mind staying here for about five minutes and watching for a woman by the name of Heather? She's my next interview, but I need to do a quick errand. I have to run down the street. "

"Sure, I have nothing better to do."

The strange look in her eye, which was gone even before he was sure he'd seen it, made him wonder if he wasn't hallucinating. He was tired enough and too strung out to figure it out. Before she changed her mind, he strode down the street to get himself one of the best cafe mochas around. Straight coffee would not keep him awake. And the exercise and cold would hopefully give him a second wind.

CHAPTER 11

HE RAISED HIS GLASS of scotch to his lips and drank slowly. Its warmth slid down his throat and heated his core like a rapidly spreading fire. It was at times similar to this, sitting in the shadows of his five-thousand-square-foot suite, that he felt almost free. A condition that was coming soon but not soon enough. He felt as though he'd been living in a prison for a long time, locked up under the thumb of his family, his father, and he was never quite good enough. Well, things were about to change. He'd show them; had shown them, in fact, but they were in for more surprises, the biggest yet to come.

It was because of certain people in his life that his movements were now restricted. It made him smile that, to his way of thinking, he was limited. He had access anywhere in the world, but he was going to have to be a tad more careful. He didn't want to be noticed by certain people, not yet. His plans for the future were at stake. He'd worked hard to get where he was. Stepping on and over people was part of business. Those who hadn't learned it would never be where he was.

The business he'd built into an empire hadn't happened because he'd been polite. He'd done it at his family's expense. There were hard feelings as he had gone against the fiber of their morals, but he wasn't in this to play nice. His family was why he had to change tactics... change course.

He refused to acknowledge this slight setback as anything more than a bump in the road. It always happened in business dealings. However, things were going to get better. He had the solution; the newspaper clipping he held in his hand had been the answer to his prayers.

He'd been there for the delivery. He'd been the doting grandfather figure that had disappeared before anyone could ask too many questions. The baby had been the answer to his prayers. Since he never trusted fate, faith, or God, he knew how to manipulate events in his favor—at least they would be, eventually. The sight of that child being born had been the most incredible thing he'd ever witnessed. He'd always wanted a son... a boy. And now he had one that he would soon groom to be his proper heir. The child would do all he had not been able to, all under his watchful and direct guidance.

It felt so good that he couldn't help but laugh. The sound was a bit rusty even to his ears. He'd not had much to smile about in his life, but all that was going to change and soon.

The thought of being able to pass on all he'd learned, to mold and create someone in the image of himself, was almost overwhelming, even for him. It meant he would live on in infamy as he would teach the boy to do as he had done... only better.

Tarin came to mind. She hadn't been what he'd wanted or expected, but he'd made do. When he hadn't been given what he'd wanted in life, he'd learned to make them happen. What made him smile, and would undoubtedly piss her off to no end, was she did not know what she had done for him. He was pretty sure she had questions; not that he cared, because she'd been a means to an end. He was pretty sure she hated him, but if she didn't, she would soon.

Parting with her son would be difficult for her, but that wasn't his problem. He wasn't letting anyone impede his plan. The boy was his and always would be, no matter what. Someday, she'd come to understand, even if he had to get a little firm with her.

He downed the rest of his drink and set it on the crystal tray on the mahogany table before pushing to his feet. He brushed off a piece of imaginary lint from his Italian silk suit before staring out the wall of picture windows that provided a clear, unhindered view of the city. To be sure, it was not the one he wanted to live in but had to until he could put his plan in place. Once he had the boy, he'd have to find a reclusive spot for a while, but he was prepared for that. In fact, he'd be moving much closer to where it had all started for him.

He just needed his heir. Waiting even one more day was almost asking too much, but he would. All the books said that early childhood was the most impressionable stage, so he wouldn't wait much longer. It was definitely time to take his son. He wasn't about to compromise on what he wanted, what was rightfully his, not for anything or anybody—even if they were family.

He picked up the phone and made the call he'd patiently been waiting to make for a long time.

"He's two now. I want the boy."

"I thought you wanted to wait until he was at least two-and-a-half?"

"Things change."

"Yes, but we have an agreement," Stephen's voice trembled ever so slightly as he responded.

The sound of his sniveling was such a sweet balm; the guy still feared him, which was exactly what he wanted. It made it easier to keep him in line. "Oh, I get it. You're worried that you won't be paid for the next five months."

"Well—"

"Nothing's changed, except I'm taking him a little early."

"Give me another week or two? And then you can have him."

"I'll meet you on Monday at the Calgary Zoo. That should be a good place to start our bonding. Make sure she doesn't come with you."

"That will not be easy."

"I don't care. Get me the boy. I'll be there on Monday to collect him."

"And the fee is now twenty million dollars."

"Really? You think you can blackmail me?"

"Well, I've been following your orders for years. I've done my job—"

"—and been paid handsomely for it. I will pay the original last payment of three million dollars, plus the five months we originally agreed on, plus the exorbitant living allowance and not a penny more. Don't screw me on this. If you need to know what I do to people who cross me—"

"Forget it. Fine. I'll have the child there in three weeks, on Saturday. My promotion party is next Friday. I need her to attend with me."

So, he thinks he has a say. How cute. He was about to argue but he still had some unfinished family business. It would be better if the boy weren't with him when he dealt with that, but he would not let this asshole think he had that much power.

"Fine. Two weeks from Saturday and not a day late."

He hung up, relieved this was finally going to be over. He could move forward with his plans. Everything would work out the way he wanted it to. Family would pay and he'd have his son.

CHAPTER 12

'YOU CAN'T DO THIS, Tarin. I'll make you pay for making me look like an ass... What makes you think you can take Chance from me... Bring him back. Now... Who the hell do you... You'll be sorry... Bring him home and I'll take you on that holiday I've been promising.'

Those had been some of the texts from Stephen that had started her day. There were at least another dozen or so oscillating wildly in their emotions. It all served as a reminder that she wasn't there on a holiday; she had work to do. She needed answers so she could cut him out of her life for good. The only positive she could glean from his texts was she was pretty sure he had no idea where she was... yet.

"So how's the job hunt?"

Tarin wanted to climb back into bed and pull the covers over her head, but then that never solved anything. "I think I messed up, Bobbie." She didn't bother to tell her friend that she'd only applied for one job because she had to get it. Most employers took their time in selecting someone, but they had seemed in a hurry and she'd made it clear she was ready to start tomorrow. That had been yesterday, and there was still no call. Maybe their sense of urgency and hers weren't quite the same.

"I thought the interview went well?"

She coughed more as an excuse to turn her head, so she didn't have to look at her friend when she answered. "It did, although I acted like a bit of an idiot." She couldn't very well tell her friend that she'd lied and cheated in the hopes of getting the position. She wasn't sure Bobbie would understand why she'd done it—or, more likely, want her to explain her reasons, something she wasn't ready to share.

"How are you doing? You seem annoyed."

"I'm fine."

"Come on. I can tell you're upset. Is it something I did?"

"God no. It's my mother. She drives me nuts. You know that Mercedes she was going to test drive?"

Tarin nodded.

"She wants to buy it for her boyfriend."

"I thought she said yesterday she wanted it for herself?"

"She does, but if it will keep young stud number three around, then it's for him. He's a whole year older than I am. So why can't I find a man? Because my mother is busy bedding them all."

Tarin snorted. "I'm sorry. That's really not funny." She tried hard to stop laughing, but she couldn't.

Bobbie smiled at her indulgently and then made a face before chuckling as well.

"She sure does like to spend money. I guess that hasn't changed." It had always been a problem when they were younger.

"Nope. That's one of the reasons Dad split. He couldn't handle being broke all the time."

"Is your mom working?"

"Oh, good gravy, no. That is such a dirty word in her book."

"Are you supporting her?"

"Me? No, not really. I've taken over her finances because she gets swamped with bill collectors when she doesn't pay. She's holding me over a barrel. She's a pro at blackmail."

"So she has money?"

"Yeah, she got a hell of a settlement and roped yo—" Bobbie's eyes opened wide. "She's got some money."

Tarin frowned. Something struck her as odd, but she was too busy with her own worries to figure out what might be going on with her friend.

Bobbie made her way across the room. "So, you're not sure about your job? Don't worry about it. I'm sure if you don't get it, there are others. Let's not sit around here moping and waiting for a call. Let's go do something."

Tarin contemplated that for a moment. If she didn't get this position, she wouldn't have access to what she need-ed; however, there were other ways to gather information. The logo on the paper that had been stuck to her back was the only clue she had to what had happened to her.

She watched her friend as she paced back and forth in her tiny room. Bobbie hadn't looked at her once. Some-thing was off. Her mom had obviously upset her. Tarin would have done almost anything to have a mother drive her nuts.

"I could get my dad to help if money is an issue?"

"God, no!" The words were spat at her almost before she was done speaking.

"Okay. I just—"

"I know. You want to fix it like you do everything. Leave it alone, Tarin. Okay?"

Tarin nodded but was taken aback by Bobbie's force-ful, hard tone. Bobbie's phone suddenly rang.

"Dammit. It's Mom. I'll be awhile."

"No worries. I'll figure out something for this after-noon." She watched as her friend walked out of her room, already talking away. She hated to see her so upset. Her mom was something else. Tarin had always thought she was a very selfish woman. Everything was always centered on her personal needs. She'd rarely come to visit Bobbie at boarding school, and when she had, she'd done nothing but complain about her life and gossip about everyone else.

Tarin gasped. If Mrs. Benson had told her dad she'd seen her, he'd know where she was. If she asked for help for Bobbie, he'd know where she was.

How did my life become such a mess?

She had to get answers before her dad discovered what was happening in her life. There was no way he was aware of the predicament she was in, or that he had a grandson. If he had, he would have taken control of her life but, more importantly, he'd have taken Chance and raised him like the son he'd always wanted.

She jumped out of bed almost in a panic. Her dad couldn't find out about her and what she was up to... not yet. If Bobbie's mom talked...

Chance squealed with delight from the other room where Kim was entertaining him. The sound was like a beacon pulling her back from the edge.

She had to do something. The pamphlet for a wine tour she'd seen on Bobbie's table came to mind. There was no reason she couldn't take a look at Caspian Winery. She might as well do something, as she'd moved across the country to get answers. Maybe she'd get lucky. Doubtful, as she had no idea what she was looking for or what she hoped to gain by going there. If she could get near a computer while there, maybe she could get information.

She fell back against the wall, surprised by what she was thinking. She, who had never stolen a thing in her life, was actually thinking of stealing something... something that could land her in jail.

"Aaaaaaaaaaaahhhhhhhh," she yelled. The sound shocked her so much that she quickly stopped, but not soon enough. Kim rushed into the room wide-eyed. She was sure she looked just as surprised as Kim. "I'm fine. I was—I'm fine."

As soon as Kim left, she bent over to take in some deep breaths. She had to do something; she couldn't live in this limbo of not knowing. Before she could talk herself out of it, she dug out a USB, tucked it into her bag, and then headed for the shower.

CHAPTER 13

"So?"

Guy plopped down behind his desk, looking almost as tired as Graham felt. "I didn't find much. I met with the resort that had received the wine, the same guy who's been doing it forever. Then I talked with the distributor, LCBO. I told them I'm from the Internal Affairs Department of Revenue Canada, and we're looking into some inconsistencies."

"And they bought that?"

"Yeah. I talked to one of the middle managers, who only knows so much, right? I told him it was so secret that only a select few knew about us. Whenever you mention anything about the government tax arm, people tend to panic. I saw a couple of pictures of a lake and casually said, 'Does the government know you own this?' The guy spilled as though a dam had burst. Nothing helpful though, at least not to us but to the government, maybe. Then I met with the employees of Caspian Winery. Not easy to ask questions like, 'Have you had any incidents of bad wine?' and make it sound routine. Grandma was very insistent that I not hint about any problems."

Graham laughed. "She doesn't expect much. Better you than me to deal with her." He smiled at his friend's grunt, knowing that Dorothea Lindell could be one tough woman to reckon with. That she was eighty hadn't slowed her down or softened her demeanor. She was an admirable lady, but he loved to rib Guy as she was quite hard on him.

"Yeah, well, now she has me doing her manager's job. I think she's having some problems with her management team, but she wouldn't tell me anything. She wants me to find out more about one of the vineyard hands that came late last year or early this year. I can't remember; I have it in my notes though."

Graham raised his eyebrows.

"Yes, I've already added him to the top of the list to follow. I need you to do a full background check. Find out all you can."

"Got it. You have fun playing mediator over there."

"Right, like I have time to do that."

"I know she's impossible to say no to. Anyway, I found nothing in the cursory background checks of any of the potential suspects you gave me. We need to narrow down the list so we can do a deep dive on a few. I'll start with that new guy. Something isn't right about this whole thing. My radar is going off the charts."

"I agree, but what? Someone has gone through a lot of work to keep us from finding answers. Ideas?"

"Yeah."

"Geoff," they said at the same time.

"Okay, so we're on the same page. Now what?"

"Can he still be alive?"

"It doesn't seem possible. They found a body. They found that ugly garnet ring he always wore. It can't be."

"Let's forget him; he's gone. It's not as though we don't have a sufficient number of enemies to choose from. Even though we keep a pretty low profile and our police and government contacts, try to keep us in the background, it wouldn't be hard for anyone to figure out who we are." Exasperated, Graham shoved his hand through his hair.

"True. We've probably made one or two hit lists. You've got to be right. And it's easy to figure out our connection to Caspian Winery. Dorothea raised me from the age of nine, and as soon as Bailey and I get married, she'll be my grandmother-in-law. If someone wanted to get back at us, it could just be me, couldn't it? Maybe it's not aimed at you at all. Anyway, what better way than to mess with our company as well as Dorothea's?"

"But what do they want? Are they trying to put us out of business, or could someone want to buy up one or both companies? Is that what this is about?"

"Or is it purely about the money? "

Graham's computer notified him of another email. Then it dinged again... and again. Sitting up straight, he clicked on his browser, stunned as thirty-five requests came in, one right after the other.

"Someone is so screwing with us."

"I agree." Guy set his coffee mug on his desk. "How'd the interviews go? Sorry I missed them."

"Like hell you are. You love them as much as I do. Not well. I'd been up a while and wasn't quite with it. And one never showed."

"And the one who did?"

He hesitated before responding. "Good. In fact, very good. She found all the Trojans I'd planted, all within the time I gave her and with no antivirus program on the computer. She searched but didn't waste time, then downloaded the same one I would have, ran it, cleaned up the problems and then she downloaded a second program and found a ransom malware I had forgotten about."

"What's the problem?"

Guy's eyebrows shot upwards, which Graham pretended he didn't notice.

"Here, read through her information."

"Looks good to me. Hire her. We need someone now."

"Yeahhhhhh—"

"Hire her. Or is there something you're not telling me? She sounds perfect."

CHAPTER 14

BOBBIE DESCENDED THE STAIRS looking as though she'd just been through a windstorm, her hair tugged in all directions. A good sign, Tarin thought, of how her talk with her mother went. Tarin winced, but rather than speak about her mother, she decided instead that Bobbie needed a distraction and she needed to do some snooping.

"I was thinking about going on a wine tasting tour. Care to join me?"

"God yes. After that call with my mom—let's not go there. I'm in. I'll make sure Kim can babysit. You're not taking Chance, right?"

"No."

After several missed turns because of Tarin's poor directions, they finally arrived at their destination.

"If you'd told me we were going to Caspian Winery, I'd have been able to get us here with no problem. They have outstanding wine. But do you realize we passed about eight or ten good ones on the way here? The Reynolds Winery right next door is fantastic."

"I saw Caspian's ad, so its name stuck in my mind. I was a bit curious. We can hit the other ones another time. You've been here before?"

"Yeah. Several times. I come here at Christmas for the tour; it's so cool. They do it up right. We'll have to come this year. We should have come by cab."

"That's okay, I won't drink. Have you ever met any of the staff here?"

"The guy who does the vineyard tour is rather hot."

"Anyone else?"

"Yeah, I guess, but I don't remember names or anything. Why?"

"I thought maybe you could get us a private tour."

"No, you've got to be family or close friends for that, I imagine."

Tarin thought about her hopeful connection through Knights Associates. If... no, when she got the job, she'd ask. There were no ifs, ands, or buts about it; she had to get that position. As she entered the building, she heard Bobbie already asking about the tour and being told the next one would start in about twenty minutes. They could wander around until then. Bobbie sat down.

"I'll wait."

"I'm going outside, okay?"

"No problem, I think I'll have a glass while I sit here."

Tarin smiled and headed out the door. The vineyards were down the hill to the left. Behind her was the area for the winemaking, but she wanted the administrative center, the best opportunity for locating their computers and data.

Walking around the building, she noticed there were several other buildings. She wasn't sure what they were for, but since there were no windows, she doubted any were offices. Around the back, she noticed there were a few workers milling about, some on machinery while others were entering and exiting the shops. Squaring her shoulders, she purposefully strode with an air of authority. At the far end, she turned the corner and found a two-story she was certain contained offices. The side and back doors were locked, so she continued around to the front, realizing they were attached to the main winemaking building. There had to be a way into the offices from inside. As she was contemplating what to do, someone walked past her and entered a side door to the winemaking building. She didn't hesitate to follow suit. Once away from the glare of the sun, her eyes had to adjust to the dimmer light. The incessant noise of the machines had her clapping her hands over her ears. Not wasting any time, she followed a hallway to her right.

"Excuse me. What are you doing?"

She spun around so quickly; she wished she'd worn runners as her heels slid on the cement floor and she slammed backward into the wall.

"Ouch."

"Hey, are you all right?"

The young man grabbed her arm, keeping her upright. She was about to pull back when she saw the darkening of his pupils. Taking a deep breath, she thought it was okay this one time to use what God had given her. She felt as though she was auditioning for a part in a play, if the nerves in her stomach were anything to go by. Bobbie had always told her as a kid she should use what she'd been given.

"Thank you so much. Do you think there's somewhere close by where I could sit down? Get out of this noise?"

"Well—"

"Ooooohhhh. It hurts." She did what she hated; she gave him her best helpless female, imploring expression that seemed to make all men think they could leap tall buildings. When he still hesitated, her lip quivered, and she forced tears to rise to the corners of her eyes. She repressed a shudder of revulsion at what she was exploiting.

"Yeah, come on. I'll take you into the reception area."

A few minutes later, she found herself precisely where she wanted to be, in the central office reception area. He got her a glass of water from the water dispenser. She bent over and rubbed her ankle as though it was painful.

"I think I might have sprained something. I need to sit for a minute." She slowly sipped her glass of water. "What's your name?"

"Cory."

"Nice to meet you. Have you worked here long?"

"I'm new this summer. I'm still learning my way around. Are you ready to go? I have to get back to work."

Tarin stood but instantly sat down. "Do you think I could sit here for a minute? You do what you have to do, come back in about ten minutes, I'm sure I'll be ready by then."

He hesitated.

"I can't tell you how much I appreciate your saving me like that. Usually, I'm not so clumsy." She eased her shoe off so he could see her passion-pink toes. It took only a few more minutes of flirting to cajole him into trusting her. As soon as he was out the door, she kicked off her other shoe and immediately went around the receptionist's desk and hacked into her computer. There was a lot to read but nothing of use. She logged off and made her way down the hallway behind her. Along the wall were several pictures. She glanced at them but didn't want to get distracted. Another time, she'd study them.

Heading for the office at the end of the hall, she took out her lock-picking set and tried to jimmy the lock. It didn't work. No matter what she did, it wouldn't open. Frustrated, she tried the other doors. It was only when she reached Oliver Gibner's door that it opened. Not sure what she had done differently, but she'd obviously missed something in the twenty minutes of YouTube videos she'd watched on lock picking. It wasn't budging. Bobbie had always been good at it when they were kids, but it wasn't a skill she could casually ask Bobbie how to do.

Tempted to go back and try the CEO's office, she decided she was wasting time and she had better be thankful for opening one. For the hundredth time, she pushed away all the guilt over what she was doing. She kept reminding herself that this was for Chance.

Oliver Gibner, the Shipping and Receiving Manag er.It only took a couple of minutes, and she was into his computer. Since she didn't have time to snoop, she downloaded several folders onto her USB and logged out. Knowing her time had to be up, she let herself out and was strolling down the hallway when she heard the door open. She scurried to get behind the main desk before sinking to the floor. As soon as she had an audience, she started moaning.

"Oooohhh."

"Excuse me? Miss? Where are you?"

"Here behind the desk. I was trying to find the bathroom."

He squatted down beside her, staring at the ankle she was clutching. "Let me see. It doesn't look swollen."

"I know. That's what's so weird." She continued to moan.

"Let me carry you." Before she could respond, he picked her up and carried her out. He stopped long enough for her to grab her shoes, and then he proceeded through the building to the front.

Bobbie jumped to her feet. "What happened?"

"Nothing." She opened her eyes wide, hoping her friend would get the message and not make a big deal about it. "But we need to go. I twisted my ankle a bit. Nothing serious."

"If you'd stop wearing those stupid things." She nodded at the stilettos dangling from Tarin's fingers.

"I know. Let's go."

After being carefully put into the passenger seat, she put her hand on the young man's arm. "Thank you." He turned a light shade of red.

As Bobbie drove away, she said, "He's young, don't you think?"

"Funny."

"What was that all about?"

Tarin hesitated briefly before saying, "I got lost, ended up somewhere I shouldn't have been. I'm not like you; I don't know how to talk my way out of that so—"

"So, you played the damsel in distress card."

"Something like that."

"If any guy would carry me, I'd play it up, too."

"It's not all it's cracked up to be, believe me."

The rest of the trip was made in silence. Tarin closed her eyes, glad that Bobbie was driving. The insanity of her actions washed over her. The last time she'd done anything this crazy, she'd been sixteen and she and Bobbie had hacked into the school's computer to change her mark, which hadn't ended well for Tarin. Sadly, she'd included Bobbie again, only this time, Bobbie wasn't even aware of it. In fact, Tarin was sure Bobbie would be shocked if she knew what Tarin had just orchestrated. She couldn't believe what she'd pulled off. The sick feeling was still present, but the excitement of what she'd done was starting to consume her.

"Stop the car, Bobbie."

She immediately slowed, turning the corner not far from her house before pulling over. "What's up? You okay? You look almost giddy." She touched her hand to Tarin's forehead.

Tarin ducked. "I'm fine. I'm going to walk—"

"What about your ankle?"

"It's fine. I need some fresh air. I think I'm only a few blocks from home, right?"

Bobbie nodded. Tarin climbed out, closed the door and started strolling down the sidewalk, even though the nervous energy bounced around inside her like a young child on a sugar high. Finally, Bobbie pulled away and waved as she passed. As soon as she rounded the corner, Tarin slipped off the heels she'd slipped on while in the car. She did something she'd never done; she ran.

The USB in her pocket sat about as comfortably as a load of bricks, and it felt as though it was radiating heat. It may not have been burning a hole in her pocket, but it sure was in her mind. Did it have anything helpful, or had all that risk been in vain? Would guilt prevent her from even going through the information to discover what she'd stolen?

Her stomach felt as if it had dropped past her knees. Her breathing suddenly hitched. She stopped, bending over, huffing and puffing like she'd run a marathon instead of a mere twenty feet.

Her phone chirped with a message notification. She pulled it out, warring with herself whether to look. Odds were that it was Stephen venting about what a witch she was—though he'd never called her anything that nice. She'd ignore it if it were from him. She'd missed a phone call. Listening to the message, she couldn't help but smile. She'd done it. She'd gotten the job. Things were going to work out.

A few people turned as she ran by in bare feet, a big grin on her face, stilettos in one hand and her cell phone in the other. It wasn't until someone honked that she even realized how ridiculous she must look... and how mortified her father would be that the young woman he'd groomed so meticulously had just thrown her manners out the window. She immediately stopped running but refused to put her shoes back on. And nothing was going to dispel the excitement she was feeling. Everything was going to work out.

CHAPTER 15

"I OFFERED HER THE job. Tarin's starting Monday. Thank God she was free to start so soon. We had little choice, but I still say there's something. She's too perfect."

"Really? I've never heard you say that about any woman."

Graham's head swiveled around to stare at Bailey, who was entering the office with a big grin on her face. "All right, that's it. I'm getting you a cowbell."

"Ah, that's so sweet." Bailey patted him on the shoulder as she passed on her way to Guy's desk, who pulled her into his lap. They both looked at the woman on the computer screen. "Wow, she's gorgeous. Who is she?"

"Someone who's causing Graham some grief."

"That's not what I said. There was something about her—"

"Yeah, she's absolutely beautiful. I would love to have that long black mane, not to mention those eyelashes, the slender body—"

"She doesn't have long hair anymore, and now it's blonde—"

"Don't you dare change anything." Guy proceeded to kiss Bailey.

Graham, feeling like an outsider, was preparing to leave when they broke apart.

"Sorry bud. Besides the fact that she should be a fashion model, what's keeping you from wanting to work with her? If all those emails you've received are because someone has hacked our system or they're leading us in a maze that has no end, we need some help. Especially with the crap that's now happening at Casp—"

There was silence for a moment before Bailey pushed to her feet and turned to face Guy. "You were about to say Caspian Winery. What's going on there? And why are you trying to hide it from me? You've never hidden anything about your cases before."

"I'm outta here. Gotta run."

"Chicken."

"Yes, but a smart one. Bye. See you in the morning." Graham grabbed his jacket and strode out of the office. He didn't know what Guy would tell her; she had finally reached the point where she'd stopped seeing Geoff around every corner. It was impossible for him to be back, he hoped, but the possibility that he might be could send Bailey back into her nightmares. He and Guy had to find out who was trying hard to get their attention.

"Dammit!" He walked out of the building, unsure of his destination. He might as well check the address in one of the latest email requests they'd received. Sometimes it paid to check things out in person. There was too much false data on the internet. In one rushed case they'd worked on for the District Attorney, a suspect had been going on trial and some new information had arisen. They'd gathered their internet research and had almost sent it when Bailey questioned the existence of a location mentioned. She and Guy had driven out there only to find a vacant lot. The lawyers would have appeared incompetent had they used their initial report and, in turn, Knights Associates would have lost credibility.The temptation to take shortcuts was getting more difficult to ignore as he didn't even have the time to get through all the incoming emails, never mind get any investigative work done. That case, though, had been a reminder that they were hired precisely because the work wasn't easy. They would have help, but he didn't feel any more confident about getting on top of everything, and he had serious reservations about letting anyone else see what they did.

Am I being territorial?

Sighing heavily, he didn't know. It would be great to have another set of eyes, but on the other hand, at what price? An image of Tarin flashed through his mind. His original thought had been how tough it would be to let anyone into their inner circle, but when he couldn't get past how attractive she was, he wondered what bothered him more. Imagining her doing this job was almost impossible, because she was definitely not his idea of a computer nerd. He couldn't help but smile as he remembered Bailey telling him the same thing not long after they'd met.

Feeling the exhaustion of the last few months, he climbed into his car. No longer concerned about checking an address, he was ready to head home, where he hoped to crash for about twelve hours.

His phone rang. Distracted, he reached for it.

"Hello?"

"Graham. Glad I caught up with you. I need your help."

All thoughts flew out of his head at the distinctive voice. "Mrs. Lindell."

"For goodness sakes, Graham, it's Dorothea. Do not call me Mrs. It makes me sound old, and I refuse to be that."

Listening to her spunky and spry voice, no one would ever have guessed she was eighty years old. Still, he felt like a young boy about to get his knuckles rapped if he didn't sit up straight and pay attention.

"Dorothea." His mother's voice played in his subconscious. *You never call your elders by their first name and never someone who has the status of this lady.* He gulped. "What can I do for you?"

"I find myself in need of a driver. Can you be at the airport at 5:00 p.m. to pick me up?"

"The Toronto International Airport?"

"Yes, please be there. Oh, and..." She gave him her flight information, where she wanted him to drive her and approximately how long she would need him, before she hung up. All of it left him very confused... and unnerved.

She had a full-time driver, so why wouldn't she use him? She often liked to drive herself or even get Guy to drive her, but she had never asked Graham. So why now? Guy was busy with his wedding plans, so maybe she didn't want to distract him from that?

Why did she want him to keep it to himself? And specifically asked that he not tell Guy... or Bailey.

CHAPTER 16

'TARIN, IT'S TIME YOU stop this foolish attitude. There are things I need to discuss with you.'

Her father had called. The one thing she'd been waiting for, for so long. He'd finally bridged the gap between them. Tarin's body sagged with relief at the sound of his voice. It was over. They could work things out. She hugged her cell phone to her chest and imagined it was her dad giving her a big hug, not that he ever had, but it was part of her new dream. Her lips stretched into a natural smile; everything was going to be fine.

Regardless of her heart's response, her mind wouldn't allow her to bask in her newfound comfort. *Why did he call? What am I missing?*

To prove to herself that it was all good, she listened to his message again, only to wish she hadn't. Though she listened to his words, it was his tone that caught her attention. She immediately became the child who had stolen a flashlight and silently hugged her teddy bear in her closet so her dad wouldn't discover that she was frightened of the dark and the monsters that came with it. Hopes of ever having a close relationship with him were slipping through her fingers like the misty layers of fog.

Reality was settling in. Instinctively, she reached up to tug her hair, which reminded her of the shorter style she'd yet to become accustomed to. Cutting her long hair had been a small sacrifice to help camouflage her identity. At least Chance didn't seem to mind it.

Leaving Chance was harder than she thought. Picking him up, he clung for a few moments with big tears filling his eyes. Then the new puppy Bobbie had just gotten came bounding down the stairs with Kim. Chance wiggled to get down and was soon playing with the dog. It made Tarin happy and sad at the same time.

Knowing Chance was okay made it easier to focus on getting ready for work and out the door on time. Her mind soon shifted to focus on one thing—her father. The weight of her father's disapproval sat heavily on her shoulders. By the time she'd pulled into her new employer's parking lot, she still couldn't shake her thoughts. *My father called. What does he really want?*

Reminding herself that she needed to get it together to start her new job, she climbed the flight of stairs. Taking a deep breath and pasting on a smile, she entered the office. "Good morning, Graham."

"Good morning, Tarin." He smiled and gestured toward the desk she'd used for her interview. "This will be yours. As you can see, this space also serves as a kitchen and an exercise room. The bathroom's just down the hall."

Tarin studied her new workspace. It was a large area with her desk on one side, a counter and fridge in the far corner and a workout machine in the opposite corner near Graham's office.

"It's great, thank you."

"To tell you a bit about us, we have a couple of companies—Knights Computers is downstairs; we fix computers there. This is Knights Associates—"

Graham explained their businesses and explained her responsibilities. He gave her access to one of the email accounts he wanted her to monitor and went on to explain their processes and security measures. It was standard but she already had the technical knowhow, so only half-listened. Her mind strayed to the thoughts that had been plaguing her since she'd received her father's message.

Why did he phone? Why now?

Something didn't feel right. It wasn't just that his tone admonished her as though she were a child; it was also the timing. Chance immediately came to mind. Did her father know about him? Every now and then, she wished she could tell Chance he had a grandfather, but the fear of giving her son the impression that he had a sweet old gramps kept her from saying anything at all.

Chance. How was Bobbie making out with babysitting him?

Tarin placed her hands on the desk in front of her and took a deep breath. It wasn't a great start to her first day at her new job. She couldn't believe she'd actually been hired. The guilt of how she'd got it crept in to dampen her mood, but she pushed that away and thought about why she was there. She was going to find the answers she needed.

Did I dress okay for work? She looked at the navy-blue blouse and beige skirt she'd finally settled on that morning after trying multiple outfits.

"And so?"

That tone catapulted her back to the here and now. Her mind was like a butterfly flitting from petal to petal, not sticking with anything.

What did he say? Graham's hard stare let her know he would not give her any help.

"So you want—"

"Hi. You must be Tarin."

She tamped down the instant sense of gratification at the interruption and stood to shake the hand of her other boss.

"I'm Guy and this is Bailey, my fiancé."

"Nice to meet you."

"You too. I'm sad to see you cut your gorgeous mane." Bailey shook her hand.

Tarin felt the color leave her face. "Excuse me?"

"I'm sorry. After Graham interviewed you last week, he was rather evasive about describing you, so I went on the internet."

Feeling shaky, she rested her hands on her desk. "Oh?"

"Hey look. I like the new blonde short style. Totally changes you, though. I'm sorry; I can tell this is bothering you. I'm here because these two don't enjoy doing paperwork, so they asked me to help you make sense of all the forms you have to sign." Bailey grabbed the stack of papers out of Graham's hands, pulled up a chair beside the desk and sat.

A distinct bell rang. Ignoring it, Tarin sat as well.

"Is that yours?"

Tarin waved her hand. "Yeah, it's my cell. It's nothing," she said, a little more abruptly than she'd meant. The last thing she wanted was to draw attention to her personal life. Thankfully, from the distinct tone, that one was from Bobbie, checking in with updates about Chance. She'd have shut it off or muted it but knew that wasn't going to happen for a while. Leaving her child behind after two years of staying at home with him was tearing her apart. Her son had waved goodbye with his porridge-filled hand and tear-filled eyes. She hoped he was okay.

"Okay, so we need to..." Bailey was all business, setting the forms down in front of her, explaining their purpose. It wasn't long before Guy and Graham disappeared into their office and closed the door. There wasn't a peep coming from behind it, which Tarin found intriguing. She was tempted to stop Bailey's awkward and stilted explanation of what the forms were for and let her know she was well versed in hiring practices. Even though it had been a few years since she'd had to deal with them, it was coming back fast. Since she hadn't shared that experience on her resume or in her interview, she kept her mouth shut and listened and signed where directed.

An hour later, when her eyes had glazed over and her mind had gone numb, she was rethinking that. She signed the last document.

"All right, there you go. You're all signed up. Graham said you handed in your criminal record check already. So that's done. I think that's it." Bailey stood and moved to the door.

"Thank you for your help."

Bailey returned her smile before knocking and entering her new bosses' office.

Tarin was tempted to stop her but watched as Bailey disappeared into the other room. If she'd kept her mouth shut, Bailey might have remained friendly rather than turning businesslike. Then she reminded herself she wasn't there to make friends. She was there to get answers. She stared at the closed door, realizing for the first time in a long time that she was on the outside, and she didn't like it. In her job in the hotel business, she'd always been in upper management, so she'd been involved in most meetings. In fact, she was the one who ran them. It was unsettling to think she wasn't part of the team that made decisions. Although as she looked around at the sparsely furnished office, she reminded herself that it didn't look as though it was a booming company—but that was precisely what played in their favor. If her cursory investigation was correct, they were pulling in nearly a cool million annually. She pushed away those thoughts; it was time to get to work.

The look that Graham had given her before going into his inner office stuck with her, as if he doubted she could do the job. It made her wonder how desperate they were, and why they needed to hire someone so quickly. When he'd called to tell her she'd gotten the job, he hadn't sounded very happy about it.

A distinct musical note interrupted her thoughts. She closed her eyes for a moment before pushing away the knowledge of who would text her. He would stop soon, she was sure. Stephen had never been one to waste his time with something that was labor intensive, at least not when it had come to her. One or two texts were fine, but that was his limit or had been until the day she'd left. It wasn't as though he loved her; thankfully, his girlfriend kept him rather busy. Was it all about losing face? It didn't sit well, but it reminded her a lot of her father. She'd sworn she'd never marry anyone similar to him and yet along comes the first man to offer his hand and she jumps in as though he's her lifesaver only to discover he's going to drown her in his obsession for status and power—exactly like her father.

Blowing out a heavy breath, she considered her new position. She felt almost giddy about it. It had been the first one she'd gone after and gotten on her own. In fact, it was the first one that wasn't under her father's thumb.

Guilt crawled over her shoulder like a slithering snake, which made her wonder if Graham knew she'd sabotaged his other interview, leaving him with little choice but to hire her. It had taken a bit of convincing to sell the other woman on the idea of the company being investigated for fraud, but she'd finally left, more than happy to get away. If Graham had known, he'd never have offered Tarin the position. His attitude made her wonder, though. From the time she'd gotten in that morning, he'd been as cold as an arctic front and as abrupt. Rather than wait for her to start her laptop, he'd reached over and turned it on. For the next ten minutes, he'd talked about antispyware and antivirus programs as though she'd never heard of them. He had taken an instant dislike to her. Or maybe he treated all women that way. She would have guessed he was one of the good guys, but her history only reminded her she had no clue when it came to men.

CHAPTER 17

CAL STOOD AT THE massive plate-glass windows and stared out over the city. He loved the view more when he looked straight down and could see people roaming the streets like so many tiny ants. It reminded him of where he had come from; a place he never wanted to return to. He glanced at his expensive jeans, which he never wore in public, and his equally expensive running shoes. Both made him feel like the jock he'd never had the opportunity to be. Living on the street hadn't left him any time for school, let alone sports, although some in his neighborhood referred to dodging bullets and taking drugs as a sport.

It reminded him how far he'd come from the filthy secondhand clothes that were fought over and sometimes even worth killing for. He was not about to give up his current life, at least not easily or willingly. Mr. J, who had found him and taken him in, held the key to this life he presently enjoyed. He seriously debated the call he needed to make. Did he or didn't he? In all honesty, that wasn't the right question. It was whether to tell Mr. J what was going on. The longer he waited, the worse it would be. If he shared the information now... he considered it but didn't see a way that he could without revealing that he'd kept secrets. Mr. J liked to know everything, and what he should have shared years ago and what he had to share now would definitely change things.

"There's a problem."

"Oh, what do you mean?"

"I mean with the package I'm watching."

"So what's happening?"

"Things are moving—"

"What do you mean 'moving'?"

"I mean changing."

"Changing how?"

"Let's just say that its lifestyle is about to change."

"When?"

"It's in progress."

"I thought you were keeping tabs on it."

"I am, but nothing has happened in a long time." He was well aware of the moment things had changed—not that he'd shared a lot of what had been happening with Mr. J. The embarrassment would harm him and his business and wasn't going to do Cal any good either. If there was one thing he'd learned on the streets, it was to take care of himself first.

"I don't track the person's daily movements. You want me to stop it or..." He held his breath as he waited for the answer. For once, he hoped that he was going to be able to do what he did best. And it would mean that 'it' would be gone, out of both their lives, for good. That would mean only one thing. He would finally be able to take over the position that was meant to have been his in the first place.

"No, not that. Find... 'it'. You know this is a bit ridiculous. I'm sure with all the security you have set up, no one is monitoring our conversations. No one will know who we're talking about."

"Better to be safe."

"I tried to call him—keep watching. Let me know of any more changes."

"All right. And if the person comes to get some answers? Then—"

"You seem to be in a big hurry to do away with it."

"Well, there's always the possibility that—"

"Your job is to keep tabs on it. To keep me informed of what it is up to. I'm not going to be embarrassed by what it is doing. You're not to do anything that can't be undone. Understand?"

"Yes." After a few more instructions, Cal hung up. Angry, he slammed his fist into the wall. The pain barely registered. 'It' was one of those things that had always been his headache, but he was sick and tired of watching and waiting. Waiting to see what it would do... which could screw up his life and his plans, big time. Getting rid of that one person would solve all of their problems, his for sure.

Mr. J had started to tell him something, *'I tried to call...'* Was Mr. J in contact with that person? That could change everything. He'd have to keep a closer eye on the one person who could send him back to the streets in an instant.

Maybe he'd act now, get rid of the problem and convince Mr. J later.

CHAPTER 18

SINCE NO ONE SEEMED to be coming back to orientate her, although she was pretty sure that's what Graham had tried to do first thing, she opened her website. She hadn't meant to neglect it, but she hadn't had much time to devote to it lately. The action on the site had dropped drastically since the sex video had been posted. She skimmed through a few pages and was about to close it out when she noticed there were messages for her.

She opened one email. The subject line simply read, 'me too'. There was no message and no signature. Tarin knew the woman had responded to the posting she'd put up about date rape and not having any memory of what happened. It had been a general article she'd found on the internet, but she'd posted it for a reason. She hadn't shared her personal story yet but wanted to find others who'd been through what she had. A faint conversation, a distant, faded memory from that week she'd lost, nagged at her.

It had better work this time.

And if it doesn't?

Well, there's always another one, isn't there? But you'd better make sure it's successful this time.

The voices faded but lingered like a song she couldn't remember the words to. What had someone wanted with her? Why her? Why had no one contacted her since then? What could they have wanted to achieve?

The depraved mind of what someone had done to her made her not only nauseous but angry. She felt as though she were waiting for the gavel to fall that would drastically change her life, and not in her favor. None of it made sense. Something told her other women had gone through what she had, and if that was so, she had to find them. Maybe they had better memories of what they'd been through. Until then, she could at least help other women heal through airing the abuse that had happened to them.

There was another message from a woman who was looking for her daughter. She sent a quick response, telling the woman not to lose hope.

A lump formed in Tarin's throat. It brought back bad memories from her childhood. She'd always hoped her mom had left temporarily and that she'd return to take her away one day. Instead, she'd been told she'd died and was never coming back, which left Tarin to live the perfect life... perfectly orchestrated... perfectly sterile... perfectly lonely.

Every day I dressed up in a frilly pink or white dress. My best shoes. My hair was perfectly curled and styled, with a white ribbon to hold it back. 'Yes, sir. No, sir.' were the only words I was allowed to speak, unless asked for more information. I had to greet any guest that came to the house 'Good day. Nice to meet you.' I had to sit for hours, staying quiet and listening. Always listen. Learn. But never talk. Never interrupt. Never yell, even if a bee stung me.

There was the barest of sounds as the door whispered open. Without looking up, Tarin swallowed a few times, forcing back her emotions before quickly logging out. Once the website was closed, she reminded herself she'd have to remove that digital footprint from the computer before she left for the day. She glanced up. Bailey was staring at her with a quizzical expression.

"Is everything okay?"

"Fine." Tarin forced herself to rein in her emotions. Now was not the time to react to the injustices these women who'd joined her site had suffered. She'd have to be more careful in the future.

There was a long pause, but no break in eye contact.

"Just leaving. Congrats on your new job. Good luck with it. Don't let these two run you ragged, and when it's quitting time, leave. They'd work you through the night if they could. They aren't like normal mortals; they forget some people need to sleep, eat and have a life."

Tarin forced a smile, glad that Bailey was back on friendly ground with her. "I'll remember that. Thanks."

She logged into the email address that Graham had given her access to. There was a ton of spam, which made her wonder how good these guys were. She waited a while to see if either of her bosses was coming out. After ten minutes, she took a chance and logged back onto her website. She read through several comments on her latest posting about believing in oneself. There was also a new message. LJ had replied.

'I've decided I'm going to look for my daughter. I need to know that her life turned out better than mine.' LJ

'I've wanted to meet my mom my whole life. Your daughter would be happy to meet you. You're doing the right thing. A mom is so important.' Tarin

With one last look, she logged out and immersed herself in the work for her new position. She spent the rest of the hour going through all the junk mail to make sure that's what it was. Deleting most, she kept a few that looked fishy. Hoping to organize things, but since they hadn't given her a clear outline of her duties, this was a good place to start. She was tempted to backtrack to where the emails were sent from, because she was sure that's where she'd find the information she needed.

"Tarin?"

She rocked backward, looking up at Guy, hoping she didn't look as guilty as she, for some reason, felt. He was staring at her in a way, though, that would suggest he'd called her a few times.

"Sorry. I was trying to get myself oriented and organized." She smiled. "What do you need?"

"Come on into our office, so we can talk to yo—"

"What the hell?" Graham yelled from the other office. A moment later, he was at the door glaring at her.

Her cheeks heated in response. He stormed over to her. Reflexively, she shoved her chair back, stood up and put up her forearm as a protective shield. When nothing happened and the room was so silent that an ant crossing the ceramic tiled floor would have been heard, she slowly lowered her arm. Her gaze darted between the two stunned men, who were staring at her.

"You're upset. What did I do?"

It took a moment, and after a quick telling glance between the two, Graham said in a much gentler tone as he stepped back, "You've started working on the emails."

Tarin could feel the red heat creep up her face. "Ah. You don't like what I've done. No worries, I can easily undo it."

"If you don't mind my asking, what exactly did you do?" Guy asked.

"She rearranged—"

"I was trying to organize—"

Guy laughed. "I've been on his case for a while to get the files in order. He says they are. Just don't ask him to find anything within five minutes because he can't."

Graham rolled his eyes before spinning on his heel and returning to his office, shutting the door behind him.

"He's stressed. Don't let it get to you. Show me what you're doing and I'll see if I can help you set up a system he can live with."

After a quick stop for lunch, Guy spent the afternoon conducting an orientation with her. He explained that they repaired computers downstairs and did internet research for companies upstairs, finding out what was legitimate and what wasn't. He went through some emails to show her which ones they might consider and which ones they wouldn't.

"So how come so many requests? Many that look—"

"That's why we hired you. We think we have a prankster out there trying to make our lives difficult, probably some fifteen-year-old who's bored. We need you to divide them into bogus, maybe bogus, could be something and sounds good."

Tarin nodded but didn't respond. There seemed to be a lot more going on, but she wasn't going to question her boss on her first day. A bell chimed again from her purse, but she ignored it. This was the fourth time it had gone off. It wasn't the one she'd programmed for Bobbie, so she wasn't too concerned about it."You can answer your cell phone. We don't want it to be a habit, but it seems someone is really trying to reach you."

"Uh... It's okay. Sorry. I'll silence it. It's only on in the case of an emergency. I'm really—"

"Don't worry about it." Guy abruptly stopped her, going straight back to business. He showed her a few more things before he got up from the chair he'd snagged.

"I hope this is okay to ask, but I noticed you have some pictures of Caspian Winery on the walls. Can I ask why?"

Guy eyed her. She was used to being scrutinized, so she held his gaze.

"It belongs to Bailey's grandmother."

A grandparent. Something she'd never had. At least not that she remembered. Her grandmother had passed several years before. She'd found the information by accident on the internet. It had made her wonder if her grandfather would ever want to see her. Her dad had always said he was a vicious old man trying to destroy his business. She'd never known what to believe, but the newspapers didn't portray him that way. He seemed to be well liked and respected by other businessmen and by his employees—not something her dad could say.

"Tarin?"

She kept staring at the picture of an elderly woman, unsure what he'd be able to read in her face. "I take it she's not very involved in it?"

"You'd be wrong. She's eighty and at the helm, steering her ship."

"Wow. That's not something you see too often. Is it a very big operation?" She tried not to sound surprised, but learning an old woman ran it wasn't what she'd been expecting. Her name was listed on the website as CEO but she'd figured that was just a figurehead title.

"Yes. They're one of the top five wineries in Ontario. They ship all over Canada, although mostly in the west and to several places in the United States and a few places in Europe."

"I'd say that's big. That must keep her very busy. I can't imagine working like that at her age."

"Most can't at her age. She's an amazing woman."

Tarin smiled but found she couldn't respond; just once she'd love to be able to talk about someone with that kind of love and affection.

"Where's the winery?" She hoped that sounded normal, as though she didn't already know.

"Oh, outside of Toronto about an hour or so." Guy stood up. "You know what? I think your first day is done."

She glanced at the time on the computer, shocked to see that it was 5:00 already. "The day went by so fast. Thank you so much for your help."

"No problem. Graham's really an easy-going guy."

She prevented herself from rolling her eyes, and instead she nodded as though she understood. *He's a jerk.* Not that she said that out loud. She needed the job for longer than a day.

The inner door flew open. "Geez, Guy, you've got to see this." Graham disappeared as fast as he'd appeared and without a glance in her direction.

It was time to leave, and that was all she cared about. She was proud of herself, although she wondered if Guy thought she had a bladder problem as she went to the washroom every hour on the hour. Since she'd been calling to talk to Chance, she figured she'd done pretty well, considering she'd never been away from him before. The tears in his eyes when she'd left that morning had almost been enough to change her mind.

Tarin was more than ready to go home. Although the closed door begged her to find out what was so urgent, she headed down the stairs instead. As she exited the building, she was sure she'd seen someone dart around the side of it. Curious, she was about to look when her phone chirped again. Frustrated, she pulled it out to find twenty-three texts from Stephen. She didn't want to read them but knew that she was going to.

Dammit, Tarin, answer me... Come on, sweetheart.

I got you a new diamond ring...

I'll take you out to your favorite restaurant. Chance can come...

I miss the little guy; at least let me see him...

You're not being fair.

It's my right... I've had it. I'm sending the cops after you... I'll find you...

You bitch. You've screwed me for the last time.

Cringing, she closed her phone. She couldn't read anymore. She'd meant to piss him off but hadn't thought beyond that. The missing clothes, the scissors sticking out of the ten-thousand-dollar dress he'd bought her, and her not being at his beck and call, seemed to have pushed him over the edge. It was so out of character for her to have done that. She still cringed when she thought about it, but she felt strangely justified when she considered all that Stephen had done to her. To him, she was nothing more than a means to an end. His arm candy. In his mind, having a gorgeous woman on his arm made him the envy of other men.

It had never dawned on her that he would want to find her. In her mind, it was over. He wasn't one to persevere; if it didn't come easy, he quit. She'd assumed that would also apply to her, especially since he had a girlfriend with whom he preferred spending time.

How much effort would he spend to discover her whereabouts?

CHAPTER 19

"THAT NEW WOMAN GISELLE hired at Wedding Rites is driving me nuts." Bailey heaved a heavy sigh.

"What now? The invitations finally went out, right? Or is it the issue with the flowers?"

"I think that's fixed, but now she's pushing me to move our wedding to one of the hotels in Toronto. She's telling me it's too far for people to drive an hour and a half out to Grandma's. Do you believe her?" Bailey was pacing back and forth across the room.

"I'm sure you set her straight." Guy stopped her and hugged her.

"Yes. Sorry. She's so incompetent. I don't understand what Giselle was thinking. I told her any more screw-ups and I go to Giselle with my list of complaints. She's promised there won't be anymore."

"See, you should have eloped," Graham tossed out with a big grin.

"And who knew you knew what you were talking about." Bailey smiled at him. "Anyway, enough of that. We have another issue. Grandma is going to place an ad for an assistant. She fired Sarah, saying the girl hadn't been doing her job. I think this time she's going to hire someone she can hand over some of the reins to. She wants someone she can groom." Bailey perched on the edge of Guy's desk.

"I'm not surprised. What do we do?" Guy asked.

"Oh, and did you know that she's had an offer to buy the winery?" Bailey shook her head.

"From whom?"

"She didn't say. And I only know because she was listening to her messages when I got there, but I only caught the tail end. She downplayed it; said it was a prank."

"Do we need to keep an eye on that?" Graham looked at them both.

"Like we don't have enough on our plates. Let me see if I can get a name and then we can investigate a bit."

"In the meantime, we need to clear up a few things. Have you talked to Detmier?" Guy leaned back in his chair.

Graham's computer dinged and then dinged again. Soon it sounded as though it was trying to create its own song. Emails were streaming in, one after another. There were twenty before it stopped. "Yeah. He says he's swamped. He can't help us. And in fact, he has a couple more cases for us as well. I told him I'm not sure we can take them on as we have more than we can handle right now. Detmier has been a PI for a long time, but he's never been this busy before. "

"How are we going to get on top of this? I've taken down our contact information from the website. I've changed our email account twice."

"Why don't we get Tarin to take all the emails and sort them into categories? Start a—"

"I'm doing that."

"I know, but your time could be better spent on the cases we know are legit. Have you found out any more about whether Mr. Amory is running an online gambling ring out of his liquor store?"

"Yeah. I'm sure he is. I didn't figure out the entire scheme. He had some high-end alcohol that he sold for five hundred dollars a bottle. Actually, I think it was cheap whiskey that he slapped a label on to make it look classier. Anyway, clients would buy that bottle. Behind the label was a code for some high stakes, illegal poker games—minimum bid twenty thousand."

Guy whistled.

"It seems the players are from all over the world, which makes it difficult. I'm sure they'll bring in the CSIS."

"It sounds so official. The Canadian Security Intelligence Service. I'm sure most people have never even heard of it."

"Yeah, not as well-known as the FBI, the CIA or the KGB. Anyway, that website will go down and another will be put up. So if you want to do some research, now might be the time before it turns into a Charlie Brown fest."

"All right. I'll see what I can find out. How are you making out in finding Mr. Hamilton?"

"I'm not. He's vanished—no sign, nothing. The heirs are like vultures waiting to rip apart his estate the minute he's declared dead. I haven't told them that could take years. They are nasty."

Graham shook his head as he went through the many incoming emails. He skimmed each one and, when he had a sense of the scope of work, he'd file it into urgent, important, or non-important/non-urgent. Then he'd determine whether it was something they wanted to take on. Sadly, all he felt he'd been doing lately was filing. As soon as he'd gotten through all the ones that had come in and maybe done a bit of checking on one or two, he had to get back to their current caseload.

"So back to my original question, why did we hire Tarin if you aren't going to let her do any work?"

Graham propped his elbows on his desk and pressed his fingers to his forehead, massaging away a threatening headache. "I'm not trying to be an ass. I don't want someone coming in and messing with this."

Guy laughed. "Look, these incoming requests are wasting your time. You go through each one methodically—which I know needs to happen—but you have several cases that you have to complete. You keep getting sidetracked by every funky new challenge. "

"I know, I know. I have to figure out what to give her."

"You set up that other email address, but all you've been sending so far is what we're sure is spam, and you're already having issues about her touching that. Forward some of these new ones but clear them so they look as though they went directly to that account. Set some limits and see how she does. She seems to have figured out that what we've sent her so far is pretty much all crap."

"Fine. I'm sending her a bunch." He did it quickly because otherwise he'd talk himself out of it again, like he had ten other times. "What do we really know about her?"

"I don't know; fill me in."

He grimaced at his friend before realizing the sarcastic remark was warranted. "She's twenty-eight and used to work for C-Lite Hotels. Her career was solid and she was well respected there. She quit about three years ago, went to work for herself doing some freelance work—setting up computers, fixing bugs or other issues the owners were having. It sounds as though she had quite a business. About a month or two ago, she quit and moved out here to take care of a friend or relative, not sure which. I can't remember what she said in the interview, to be perfectly honest. I found an article she wrote for the *Vancouver Sun* a few years ago about the computer industry and where it's going. Pretty interesting."

"So, you did a thorough check."

"Yes, and No. I went back ten years. All seems to be hunky-dory."

"And nothing came up. No jail time? No parking tickets? No man in her life?"

"Funny. No, nothing in her adult life—criminal record check was clear, no arrests, no warrants, nothing suspicious. I didn't dig into her younger years or childhood or family background. Yet. I did all the security checks, and nothing showed up. Her references were awesome." Graham rocked back in his chair.

"If this is bugging you, I can do some digging. Or we could ask Walters to check through the police database, see if there are any juvenile records? And yes, I know you can hack it but sometimes it doesn't hurt for us to follow the rules. Well, sort of anyway. Shelby, the head of homicide, is not sure how you do it, but he knows it's you, and he's determined to catch you. And it's not worth explaining that we only do it when requests come in that are over his pay grade."

"All right. Forget it for now. Do you have a good feeling about her?"

"Yes, I do. I know there's something, but she doesn't strike me as the type of person to be involved in anything bad. She's a little too strait-laced, uptight, by-the-rules. And we could stop being so paranoid and accept that she's legit. Cripes, the guys we hire downstairs to work on other people's computers don't go through this much security. You've done all the checks and have a bunch of safety nets in place. Monitor her but let her do her job."

Graham shrugged before he stared into space. An un-settling feeling pressed against his breastbone. He wasn't sure what it meant, though. He'd never been all that good at judging a person's character. His reaction to Tarin was different. One thing he was good at was telling when someone was holding back, and she definitely was.

The sound of another email coming in, had him auto-matically lean forward to check it.

"Walters says Mrs. Neilson wants to know when he's going to nail her son for fraud. Which means, where are we with it?"

Guy shook his head. "I have to say, when Walters first approached us with this, I thought it was silly. But it appears that faking her death was the key to catching him. He stole the dog she left her fortune to; the mutt was supposed to go to her sister. That was what I was going to tell you when I came in. That all went down last night. I guess the son got caught hacking into her account and draining off the money. It appears the dog was tied up and not in good shape, with no food or water for days. Obvious he was going to kill it. I guess he was waiting until he'd made sure he didn't need it anymore. Totally warped. Kind of makes you want to lock the son in a cage with a few starving dogs, doesn't it?"

"What an ass! The dog's okay?" Guy nodded. "Okay, I'll make sure Walters gets our report so he can let her know."

The computer started dinging non-stop.

"My ol' boy, we got a flood a happenin.'" Graham sat back so Guy could see the ten emails that came in one after the other.

"That's why you need to start using Tarin. She seems to know computers. She doesn't know all that we do, so what if she goes through these and determine whether they're legit?"

"Look. I'm being cautious."

"Oh man. Is that what you're telling yourself? You've been spending a minimum of four hours a night going through everything you've asked her to do during the day. And it's stuff we know is crap. I thought we hired her to take some of the load off, not to add to it."

"Well, don't you think it's just a little too perfect that we need an assistant and we get the mother of all assistants? I think there's a thing or two she could teach me."

Guy gasped, clutching his chest in mock pain. "What? You've got to be kidding. Oh, my—"

Graham chucked a paperclip at him, nailing him in the forehead. They burst out laughing.

"Okay. Maybe I am a bit overprotective of my baby." He patted his computer. "But I don't want to get taken for a ride. The thing that freaks me out the most is suddenly, those email requests that were coming in like gangbusters slowed down to a trickle and then boom."

"Meaning... you think she has something to do with that and it's not just timing? Don't forget we went through this a couple of times already this year—the volume is cyclical."

"Yeah-yeah. I know but—"

"So give her a break. Have you found anything yet?"

Graham looked away in disgust before quietly saying, "No. But come on, you have to admit there's something."

"She's harmless, but she's been hurt. Someone did a number on her," Bailey said as she entered the office.

"And if anyone has good instincts about people, it's Bailey. Kind of reminds me of someone else."

"Get out. Melinda—"

"—was a bitch and hurt you badly. Used you. Kicked you to the curb. Stomped on—"

"All right, for crap's sakes, man. I hear ya. And I got over her," he said in his best Sean Connery voice.

"Sorry, I haven't been in the office much."

"Forget it. I know you've got all the lovey-dovey wedding stuff to go through." Graham pursed his lips and mimicked in a high-pitched voice, "My god Guy, what do you think of this frilly white stuff? Oh, and these crab cakes? Oh, and the scent of Freesia?"

"I do not sound like that, Graham." Bailey lowered her voice to mock him. "And I sure as hell don't give a damn about frilly things. And I think this is about a woman who is not only attractive but is smart too."

Guy chuckled. "Maybe I should talk to his mom, let her know he doesn't like beautiful, intelligent women—"

"All right. All right. I'll back off the poor thing."

"Me thinks he doth protest too much." All three laughed.

There was something about Tarin that grabbed his attention. And it wasn't just her form-fitting skirts. What really got to him was that her computer was wiped clean every night. There was no trace of her even having used it. But why?

CHAPTER 20

"TARIN, CAN YOU COME in here?"

She took a deep breath as she walked over but stopped in the open doorway.

"We've decided—" He stopped and looked at Guy and Bailey, who were watching him expectantly.

Tarin glanced back and forth between them, wishing she could read the unspoken messages.

"All right. These two believe I'm wasting your talents, and we're not getting any further ahead. I need you to go through the eighty emails I sent you a little while ago. Read them. Figure out which are real and which aren't."

Her gaze flew to Guy and Bailey, who looked back at her with respect. Unsure of what was going on and unsure if she should mention it, she took a deep breath before asking them to come to her desk.

"Look, I know I kind of did this without permission, but I want you to see something." She sat while they huddled behind her. She flipped through the websites. "Now I'm not sure, but there's something odd about this one, this one and this one and potentially these other five. I don't think any of these are real."

"What makes you say that?" Graham leaned over her shoulder. Neither noticed that Guy and Bailey silently made their way out the door, leaving them alone.

Graham soon got a chair and his laptop and set up beside her. For the next hour, he and Tarin worked together, going through the websites and identifying not only what seemed fake about them but what made them special. Graham attempted to backtrace the IP addresses, but most had been blocked. Tarin checked the hosting services, and all were legitimate. Next, she pulled up the yellow pages and then reached for the phone. She hung up and dialed the next number on the list.

"Hi, can I speak to Cory Genner?"... "He doesn't work there?"... "Okay, thank you."... "Hi, is Penny Thornton there?"... "Oh, there's no one there by that name. Uhm, could you tell me who your regional manager is?"... "You don't have one. Oh, I'm sorry. I think I might have the wrong number. What is it that you do there?"... "Could you give me your website so that I can learn more?"... "Thank you for your help."...

She was about to call the next one when Graham took the phone from her and set it down. It seemed to take forever for him to remove his hand. He withdrew, settling back in his chair. She turned her attention back to the screen, but the heat from his steady gaze was like a gentle tapping on the base of her skull, telling her that someone wanted her attention but would wait her out. Taking a deep breath, she turned to ask what he wanted, but the words never came out. His green eyes were intensely focused on her. There was a new, questioning expression in their depths. His chair was snug up against hers.

Clearing her throat, she turned away and stood. "I need a drink of water. Do you want one?"

He waited until she had the fridge door open before replying, "Yes, please."

The walk back to the desk was the longest ten steps she'd ever taken. She was trying to look anywhere but at him, fully aware that he hadn't taken his eyes off her. At the far edge of the desk, she tossed a bottle to him. Opening hers, she took a long drink.

"I'm sorry if making those calls was the wrong thing to do. I know I should have asked first, but it made sense."

"Yeah, too much sense."

She met his gaze. *Who did he think he was?* "I don't need—"

He put up his hand. "Look, I owe you an apology. I've been a real butthead. I'm sorry. That was brilliant to call those businesses. I'm embarrassed to say it never dawned on me, probably because I knew I didn't have the time. And I get so accustomed to using the internet, tracing and tracking everything electronically, that I forget there are other ways to get answers."

He shook his head but finally chuckled. "What did you learn?"

Reluctant to close the distance between them, she leaned against the far edge of the desk.

"Well, I learned in the second phone call, I should have asked way more questions in the first. I learned Cori Genner had never worked there. So that's probably a bogus request. As for the second one, there is no Penny Thornton, which I'm sure means it's crap, too. In both cases, the companies exist. Hey, wait." She sat down in her chair and clicked open a new browser, typing in a URL. Then she went back to the emails and found the one she wanted and clicked on the link. Then she flipped back and forth between the two websites.

"Okay, so what are you doing?"

She turned her head; her focus still on what she'd been looking at on the screen. It was a bit of a surprise when she found herself almost nose to nose with Graham. His eyes widened ever so slightly, while hers peeled wide as she jerked back in her chair. To hide her embarrassment, she waved at the monitor.

"They look identical, don't they?"

Graham studied them. "Yes, but I take it they aren't?"

"You got it. Look at this." She pointed to the two URLs—cornerstone and cornerstones.

"Holy crap. How did I miss that?"

"I'd never have missed that kind of a trick before. Dammit. So why is someone setting up almost identical but bogus websites? What the hell is going on?"

CHAPTER 21

I WANT TO MEET you.

The message sent her heart racing. This was it! With shaking fingers, Tarin replied. The woman hadn't said where she lived but that she could meet in or around the Toronto area, no problem. Evenings or weekends were fine.

Excited, Tarin had to correct her typing mistakes eight times before she was able to form a coherent sentence. Not sure where the woman had to travel from, she considered possibilities. Toronto wasn't a city one wanted to travel around in, because it took a lot of time—especially downtown. She kept picking and rejecting places—Tim Hortons, which were all over the city but they were always so busy... and noisy. She wanted something public yet private. Opening a browser, she scrolled through various places to meet. Parks brought up some interesting places. She read through several when she came upon Bronte Creek Provincial Park. It was outside Toronto, was public but would give them a quiet space if they needed it. She typed directions from the outskirts of Toronto heading southwest and set it for 10:00 Saturday morning. The traffic shouldn't be crazy at that time. The only problem was it was still a few days away, and she didn't know if she could wait that long. Before she could change her mind, she sent her reply.

A rush of tiny waves of anticipation mixed with a niggling stab of fear coursed through her. She didn't know if she'd done the smartest thing in her life or the stupidest, but she couldn't stop the voice that kept saying, 'You did it, now you'll get answers'. The thought of finally knowing what had happened to her three years ago was almost overwhelming. After she'd initially figured out some of what had happened, she'd been so frightened that she'd wanted to distance herself from it. Then things had snowballed on her. Finding out she was pregnant and alone, then having Stephen propose and then marrying him, only to have him change overnight... it had all been too much, but now she needed to know. She needed to find out who the sick bastard that had locked her up for a week was . Who had drugged her? Who had taken away her memory and left her with only fleeting glances into what might have happened? And that's what scared her the most—what might have happened? What had actually happened? She knew only a small part of the whole situation—the outcome. But who else knew?

The USB that she still had hidden away came to mind. She so badly wanted to see what she'd downloaded from the winery and, she was having a hard time making herself snoop into someone else's business. It felt so slimy and wrong. If she could, she wanted to figure things out without having to use information illegally gained. There may be absolutely nothing of value, and then how crappy was she going to feel for stealing it? She was so morally torn between the urgent need to check it out and her conscience telling her not to touch it.

Overcome with emotion, she sank into her chair as the reality of her actions hit her. On Saturday, she was going to meet someone who may have gone through the same thing she had. Could that be possible? Was there a sicko out there targeting women this way?

Suddenly she sat upright and reached for her cell phone. She pulled up her calendar; she was already booked. She'd made a playdate with Chance to take him to the Toronto Zoo. He loved animals, and she thought it would be a great way to make up for being absent so much. Thankfully, he was adjusting to Bobbie and Kim as babysitters. He no longer cried or held onto her with a stranglehold when she left in the morning. That alone instantly brought tears to her eyes. Things were changing. He was already becoming independent of her. And she was becoming more independent of him. The flood of emotion that hit her was like a dam about to burst. Pressing her hands in a steeple over her nose, she took some long, slow breaths, willing away the feeling of despair.

After a few moments, she was able to think about it rationally. She could change her time with Chance to Sunday. The accompanying guilt almost had her throwing up. He wouldn't know the difference, but she sure would.

Sighing, she clicked on the email to send a new one and adjust the meeting time and day only to discover when she looked at her calendar that Sunday was booked as well. They were having brunch at Bobbie's and then going to the lake. That meant she'd have to wait another whole week to meet this woman. An instant sense of dread bordering on panic at the thought of putting it off let her know there was no way she could do that. She'd have to come up with an alternative plan.

"Good morning. You're in early."

She'd barely had time to close out her emails and open the company information at the sound of the key in the lock. She hadn't had time to get through many of the other messages she'd wanted to.

"Morning, Graham. I hope it's still okay that I deal with a few personal emails on this computer?"

"Yes. We talked about it, and I'm okay with it. What I'm not okay with, however, is you thinking you have to come in before 6:30 to do it. You can do it on your break that you never take, or during the lunch that you work through."

She was tempted to press her hands to her heated cheeks, but she refrained. "I don't see you taking breaks, either."

"I'm the boss. It comes with the territory."

"All right. Thanks."

He headed to his office.

"Uh, Graham?"

"Hmm, yes?" He glanced over his shoulder.

"Is there anything new in those emails I followed up on?" Things seemed to have shifted between them since she'd shown him what she'd discovered.

"Well, so far, I think you've discovered almost four hundred fake companies and requests. About one hundred and fifty that are maybes, which I think we'll ignore—they're taking too much time. And then there are twenty-five legit and thirty questionable ones. I'll get you to do some more digging on the questionable group. I don't know how we're going to take on much more work, but we'll see what we can do. Sorry I haven't said anything, but that's damn good. You've saved me countless hours."

"Even though you've gone through everything I've done with the utmost care to make sure I haven't been messing with you or making mistakes?"

His eyes widened, but she was sure not as wide as hers. There was a stunned silence.

"Oh my God, I'm sorry. I had no right to say that. I don't know why I did. Just ignore it. It's—"

"A fact." Graham started laughing. "So you know, I quit doing that a while ago."

"A day ago." Tarin slapped her hand over her mouth.

"No, a little longer than that. I might be a bit narcissistic, but I'm not quite that bad," he said in his best western drawl.

It reminded her of the John Wayne movies she used to sneak out of bed and sit on the stairs to watch. Her dad had loved those old shows. For her, it had been a way to feel she was doing something with him, although he'd never known she'd been there.

She wasn't quite sure how to react to Graham, since their relationship had begun as anything but friendly. She couldn't help but smile, though, as he took a few steps in a comically awkward gunslinger's swagger. Her eyes automatically gravitated toward his. The green of his eyes was as intense and arresting.

"Hey, you guys look as though you're having too much fun."

Tarin tore her eyes away from Graham's, sure they would show too much, and concentrated on her monitor.

"Morning, Guy. Bailey." She started opening emails, clicking on websites. She glanced up briefly to smile at them as they passed through to the inner office. Once the door was closed, she wilted, laying her forehead on the edge of her desk.

She felt like a teenager who'd been caught mooning over the cute boy down the street. She hadn't been exact, but she was so touched by his praise and his taking responsibility for his over-the-top actions. In the past, she would have been made to feel at fault.

Rather than go down that dark hallway of her past, she allowed herself to bask in the warmth of finally being appreciated for something she'd done. She worked steadily throughout the day, able to get a lot of work done. Before she left for the day, she quickly checked her emails to see if the woman had responded, eager to see whether she had agreed to the time and date. She was finally going to talk to someone who might have gone through the same experience. The odds of it being the same man—she chose not to go there. It was having someone who totally understood what she was feeling coupled with the off chance their situations were the same. Her knees were shaking so strongly they almost knocked together.

I can't meet. Not this Saturday. I'll get back to you.

Tarin slumped in her chair, feeling as if all the wind had been taken out of her sails as she read the woman's reply. *Damn.*

After sending a quick reply, she got out of there. About to call Bobbie, a text from Stephen.

'Thanks for leaving my car at the airport. Real nice of you. You're lucky it hasn't been harmed. Good riddance. Not impressed. I can't believe you're standing me up. I had to find a replacement date. It wasn't easy to explain...'

CHAPTER 22

"WHEN WERE YOU GOING to tell me she's gone?"

How the hell does he know already? "I... look—"

"No, you listen. I paid you handsomely to keep track of her. To take care of all that, she needed. To ensure that she stayed in one place. That was too much to ask?"

"Well, how was I to know she was flighty? She was following all my orders." Stephen dropped into his leather chair. He'd been dreading this conversation. "Cripes, she was always at home or busy with—"

"You're not very bright, are you?"

"I'll have you know—"

"Oh, believe me, I already know. I know that you're a Harvard grad. Your father believes you can do no wrong, although he is making you pay your own way, which you're finding rather difficult. Oh, and you have a mistress at 142—"

"How the hell do you know that?" Stephen's left knee bounced rapidly as he listened to the man he'd been eager to meet four years before. All he'd had to do was to meet this young, attractive woman and convince her to marry him. Not only was she from money, but he'd be paid handsomely to keep track of her and keep her in line. It had sounded so simple, and although Stephen had never been told, nor asked what the man's relationship was to her, he'd known it had to have been a close one. It hadn't bothered him that he didn't know that or even the man's name.

At the time, Stephen had been trying to prove to his father he didn't need his money or his help to bail him out every single time he made a mistake. Stephen had decided he could look after his own problems. Besides, it hadn't hurt to bring home a beautiful daughter-in-law. The grandson had been his security blanket. Stephen had never seen his dad so proud of him. The family money was now his to spend. If his father ever found out Tarin and Chance were gone, he was pretty sure the finances would disappear as well. And now his only source of income was going to vanish faster than he was prepared for, leaving him with the pittance he got paid on his regular job. It didn't even come close to meeting his needs.

"Do you think I'd have hired you without knowing everything about you? I thought I made it clear that you weren't to see other women."

"I didn't. Well, not for the longest time. But God, she was like bedding a cold fish. You can't expect a man in his prime to put up with that."

"So getting a piece of tail was more important to you than receiving the healthy cheque I sent you each month."

"No... well... look, I'll find her. I promise. We have a good arrangement. I'll get her back and we can continue as it was. My life is no picnic without her, you know. I've missed out on some things because she's gone. I've had to put up with embarrassing moments. I've had to make up stories."

"Ah, but in the week or two she's been missing, you've done nothing to find her, have you? I don't do well with being taken for a ride."

"Not true. I hired a private investigator to search for her."

"Oh?"

"Yeah. He hasn't found anything yet. I was hoping to get her back before I had to tell you about it. Don't worry; I'll fix this."

"You don't, and you'll be swimming in the fish tank at the zoo."

Stephen sank against the wall as he listened to the buzz indicating his caller had hung up. When he finally felt as though he had some control over his muscles, he stood and walked to the wastebasket beside his desk. He rooted around in it until he found the card of the guy he'd actually met with but had to refuse because of his exorbitant fees. It looked like he didn't have a choice now.

That bitch has humiliated me for the last time. Dammit. Where the hell could she have gone?

CHAPTER 23

YOU SO CALLOUSLY THROW my love back in my face and vanish without a trace...

A chill invaded Tarin's core. Stephen had changed tactics again. That wasn't surprising, but he'd never used the 'L' word before. He'd even skipped it in his vows, rather than 'love, honor and cherish', he'd said, 'I'll cherish & honor you'. She'd been too busy saving her own skin and so thankful to him for wanting to be with her she'd overlooked it.

I've hired a private investigator.

Now she had to step things up.

What she was planning was not smart, but she didn't know what else to do. She'd finally earned their trust and was now throwing it out the window. The thought of Stephen finding her, though, was keeping her from sleeping, and she felt she was developing a nervous tick—looking over her shoulder every five minutes. He'd take Chance from her just to bend her to his will; she was sure of that. She felt caught in this vortex of the need to find answers, to resolve some issues in her life and for once bask in a normal, carefree life. She'd had fleeting moments of normalcy—raising a son, going to work, paying bills, a myriad of responsibilities that came with adulthood. But then Stephen kept reminding her that her life was anything but normal.

She had to quit lying to herself that everything would just fade away without her having to do anything. Certainly not break the confidence of others that she'd just gained. She had to be sure she could be free of Stephen legally, but unfortunately, she did not know if that was possible. The week she'd lost kept her mired in a thick swamp of gloom and monsters lurking in the dark. Until she knew what had happened, until she was sure Stephen had no part in it, until it was clear who was responsible, she would never be free.

Acid roiled in her stomach as if it was her new best friend. It was the game she was playing, the lies she was telling, or actually, the omissions that were causing her so much grief. They were so good to her at work, and she felt as though she was selling them out. If she believed in luck, she would hope she was lucky enough to remain undiscovered, but since luck had never been a part of her life, she hoped they wouldn't find out until she was long gone.

Some spoils are inevitable in business, Tarin. Get used to it. Her dad's words echoed in her head. That was how he operated, but not how she ever thought she would. What scared her was the thought that maybe she was more like him than she wanted to be. Sighing, she brushed her fingers over her son's wispy hair. It was so soft, so comforting. It reminded her of how life was supposed to be, what she was working so hard for, to make it easier for him. He made the slightest of cooing sounds as he slept. It was a good sign that he was out for the night. She kissed him and then crept out of his room. She stopped long enough to talk to Kim, Bobbie's teenage niece, who was now her stepdaughter and who was going to babysit while she was out.

"Uh... Mrs. Roth?"

"Tarin, please."

"You look great and all. I like that rad haircut. It's cute, but it could be sassy and short, you know, not just cropped." She tilted her head as though she were contemplating how she'd make it look. "Hmmm, anyway, don't you think you should put on something nice for your date?"

Tarin looked at her wide-eyed before glancing down at the baggy sweats she'd pulled on when she'd arrived home. They were an old pair of Bobbie's, baggy and short, but she loved them. She'd never worn anything like them before. She had her usual skirt laid out on the bed to wear with the USB in the pocket.

"I don't—"

"I know you didn't want her to know about your date, and you're trying to keep it hush-hush because you left that dimwad of a husband. But she's thrilled for you. Aren't you, Kim?" Bobbie glanced at her daughter.

"Don't let that jerk get you down or keep you from finding the right guy. I was hoping men got better as they got older. All the guys in my class are idiots. There has to be at least one out there who isn't. Don't worry; I'm sure you'll find someone."

Tarin was a little stunned at that speech from a fifteen-year-old. "Thanks. I hope you're right." She didn't want to disillusion the girl that in her experience, there wasn't one.

"Hey, I have the perfect stuff for your hair. It'll give it that sassy look I was talking about. Oh crap. It's at my other house."

"Kim." Bobbie stared hard at her.

"Hey, love your dimpled chin. Yours looks just the same as mine. Soon life can get back to normal for all of us." Kim grinned and went into the living room.

"Dimple chin?"

"It's cute. I've always thought so anyway. And it's this kid who I think has a crush on her said she had a butt chin. She changed it to dimple chin. She's been making his life hell," Bobbie whispered.

Tarin chuckled as Bobbie linked her arm in hers and steered her down the hallway to her bedroom. She'd been grateful to her friend not only for taking her in but for letting her rent her basement suite. And the best part was she had a built-in babysitter. Bobbie closed the door behind her.

"Her house?"

Bobbie hesitated as she looked away. "Oh, Mom's. She's always leaving stuff there. Sorry about the misunderstanding—what she thinks is happening for you. I had to tell her something. She's bright. She was asking why you looked so sad. Of course, she assumed it was because of a man. So I went along with it. I didn't tell her what had happened."

She was asking for answers herself, but Tarin wasn't ready to share everything with her old friend. Things were still a little stilted. She felt bad having her babysit every day, but Bobbie had insisted, and Tarin really didn't have any other choice.

"She says you're too beautiful to be a wallflower."

"Oh, my God. Where does she get this stuff? By the way, she's a great kid. You must be proud of her."

"Yeah. She's nothing like me. A lot like hmmm—"

"Your sister?"

"No. No. Not like my family at all. More like... h-her father's."

Tarin squeezed her hand. It sounded as though it had been tough when her sister died at twenty-four, leaving Bobbie at nineteen with a six-year-old to raise. Tarin was pretty sure she wouldn't have been able to do it.

"Okay, let's get you changed. Jeans should be fine."

"I don't have a date, Bobbie."

"I know that. And you know that. But the man you might meet on the street doesn't know that. And men who think women are taken are more likely to be interested if you appear as though you're unavailable."

Tarin laughed as her friend grinned at her. "You're nuts, but all right. Then, I need to go. I have a lead on my mom; I'm hoping it will help me find her, but it's kind of freaking me out. The security at work is top-notch, so if someone doesn't want me connecting with her, I should be able to search undetected. I don't want anyone to know that I'm trying to locate her." She hated lying to her friend; reconnecting with her mom was one of her goals but not something she had time for right then. And it would keep her friend from asking too many questions.

"Especially your dad. I could help?"

"Thanks, but this is something I've got to do myself. Tell Kim to sleep in my bed. I'll crash on the couch when I get home. I have no idea how long I'll be."

"Are you sure you need to do this?"

"Yeah, I don't trust that Stephen didn't put a tracer on my computer. I have an uncomfortable feeling. The last thing I want is for that son of a bitch to find me because I was too arrogant to think he doesn't have the brains to put spyware on my laptop—or track me somehow. I'm even scared to check it or remove it, because it might give me away. I'll be safer at the office. They have every kind of security. I won't have to worry." Thankfully, Bobbie seemed to understand that she also didn't want to do it when her bosses were around. She also appeared to have bought her story about Stephen being abusive and ruthless.

Tarin's phone buzzed. She'd silenced it but left it on vibrate so it wouldn't wake Chance. She pulled it out of her pocket and checked the phone number. An involuntary shudder shook her body. Bobbie rested her hand on her forearm, looking at her in concern.

"I think I said Stephen's name too often or worried about him too much. He's kind of similar to Beetlejuice; say his name three times and he appears—or calls in this case."

"Why don't you get rid of that phone? Cancel that plan. That's how he'll find you, if he's going to."

"I've disabled the GPS. I know he might still be able to track me, but it's the only way Dad can get hold of me." And it was her way of keeping track of Stephen. His comment about hiring a private investigator had freaked her out a bit. She needed to find out more.

"Here's a thought. Call him. Give your dad your new number."

"I want to, but I can't. He has to be the one—" She hadn't mentioned that he had called, but she hadn't responded. To her, it hadn't been the call she'd wanted. She knew things weren't going to change between them, but that phone number was the last link she had, no matter how bad it was.

"Look, I know he's a jerk. I've known you for a long time. The man is as cold and emotionless as a wall-mounted fish. And he was scary as hell when we were kids. But come on, you're his only child. And if it hadn't been for him, we'd have been separated a long time before you turned sixteen. Don't you think he owes you some explanations?"

"I'm forever grateful that the only wish of mine he ever granted was to talk your mom into sending you to boarding school with me."

"You know he paid for me too, right? He paid everything."

Tarin frowned at the intensity of Bobbie's expression but put it down to guilt. "Yes. I hoped you didn't know."

"My parents weren't poor, but they weren't rich enough for something like that. Mom always wanted that kind of lifestyle though." Her voice caught. "I think they were just happy I left and went away to school. They were always fighting, and if they weren't, then I was doing something to screw up their lives. Or so they kept telling me. They split up a few months after we started school."

Tarin took her friend's hand. In truth, the only reason he'd done it was to ensure she wouldn't run away. It was his excuse to send her away in the first place. She'd played in the sand in her fancy clothes and rolled in the mud with the neighbor's puppy. She'd run away with her stuffed teddy bear and her red sneakers. He'd found her—or rather, one of his men had found her—in the park under a bench, which she'd turned into a fort. Her rebellion hadn't lasted, but it had been enough for him to enroll her in a private school; banishing her to a place as cold and lifeless as he.

"I'm surprised my dad didn't exact some kind of payment from your family in exchange. Who knew he'd do something nice for me, just because. Hey, are you okay?"

Bobbie's face was so pale it reminded her of the white, sterile walls of her childhood bedroom.

"Yeah. I need to sit. Crazy day. It's catching up with me."

Tarin smiled at her friend but noticed she wouldn't look at her. She shrugged it off, happy to finally have time with her. It had been apart a long time; they needed to get to know each other again. Bobbie's life was a mystery to her and she didn't know what it meant for her that Tarin vanished from her life.

The dumbest decision I ever made.

Her father had convinced her that her friend wouldn't forgive her for what she'd done and, besides, with all the embarrassment she'd brought to the family, she owed him. There had never been any real love between them, but the one kind gesture of paying Bobbie's tuition had bought him her loyalty for a long time. He'd been a master at convincing her that the one stupid thing she'd done at school had cost him dearly. He'd kept her out of juvenile detention, but she'd needed to start acting like his daughter and someone he could groom to take over his company one day.

She'd tried but had failed.

Somehow, she still believed a heart beat in his chest and that he had the ability to care for her. All she'd ever wanted was for him to believe in her, to love her. She still prayed for it, which was why she couldn't totally break ties with him. He was the only family she had. Her grandfather immediately came to mind, but she had no idea if he was an older version of her dad or not. It was something she'd been too scared to find out.

"I know I need to call my father, but not right now. I've disappointed him enough. Soon. I promise. Okay?"

"Let's get you dressed and out of here. Here, put these pants on. They'll not only look good but will be easy to get around in." She tossed them to Tarin and then showed how easy it was to move around in pants.

Tarin grinned at her friend's silly antics as she dressed. She gave her a quick hug before she thanked Kim, made sure she had all her contact information and headed out the door. The thought of leaving Chance after a long day away from him almost had her turning around. Taking a deep breath, she strengthened her resolve and climbed into Bobbie's eight-year-old Camry she insisted she use. She hadn't bothered to tell her that it had been almost two years since she'd driven, other than the stint to the airport the month before. Stephen had insisted on having a driver at her beck and call. The new job was thankfully giving her the excuse to drive regularly, and she was loving it.

Tonight, though, was one of those times she wasn't looking forward to; at least not to what she was doing.

Things had been so crazy at work, though Graham had come around, as much as he could with allowing her to play in his computer world. Guy was often trying to be the mediator, but between the wedding and following leads, he wasn't present all that often.

Twenty-five minutes later, she parked down the street from the office. Knowing that her bosses liked to put in long hours, she watched the darkened windows for several minutes before she was sure no one was there. The fact that the lights were off wouldn't have even fazed Graham. She'd been watching for any sign—flickers of light—just in case he was on his computer.

Finally, having determined it was safe, she made her way to the outer door. She couldn't resist looking over her shoulder, but that made her feel all the more slimy, as though she was stealing the family jewels. Using the key she'd been given at the start of this week, she let herself in, shutting off the alarm. Once in the office, she quickly booted her computer. She glanced a few times at the closed and locked inner door. That was a room she wasn't allowed in, even during business hours.

She quickly hacked into Stephen's email account for clues on what he was up to. There were several; some were from his girlfriend with pictures that weren't fit for anyone's eyes; however, they were great for Tarin for future negotiations. His girlfriend said she was emailing them to him because his work cell kept blocking her. Tarin copied and pasted the photos into her own file. Skimming through a few more messages, she finally found what she was looking for—Kevin Johnson, Private Investigator. His name and address were included in the message.

Sitting back, she considered her options. Since they had only found the car so far, she decided to have all of Stephen's emails forwarded to herself so she could stay in the loop. It didn't help her with text messages, but hopefully the PI, Johnson, would send reports. She decided not to leave that to chance. Posing as Stephen, she sent Johnson an email asking him to email a report of anything he found but not to bother to respond to the message she'd just sent. It was a bit risky, but she needed to take the chance. She erased all her footprints and logged out.

Sighing, she wasn't sure how to handle this latest bit of news, the P. I. that was to find her. Since she was there, she decided to quickly check out her site. There hadn't been much time to check or post anything. Forty more women had sent a request to join, and several had shared their stories in their application. After reading through them all, she allowed fifteen of the women into the inner circle where the real stories were shared. Or at least, she hoped they would be. So far she'd been the only one to post any of her history publicly, which she'd kept rather sketchy. She did share a lot about being in a controlling, overpowering relationship, though.

This group was something she took seriously, and she did what she could to ensure it was safe and secure for women to share and learn. The women who were allowed to join had been traumatized in some way, many for a long time.

Who they were and what they were sharing seemed to hold true. All the women had awful stories of what they'd been through, but there were two emails that grabbed her attention.

I ended up pregnant, but I don't think Don is the father. I've never told him, but... I went away for the weekend to that convention in Vancouver, and I don't remember a damn thing.

Tarin sat up straight. An eerie icy feeling crept up her back. Vancouver was where she'd lost that week of her life. She read the other message.

'I sat down beside him at the bar; he ordered me a drink, and that's all I remember. It was some time later that I woke up. I'm sorry, I shouldn't have shared this much.'

Tarin wished the woman had left more information. She immediately responded to both women.

'Thank you for telling me a bit about what you went through. I'm so sorry it happened to you. I would love to hear more about your story. When did this happen? Where exactly? Do you know the name of the hotel?'

She hit send before she could talk herself out of it. But of course as soon as she sent it, she Had she just scared both women off?

She closed her eyes, trying to shrug off the tired feeling and wishing she had more time to interact with the members. The time on the computer said 2:00 a.m. She quickly posted information about some services she'd found to help women leave abusive situations, along with articles on empowering oneself. Then she logged out.

She needed to find out more about Caspian Winery. She'd glanced at their website before, which had given cursory information about its founding, ups and downs in winemaking and a bit about the current owner and the managers.

Dorothea Lindell - owner and CEO

Cara Wilson - Financial Administrator

Martin Dey - twenty-two years as the Chief Winemaker

Oliver Gibner - fifteen years as Shipping and Receiving Manager

Tom Nelson - almost three years as Vineyard Manager

She skimmed through these and the rest of the employees' bios, but nothing led her to believe that any of them were the kind of man she was looking for. The kind of man who had done what he had. She studied each of their faces, searching their eyes, but she didn't recognize any of them—although seeing a picture and seeing someone in person were totally different. Somehow, she'd have to meet each of them. She started some background checks on everyone of them.

The reason she'd gone there was bothering her like a woodpecker pecking at her skull. She reached into her right pocket to pull out the USB, only to realize it wasn't there. She reached into her left one. When she came up empty, she patted her front pockets and then her back ones. Frantically, she slapped at all her pockets and then shoved her hands in. *What the heck?*

Suddenly she remembered where it was. Her head dropped backward as she clapped her hand over her mouth. It was in the skirt's pocket she'd been planning to wear.

What am I doing?

Exhaustion rolled over her like a wave crashing on the shore. Wearily, she wiped her computer clean, shut it down and with one last thorough look around, she left. She closed and locked the office door before heading down the extensive set of steps, using her cell phone to light the darkened stairwell. When she was about halfway down, there was a loud bang outside. She flattened herself against the wall as she listened intently, having no clue what she'd do if someone came through that door. She stuffed her cell phone in her pocket.

Five minutes later, when nothing else happened, she made her way silently down the rest of the steps. Unlocking and then slowly opening the door, she peered out before stepping through, closing and locking it behind her.

She hadn't taken two steps when she felt something sharp touch her neck, and at the same time an arm slid around her waist like a cinch that tightened with each movement.

"You hold it right there or I'll cut you. Give me all you've got. Your cell phone first."

CHAPTER 24

"You scared the crap out of me. You had that man accost me. Then you casually stroll in here as though nothing has happened?"

Graham stared at her. If he opened his mouth, he'd deafen her with his tirade, and he wouldn't get the answers he needed.

"You hired that guy to guard this place?"

"Yeah, is that a problem?" He ground his teeth as he turned away from Tarin. Bill stood like a silent sentinel off to the side. Graham handed him the bag of new socks he'd been carrying around in his Hummer for a few days. He watched as Bill's blackened, aged fingers slowly wrapped around the offering before he shuffled off, disappearing around the side of the building. Once he was out of sight, Graham unlocked the door, gesturing for Tarin to precede him. Her thrust chin told him she wasn't any happier than he was. He almost laughed because she had no idea what pissed was. But she would soon.

Once inside his business, he went past her and into his office, holding the door wide for her. He waited her out, making sure it was clear he expected her to come in. Some of the starch had gone out of her. Her posture was less intimidating, but the second she noted he was watching her, she squared them. The look of resignation on her face was a little harder to hide, though.

Striding across the room, he gave them both some space.

"So, what? You let him hang out in your alley and you give him a few tokens of appreciation?" Her eyebrows drew together with force.

He held her gaze without blinking. It probably looked bad, his handing Bill that bag, but he'd noticed it when he'd gotten out of his Hummer and realized he'd forgotten again that day.

"I'll presume you do the decent thing and at least give him clothes and food?"

He sat down on the edge of his desk and crossed his arms.

"Geez. Can't you at least do something right and give him somewhere to live?"

"You sure do make a lot of assumptions, don't you?"

"Oh? You've given him a room at the Hilton?"

He shrugged.

"You cheap son-of-a-a-a—jerk. You've got money and yet you can't even spare a little for a guy down on his luck. A homeless guy means nothing, does he? Big deal. You rich men are all the same." She spun around and was headed for the door, but it slammed shut before she reached it. Forced to stop, she refused to turn around. "Cute trick."

"I thought so. I can close it without leaving my desk. It keeps some people out and others from leaving before I'm done talking to them." He looked at the gizmo he was holding in his hand, feeling quite proud of himself. "Never had to use it before, though."

"So now what?" She turned slowly to face him. The bravado was there in her voice and on her face, but her drooped shoulders and the constant rubbing of her thumb against her index finger suggested she was unnerved.

Good. He needed to know what she was up to.

"What are you doing here in the middle of the night?"

There was a flicker in the depths of her hazel eyes, but he wasn't sure if it was fear or determination.

"The truth? I needed to do something on the computer; something personal, and I don't have one."

"And you had to do it now, because?"

"Because during the day, you'd haul me over the coals naked if I did that."

A clear image of her bare backside flashed through his mind. It was so intense that he had to either look away or let his eyes wander down her body. His thumbnail suddenly became very interesting. He walked around his desk and sat down. It took a moment to get control of his wayward thoughts. He glanced up. She seemed to take his actions as a sign and sat in the chair beside Guy's desk, where Bailey often sat.

"What the hell is your problem? You're touchy. You lie—"

"And you're so darn arrogant; you think you're something else. You may look as though you're a pauper in your worn jeans, your tight t-shirts, riding your ten-speed everyday like some fit fanatic—"

"You don't even know me—"

"And you don't know—"

"What the hell are you hiding?"

"None of your damn—"

"It is my damn—"

"Go take a flying—"

He stood abruptly, his knees snapped back like a cadet coming to attention, hitting his chair and sending it spinning backward into the wall. It had the effect of a judge slamming his gavel in a quiet courtroom.

Graham and Tarin both went utterly still but didn't look at each other. The silence that ensued was a throbbing presence that had its own pulse. Neither moved.

"Sorry." Graham reached for his chair, not to sit in it but to move it to the side. He did not want a repeat, but this woman was driving him nuts. Resting his knuckles on his desk, he looked at her. She hadn't moved, although she was a lot tenser. Her body was as still as a statue, her face expressionless, but tilted her head in defiance. Tension emanated from her in waves, like the blistering sun off asphalt.

"Are you okay?"

She made a slight movement of her head. "Fine. Actually, I'm sorry. That was uncalled for. I don't normally use that kind of language."

"Uh—" He felt totally off-kilter. He was not handling this well. "Would you like something to drink?"

"Yes, do you have any wine?"

He blinked twice. "No, but I have some Jack Daniels. Will that do?"

She gave a brief nod. "I'm sorry for my behavior; it was uncalled for."

Her attention was focused on the floor, but her posture was as rigid as the chair she sat in. He opened a cabinet in the corner of the room and pulled out a full bottle that had been a Christmas gift from a client. After retrieving two mugs from the outer office and some ice and bottled water for mix, he poured her a drink. She downed the first one before he'd barely poured his and had time to sit at his desk. She didn't ask for another one but didn't argue when he poured her another one. The third and fourth ones, she helped herself to.

She didn't say a word, so neither did he. It was like being out in nature with a timid animal he wanted to get close to, but had to take his time and keep his movements slow and steady. He didn't know what to do with her or how to approach her.

He could just fire her.

"You know. I'm a damn good worker. Been working my butt off since... a long time. Yeah. A long time. I was little. But if I wanted to be seen, I had to work. Always work. Never fun." Her speech was slurred, yet she was sitting ramrod straight. If he hadn't known she'd drunk so much booze in such a short period of time, he'd have been sure she was faking it.

"You ever have fun? I mean as a kid." She was looking at him earnestly.

"Yeah. I have brothers and sisters. We got into a lot of trouble. Did some crazy things. Played superheroes a lot."

"I wanted to be Cinderella. Well, no, not her, the one in the tree with the long hair. You know Rapunz... or something. Her anyway. I wanted to let my hair down. Have fun, you know. Party. Do girl things. And find me a man." She laughed a sharp, huffing bark. Or at least that was what it sounded like to him. It was the most unnatural thing he'd ever heard.

He poured her a glass of water and handed it to her. She wanted to be the fairy tale character Rapunzel. He wasn't sure what to make of that.

Tarin took it and downed it.

"Yuck. That tastes like crap." She got to her feet and made a beeline for the bed in the corner; obviously taking it as an invitation, immediately climbing into it. Although it was more like falling onto it. She was sprawled out on top of the covers. It didn't take long for her to start making the funniest cooing sounds.

Wondering what the heck had just happened, he looked around to make sure there wasn't a camera recording, and he was part of a gag. The snoring coming from the corner was the only thing that seemed real. He sat at his desk while watching the sleeping woman he'd hired just a short time ago.

Unsure what to do, he turned on his computer. It was now 4:45. He glanced longingly at the occupied bed. If things had been different, he'd have climbed onto it and gone to sleep. The person who was currently sleeping peacefully rolled over at that moment, giving him a great view of her blouse, which molded to her nicely formed chest. The images that ran through his mind in quick succession were not ones he should be having—most definitely not ones about an employee.

Getting up from his desk, he headed to her computer. After logging on, he checked through to see what she'd been doing. But like every day when she left work, her laptop was scrubbed clean as though she'd never been on it. He'd finally gotten a little smarter, though. Opening the hidden tracer he'd installed to track her movements;

he flipped through what she'd been doing. He clicked on the website where she'd spent a fair amount of time. It was a membership site exclusively for women looking to change their lives. There was a lot of information about empowerment, standing on your own, and standing up for themselves. *Believe, and your life can change.* He flipped through all five pages; they were pretty basic. Not too much information. One had links to websites that helped women dealing with abuse, getting back on their feet, shelters, counselling. To get any information, he had to be a member. There was a place to sign up to receive monthly newsletters. Using an alias, he did just that.

As he was finishing up, a kid's song started playing. His head whipped around. It was coming from inside his office. He followed the source and soon discovered her cell phone tucked inside her jacket, which she'd set on the chair. Tarin hadn't and wasn't moving. The number meant nothing to him, and he only debated for a quick second but realized that it could be her family before he answered it.

"Hello?"

"Who is this?"

"Who's this?"

"Where's Tarin? I know I called the right number. Put her on. Now."

"I can't. She's sleeping."

"What? What did you do to her? And who the hell are you?"

"I'm Graham."

"Oh, her boss."

"Yes, her boss."

"If you hurt her—"

"What the hell kind of thing is that to say—?"

"Well, it's the middle of the night, and you say she's sleeping."

"She is. She drank too much whiskey—"

"Since when does she drink that?"

"How am I supposed to know? Look—"

"No, you look. I don't know what happened there and whether she's all right—"

"I'll take a picture of her and send it to you if that will help, but we'll have to switch to my phone as hers I'm sure is locked."

"Swear to me she's okay."

"I swear she's fine. A little uptight and very drunk but other than that, fine."

"I know what she did was wrong, but you can't fire her. Promise me you won't."

"Not your call. And what do you think she was doing that was so wrong?"

Graham tried to get her to divulge some information, but he got very little. Taking a chance, he hooked Tarin's phone up to his computer to see what he could find. Five minutes later, he put her cell back where he'd found it. Someone was pissed at her. Rather than read all the texts, he copied them and decided he'd only broach the subject if she turned out to be doing something more devious. Exhaustion pulled at him with the force of a semi pushing against him. The thought of sleeping in his chair had him looking longingly at the single bed Tarin was taking full advantage of. Sighing, he sat and leaned back, resting his feet on his desk. He tried not to think of the fact that the last time he'd slept like that it had taken several days to work the kinks out of his neck.

He'd barely closed his eyes when he sensed movement or heard something. He wasn't sure, but it was enough to force open his weighted lids and peer at the blurred body tiptoeing across his floor.

"You're not leaving yet."

Her whole body jolted like a springboard and stopped suddenly as she whipped around to face him.

"I already know I'm terminated. Let's save the hoopla. I know I messed up. You know I messed up. Let's leave it at that. I can dole out my own lumps." She reached for the doorknob.

"God, you're a pain. Do you ever let anyone make decisions?"

"Never again." The viciousness with which she said those words was nothing compared to the gritted teeth and her rigid stance with clenched fists.

He stepped back. His computer dinged. He'd set the alarm to wake him.

"What time is it?"

"7:00 a.m."

"Oh, my God. Oh, my God. Chance. He's going to freak out. He's going to freak out. Oh, my God. I'm so in over my head. I'm dead." She repeated that over and over as she grabbed her jacket she'd forgotten and raced out the door, leaving it wide open as she ran.

He chased after her and yelled down the stairs to her. "Hey. I need you back at work. You can't fire yourself. And I'm not firing you. Be here or I'll come and get you. Be back Monday."

She stopped for a brief second with her hand on the doorknob, but she didn't look back. After a brief hesitation, she pulled it open and disappeared through it. Graham stared at it long after she'd gone.

What the hell happened?

****

"Graham?"

"Hi Mrs—Dorothea."

She laughed. "You're getting it. I need your driving services again."

Graham made a funny face as he looked around his empty office and wondered why he had been chosen as her personal chauffeur—and what she was hiding that she needed his services.

"Uh. Yeah. Sure. When?"

"Now, thank you. See you in an hour? I know most people take an hour and a half. If you're going to bring that monstrous Hummer, please bring steps so I can get into it with dignity."

"Okay. I'll see you soon." He closed out the game he was playing, Kingdom of Amalur, and all the other things he had opened for work but hadn't touched. Once he'd shut everything down, it wasn't what he wanted to be doing on a Sunday, but it beat sitting in his office pretending to work or wondering what was going on with Tarin.

Chapter 25

Dorothea entered the beautiful Carina Hotel. It was one of her favorites and the first in the Cooper-Lite Hotel chain, not a hotel most people would have expected to see her in, though. It was an acceptable place, but not in the league that someone of her stature would normally grace. In her younger days, she'd spent many an hour at the hotel. It was the first in a long chain that she and her husband Jonathon's friend Calib—better known as Charles Cooper to his rivals—had built. In fact, he'd given them the first key to a room fifty years before, when she'd taken over the family winery business and he'd taken over the family hotel business. She still had it tucked away in her wall safe at home. It was symbolic now, as all the locks had been changed and updated. Since then, he'd given them a master card that could be used at any of their hotels. He had trusted them, but she'd never before had an occasion to use it. This situation, however, required it.

Old memories flooded back. She and Jonathon had been the first guests at this very hotel after Calib had purchased it. They had been young and so much in love. The world had been theirs. It saddened her to think her best friend and love had died so many years before, and she'd stopped going there. Life had gotten in the way of old friendships.

Walking up to the dark, ornately carved front desk, she handed her key to the man, letting him know there was a code on the back. As a professional, he did well at remaining jovially stone-faced, his eyebrows only lifting slightly. A minute later, she had a programmed card that would let her access any room in the hotel; but she only needed to access one.

The elevators were on the right and around the corner. She made her way to an empty one, slid her card into the slot and the doors closed. She hit the button for the seventh floor. The ride was brief but long enough for her to know this might be something foolish. It had been a long time since she'd done anything this rash, but somewhere in her gut, there was some truth to what the woman had told her. There had definitely been enough information to pique her interest. Leaning heavily on her cane for a moment, she let her years get the best of her. The weight of all she'd been living under weighed in, drooping her shoulders even more than the normal age-related slouch.

It was long past time for her to retire. At eighty, she should do what her friends were doing: going south for the winter, visiting and playing cards. But in her heart? That wasn't her. Although she did realize it was time that she stepped down and found something a little less stressful, like maybe skydiving.

She smiled at her own joke, knowing her family would have a fit if she did anything like that. But the truth was that it was time for someone else to take over. Since her family had all turned her down, she needed to look elsewhere. It left a bit of a bitter taste in her mouth, but she couldn't blame them.

Being the head of Caspian Wine had been her dream and, thanks to her brother Geoff, her nightmare as well. Since she was the oldest, it only made sense that it went to her, even back in the day when women were not in charge of businesses. But to him, she had always stolen it out from under him. In reality, he'd always hoped to be able to use it to redeem himself in their parents' eyes. An innocent child, badly abused and humiliated, he was the offspring of the patriarch and the maid. A young, tender-hearted Dorothea had always felt guilty that she hadn't stopped her parents from making a mockery of him. And Geoff had used her soft side against her. He'd taken so much from her.

The guilt of all he'd been through was her cross to bear, but never again would she let him almost destroy her family. She was still bothered about his death, though; something about it hadn't seemed real. She had grieved losing him, but she'd never had the sense he was gone. Not that she'd shared her thoughts with anyone, but no matter how many people she'd hired to find him, he was a ghost—one who may have finally decided he wanted back in her life. Hopefully, she'd soon get answers about who was attempting to sabotage her business.

When the elevator doors opened, she made her way to room 712. Bracing herself for the tale she was about to be told, she knocked. The door opened, and a mature woman stood there; the only telltale sign she wasn't as confident as she appeared was the slight involuntary tick at the corner of her eye. She waved Dorothea in.

Dorothea entered the suite, glancing around the room. There were just the two of them as promised. It didn't mean there wasn't someone hiding in the bedroom or bathroom, though. The woman never let her gaze waver but stared openly at her. It had Dorothea rethinking her own actions. But there had been something in her voice, in her story, that convinced Dorothea she had to see her alone. Taking someone at their word was not something she was usually so gullible about. Dorothea sat in a high-backed stuffed chair.

"Before we start, I'd like a glass of water, and please turn on the television. I don't want this conversation overheard or recorded."

The woman appeared startled. "I would never... I promise you that's not why I contacted you. There is a potential problem at your winery, but I'm not sure you have any clue about it. What I need to share with you—" she drew in a shaky breath, "may shock you beyond anything, but I promise you I'm not making it up."

She spun away, flipping the television on as she passed on her way to the mini-fridge. After taking out a bottle of water, she poured half of it into a glass. Once there was noise to mask her movements, Dorothea took out her phone and snapped pictures from her hip. She hoped her aim was good. She slipped it back into the pocket of her trench coat as the woman started making her way toward her.

Blue-green eyes, dark, dowdy brown hair that was the poorest excuse for a wig. The clothes were cheap—torn jeans and a white simple but stylish blouse. She'd never seen the woman before; nor did she resemble anyone she knew.

She accepted the glass of water and took a sip. The woman moved to the window, pulling back the lace curtains to stare out. Finally, she moved to the sofa to Dorothea's right. She clasped her hands in her lap and curled her bare toes back, resting her feet on the Berber rug.

"Thank you for meeting with me. I know that my story will seem unbelievable... but I—"

Dorothea nodded. "I want to listen to your tale, but please make no mistake; I'm here because I want to know why. Why are you telling me, and what do you have to gain? If this is a plot to blackmail me, there is nothing that can implicate me. Now, you mentioned Caspian Winery and my brother. I've seen it all. I've heard it all. Tell me your name. Your real name and how you know so much about my business and my family."

"I don't know where to start. Let me go back a couple of years. I need you to understand how this came about..."

Forty-five minutes later, Dorothea was thankful her heart was in decent shape because otherwise she wasn't sure she could have survived what she'd heard. It was unbelievable, but something had been coming. Life had been almost normal for a short while. She had high hopes the fairytale life Guy and Bailey were living would continue, but with what she'd heard, that might not happen. At least not without at least one or two more mountains to climb. She clutched the pages and the receipts the woman had given her, unable to believe what she'd heard and what she was reading. She stuffed the papers into her purse. Leaning heavily on her cane, she came to her feet. The woman who towered over her diminutive 5'3" immediately rose to help her, providing a steadying hand. Dorothea grasped it more firmly than she needed to.

"I have some things to work out. I'll get back to you. Do you have somewhere to lie low where you'll be safe?"

"You believe me?"

"I have some things to look into first. I'll be in touch."

"I can look after myself. I've been doing it a long time. I've closed down my business and vacated my apartment. I don't think I'm in danger. My daughter, however, I'm not so sure about. I need to find her. I'm close to locating her. I'm scared if I don't get to her first, he will. I already know he's capable of some pretty sick stuff."

"You have my number. If something happens, call me immediately. The fewer people that know about this, the better. Give me a day or two. You do not know who the father of your child is—or the identity of the man threatening you?"

"No. I know you want to confirm the story I've told you is true, but I promise you I've told you everything. I want my daughter, but I want her to have a different life than I've lived. That's why I gave her up for adoption. It seemed like the best idea a the time; I never imagined her life would be in danger. He'll follow through on his threat if I don't do what he asks. It's not in my nature to intentionally hurt someone. Why does he want me to damage Caspian Winery?" She raised tired shoulders. "My life is not pure: owning an escort service puts me out of that category, but I promise you, I've tried to live an honest one."

"Someday I want to know how you got into that kind of life. I assume you made a living at it?"

The woman frowned. "Before I closed it down, around $120,000 a month."

"You're sure this man who is threatening you wasn't one of your clients?"

"I'm sure. I'm cautious with clients, screening them thoroughly before I take them on, and I haven't had a new client in well over a year. And I haven't heard from the man who did this to me in almost eight years. My daughter turned seven. I know it seems unbelievable, and I can't give you a description, but I've paid some private investigators quite well to find what they could. Their search led me to you and who I think is behind this. I don't want your money; I want my daughter to be safe, and she won't be if I don't follow through with something destructive to your business. He killed my cat—" she wiped a tear from her eye before continuing, "in the most heinous way so I would get the message."

Dorothea nodded. "I'll be in touch." She slowly made her way out of the room, her limp more pronounced and her movements slower. In the hallway, she continued to an alcove, where she sat heavily in an armchair. Pulling out the smartphone Bailey had spent hours teaching her to use, she flipped through the telephone numbers until she found the contact she needed and pressed call.

"Hello."

"Calib?"

"Yes, hello, Dorothea."

The sound of his voice brought back so many happy memories. He had been a good friend to her and Jonathon. She took a deep breath before slowly letting it out. "It was good to see you last week. Thank you."

"Indeed. What's going on? Things were happening so fast when we met, I never got a chance to say I was sorry to hear about your brother. Such a tragic death."

"Thank you." She couldn't change the past, but she could change the course of what her brother had put in motion before his death. This time, she would not be so gullible. She would not be taken in by him or whoever was behind this sick game, and she would not be killed because of him. Not that she was going to share any of that with Calib. He was a man she could trust, but she didn't want to get him any more involved than absolutely necessary.

"Did you have time to look through the names I sent you? I split the list into who would be suitable candidates and who would be great."

"I did."

"And?"

"Thank you."

"But none quite fit what you're looking for."

"I know they are all qualified and doing outstanding work, but no, they aren't what I'm looking for."

"It's difficult to leave a business you started and built up and have taken care of it, all your life. I know."

"You're lucky you had—I mean, found someone."

"Yes, sadly, it should have been my son. Alas, but he thought it more important to go into business for himself in an attempt to put my company out of business."

"I'm so sorry."

"Me too. My fault for being away so much. His mother did a lot to make him the bitter man he is. Anyway, let's not talk about him. I may have another suggestion for you on someone to hire, my granddaughter. She's smart, has run a portion of my son's business, C-Lite Hotels, and she's savvy. I have to find her. My butthead son has lost track of her. How can you lose your own daughter?"

"I'm sorry, Calib."

"Let's not talk about it. You called me because—"

"Do you still have that computer genius working for you?"

"Yes, but I'm sure he's nowhere near as good as the fellow working with your step-grandson."

"I know, but some things can't be shared with family. At least, not yet. He needs to do a background check, one that digs deep. Her information won't be all that easy to find. What I do have might not be true. I'll text you some pictures shortly as well."

"No problem, I'll have him check her out. When do you need it by?"

"Today? Tomorrow? As soon as he can." Dorothea closed her eyes as a glimmer of hope was finally shining through. "Thank you. You do this, and I'll find your grand-daughter. Deal?"

"Deal. Always a pleasure talking with you." There was a slight hesitation. "I got the invitation to your granddaughter's upcoming wedding. Congratulations. If you need help with any of the arrangements, please ask. I know you already have the best, but sometimes things happen, and I want you to know my hotels can help if you're stuck."

"Thank you. I—would you like to come as my guest?"

"I wasn't fishing."

"I would be honored if you came as my escort; it'll give me someone to talk to while my family is off having fun. It would be wonderful if you sat with us?"

"I would love to. Maybe we can even dance."

"That would be lovely. And discuss business."

A few minutes later, she hung up. It wasn't until she was back in Graham's Hummer that she let the reality of what she'd learned hit her. Life was going to get a lot rockier.

"Graham. I need you to find me a nanny."

"A... nanny? Uh... is there something I don't know about? Guy and Bailey?"

"No. Not for them. Find me one that is trained in martial arts too, okay?"

CHAPTER 26

THE HEAT OF THE day slapped her like a wet rag as soon as she stepped out of the house. Beads of sweat popped out on her face, and she could feel the dampness pooling between her breasts. Tarin was tempted to turn around, play hooky from work and instead, take Chance to a waterpark to play.

Stephen hadn't called or texted in a little over a day. It was what she had hoped for, but it also left her feeling all the more unsettled. He'd texted continuously almost since the day she'd left, and now nothing.

Climbing into Bobbie's Camry, she immediately turned on the air conditioner. Once she arrived at work, she parked around the side of the building in her usual spot. Her stomach felt queasy, which it had for the whole weekend thanks to the whiskey she'd downed and the guilt she wasn't digesting very well. The thought of facing her boss wasn't sitting well either. If it weren't imperative that she find out what the hell had happened to her life and ensure Chance's safety, she would have run long and far. It almost made her proud that, for once, she was going to deal with her own mess. Well, if she didn't throw up first.

She got out of the car and grabbed her bag and lunch. When she turned around, the guard she'd encountered the other night was standing less than two feet away. She jerked back, sending her bag flying out of her hands. Her heart thudded rapidly beneath her hand as she leaned back against the vehicle's hot metal.

"Bill. Right? Is it okay if I call you that?"

His steady gaze never wavered.

"What can I do for you?" She made a motion as if she were going to step forward, but he didn't back up. Taking a sidestep, she scooped up her bag and closed the door, locking it. Hugging her arms to her chest, she slowly continued to edge sideways.

"You're late."

"I know. I had some things to do—" *I was just avoiding coming in.*

"Not good to be late." He walked away, disappearing from view around the corner of the building.

She frowned as she looked around to see if she'd missed something. It wasn't odd to see Bill, she supposed; she only wished he hadn't snuck up on her. It made her wonder if he'd always been watching her and was adept at fading into the background—until he'd decided she'd crossed a line and accosted her. Feeling uncomfortable, she sprinted up two steps at a time. She'd just stuffed her bag in the desk drawer and turned on her computer when the inner door opened. But it wasn't Graham or Guy who came out but Bailey.

"Hi."

She almost sagged in relief. She was not looking forward to seeing Graham. The text he'd sent her—*Please come back to work. We appreciate all the work you're doing. You've helped a lot. We can't get through this without you*—that was why she was there. No one had ever appreciated anything she'd done before. It had been expected. She wanted to delay the inevitable moment when she came face to face with him. She was sure she'd look sunburned because of the embarrassment she felt.

"Hi. Sorry, I'm running behind."

"Hey, don't tell me, because I can plead ignorance if the boss questions me." She winked as she walked by.

"Uhm. How are things going with the wedding?"

Bailey stopped but didn't do well at hiding her surprise. "Good. It's all coming together, I think. There are a few hiccups, but I guess that's normal, right?"

Tarin's eyes widened. For a split second she thought her statement implied she'd been through it herself, but she hadn't shared that she was married. She was being crazy. There was no way Bailey could know she'd just left her husband. "I guess whenever you're planning something big like this there will be a few problems. Nothing serious, I hope?"

"No. No. It's the wedding planner who has hired a new staff, and since we're so easy to get along with, she assigned her to us." She shrugged. "I don't know if I've been called easy to get along with before—anyway, there have been a few issues that have cropped up since she's taken over. Things were going along smoothly, and now—I'm trying not to be judgmental, and I'm sure they aren't her fault but—"

"But it's all happened since she took over."

"Yeah, everything was going smoothly and then suddenly there's a problem with the band. But it didn't stop there. The flowers were next. Then with the invitations. Then with—I don't even know what. It's one thing after another, and then of course she has her own ideas. I've had to rein her in a bit. She wanted us to change the venue from Caspian Winery—actually Grandma's mansion—to something closer to Toronto. Anyway, I shouldn't be boring you with all of this. It is what it is, and the wedding will happen no matter what. You know, I wanted something simple, but Grandma got in the mix and there was no way an intimate gathering was going to happen."

Tarin smiled at the affection in her voice. She couldn't help but be envious of her. Bailey seemed to have it all, money, a great guy and a loving family. Some people had no idea what a tough life was like. Not that she could complain; she'd grown up with money too. And when she looked at someone like Bill, her upbringing might have been emotionally bereft, but her physical comforts were more than he currently had.

"You mean her?" Tarin nodded toward one of the many wall pictures of Dorothea Lindell.

Bailey's expression softened as she looked at the woman. "Yeah. She's something." There was a sad hitch in her voice. "I'm forever grateful to that woman. She's amazing, and I am truly blessed to have her in my life."

Again, something sounded off. "She's okay, isn't she?"

"She'll outlive us all. She's someone who radically changed my life."

"You're lucky."

"You know I never used to think that, but you know what? I am." Bailey glanced at her cell phone. "I have to run. I have a new client I'm meeting."

"Have a good day."

She was at the door before she stopped and turned around. "Are things okay with you?"

Tarin blinked at her a couple of times, tempted to look over her shoulder to see if there was someone behind her. "Yes. I'm fine. Things are good. Graham and I have come to a bit of an understanding. We still have a few things to work out."

"Yeah, he barks and you—"

"No, it's not like that anymore. He's mellowed some. I guess I brought out the worst in him. Guy has said a few times he'd never seen him so growly in the eight years he's known him."

"Oh? Hmm. Interesting. Anyway, I do have to run. Hey, do you want to do lunch sometime?"

"I'd love that. Do you think you could show me Caspian Winery at some point?"

"Sure," Bailey nodded. "I'll call you."

Tarin rattled off her cell number before Bailey slipped out the door. Feeling a little out of sorts, she was tempted to sit there and contemplate their odd conversation, but maybe it was awkward because she'd never talked to Bailey before. The soft ding from her computer reminded her she had a lot of work to do.

She quickly logged on to her site. There were fourteen more women who had asked to join. A few shared their story but none were what Tarin was looking for.

I shouldn't be sharing this with you, but I'm being asked to do something that is so wrong. But if I don't, he'll hurt my family. He's hard to get rid of. There's something I did that might end everything for me. He's a bully and I hate being bullied. I'm standing up to him in a roundabout way. I didn't know what else to do. Sorry, I needed to vent to someone. LJ

LJ, I'm sorry you're in this situation. I know what it's like to have an abusive man in your life. I'm currently trying to leave mine. Can you go to the police? I know he's probably threatened you if you do but if you don't... I don't know what to tell you to do. I ran. I don't know that it's the best advice. Maybe you've done the best thing. If I can help, I'm here. Tarin.

After she replied, she wished there were something she could do. There were way too many women in situations similar to this. She hated feeling so helpless. Skimming through the other information, there was nothing more from the other two women. She sent a personal email welcoming each new member. She posted some new information. There was nothing new from any of the women. None of those she had questioned had responded, so she logged off.

Graham hadn't come out to check on her, but he wouldn't be pleased that she was over an hour late. For whatever reason, Chance hadn't wanted her to leave that morning. He'd clung to her, crying. It made her feel all the more guilty for what she'd put him through and, if truth be told, she hadn't wanted to go to the office at all.

Pushing away her thoughts, she quickly opened K.A.'s emails. The first one stopped her. There was nothing special about it except for the banner that had been included. It was the same logo on the paper left underneath her when Tarin had awakened from her week-long drugged state. It was one of the few clues she had.

The logo for Caspian Winery wasn't out of the ordinary; but seeing it on something sent to Knights Associates looking exactly like that piece of paper stuck to her back, hit home like nothing else had.

It's run by an eighty-year-old woman. It didn't even make sense, but it was all she had to go on. She couldn't stop staring at it. Her gut told her it was the link she needed. She was tempted to connect the USB from the winery. There was no way she could do it during the day; she didn't want to be found with something so incriminating. It reminded her of the information she'd been accused of stealing at school, only that time she hadn't stolen it. She'd barely been able to use computers back then. She still had no idea who'd set her up.

Being caught was not something she was ready to go through again. The best place to look over that information would be through the office, but how was she going to do that? Her brilliant midnight run had turned out to be her usual screw-up. She'd have to try again. She didn't have a choice. She needed to know what connection Caspian Winery had to her. One question from that situation three years ago that reverberated through her mind: Had she gone willingly?

CHAPTER 27

"GRAHAM. CALLING TO LET you know your suit's in. Go down to Jasper's Menswear so they can get you measured and fitted. Today. Tomorrow. That would be great."

Graham hit the delete button on the message. Guy was going to drive him just a little crazy with his wedding. The good news was he only had two months or so left to listen to him. Not that he begrudged the guy the awesome woman he was marrying or the fact that he was getting hitched. Graham stopped himself in mid thought. *That's bullshit.* Jealousy head had reared its ugly head; something he'd sworn would never happen to him.

Guy and Bailey were good together. It had taken Guy two years to wear down Bailey's adamant resolve that they needed more time to get to know each other. She wanted to make certain she wasn't suffering from the woman-in-jeopardy syndrome, since Guy had rescued her from her uncle. The whole thing still made him scratch his head. Crazy didn't even adequately describe how they'd met or what they'd been through. Graham was thankful that they were going to have a happy ending. What concerned him was all they'd gone through to find each other. The whole concept was a little off his radar, and if the only way he could find the same kind of happiness was to go through a similar ordeal, no thanks. All he had to do was show up, be the best man and then run like hell.

He checked over the email listing all the tasks Tarin had completed the day before. The little lull they'd had in business requests hadn't lasted long. They'd been hit with a deluge again. It was bizarre, and he didn't understand why. He didn't have time to ponder it, though, but he had to admit Tarin had made it much easier. She'd honed it to an awesome science. She'd open the emails and put them through a ten-step crap test—his title for it, not hers. The ones she could eliminate, she put in a file in case there was something there they could check out later. Those that she was pretty sure were bogus went in their own file. Those that appeared both promising and legit despite remaining questions would go into another. That left those that were definitely legit—or at least as much as they could tell without a deep dive. The interesting thing was that about twenty percent of them now seemed to be real—way up from the five percent when they'd first been hit.

It made him wonder if they were being tested, perhaps to see if they were any good before they were hired. He needed to figure out a way to configure a trap, tracing some of the emails back to their source.

"We've got a problem."

Yeah, and I'm looking at them. Graham looked up and nodded at Guy, who was just entering the office. "What? You put on too much weight? You're turning into a fat, married man before you've even gotten hitched?"

"Ha-ha. Funny. No, unfortunately, it's more serious than that. A wine shipment headed for Calgary got hijacked."

Graham's head jerked up. "Who steals a truckload of wine?"

"Wine lovers?"

"Is there really a demand for that kind of alcohol on the black market?"

"If it can make money, I'd say yes."

"Jesus, something is fishy. I mean fishier than normal fishy."

"I couldn't agree more. We need to see if we can help in any way."

"Any leads?"

"Nope. The truck was stopped by two armed men. The driver said he was sure they were using machine guns."

Graham looked at him in disbelief. "Really? In Canada? That's got to be a new one. The driver is okay?"

"Yup. It happened late in the evening, when there was little traffic. Well planned, from the sound of it. They took his cell phone and smashed it and then drove away in the truck. They left him by the side of the road in the middle of Saskatchewan. Another trucker stopped about an hour later and picked him up."

"So they had a good head start?"

"And no leads. The driver is being questioned."

"'K. Let me see if I can find anything about a black market for wine. That still sounds odd to me but I guess if it'll make money, it's up for grabs. How's Dorothea doing?"

Guy shrugged. "Upset. Never has anything like this ever happened before. Two incidents in a little under a month is too much. Oh, and guess what I found out today? She's already hired an assistant. Her name is LJ Brown."

Graham looked at Guy's drooping eyelids. The long days and late nights of trying to catch the bad guy were wearing on him. "Oh-oh. What do you know about her?"

"Dorothea interviewed her, checked her out, or so she says, but hired her immediately. She's convinced this woman is legitimate. Grandma says she has sources besides us. God, I'm worried about her."

Graham thought back to the rides he'd given her. *Oh wow, is that what she was up to?* He was tempted to mention it to Guy, but the way Guy was pacing and rubbing his forehead, he didn't look like he could take too much more.

"Your grandmother is a smart woman who's been running that business for what, fifty years? She's pretty savvy."

"Yeah, but since Geoff—" Guy suddenly dropped into his chair behind his desk, leaning back.

"She won't make the same mistake again. And don't worry, I'll check out the woman."

"Thank you."

"Oh, and Dorothea wants us to find someone—the granddaughter of Charles Cooper, owner of Cooper-Lite Hotels."

"I'll add it to the list, but do we have to make it a priority?"

"Well, to her, everything she asks us to do is top priority. Add it to the list; when you have time, look into it, but we have a few other things to solve first. I'll stall her on it. I want to know more about this LJ first."

Graham was about to close out the email account he'd been browsing when one of the subject lines caught his attention.

'Shipment of wine for sale, 70% off.'

He glowered at it. Finally, he looked up and was about to mention it to his partner when he discovered Guy's chin had dropped to his chest and he was snoring softly.

Why would someone drop this in our lap?

CHAPTER 28

TARIN POURED HERSELF A glass of wine and sat on the couch. It had been months since she'd last enjoyed a drink—well, except for that slight slip at the office that still made her want to bury her head in shame. Thankfully, Graham hadn't brought it up.

Chance had finally fallen asleep, and she hoped he stayed that way. He'd been quite fussy earlier, whining and clinging, signs she wouldn't get anything done if he woke up.

"Tarin? Kim and I are going out for a couple of hours."

"All right. Is everything okay?"

"Yeah, just going over to Mom's."

Tarin stiffened. "Uh, she hasn't or won't—"

"Don't worry. She hasn't talked with your dad... in... umm, a while. She'll keep quiet. I promise. She's on one of her usual spending sprees, and I need to put some brakes on her. In her bubble, money grows on trees. Anyway, we'll see you later."

"Have fun."

She had wanted to return to the office, but she couldn't figure out what lie to tell Bobbie this time. As they prepared to leave, Tarin had a brainstorm to use her friend's computer. She should be able to wipe it afterward so Bobbie wouldn't have a clue she'd used it. She didn't want to involve her friend any more than she had to.

She waited a good ten minutes after they left before coming to her feet. After a quick check on her sleeping son, she made her way upstairs. She plugged the USB into the port and logged on. There was a lot of information to sift through, and since she had no idea what she was looking for, she snooped through a lot. Most had to do with sales, business contacts, shipping logs, nothing that was overly helpful.

She skimmed through nearly everything she had, but there wasn't anything that jumped out at her. Sighing heavily, she rested her elbows on the table and placed her chin in her hands. Disappointment filled her as she stared at the screen. What had made her think she'd find anything there? As she was about to close out the files, a niggling little voice urged her to keep looking, so she opened even the deepest buried files, some of which were twenty folders deep. But there was really nothing; just drafts and old files that should have been deleted and some information stored in a backup file and archived. Frustrated and bored, she skimmed through about five more. Fed up but not quite ready to quit, she clicked on one, not expecting anything of importance. When she saw it was a group of pictures, she was about to close it out when what she was looking at finally registered.

She blinked a few times in disbelief. She flipped through a few of the fifty or so pictures that involved the man from whom she'd stolen the information—photos she would never have guessed in a million years that he would be involved with. He appeared like someone's middle-aged, kind-hearted uncle in contrast to what she was viewing now.

Could he be the creep behind her lost week? There was nothing familiar about him, but as she skimmed through a few of the photos and the vulgarity of the acts, anything was possible. He was doing unspeakable sex acts. She clapped her hand over her mouth and had to look away for a long moment as her nervous stomach threatened to lose her supper.

They were perverted, but they weren't illegal. Realizing everything she was staring at would most likely remain in her subconscious forever, she finally closed it out. A few other files were encrypted. It struck her as odd that he wouldn't have encrypted the photos, as potentially damaging as they were. She tried a few procedures to open the files, but nothing she did worked. It would take a special program to break the encryption. She hoped they were answers, maybe even financial files that would show some payments to help her figure out who was behind all that had and was going on with her life.

Her computer downstairs would work, but she didn't want to chance it. She had discovered that Stephen had secretly accessed the GPS for her car, which was still in Calgary, so it didn't matter, but the one on her phone did bother her. Both had been disabled, but she wasn't taking a chance—with him being the control freak he was; he could well have installed something that she hadn't found on her computer.

The only other place that would have the software that she needed was at work. She dropped her head into her hands. *What am I thinking?*

Deciding she had a good opportunity to see if anyone had responded, she logged onto her website. There were several requests to join, some sharing some basic information and appreciation for her website, but there weren't any in response to her emails. Sighing heavily, she was about to close out when an email came in.

'I'll meet with you, but don't expect me to spill my guts. I want to know who you are. And more about your story. Maybe then I'll tell...'

The email went on to suggest a little restaurant where they could meet on Friday morning. Excitement coursed through Tarin like an electric charge. She hit reply, agreeing to the time and date. She had no idea how she was going to get out of work, but she'd think of something.

As she was logging off, she remembered that she'd intended to get a new birth certificate. She accessed the government agency website and read what information was needed. Of course it was information she didn't have, at least not yet.

She heard Chance whimpering and hurriedly closed out everything, quickly erasing her tracks from Bobbie's computer while praying that she hadn't made a big mistake.

She went downstairs to check on her son. He was sitting up crying, his little cheeks bright red. His arms thrust into the air at her. He was her reason for everything she was doing. She crawled into bed beside him and snuggled with him. Several lullabies later, he finally fell back asleep while she lay wide-awake for hours, trying to figure out how to use her computer at work without getting caught again.

CHAPTER 29

"I THOUGHT YOU SHOULD know she's applying for another birth certificate. Or was trying. I stopped it of course."

"Dammit. Why now?"

"I don't know. You also need to know that she's living back in Ontario."

"What? Where?"

"I'm still checking on that. I happened to catch her as she was applying. My first thought was to shut her down quickly. I never really thought about her address. Sorry."

"Jesus. Get me that information. I want Tarin found. I want her brought to me before she causes more problems."

"Oh?" Cal felt sick to his stomach. This was what he'd wanted to avoid.

"I'll straighten her out. A little time with me and she'll start acting accordingly, doing as I ask. Find her, bring her back. I want this to end."

"Yes sir. I'll find her." Long after the call had ended, he sat immobile. What if Cal found her and then HE didn't want him around anymore? The streets were a great place to learn to look after oneself, but there was no way he was going back to that way of life. The man who had saved him and had told him he was the son he'd never had but always wanted. But the truth was that nothing ever replaced blood ties.

He clicked on his computer and opened his email. He flipped through the twenty or so that he normally got. All were from different websites where he'd registered to receive their information. He clicked to open a few more in an effort to distract himself more than anything else. His monitor started displaying a message that flashed across his screen—'your computer was locked.' It also said some crap about he'd been caught performing cybercrimes and if he didn't pay within a short period of time, the RCMP would be at his door to arrest him.

"Son-of-a-bitch." He wanted to chuck the damn laptop across the room but managed to stop himself. Someone had sent him a ransomware virus. Standing, he kicked his chair, which spun into the far corner, slamming against the bookshelf. His prized bronze statue of a bum lying on a bench, a reminder of what he wasn't going back to, tumbled off the shelf and landed with a loud thump on the floor. "Dammit. Dammit. Dammit."

He didn't bother to pick it up. For the most part, it would be okay, but it would be marred. Everything in his life was marred by *her*. The only bright light had been that things hadn't been going well with her for a while. Not that he'd shared any of that. But now he wasn't sure where she'd gone. She could show up on her daddy's doorstep tomorrow, but he wanted to make sure that didn't happen. That it never happened again. What if she went home and was ready to be Daddy's girl? Or worse, bring *him*—the one person who could destroy his future faster than she could.

Clenching his fists, he focused his attention on controlling the anger that had gotten him into more trouble than he cared to remember. He would not let it destroy his future. He reminded himself how important he was to Mr. J; without him, the man and his business would both be lost. The reason Mr. J was doing so well was because of him. Besides, he'd make sure he could acquire that other winery he wanted. There's no way he'd get rid of him. Tarin's return would change nothing. After a few minutes, he felt a little calmer. The first thing he needed to do was get his computer fixed, so grabbing it, he headed out the door to find a repairman.

CHAPTER 30

"GRAHAM, I CALLED—"

"Hello. Dammit. Shut off. Hello."

"Oh. Hi. I didn't expect you to be in so early."

Graham could hear the unease in Tarin's voice. "What's up?"

"I... umm... can't come in today. Sick. Sorry. I'll call you later. Bye."

"Wait." But Tarin had already hung up. *That was odd.* He looked at the time; it was barely five o'clock. She'd deliberately called that early to avoid him. But why? He was only in the office that early because he was desperately trying to get on top of what was going on at Caspian Winery; plus there were several of their other cases that he had been neglecting.

Logging onto his computer; it was way past time he did some serious digging on Tarin. It was time for him to listen to his gut. He'd done a basic background check but nothing too deep—partly due to his ever-present time constraints and partly due to misplaced guilt, as if he was betraying her trust. In truth, he felt like he was betraying himself.

He typed in her name; Tarin Roth, not a common name in his opinion. There wasn't much on her. He scanned through the first page of search engine links. At the bottom was the article in the *Vancouver Sun* he'd read before. He opened it and skimmed it again. The information was interesting and relevant, but something about it bothered him, though he couldn't put his finger on exactly what or why.

He flipped through several pages on the website. As he was reading another article, he noted something interesting and, on a hunch, he hacked into their system and did some snooping around. The information he discovered was eye-opening, but just as he was about to do more sleuthing, Guy flew through the door looking steamrolling mad. It was something he'd only seen twice before with Guy—when someone had been shooting at him and when Geoff had taken Bailey with the intent to kill her.

"What's up?"

"Another two trucks of wine en route to the East Coast have been hijacked."

"Shit!"

"Yeah. Same kind of scenario, late at night, two armed men."

"And that IP address you had me track down. It's in the middle of nowhere, Algonquin Park to be exact. I don't think they even have internet capabilities in that area. There's nothing for miles. So no way it came from there. Another was at the Toronto Public Library. Doesn't look like it came from there either, at least not the one on Yonge St."

"Someone knows their way around faking IP addresses and using proxies. This is nuts."

"Right, so where do we start? We need to get on top of it. Maybe Tarin can help with—"

"She called in sick."

"Oh. I can help you today, at least for a couple of hours."

"Gee thanks there, buckaroo. Sure you remember how to turn on your computer?"

"I'll show you, you young whippersnapper."

They both burst out laughing at their really bad impressions.

Guy sat and logged onto his laptop. Graham watched him for a few moments, enjoying the old camaraderie.

It was like when they had started the business five years before. They'd always made it fun.

He wondered where that had gone. There was very little joy in his day now. He used to laugh and joke all day, every day, and still get lots of work done. Now, it was all about trying to stem the overwhelming flow and keep his eye on the bottom line.

It hit him he couldn't remember the last time he'd taken a day off. "Uh. I will not be in tomorrow. I'm going to take the day off."

"About damn time."

Graham nodded before turning back to his emails. "Walters wants to meet with us to discuss what's going on with the stolen wine. Wants us to meet at a coffee shop on Queens Quay in about an hour. Okay?"

"Yeah. Let's hope he can tell us some more about the hijackings."

CHAPTER 31

THE BIRTH CERTIFICATE WAS a bust. Not only had the site kicked her out, but she didn't have her mom's name, never mind her maiden name. How was she supposed to get that?

Most people would already know that.

She bet even Bill knew who his parents were. Maybe it really was time for her to contact her father... to get some answers... to stand up to him. Her hands trembled as she ran them through her hair. Her fingers slid through the short strands so fast; it caught her off guard. As a child, she spent hours lying on her bed and playing with her long hair. It had been one of the few things she could do without having to ask for permission. It had become one of those go-to habits when she needed to think or de-stress.

The little body beside her snuggled into her side as his little hand came up to tickle her under her chin. She giggled. He pounced on her.

"Ooommph."

"Got you, Mommy."

"Help me. Help me." She poked her fingers into his sides. He exploded with laughter while he squirmed. A day of quiet had done him wonders. There was still a bit of pink to his cheeks, but the tooth that had been causing him so much grief appeared to have poked through and wasn't hurting as much.

They play-wrestled for a good twenty minutes until they were both pooped.

"Honey, I have an errand to run this morning. So, we'll go to the zoo later today. Okay?"

"Zoo, Mommy, zoo."

"Yeah, sweetie. Soon."

After she put him in Kim's care, she showered and dressed. The reality of her expectations made her hands shake so badly she could barely button her blouse. Once dressed, she opened her sock drawer and pulled out the sheet of paper she was sure would lead her to some answers. Could the police have gotten any fingerprints off it? Had she made a big mistake by not going to them?

For the hundredth time, she berated herself for not doing so. But the fear of what her father would have thought and the fact he may have disowned her had stopped her. In fact, the statistics for women reporting rape, abuse and other violent acts against them were estimated at less than ten to twenty percent. It sickened her to think that others had similar experiences. No woman should be treated that way.

The ever-present question was why? And did they know about her son?

At the restaurant, she sat at a table that gave her a good view of the entrance. She was over half an hour early, but she wanted to be there when the woman arrived. There was no way she would miss her.

The restaurant was about half full of people eating breakfast. She scanned each table and person to make sure the woman hadn't arrived there first. The only description she'd given was that she'd be wearing a silver necklace with a snowflake-shaped pendant.

Tarin also shared the woman's fear of disclosing what she looked like. Tarin had only told her that she'd have a pair of white-framed sunglasses perched on top of her head. Currently, they were tucked in her purse. She'd pull them out, ready to put them on, if she found the person she was to meet. She had so wanted to tell her more, but something held her back.

There were eight other women present. She studied each one.

One sat by herself reading a book as she ate. She was wearing a heavily beaded necklace.

Another was sitting with a man; she was doing all the talking and he was doing all the eating. The woman was sitting, so the only way Tarin could see if she wore a necklace would be to walk past their table. But she didn't feel right. It was doubtful she'd bring her husband or boyfriend along to talk about abuse.

Four women who appeared to be on a regular get-together were laughing and talking. None of them appeared as if they were hiding a dark secret, but that almost made Tarin laugh. People would say the same thing about her as well.

Two other females were sitting together. Every now and then they'd look in her direction, as if they were questioning what she was doing. Unsure what that meant, Tarin realized she'd been sitting there for fifteen minutes without so much as taking a sip of water, reading the menu or ordering. Doubtful she could get anything past her tight throat or keep it down; she opted for a cup of tea and a biscuit. It would give her something to pick at, and she'd look like she should be there.

Forty-five minutes later she had fully shredded her breakfast, so it looked like a snowfall of crumbs on her plate, but still she didn't see the woman who she was to meet. Glancing around carefully to see if any woman was wearing a snowflake necklace. She tilted her head. The woman could be doing the same thing as her. Pulling out her sunglasses, she perched them on top of her head.

A few ladies left, and a few more came in. No one really even gave her any notice, and yet, she felt like she was being watched. The waitress stopped by with that sympathetic look one gets when one is stood up and wanted to know if she could get her something else. Translation: eat and then get out. They were filling up; only two tables were vacant. Unfortunately, all the women appeared to be old enough to be her mother or grandmother. Not the woman she was searching for, and none looked her way.

After another ten minutes, she finally gave up. People had come and gone; not one was the same, yet she still felt like someone was waiting for her. Desperate now to get out of there, she paid and left. Wondering if the woman had emailed cancelling, she headed to the office, praying no one would be there. Graham usually was, but hopefully she could come up with something that would appease him. Or she'd cough a few times, so he'd really believe she wasn't feeling well.

Opening the office door slowly, she peered around it. There was nothing but silence. Surprised but happy, she looked toward the inner office, reminding herself he could still be behind those doors. The need to know what was going on loomed larger than worry about confronting her boss. She quickly sat at her computer and logged into her website. Nothing. There was nothing from the woman who had agreed to meet her.

So what happened?

Her cell phone rang. She jerked so hard that if some-one had seen her, they would have thought she was having a seizure. Her first instinct was to ignore it, but then she realized not many people had it. She checked the caller ID. It was Bailey. Frowning, she answered the call.

"Hello?"

"Hi Tarin, it's Bailey. Hey, I know you're new in town and all, and I know what it's like not to know a soul. And you seemed interested."

Confused, Tarin wasn't sure what to say or if they'd lost the connection. "Hello?"

"Hi. Sorry. I didn't mean to disappear on you. I realized I suck at this. Look, I have to go out to the winery on Monday to look over some things for my wedding. You seemed interested, and I wanted to know if you'd like to come with me?"

"Yes!"

"Meet me at 4:00. Do you need me to talk to Guy or Graham so you can get off early?"

"No, I've got it."

"Right. See you Monday." She gave her directions of where to meet and then hung up.

It took a moment for the stilted conversation to work its way through her brain. She was going to Caspian Winery again, but this time with family. Her heart sped up. Images, thoughts and feelings all flooded over her at once. It was all so fast and furious that she sat there, staring off into space. She couldn't even comprehend that she was going there and would very possibly meet the staff—especially the one whose pictures she'd stolen. She wondered if she saw the person responsible for her lost week, she'd recognize him.

The ding on her computer slammed her back to the present. She still had emails open, and she needed to get out of there. Not sure what to do, she finally decided to send off another email to the woman, suggesting they reschedule for next Saturday. She didn't want to wait another week, but if things went well, she'd be meeting with the first person to hear her story, or at least enough of it so the woman would open up about hers.

She sent emails to four more women, asking if they'd share more or be willing to get together. None had replied to her previous messages. She was close to feeling like a stalker. She was trying to respect each person's privacy and hoped they'd come forward on their own, but the need for some clarity in her life was almost overwhelming.

Tapping her fingernails on her desk, she contemplated hacking their accounts to see what she could find out about each of them. The thought of someone doing that to her, especially after what she'd been through, would not make her happy. In fact, she would shut right down, which was the last thing she wanted to have happen with these women. The conflict between figuring out what the hell was going on and respecting the women's privacy pummeled her stomach as if an ulcer was being drilled out with a jackhammer. She decided she would wait a while longer and pray that someone would come through with helpful information. She needed something—anything—that would finally help her solve that gigantic puzzle. Otherwise, she felt as though she would go through life like she had a target situated right between her shoulder blades.

Tears filled her eyes as she realized that yet again, she had to go home empty-handed. Choking back her emotions, she closed it out. As she was about to shut down her computer, she remembered the USB and the encrypted information. Once she had it open and was looking at the files, she found she couldn't go any further. *What if all it is, is confidential business records? Winemaking recipes?* Closing her eyes for a minute, she waited until she'd been to the winery with Bailey. She wanted to meet the man up close that she'd seen do unspeakable things and see if she could tap into her memories to determine if he had been responsible for her abduction.

Ready to get out of there, she was about to shut down when she realized she'd gotten another message. It was a reply to hers. She quickly opened it. The woman said she could meet the next day. There was no explanation for not showing up. Tarin pressed her hands to her face and tried to get her ragged breathing under control.

It's really going to happen.

She wasn't sure if she had heard something or if it was guilty paranoia, but her head jerked up and turned from side to side. It was time to leave. She put everything back in its place, locked up and left. Stepping out of the building, she'd only made it two steps when she smelled a familiar, strong, pungent odor. She was about to turn when she was grabbed. Something jabbed into her back while a foul-smelling arm wrapped around her neck.

"Hold it. You're not going anywhere. Graham said you called in sick. You're coming with me."

"Look, Bill. They must trust me, or they wouldn't have given me a key and the codes."

He stubbornly stabbed her in the ribs again. Fear slithered through her belly as she pondered his mental stability.

"Move."

"Where are we going?"

"Just go. Oh, and give me your cell phone. I need to make a call."

Not sure whether to laugh or cry, she let him push her around the side of the building, directing her to walk down the alley. That's when her nerves kicked in, stopping her forward motion.

"I don't think this is goo—"

"I won't ask again. Now."

She didn't sense that she was in imminent danger, but she also knew nothing about him. "Graham won't be happy if anything happens to me."

He kept her walking until they came to a door at the back end of the building. He fumbled with the lock before pushing her inside. She stumbled through the opening only to stop dead.

What the—

CHAPTER 32

CAL STEPPED OUT OF the building, his head bowed as he looked at his cell phone. It was only when a car's rude blaring caused him to glance up. Traffic was in its usual frenzy with irate drivers leaning on their horns in an effort to scatter others out of their way. Fascinated by the skirmish, he watched as drivers revved their engines with their foot to the floor before abruptly slamming on their brakes after gaining mere feet. It was like watching a game of chicken. He loved it.

He wiped the sweat off his brow. Thanks to the heat, he'd be spending another day indoors enjoying his air conditioning. After living on the streets since he was about eight, he'd come to hate the oppressive summer heat. He glanced once more down the street before turning in the opposite direction to head to his car. Something triggered his mind in that split second. He spun back around only to duck his head when he realized what he was seeing. Luck had never been part of his life; he'd had to work hard and dirty to get everything he had. So he was a little puzzled but over the top excited about what presented itself. He leaned against the building in an attempt to use the natural design of the pillars to hide behind.

It's her!

Three people were standing at the far end of the block and appeared to be in the midst of a heated discussion. One of them reminded him too much of his old life. What he didn't understand was what she was doing with a man like that. She'd never given him the time of day.

The two men glared at her with angry expressions. It made him smile because she was obviously in hot water, something he relished seeing. The best part was he now knew where she was and would soon know where she lived—not that he was going to share any of that, at least not anytime soon. He had to figure out what she was up to.

Maybe it was a touch of paranoia; he thought she'd glanced his way. Concerned if she spotted him it would give her the upper hand, he quickly ducked around the end of the building. A heartbeat later, he looked again only to discover that all three of them were gone.

****

"You have some explaining to do." Graham quirked an eyebrow at her.

"I do?" She dropped her gaze to the glass of wine in front of her. "Same thing as before. I needed a secure network. I was contacting a woman who is going through a bad time. End of story."

"And yet you called in sick because?"

"Because I wasn't feeling well."

"So you come into the office, and now Bill feels he has to call me every time you show up when I'm not here. Are you sure that's all?" Why he'd brought her to the little pub down the street from the office, he wasn't sure, but he did know it was time to clear up a few things. She'd been reluctant, and not only because he wanted some answers. She kept saying she had to get home; someone was waiting for her. Probably that Chance guy she'd been mumbling about the morning after she'd gotten drunk in his office.

She met his gaze. "Yes. I'm not selling company secrets. You can check my computer or put me through a polygraph test. I had some errands I had to do, and I said I was sick because it was easier than explaining. I thought I'd clear it up when I got in."

Graham observed the tightening of her facial muscles, especially under her left eye. If he hadn't been watching her closely, he'd have missed it.

"Please explain to me why a guy in bad need of a shower and laundry services is living in an apartment I'm sure the city doesn't know exists?"

"Are you threaten—"

She waved off his reply. "No. I'm trying to understand why you made that place for Bill. I thought—never mind, it doesn't matter. But it's nice. He's got a bed, a bathroom, toilet, shower—which he obviously needs someone to show him how to use."

"Huh." Graham nodded his head as he thought about her words.

"What's that supposed to mean?"

"Guy and I have been trying to get him to take a shower, but he won't. It never dawned on us that he doesn't know how to use it. Or maybe it's something else."

"Okay. So why have you set him up so well? He doesn't pay rent, does he? You guys are looking after him. Why?"

"Because he's a good guy. He deserves a break. And because we can."

Her face softened. She smiled in acknowledgement. "That's nice. So what's his story?"

"He's been on the street since he was young. As far as we can tell, he left an abusive home. At some point, he joined the army. We don't know how or why, but he ended up back on the street. He's seen a lot in the forty or so years he's been out there. He never talks about it. We're not even sure of his name."

"And you tried to get him help, and he refused it."

Surprised by her insight, he took a swig of his beer. Bill had been one of those people they'd noticed right away. He wasn't the only homeless person in the area, but he definitely was one of the honest ones, one that Graham and Guy too had felt drawn to. It had started simply enough when they had witnessed him eating food out of a dumpster. It made them realize how good they had it. And they had learned he was a war vet, which made it all that much more important to them to help him. They were still searching if he had any family.

"So why are you helping women who've been abused?"

It was as if the lights went out. Though her friendly expression never wavered, almost as though it had frozen in place, her eyes darkened and became distant and veiled. A telltale sign that his comment had hit home was her hand shaking ever so slightly as she picked up her glass—and the fact that though she'd been sipping her wine, this time she downed half of it. "Same as you. I wanted to help someone. The website seemed like an ideal way to do it; I could give them a safe place to vent, to talk, to learn, to find help. Kind of like what you did for Bill."

He doubted that. There were a lot of questions he wanted to ask her, but he didn't know where to start, and he was quite sure she wouldn't be all that forthcoming. Besides, if he hadn't accidentally seen a few of the nasty texts she'd received, he might have wondered more about her involvement. But knowing more kept him from asking deeper questions. They sat in silence for a while, but it wasn't the awkward silence that always seemed to hang between them. Graham drank his beer and casually glanced around at the few other patrons at the pub. He was glad it was a quiet Friday afternoon.

"Are you glad you moved out here? You must find it very different from Alberta?"

She tilted her head. "Actually, I used to live here. I'm used to the gross, wet summer heat and the cold winter snaps, but yeah, it is different from Alberta. They have longer, colder winters, usually. Later spring. But they have the Rockies. So—" She shrugged.

"Don't tell anyone, but I've never been there."

"You should go sometime. It's a very unique province, with prairies on one side and mountains on the other. There is a kind of desert in the southeast and forest, swamp in the north. The south doesn't get nearly as much snow as the north. Well, not usually anyway."

"Sounds like you enjoyed living there?"

"I did. All the large cities have a river running through them. Downtown Calgary is a bit crazy, but then what city's isn't? The river valley is gorgeous."

"Miss it?"

Her eyebrows drew together, and then she glanced at her phone. "I've got to get going. Jesus, I did it to him again." She dug in her purse and tossed down some money before jumping to her feet. "Sorry."

She ran out the door before he barely made it to his feet. He quickly pulled out some money only to realize she'd left enough for the full bill. He ran after her, but by the time he reached the office; she was pulling out of the parking lot. She either didn't see him waving or deliberately ignored him. He was tempted to follow her but knew that would be pointless. Friday afternoon traffic could sometimes be more crippling than the weekday rush hour. Sighing, he returned to the office. As he walked by her desk, he glanced at her computer but kept going. When he reached his door, he remained there. Did she or didn't she?

It was something that would piss him off to no end, but he was only trying to protect her. He suspected she had as much firsthand knowledge as the women she tried to help, and he needed to protect his company. He sat at her desk and logged onto her computer. This time she'd forgotten to clear her tracks, which made it so much easier to hack into her website.

The information he read and the stories the women told made him nauseous and sick, reminiscent of a morning after a heavy binge. He'd read about incidents of abuse but, thankfully, it had never been a part of his life. He'd never been exposed to it and certainly had never been this close to it. It was too unbelievable for words. He had to close his eyes at one point or he thought he'd throw up. About to log out, he noticed there was a message center.

Guilt started thumping at his chest, shouting that he was making a big mistake when he opened her emails. What he read, though, stopped his heart almost completely.

What was he supposed to do about it?

CHAPTER 33

MEET ME AT 10 a.m. at Bronte Provincial Park, near the hole.

Graham stared at the message. It hadn't been meant for him, but he was certain the result would affect him and affect his business. Ignoring the twinge that told him he'd be sorry, he shut down Tarin's website and logged off the computer. He grabbed his bike and headed home. Invited or not, he planned to be there first thing in the morning.

Of course, the next morning, things didn't go as planned. Since he'd forgotten to fill his tank the day before, he had to stop for gas, and then he got behind someone poking along below the speed limit. So when he finally reached the destination, he was a good ten minutes late for the rendezvous.

The park was huge, but thankfully the person had said near the swimming pool. Or at least that was how he had interpreted the reference to the hole. Once he parked, he didn't even need to follow signs; the clamor of kids yelling, screaming and splashing was easy to follow. The enormous sign read, 'Now Open'.

No wonder I had to park a mile away.

Since there was a fee to use the pool, he was pretty sure he wouldn't have to enter the inner confines of the pool area. He'd better check just to make certain. His eyes tracked over the heads playing in the water, difficult to do with all the splashing. Then he looked over the ones who were lounging on towels along the beach area. There was no sign of Tarin's blonde, sassy hairdo anywhere, but he could have easily missed her. Or that wasn't where she was going to meet her mysterious person. He started walking; standing around gawking wasn't getting him anywhere. A woman brushed past him, as if there weren't two feet of path on the other side of her. He shook his head as he continued on but then stopped to look at the person. She was wearing a summer hat. It hadn't occurred to him that Tarin might have something on her head. Feeling like he was hunting for an ant in a tropical forest, he continued around the edge of the pool area.

Twenty minutes later, he was confident that he had checked every one of the few hundred people in and around the pool, and yet there was still no sign of her. He expanded his search area but still came up empty. Seeing the main office, he headed over to it.

"Excuse me. Could you tell me where the hole is? I'm supposed to meet someone there, and I thought it was the swimming pool, but I can't find her."

The young woman, who had to be barely out of high school, smiled as if she was a witness to a surreptitious tryst. "Oh, that's funny. Your friend was here a little while ago. Blonde. 5'8?"

"Yeah. That's her." His heart rate quickened.

"There's a little-known fishing area on the creek that some people call a hole. There's trout, walleye, pike—"

He tried not to go cross-eyed listening to her, but he didn't interrupt. Finally, she gave him directions. There were several paths; thankfully, all were labelled. He ran toward the old Spruce Lane farm buildings and then followed the Half Moon Valley Trail. He hadn't planned on a three-kilometer run but jogged the first couple of k's, then sprinted the last half kilometer. By the time he reached post number four, he realized he was only about one hundred meters from the stream. He slowed down, taking deep breaths to calm his ragged breathing. The thick trees concealed him. He quietly made his way down to the water.

"Ugghhh."

It wasn't very loud, but it definitely sounded as though someone had fallen. Since he had no idea where Tarin was, he headed in the direction of the noise. Knowing he was probably foolish, he forgot his stealth and hurtled forward. At first, as he came over a slight knoll, he didn't see anything, but a quick area scan revealed someone lying beneath a tree. He raced over to her and knelt beside her. He glanced over his shoulder, but no one else was around. She moaned and rolled onto her side.

"Tarin, are you all right? It's Graham."

"What?"

"It's Graham. You hit your head."

She pushed away and sat up, swaying slightly. He rested his arm behind her back as he sat on the ground slightly behind her so she could lean against him. A slow trickle of blood made its way down her cheek from a welt high on her temple.

"What are you doing here?" She pressed her eyelids shut.

"I was going to ask you the same question."

"No. No-no-no-no-no. Dammit! You scared her away." She tried to struggle to her feet, but her legs were too wobbly to sustain her weight. He grabbed her even though she tried to pull away. "You've ruined it."

"What, my business?"

She pressed her hand against her head and winced.

"You might not want to touch that."

"Really. Why? Because it hurts like hell? I think I got that."

"Care to share what happened?"

"I need to sit. No, I need to find her." Determined, she pulled away and weaved her way up the gentle incline.

Swearing under his breath, he caught up to her and wrapped his arm around her waist.

"Leave me here. Find her. She's my link. She has answers."

"What I need to do is get you some medical help."

"No. Just go. I'm worried. She left so fast, I want to make sure she wasn't injured too."

He had to stop her every five seconds, not only so she could catch her breath in a vain attempt to stop the dizzy spells, but also so he could tell her he wasn't about to leave her to chase after some stranger. He had no idea what she even looked like, and he wasn't completely convinced that she hadn't been the one to cause Tarin's head injury.

After arguing with her for a good five minutes, he finally convinced her to let him take her to someone who could look at her injury. Since the person he was thinking of was only ten minutes away, she finally relented. It hadn't been easy to convince her because she was adamant there was no way she was leaving her car and there was no way he was letting her drive.

Finally arriving, he pulled into the driveway of her townhouse, beside a bright red car. After a brief look at Tarin, who was resting her head against the seat, he climbed out. The neighbor's dog gave an excited yap and looked at him eagerly through the fence.

"Sorry, buddy, no time today. I promise to bring a treat another day." Walking up to the door he wanted, he knocked.

The door opened almost immediately. "Hi. What brings you here?" A young blonde woman, dressed in a nurse's uniform, was holding a set of keys in one hand and her bag in the other.

"Hi. I can see you're on your way out. I know I shouldn't have just dropped in, but I have a friend who's been injured. Can I bring her in?"

"Of course you can, you colossal idiot. Where'd you leave her, in the car? It's sweltering."

He trailed behind as she barreled past him to yank open the passenger door. "Hi. I'm Jen. Are you okay to walk? Come on, let me help you into the house."

"I'm fine, really. Just a little bump." But she didn't protest Jen's assisting her into the house and disappearing with her into the bathroom off her bedroom.

Unsure how to help and figuring she'd give him hell, he called Guy.

"Jen, I'm outside on the phone. Call if you need me." When no answer came, he took that as silent consent and stepped outside. The only problem was how he could explain to Guy what had happened—and have it make any sense.

CHAPTER 34

"I'M REALLY SORRY TO barge in on you. I'm okay."

"Yeah, don't worry about it. He's a little overprotective. Always has been. Always will be," Jen said. Though her words were accompanied by an exaggerated eye roll, deep love and affection were evident in her voice.

Tarin smiled wanly and tried to hide the pang of jealousy that pressed in on her.

She wet a facecloth and dabbed at her cut. "You actually have quite a long gouge. Did someone throw something at you?"

"No, I fell. I didn't see anything, but I sure felt it."

"Where were you?"

"Down the road at Bronte Provincial Park."

"It's beautiful there. I bet it's packed too, it being the first day for the pool and so hot."

"Yeah, it was busy." Tarin frowned, but stopped when the movement made the side of her face feel like it was on fire. Is that why the woman had chosen the hole, because it would be swamped with people? They had barely gotten started. Tears filled her eyes. She hadn't learned anything.

"Oh, hey. Sorry if this hurts. I want to make sure it's clean."

When she was done, all Tarin wanted to do was leave, but she couldn't very well turn down the woman's hospitality after all her help. And that she was Graham's girlfriend meant Tarin couldn't afford to offend her, like she had pretty much everyone else she'd met.

"Can I get you something to drink?"

Tarin nodded. "Whatever you have that's cold would be great." She sipped the iced tea that was offered before placing it on a coaster on the glass coffee table. Exhausted, she sank into the soft, embracing folds of the sofa. The throbbing ache that had taken residence in her temple eased slightly as she laid her head back. Her eyes automatically closed. Her mind wandered, and she lost touch with everything as she drifted. It was so relaxing and comforting, like being cuddled by a large fluffy cloud. She allowed herself to flow... not to think... not to want... not to pretend. And she did... for a while. But then things changed. The meeting with the woman came to her as though watching a movie.

****

She was standing by the water, wishing she'd worn her runners and not her heels, even if they had been the low ones. Some habits were very hard for her to break. Years of having to be dressed up and polished weren't overcome in a day. That she owned a pair of running shoes was a testament to that. And one day she'd even put them on. While she'd been standing on the matted, grassy bank, she'd gotten a strong sense of someone watching her, though she didn't see anyone at all. The sensation persisted until she began to wonder if it could be wildlife, perhaps a bear or a fox or a deer. Maybe she was invading their home. She'd never been comfortable in nature. The downtown streets of any city were safer to her than out there. But she waited.

Finally, a tall, slender woman had walked down the gentle slope toward her. At least she assumed it was a woman. The hoodie concealed her hair and shadowed her face, but the build was slender, feminine.

"Thank you for coming. I really appreciate this. Can you tell me what you know?"

"Why are you so interested?"

"Because I think we had the same things happen to us. I was drugged, kept in a hotel, naked for a week. I have disturbing memories, but I'm not sure if they are real or imagined. I don't remember how I got there. And I was left with a code similar to yours," Tarin said.

"How do I know you're telling the truth?"

"Who could make this up? How do I know I can trust you, either?"

She nodded. *"My story is much the same, but I met a guy in a bar, an older guy. He bought me a drink. I didn't pay attention to what the man looked like, but he was old enough to be my grandfather. I thought... hell, I don't know what I thought. It was the stupidest thing I've ever done. When I awakened in a hotel room several days later, I discovered the room was in my name and paid for, but that's impossible. I didn't have that kind of money. And I'd never been there before. In fact, I'm not sure I could find it again. I wanted to run and hide."*

Tarin took a step forward, but the other woman stepped back. *"I wanted to offer you my sympathy."* She hadn't blamed the woman for stepping back. That was definitely not her strong suit, offering a shoulder to lean on. She had no idea how to do that.

"Anything else that you can remember? Or that happened afterward?"

The woman's piercing blue eyes studied her suspiciously. And that's when it happened. Both their heads swiveled to look across the creek at a snapping sound. The movement beside her had Tarin turn back in time to see the woman sprinting away. Tarin ran after her, but her heel got tangled in the grass. She thrust out her hands as she started to fall.

****

"Whoa!" She sat upright, her eyes wide open.

"What is it? Are you okay?"

Tarin looked wearily at Jen, who was standing across the room, her hand on Graham's arm, leaning in close as though in an intimate conversation with him.

"I'm fine. Sorry, I nodded off. I really need to be going."

"Actually, I have to get to work. Nice meeting you. See you later." Jen stood on tiptoes to kiss Graham's cheek before hurrying out the door.

Tarin blinked a few times, partly to wake herself up but also to convince herself she was safe now. She shuddered as she realized how close she had come to being seriously injured or even killed. She wasn't sure it had been an accident or if events had unfolded on purpose—and if they had, did the woman set her up?

CHAPTER 35

"WHERE ARE YOU GOING?"

"I need to get home."

Graham crossed his arms and rested on the edge of the stuffed chair beside the couch. "Not before we talk."

"Why? What's there to talk about? Unless of course you mean about your following me? You show up at the place where I just got hurt? Know anything about that?"

"Actually, I do."

"What?"

"I followed you."

"Why?"

"Because after you told me you were helping abused women, it got me thinking that men behind power games probably wouldn't enjoy having their stories aired."

"You were worried about me?" She looked surprised.

He shrugged, looking away for a moment before meeting her gaze. "Do you know what happened?"

"Not really. We'd started talking. Something spooked her, and she took off. When I went to follow her, I tripped and fell. I guess I hit my head." She clasped her hands tightly in her lap. "Do you think her husband or boyfriend could have followed her there?"

Without a word, he went to a table on the far side of the room. He picked up the item he'd found and returned to her.

She frowned. "What are you doing with an arrow?"

"Take a look at it."

She tentatively took it from his hands. He watched as she studied the length and the feathers. It was obviously something she'd never seen before. She turned it around, shrugged and looked back at him.

"Okay. So?"

He took it from her and turned it so the tip faced her. The color drained from her cheeks. Her fingers hesitantly touched the sore spot on her head.

"Is that what hit me?"

"I think so. It has blood on it. Some blonde hair that matches yours was sticking out of a tree near to where you were standing."

"Jesus. You'd think they'd have regulations against people using a bow and arrow to hunt in the park."

"Hunting of any kind is illegal in that provincial park." He could tell she was totally baffled and wasn't putting the pieces together. It almost bothered him to be the one to tell her what he thought had happened, but then he remembered she might be the one sabotaging his business. If she were, they wanted to know who she might be working for and why. Now, it appeared that someone was after her. He straightened up, staring down at her.

"I think you need to be more careful with these women you're trying to help. Could she have...?" He'd been sure that she'd been playing him, but her stunned expression couldn't be faked. She masked it, but not quickly enough.

"You must be mistaken." She went silent momentarily. "Which reminds me, you haven't told me how you came to be there?"

"I want to know who you were meeting."

"Don't worry, I'll be more careful." She attempted to jump to her feet, but quickly grabbed the couch arm to steady herself. He reached for her, but she jerked back, almost sending herself toppling backward. This time he gently grasped her upper arm to keep her upright. She swore but didn't pull away.

"This isn't a joke. Someone tried to hurt you."

"No kidding. I'm tired of the games. I swear I don't know why someone shot that thing at me but come on—people break the law all the time and hunt where and when they're not supposed to. Now tell me why you're following me."

His gaze locked on hers. The friendly air that had sprung up between them in recent days turned darker and deeper before her eyes. An awareness that he realized had always been waiting just below the surface came to light. Ignoring the voice telling him this wasn't a good idea, he pulled her forward and lowered his head.

He could see the hesitation in her eyes, but her eyelids languished as his mouth touched hers. It was soft, sensual and so damn hot. His arms clamped around her, drawing her in, pulling her closer. Her arms snaked around his neck, clutching at his back, pulling him close before she abruptly thrust him away. She flopped onto the couch and then scooted down it and stood up at the other end of it. Stunned, he stood there with his arms still in the air.

"You're like all frigging men. If you want it, take it."

"I didn't see you complaining."

Her face turned crimson. "Yes, because I'm an idiot."

"I'm sorry if I came on too strong, but I don't understand. If anyone should be pissed, it's me."

"Why? Because I bruised your ego by saying no?"

God, he wanted to throttle her. He'd never met anyone who'd exasperated him so much. He stormed toward the door. It flew open before he reached it.

"Hi. Sorry. I forgot a few things. Man, I'm going to be late." Jen stopped over the threshold, but he ignored her and kept going. "I don't think I've ever seen my brother so annoyed."

He climbed in the car and started it, turning the air conditioner on full blast in an attempt to dissipate the sweltering heat. Five minutes later, the two women finally came out. Tarin climbed in without saying a word. He backed up and headed back to the park.

"We're going back to your car. You're going to drive it to the city, to the office. We're going to talk about what's going on with you. Why did someone shoot an arrow at you?"

"Look, it wasn't aimed at me. It was an accident. I think you've been doing the PI thing for too long. I'll report it. Okay? I'm going home. I'm fine."

He was tempted to say something, but when he glanced at her, she was lost in thought. Did she know something she wasn't sharing? When he pulled behind her car, she sat there for a moment, staring out the front windshield. Since it was only a view of all the vehicles in the parking lot, he doubted she even saw them.

"I didn't know she was your sister." With that, she got out and climbed into her vehicle.

He followed her all the way into town. During the hour-long drive, three thoughts played incoherently in his mind.

Who wants to hurt her? Does that mean I'm not a two-timing pig? Or is she telling me it's okay to kiss her again?

As they reached the city, he slowed for some lights, seeing that Tarin was doing the same. At the last second, she bolted through the intersection. That was the last he saw of her. Heading for the office, all he could think was, '*This is why I stick to computers. They aren't this confusing.*'

CHAPTER 36

"WHAT HAPPENED? I WANT all the details, and I want to know she's been shut up."

"Uh—"

"You missed? God damn it. I thought you were a crack shot with an arrow."

"I've never shot at moving targets before. If you'd have let me use my gun, the outcome would have been different."

"Too easy to trace. An arrow is nice and quiet, not easily traceable and could easily be considered a stray, not a deliberate means to kill someone."

"I know I screwed up. I went back to Carol's place, and she's cleared out. I don't think she'll be a problem."

"Make sure she isn't. If she contacts Tarin again, stop her before she does any more damage. And Tarin?"

"She fell."

"Where is she?"

"Since I missed, I thought you'd want me to make sure that Carol wasn't a problem anymore. The whole point was to shut her up, wasn't it?"

"Jesus, you incompetent ass." He couldn't believe the kind of people he was forced to work with. Many of the men he'd used in the past had wanted to charge him an astronomical fee for such a clandestine operation. He was almost sorry he hadn't been willing to pay it.

"Find Tarin. I'll let you know when you can finish her off. Make sure there are no more screw-ups, or you might find yourself on the receiving end of a bullet." He flung the cell phone across the room and watched as it shattered against the wall. An old injury instantly sent a shooting pain down his arm, and he immediately grabbed his shoulder. His fingers curled reflexively. The skin from his third-degree burn pulled taught, hurting. A smile curled his lips. Soon, those responsible would pay.

He reached for his landline phone and called Stephen. "What have you found out?"

"I'm waiting for the PI to get back to me. He texted me he had good news, so I guess he's found her. I'll call you as soon as I hear from him."

"It had better be soon, Stephen. I want that boy. He's mine."

"Soon. Just be patient a little while longer."

That was not his strong suit. He so wanted to blast the son-of-a-bitch who couldn't even keep track of a woman and her child. But he had better plans for Stephen's demise. His daddy wouldn't be too thrilled to learn that his son was selling secrets to his competitor. He was finished; he just didn't know it yet. The strain of waiting to pull that plug was almost excruciating, but he wanted his son first, then he'd do away with Stephen.

****

Tarin's neck was so tight she felt like her shoulders were on the receiving end of an eagle's talons. An archer in the park frightened her, although she still couldn't believe they'd meant to hit her; the woman she was with, maybe. Since Graham wasn't sharing how he knew her location, it was enough to convince her it was time to get a new phone. He must have used the GPS on it, even though she'd disabled it. She couldn't figure out how else he would know. Avoiding him had been her only thought after they'd left his sisters. It wasn't until they reached the city that she took advantage of being the first in line at the lights and bolting through them. Graham hadn't followed. She'd have to face him, but getting some rest, making sure

Chance was okay and trying to figure things out on her own were higher priorities.Chance was fine and more than happy to play in his wading pool in the back yard. It had been a distraction for a while. Tarin was able to push away all that had gone on. At least, until Graham's text had come in. She should have ignored it.

Tarin, I need you to come in to work tomorrow. There's a lot going on. She still had a job commitment. And answers she needed to find. It also meant she had to come face to face with Graham. What was she going to tell him? After that, her day was ruined. Thoughts of her messy situation assaulted her from every angle, leaving her exhausted and grateful to go to bed at 7:30 with Chance.

3:00 a.m. and now she was wide awake. Her skull was throbbing. She gently brushed her fingers over her injury. It was another reminder that she had a lot to figure out... in a very short time.

Looking at her cell phone, she considered what she was going to do with it. It was more of a liability than an asset. Too many had her number, and all were using it except the one she wanted. There were miracles every day, and her dad might reach out to see her again. But with a sinking heart, that what she waited for was like believing a Canadian winter lasted only a week.

Flipping open her cell, she intended to ensure the GPS was off. She got a bit sidetracked, however, when she discovered Stephen had sent her a lot of texts.

'You can't avoid me. I'll find you.'
'You're mine. Remember that.'
'I know who his father is.'

That one sent chills down her spine. Did he really know, or was he bluffing? She wanted to finally know the truth. If for one moment she believed he knew something, she'd contact him, futile as that may be. The good news was she was sure there had to be another way to find out.

She skimmed through his other texts, in which he called her a multitude of inventive names and warned her that when he found her, she would pay. It left a bilious sensation in the pit of her stomach and a pulsing throb in her temple.

About to delete the crap he'd sent her, her gaze snagged a few words from the last message.

'Your mother might still be alive.'

Thankful she was sitting on the bed, she zipped back through his messages to see if he'd given her any more information. There was nothing else beyond that one tantalizing tidbit.

She felt catapulted back to the five-year-old child hiding in the closet because she'd be safe from the big bad night monsters. Her dad had taken away her nightlight and teddy bear because he said it was turning her into a sissy. The teddy bear had been her replacement for her mom hugging her. It had meant too much to her, so she'd snuck out and taken it out of the garbage bin where he'd thrown it. It had become her safety blanket, her mom blanket, the one thing that took away all the loneliness and kept her company. Her tears had soaked it many times. Tears that were shed by a scared little girl who was praying and trying to be the best little girl she could be in the hopes it would bring her mom back to her. Or *any* mom; she didn't care whose. She'd just wanted one.

The thought of her mother being alive was overwhelming. Tarin's breath became choppy, shallow, until she was nearly gasping. She took a few moments to focus on her rapidly beating heart and her erratic breathing. It was when she pressed her hand to her mouth that she realized tears were streaming down her face.

If she's alive, where in the hell has she been?

Tarin paced the room. Was Stephen lying? Was he trying to bait her? What did he really know?

Why she'd felt the need at four in the morning to look at his texts was beyond her and something she wished she could go back and change. If what he said was true, he knew a lot... if she was to believe him. She didn't want to know what she now knew. It meant that she could no longer pretend her life was normal. It had never been and

never would be. The blow sent her to her knees but only
briefly. If there was only one thing she'd learned from her
father, it had been how to get up and keep going. So that's
precisely what she was going to do. Knights Associates
was her best connection to Caspian Winery. She had to
find out whatever she could through them. The owner
of the winery employed them for employee background
checks, based on what she'd overheard Guy and Graham
discussing more than once. No longer was she going to
putz around at center field; she was going for the goal.

It was past the opportune time to find answers; now
every second counted. She winced when she considered
her bosses' reactions once they knew she'd been using
them. It was almost enough to stop her.

After combing her hair forward to hide her cut, she
woke Bobbie, saying she had to go in early because of
a crisis at work. Bobbie's expression let her know she'd
accept the explanation for now, but at some point, she
wanted some answers. Yet without question, Bobbie had
risen from bed and moved downstairs, agreeing to watch
Chance and keep him indoors all day.

Tarin headed out. She parked down the street, studying the path to the office for signs of movement. Not seeing
anyone, she quietly exited the car and, sticking close to
the buildings, she made her way to the office. Once there,
she walked past and peeked around the corner, hoping
Bill was nowhere in sight. When she didn't see him lurking
around the alley, she took that as a good sign.

Sitting at her desk, she logged onto her computer.
With shaky fingers, she opened the Knights Associates
website and the email account they gave her access to.
It took her a while to back-trace the emails he sent her
every day as he had several blocks up, but she was finally
able to discover what email address he was sending them
from. Taking a quick breath, she spent the next twenty
minutes figuring out how to hack into his account. Once
in, she quickly snooped through his emails. There was
a lot of information, but nothing that really looked like

it was going to give her any answers. There were a lot of messages and folders, but she didn't have time to go through them all. She scanned through twenty or so files and finally found something of interest, Caspian Winery.

She reached up to twine her hair around her finger only to feel a deep sense of disappointment that it wasn't there. She tugged hard on the short strands before taking a deep breath and opening the file. There were at least ten individual folders in there. A quick glance at the time let her know it was already past 5:00 a.m. She didn't have much time. She opened the newest folder, dated a few weeks before. There was a list of the winery staff, their company history, some personal information. It was really quite detailed, but it appeared to be recent information. She couldn't read it all in the short time she had, so she copied all of it to her USB. Once she finished, she found information on the companies that contracted with Caspian. Deciding this might be her only chance, she copied several more files.

Logging off, she used every trick she'd ever been taught to hide her tracks. She prayed it was enough. Feeling sick, she put her USB in her pocket and, careful to ensure that Bill wasn't around, she left the building. Once outside, she'd only made it a few steps when she realized that the shakiness in her legs wasn't going away. She leaned against the side of the building to catch her breath and steady her nerves. She waited several heartbeats to calm down, but she couldn't stay too long. Traffic was already starting to zip by on the street, and she had no idea when Bill would show up. She did not want to be found there at that hour. Feeling a tad stronger, she pushed away from the wall and straightened up.

"You're early."

CHAPTER 37

TARIN'S LEGS ALMOST BUCKLED as her head whipped around to the right and her hands pressed hard on her chest. "Bill," she squeaked out. She dropped back against the solid support behind her for fear she'd be a puddle at his feet.

"You're early."

She schooled her features before giving him her best smile. "I am. It was a glorious morning for a walk, so I thought I'd beat the traffic and go for one here. Any suggestions? After I got here, I realized I didn't know the area. So my plan wasn't a good one."

He fixed her with that unsettling, unwavering stare, and then, without another word, he left. She sagged into the building; certain he'd noted the heels, which weren't made for strolling.

"You're early."

She snapped upright so fast that she whacked her head against the brick siding. "Ow." Pain exploded through her skull.

"Hey, are you okay?"

Her hand cupped the area as though it could ease the ache. "Fine."

She opened her eyes only to have them stretch wide open. Graham in shorts was something new. Graham in a close-fitting shirt and skintight shorts was enough to get her heart rate pumping as though she had just gone on the bike ride for which he was dressed. Perhaps it was because he was standing so close and peering into her face or perhaps it was her own common sense rising, but she realized she was ogling him. She was tempted to wipe her chin of real or imaginary drool.

She snorted in an effort to choke back the laugh that was threatening. She pressed her fingers against her lips in an attempt to stop anything else from escaping. But it did nothing to discourage her eyes from trailing the long, lean line of Graham's chest down to the form-fitting shorts. She wished he'd turn around.

Oh wow.

She blew out a breath as she pushed herself away from the wall and stepped away from temptation. When she saw his gaze linger on her temple, she brushed her hair forward to ensure it hid her injury.

"I'm fine. I was going to get myself a latte; can I get you something?" She'd never been to the coffee place down the street but was sure it couldn't be that hard to find as Graham often walked there. She started strolling before he even answered.

"If you wait, I can come with you? Or pay you?"

She waved over her shoulder.

Finally, he yelled after her, "A mocha latte would be awesome."

She wiggled her fingers to let him know she'd heard. A few minutes later she returned with one mocha latte, having downed what she hadn't spilled of hers.

"Here." She set his cup on his desk before returning to her office. The door was now left open unless Guy and Graham were discussing sensitive information. She slumped at her desk, feeling out of breath and tired; even muscles ached that she hadn't even known she had. Running after a two-year-old should have kept her in better shape, but she didn't realize she'd have to walk halfway across the city to reach the coffee shop. She kicked off the heels that had become a second skin and realized for the first time how painful they really were.

Wiggling her toes, she logged onto her laptop. She had no idea how long she sat there listening to Graham tap away at his keyboard. A sense of doom hung over her like the rain cloud that followed Linus around in the *Peanuts* comic strip. When no explosion came, no swearing, suggesting he hadn't discovered her snooping, she figured she had a temporary reprieve.

A quick glance at the time and she realized she'd just wasted an hour. She first followed up on Graham's responses to work she'd completed the prior week before starting on a new list of emails.

It was the third one that stopped her. She'd read it three times but still couldn't comprehend its meaning.

02 CW 2013. It triggered a memory. Someone who had been there and who had a conscience, when she'd been drugged and lost that week of her life, had given her a code. It struck her that he had been trying to help her. It might not be exact, but it was familiar. Excitement coursed through her as she realized she might be onto something. Whatever had been said to her wasn't coming to her fully, but it was there; she could feel it.

"You look—uhm—did you find something?"

She quickly schooled her face into the professional expression she'd been well taught before looking at Graham. "Uh—no. Just thinking of something else." Her hand was busy moving the cursor to close out the email and open the next one, in the event he decided to step around and check it out. She was trying not to be obvious, but she noticed he glanced at her hand.

"You never told me why you were in so early?"

"I need to leave at 3:00 if that's okay? Something came up, but I didn't want to bother you with a phone call. So I showed up a few hours before I'm to start. I hope that's all right?"

"Yeah. It's not like we keep regular hours. I want the work done. Is everything okay? Are you okay? How's the head? Anything else happen?"

"Yes, things are good. Nothing serious. Thanks." She smiled, glancing briefly at him before refocusing on her screen.

"Did you hear from the woman you were to meet?"

"Yeah. She sent me an email; said she'd panicked that her ex had followed her." In reality, Tarin knew she'd never hear from her again, but she really needed Graham to drop it. The last thing she needed was for him to look closely into her life.

His reluctance to go was palpable, but she refused to look up. Once he was gone, she resisted the urge to flop across her keyboard in relief. Before getting back to work, she leaned forward, peering as far into his office as she could. The open door made her feel unsettled. When she didn't see or hear him, she assumed he was seated at his desk. She reopened the message containing the code. Scanning it quickly, she noted all the information, copied it, forwarded it to her personal email and then deleted any trace of what she'd done. Her hand shook as she opened the next one, hoping he wouldn't ask about it.

Working like crazy, she got through over seventy messages, researched and discarded just about all of them as fake. It was quite a jolt when she heard the soft sound of bells ringing. It took her a moment to remember she had set the alarm. Noting it was almost 3:00, she grabbed her bag and raced out of the office to meet Bailey. She'd been so tempted to cancel, but this trip to Caspian Winery was what she had been waiting for. Finally, she'd meet the people behind it and the one who might be connected to the nightmare in her life.

But even as she hurried away from the building, she wondered how she could use the code or anything she'd find at Caspian Winery. She had no proof of anything.

CHAPTER 38

"WE'VE GOT A PROBLEM," Guy said as he set down his coffee.

"Yeah, I know. Those two shipments, oops, I mean three stolen shipments, have been discovered in a farmer's field in Quebec. He swears they weren't there last night, but they were this morning when he checked his crops. He's lawyered up, says there's no way in hell he's being blamed for something he didn't do."

Guy sat across from Graham at their usual table in the back corner of their favorite coffee shop. It was a good place to meet at 4:00 p.m. on almost any weekday as it was usually fairly quiet in the dining area, so they could talk without worry of being overheard. Once in a while they went there just to get out of the office.

"And the trucks are full? Empty?"

"That's the bizarre part. Full. Nothing looks as if it's been touched. So the email we got doesn't make sense for the 70% off."

"But they can't take that chance as someone could have spiked the bottles somehow, right?"

"Yeah, but the packaging looks intact. It's going to be tied up as evidence for a long time, anyway. What the hell is going on?"

"No, the big question is who the hell is doing this? Do the cops have any ideas?"

"None they're sharing. Walters says he doesn't have anything new to tell us."

"I'm going to contact our bootlegging swindler, Mr. Amdory. Maybe he'll work out as an informant. The police are having a hard time finding any solid evidence that links directly to him. I figure we use him. Did you get anywhere with that email about the wine?"

"No." Graham's gut clenched as he considered that he hadn't been able to trace the source. Someone was very good. "And Dorothea?"

"You know how she likes to slam her cane on her desk when she's irked? I think she might have actually broken the thing this time."

Graham choked back a laugh. "I'm sorry, it's not funny, but it is."

"I know, Bailey and I had a chuckle about it, too. She has a temper. In this case, I don't blame her. We really have to figure this out. And now."

"I agree, but we also have another problem."

"Oh?" Guy took a bite of his cinnamon bun.

"Yeah, our new employee has been hacking into our emails."

"What?" Crumbs spewed out of his mouth.

"Gee, thanks for that shower, buddy."

"Sorry."

"Bill has caught her a couple of times here—"

Guy raised his eyebrow.

"Yeah, I know I should have told you, but you've got lots going on—"

"I know my life is interfering with work right now, but you need to keep me in the loop."

"Okay. Anyway, Bill has caught her a few times leaving the office when we're not there. I'll give her credit—she's good—but I have my safety net, so I'm alerted when someone has been into our account. And I know it's not you—getting up before dawn is the last thing you'd do unless Bailey was the reason."

"Shit. So now what? Fire her?"

"Believe me, that was my first thought, but there are too many coincidences. That incident at the park is still a mystery. An arrow almost hits her, and she says it was an accident. She acts as if it's nothing. Would you?"

"I'd be pissed and want to know who shot the damn thing and why that woman ran."

"Me too. She said that the woman she met sent her a message showing she was scared her ex might have followed her. I checked her email, and she never got one. So why tell a lie? Why not ask us, since we investigate for a living, to help her find out who did it? Why not go to the police? Although again, she said she'd report it."

"This is too crazy. You think she's behind all the emails we've been getting?"

"They started before she came, but what better way to ensure you get a job?" Graham thought back to the day he'd interviewed her and realized he'd played right into her hands. He'd left her to talk to his next candidate. "Oh, man."

"What?"

He explained to Guy what had happened when he'd hired her, how he'd left her to catch his second intervie-wee while he ran to get a coffee. She said the woman had never arrived, but she might have scared her off.

"Sorry man. I know I haven't been much help lately. Damn, this is crazy. Why would she do this, though? Just for a job? There has to be more to it."

"Yeah, that's why I suggest we don't get rid of her yet. We need to know what she's doing and why. There has to be a reason. And it better be a damned good one."

"Hey, Bailey's taking her to the winery today. I could ask her to find out what she can about her. We really don't know much, do we?"

"No. Although I have discovered the article I read in the *Vancouver Sun* was planted by her. It was never in any of the newspapers. I found another one in the *Edmonton Journal*. She has set a trail for us to follow, and she's kept us swamped so we have no time to check her out."

"And we fell right into it. Man, this sucks. Okay, let's figure out what we're doing. I'll call Bailey and apprise her of the situation—at least part of it. I'll have Bailey take her to Grandma's instead."

"I'm pulling in that favor from Detmier to check out Bronte Park; see if he can track down where the arrow was bought. I've also discovered a website she's operating. I'll go in and see what I can find out about her past. I checked back ten years on the internet and there was nothing out of the ordinary, but maybe she's shared information on her site that will give us some answers." Graham had only skimmed a few posts, but now he'd dig deeper. He made his way back to the office but walked past the entrance, rounding the side of the building and heading down the alley to the back door. He rang the doorbell four times with a certain break so Bill would know it was him. The security camera he'd installed would have shown Bill who was there, but Bill didn't trust it, said it could be manipulated. Graham was beginning to realize how easy it was to be played. Two minutes later, the door finally opened.

"Hi Bill. I brought you some cinnamon buns."

"From Caspers?"

"Would I get them from anywhere else?"

Bill snatched the bag and started to close the door.

Graham got the hint. "Good night." He turned and headed back the way he'd come.

"She was here this morning," Bill said.

He retraced his steps. "Tarin?"

"Yup, standing outside the door."

"Did she go in?"

Bill shrugged and closed the door.

Unsure what to make of that, he made his way to the office to get his bike. It confirmed what he'd discovered when he'd opened his account that morning; Tarin had been in the office early. Had she been leaving when Bill saw her? Or when he had? What was she doing going through the company's emails? He sent most of them to her, anyway. He hoped he was wrong about her, but it wasn't looking that way. And someone was after her—the arrow proved it. But who—and why?

CHAPTER 39

"Wow, THIS PLACE IS amazing." Tarin forced a smile. It really was awe-inspiring, but she was trying to tamp down disappointment that they hadn't gone to the winery first as planned.

"Yeah, it kind of knocked me for a loop the first time I saw it. I imagine it's like entering the White House."

Tarin looked around the immaculate mansion. The marble steps they were walking up were as impressive as the massive fountain sitting in the middle of the driveway behind them. She wanted to click her heels just to make sure she hadn't been transported from Kansas and to see if it really worked. This wasn't new to her and, in fact, was what she had left behind. That sad, lonely kid she thought had been long forgotten suddenly appeared, filling her with angst and making her feel like the outsider.

"Are you okay?" Bailey's quick smile soon turned to a frown.

She forced away the feeling of not really belonging and pulled out all the stops to put on her best friendly face, as her dad had called it.

It is always important to be able to pull that out of your bag of tricks, Tar.

The memory of his words jolted her a bit, causing her to stumble on the last step. Laughing self-consciously, she said, "I'm fine. A bit clumsy. Are you sure it will be okay with your grandmother if we come to her house? I wanted to see the vineyard."

"Oh, well, we might stop there later. Sorry, my plans have changed. I should have told you. Things are so crazy." Bailey rang the impressive doorbell before opening the door and walking in.

A small woman, who appeared to be in her sixties or older, scurried from the back of the house as they entered the massive foyer.

"She's waiting for you on the balcony. I'll bring refreshments right up."

Bailey gave her a big hug. "Penelope, this is Tarin. She's the new assistant for Guy and Graham."

The woman stared at her for a long moment before nodding and grinning. "You'll do. Nice to meet you." And then she was gone.

"Umm, hi."

Bailey laughed. "Don't worry about her. She's like the wind. She whips through, makes sure everything is the way she wants it, and then she's gone. I hope I have her energy at her age. She exhausts me just watching her."

Tarin thought of the household staff under whom she'd grown up, but she couldn't recall any ever smiling or touching her, never mind giving her a hug. "You obviously care for one another a lot."

"Yes, we do. Come on." She led her to the elevator tucked in the corner.

Tarin eyed the stairs with longing. They were long and winding and reminded her of the bannisters she'd always wanted to slide down but never had the nerve to do so.

"Do you want to walk up?"

Startled, she turned to Bailey. "Actually, I was thinking how much fun they'd be to slide down."

Bailey chuckled. "That's what I said when I first saw them. Maybe this time we can try it. I'm game if you are? And of course, if we have time."

They got off the elevator on the fifth floor. Tarin followed Bailey through a room and onto a large marble balcony. She gasped as she wandered to the edge and peered at the view. Vineyards for miles, a few houses, a stream winding through the countryside, the gentle hills. Tears threatened to flood her eyes as she considered how much fun a kid could have exploring. The gated fence between the outside world and this one, however, reminded her again that she had come from this world and no longer wanted to be caged within it.

"You look very determined."

Tarin spun around to face an elderly woman sitting beneath an umbrella that shielded her from the hot sun.

"Just in awe. It's a exquisite place you have here."

"Tarin, this is my grandmother, Dorothea Lindell."

"Very nice to meet you, ma'am."

"Dorothea, please. That makes me sound old, like I'm from the eighteen hundreds."

Tarin's face went instantly hot, which she'd have thought would be impossible to notice in the raging heat. She hoped that any red tinge would be hidden by the sweat beading there.

"My apologies, Dorothea."

"Please come and sit. Join me. Refreshments will soon be up. I hope you're up for a glass of red wine, Cabernet Franc, which I don't think gets the recognition it deserves. It's one of our best."

"I really don't drink—"

"It's late enough in the day, you're fine. Besides, if you need a driver to take you home, I'll send Stan."

Tarin sat across a table from the elderly lady while Bailey gave her a quick hug and a kiss before she took the chair beside her. For a moment, Tarin almost felt they'd ganged up on her, them on one side, her on the other. She wasn't sure what it was about the place, but it was making her very maudlin, like she was carrying her emotions close to her chest, and with each breath, she was exposing a little bit of who she was. Closing her eyes for a brief second, she used an old trick she'd learned at a young age that helped her focus and dispel her emotions. She'd gotten it down to an art. She visualized flipping off one shirt—her emotions, and pulling on another—her shield.

Dorothea clasped Bailey's hand and held it. The love the two exchanged with their eyes almost undid Tarin's recently suppressed feelings.

"So tell me about yourself?" Dorothea's piercing blue eyes caught her off guard.

"I'm originally from Ontario. I moved to Calgary a few years ago. I've been working in the computer industry—"

"Okay. So, you lived, and you moved. Who are you?"

"I—well, I don't know what you mean."

"I mean, you've had a strict upbringing. You're used to money. I'm betting that you either didn't have a mom in your life or she came right out of the eighteen hundreds I mentioned earlier."

Her eyes widened. "I don't—" The knowledge in Dorothea's expression let her know she'd have to play this one carefully. The woman was as quick as a whip and noticed way too much. "How?"

Her smile was warm and open. "Your carriage, really. Your manners. Your language. How you address me. All are signs that you have been well trained. And—"

Tarin tried not to squirm under her raw assessment as she wondered what else the older woman could see. She was starting to feel as if she were being stripped naked.

"All right, enough of that. So I hope we won't bore you if we talk about the wedding?"

Tarin shook her head now, thankful for the reprieve. When the wine arrived, she had never been so glad to have something to do with her hands, and she was grateful for some liquid courage. Although she hoped her demeanor would have them thinking she was paying close attention, her mind wandered. She'd hoped to go to the winery. Although what good it would do her, but if she could meet the staff, maybe she'd know. Slim as it was, it was all she had to go on.

The women's animated talk broke through her reverie. There was so much love and affection between them. She wondered why she'd never been allowed to know her grandparents. She'd never even heard them mentioned.

There was one time she thought she might have had a male cousin, but she didn't know if that was true or just another one of her fantasies.

Feeling like an intruder, she needed to find a moment to herself. "Excuse me. Sorry for interrupting, but is there a bathroom I can use?" After declining Bailey's offer to accompany her, she entered the house, walked through the room and down the hallway. *Did she say the fourth or fifth door down?*

Since all the doors were closed, she knocked on one and opened it to reveal a massive bedroom. It was warm and inviting. Delicate lace doilies covered the mirrored oak dresser, the delicate antique table in the corner and the bedside stands. Warm hues of pinks, yellows and oranges invited her in. She was in the middle of the room before she realized she had entered. Turning slowly, she took in the beautiful decor. As she did a full three-sixty and was facing the door, she noticed some pictures on the wall.

Some were very similar to those at the office. The one that really grabbed her attention was an aged black-and-white photo of a well-dressed older man. He looked not only wealthy but regal, gallant even. But it was his eyes that caught her attention. They were like obsidian glass. No warmth. No depth. No emotion. She knew that look well, because her father had perfected it. After what she'd witnessed between Bailey and her grandmother, it made her sad to think they had someone as cold and unfeeling in their family as she had in hers.

A sound from the open window drew her to it. She glanced over the most incredible garden she'd ever seen. Victoria's Butchart Gardens would have been envious. When one of the several groundskeepers looked toward her, she quickly stepped back, grimacing at the thought of being caught. The last thing she wanted to do was hurt this wonderful lady, or be perceived as a snoop. She hurried out of the room, closed the door and moved down the hall to the next door.

Fifteen minutes later when she returned to the balcony, neither Bailey nor Dorothea was there. She was reentering the hallway when Penelope showed up.

"Come with me."

Not having a choice, she followed the quickly disappearing woman down the hallway and stairs. She couldn't help but trail her hand along the long-curved banister. It took all of her willpower to keep from jumping onto it and going for the ride of her life. Deep down she knew she wouldn't; she was always dreaming, never doing.

"Wait here."

Penelope left her in an office. There was a massive cherry desk to one side, a leather sofa and two chairs. A huge plant in the corner appeared forlorn and forgotten as the heavy drapes were closed against the sunlight.

Unsure what to do, she perched on the edge of the couch. After about ten minutes, she got up and walked over to peer out the window at an immense green lawn. Sprinklers sprayed in earnest, the mist blocking her view of the distant landscape. Turning away, she wandered to the opposite edge of the room. There was beautifully framed art on every wall. She followed them, going from one to another. It was when she was behind the desk that she happened to glance at it. Her eyes immediately gravitated toward the paperwork. A quick glance at the door confirmed it was still firmly shut, so she stepped closer so she could read the information lying there. On top was a memo addressed to employees. She gently pushed that aside to see what was underneath. Disappointment slammed into her when she realized there was nothing of value—nothing that would give her any clues.

Another dead end. What compelled her to do it, she wasn't sure, but she was opening drawers. There wasn't anything too exciting. In fact, they were fairly empty, holding only pens, paper and a few plaque awards. But when she tried to open the bottom right-hand drawer, it wouldn't give. She yanked harder. She quickly went back through the other drawers searching for a release. She'd been good at discovering her dad's secret compartments and the hidden buttons that opened them. There were none that she could find, and there were no keys.

Leaning on the desk, she decided to do a last sweep around it. Just as she was getting started, she heard the faintest of sounds. She slid the chair back into place tight against the desk and hurried to sit on the couch. Her eyes widened when she realized she hadn't put the sheets back quite the way she'd found them.

"Sorry to keep you. I had a few things to take care of. I've sent Bailey off to do some errands for me. She'll be back in a bit. Can I get you anything else?" Dorothea sat in one of the leather chairs facing her.

"No, thank you."

"Your eyes are very arresting. And your smile. Or maybe it's the way you hold your chin—hmmm."

Tarin didn't move but felt very much like a bug under a microscope as Dorothea stared at her. "There's something about you that looks familiar. What did you say your last name was?"

"Roth."

"No. Never heard of it."

"You have a beautiful home here."

"Thank you, my dear. I recognize that chin tilt, the posture. I know four places that teach that. Mrs. Daniel's Young Woman's Etiquette, St. Anne's Girls Boarding School, Proper Young Miss and... hmmm, no, not the fourth one. You're not old enough; it's only been running about ten years."

"I'm sorry, I'm not familiar—" The steady gaze was too honest, too knowing.

"It's okay, dear. I know I'm a little pushy, but I haven't gotten to this age without having to fight a battle or two. I find being direct is the best way to be. I think the new term is 'the elephant in the room.'" She shook her head. "I don't understand some of the slang these days. You can't even fit an animal of that size in a room, and I know what they mean, but—oh, forget it. It's nonsense."

"Look, Mrs.—I mean, Dorothea. I'm not sure what you want to know?"

"It's okay, dear. I think I know all I need to." She stood up. "Walk with me, if it doesn't bother your head too much." She put out her arm and hooked it through Tarin's, leaning ever so slightly, although Tarin was sure it was her way of saying she approved. Or at least she hoped that's what it meant.

Tarin's fingers automatically touched her injury. "I'm fine. Just a bump." She'd been hoping she wouldn't notice or at least she wouldn't feel comfortable enough to ask. It seemed no topic was off-limits to this lady.

"You will come to the wedding, won't you, dear? There's someone I'd like you to meet."

"I don't know if Bailey and Guy—"

"Don't worry about them. I'm inviting you. I know they'll give their wholehearted approval."

"I—"

"I'll get you an invitation and put your name on the list." She patted her arm.

As they left the house, Bailey was coming up the steps toward them. When she caught sight of them, she hesitated. If Tarin had to guess the emotions that crossed her face, there was a moment of guilt written there.

Had she been set up? But for what?

CHAPTER 40

'TARIN, WE NEED TO meet with you as soon as you get in.'
The text sat like a pot of espresso on an empty stomach, the acid churning and burning her insides. As she walked into the building, she felt like hanging her head. She was the young child who had to follow her father into his office knowing she was in trouble again, praying for once it would be different; praying she wouldn't feel like a world-class failure again. The sick feeling clung to her insides like bubblegum to a shoe sole. Whether she was overreacting and her guilty conscience was making her believe the worst, she didn't know.

Really, what could they do? That thought didn't do anything to make her feel better. She entered as quietly as she could, wanting a moment to herself. Graham appeared the moment the door clicked shut.

"Good morning."

Unable to meet his gaze, she half-smiled before she squared her shoulders and walked toward his office. Nothing was said as he gestured her in. Not really paying attention, she entered and then looked up and suddenly stopped. Graham slammed into her back, and she stumbled forward. His hands grabbed her firmly to keep them both from falling. It was such a good feeling to be held against a strong, solid chest that it took her a moment to remember she didn't belong there. And he was her boss, one who was pissed at her. For what, she couldn't even guess. Reluctantly, she pulled away but imagined his fingers tightening, not wanting to release her.

"Hi." She said absently to the room, but her gaze was pulled to Bailey sitting to her left, appearing slightly guilty. Something was up; it hadn't been her imagination, because why else would Bailey and Guy be sitting there waiting for her? Both looked as uncomfortable as she felt.

Do they know I stole information from Caspian?

"Hi, Tarin."

"So, is this an interrogation or a firing?"

"Neither. Please sit."

Feeling sick, she perched on the edge of the hard chair just inside the door rather than the one beside Graham's desk that he'd indicated. She might be required to be present, but she didn't have to be up close and personal. The training she'd been trying to shed was now her shield. The scared little girl could be hidden away in the deepest recesses. She could be the ultimate professional, not taking anything personally, not allowing emotions to get in the way. This was purely a business transaction and not the first time she'd been in the hot seat. She'd been told off by the best and the wealthiest of them. The ones who hadn't liked a smart, savvy businesswoman who knew how to put together a business deal. Sadly, her father had probably been the worst. It hadn't mattered that she'd managed to snag multi-million-dollar deals; no, it had been why hadn't she been able to snag more?

She sat up straight, placing her hands in her lap and pasted on an attentive expression while vowing not to be run over. She stared back at Graham who was looking a bit uneasy.

"Look, there are some things happening that we don't understand."

She turned to Guy, who was sitting behind his desk but was leaning forward. He didn't seem very comfortable either. This could take all day.

"So what exactly are you accusing me of?"

"You don't pi—uh, waste time, do you?"

"No."

"How did you come to work here?"

"I saw your ad online, so I applied."

"Why here? Why not out west where you were living?"

Graham's hard look almost pierced through her armor. If she was going to get through this, she couldn't look at him. "I wanted to move back east. The job I wanted just happened to be one I applied for."

"What did you say you did before you came to us?"

"I ran my own business. I did contract computer work."

"Do you mind giving us their names?"

"You're asking for more references? Now? A little late, isn't it?" That had to mean they thought she was doing a lousy job. She dropped her gaze to her fingers clasped in her lap.

"You didn't tell us you were married, either?"

Her head snapped up, and she looked at Graham. "Anything else of interest you learned about me?"

A light flush crept up his face, but he didn't break eye contact. "Are you behind who's sabotaging our business?"

Of all the things he could have asked her, that one hadn't even entered her mind. Her eyes widened as she realized what he was accusing her of. Her nose flared, which meant the waterworks weren't far behind.

"Oh, I get it. Since I showed up a few months after things went crazy, I have to be responsible for it happening."

"You have some secrets."

Clenching her hands into fists, she replied, "No. What I have is a life. One I didn't know I had to share with my bosses. I haven't done anything to hurt this place. And I wouldn't. Did it ever occur to you that you've probably made an enemy or two with the number of guys you've helped to put behind bars? Why are you accusing me?"

"We don't mean it like that, Tarin. But we are a bit confused, and we need some answers. Look, we don't know much about you, and we need to know it isn't you. We've checked with our major clients, and none of them have been hacked. Yes, there are people who spam others for the sake of it. We've put up the necessary blocks, and we're still getting bogus requests. Yes, you're right; we probably have a few enemies out there. Let's just say someone is screwing with us, and it feels like it's closer to home," Guy said.

"So I had to be a good bet." She stood. "Maybe there's someone else you haven't checked out—someone else you've done work for that might have been hacked. No, it was easier to assume it's me, right? Too many things add up. I'll clean out my desk." She walked out but stopped long enough to stare at her desk, where she had no personal items. Not one.

"Why didn't you tell me you had a husband?" Graham was standing right behind her.

Funny, the one thing he was hung up on had nothing to do with her supposedly destroying Knights Associates. And he had to have dug for that information. She'd hidden it well. It made her wonder what else he knew about her.

"Because I didn't think it was your business."

"Oh? Yet you got all in my face, thinking I was two-timing you with my supposed girlfriend."

She took a couple of steps before facing him. "Funny, the things we believe, isn't it? Evidence just seems to add up, and it's easy to come to a wrong conclusion. I didn't tell you about my marriage because as far as I'm concerned, it's over. And it was none of your business. One kiss doesn't give you the right to my entire life. Thank you for the job." She smiled and walked out, ignoring his pleas for her to wait. Once in her car, she put herself on autopilot and drove home.

She was almost there when she realized the car was pulling to one side. Driving into the nearest service station, she filled the rear right tire. She wondered if it had a slow leak; if so, if she didn't fix it soon, she was going to find herself stranded. Not something she really gave a damn about right then. As she was leaving, she noticed a man in a silver rental car pull in to fill his tank. As she climbed into the driver's seat, she was vaguely aware of his head swiveling toward her. Maybe it was her imagination, but he looked a bit stunned; but in her current agitated state, she didn't bother to get a good look at him. Sighing, she pulled out and shot down the street. Arriving home, she parked and made her way slowly to the house.

"Uhm, you okay?"

She had hoped to sneak into her basement apartment and take a few minutes for herself. She'd been able to avoid Bobbie for a few days now, but her friend had obviously seen her arrive.

"Fine. I came to get Chance."

"Something's up. What is it?"

"I don't know."

"What's that mark on your forehead?"

She explained at an edited version of what had happened—she'd stumbled and hit her head on a tree and now had a raging headache. She didn't bother mentioning it had been a few days before.'

"Leave Chance with us. Pamper yourself; take a hot bath and relax."

"No, I'm going to spend time with him." She grabbed Chance and headed to the park. It was already 7:00 p.m. and she had one hell of a headache, but she couldn't disappoint him again. Hopefully, an hour at the playground would make up for her absence.

"I'm gonna get you." She growled and crouched as though stalking him. He squealed, flapping his arms as he ran away from her. She couldn't help but smile, the emotion spreading from her lips to her entire being.

She tentatively touched the sore spot on her head, trying to massage the dull throb away. Her day may have been crappy, but this was what she needed. Chance giggled. He was the best medicine. She forgot about everything else and let the laughter of her son soothe her wounded body and soul.

CHAPTER 41

"THAT WENT WELL." GRAHAM sank down at his desk.

"Is there any chance you guys are wrong? Couldn't she have just needed a job?"

"Too many coincidences, Bailey."

"Maybe. But let me tell you something, Graham, I can read people. When I was a kid, I had to learn fast who I could trust and who I couldn't. I learned quickly how people dress, how they appear, has nothing to do with who they are." She walked over and sat in the chair beside him. "I think Tarin is good. Grandma likes her. Says she's had a strict upbringing and not to worry about her. That was all she would tell me."

"Jesus. Caspian Winery!"

Graham and Bailey turned to look at an excited Guy. "We checked out our list of contract companies but we never checked out the winery—at least not in connection to us. We've done a lot of business for them—never mind the family connection and the upheavals they've been going through."

The look that passed between them told him Guy shared the same thoughts 'about Geoff'. They'd both pondered him in the beginning but they couldn't believe he might still be alive. Knowing it was a sensitive subject with Bailey, he didn't pursue it. Behind the tailored suits had hidden a frightening and devious man. Graham would trust the homeless guy, Bill, with his bank account before he'd ever trust Geoff with a dollar.

On a whim, he opened the Caspian website and tried to hack into it. Twenty minutes later he was in. "Shit. I think we may have discovered a problem, one that may have something to do with us." It had been way too easy to infiltrate.

"Okay, so our perpetrator has to have some skill, but it doesn't require rocket science to get in here. I thought we'd fixed their site, their information."

Are our problems tied to Caspian Winery? Instinct shouted that yes, they were. The issues Dorothea had appeared to be tied with their own. He wasn't sure why, though he had a strong feeling about who might be behind it. Glancing at Guy, it was obvious he was having the same thoughts.

The office phone rang, and Bailey answered it. A few minutes later she hung up. "Okay, two things. Grandma says for you guys to stop looking for Charles Cooper's granddaughter. She already found her."

Graham looked at Guy as he shrugged. It reminded them both that she was clever and when she wanted something done; it meant now.

"Oh, and Oliver is threatening to quit. He says someone hacked his computer and planted something on there but won't say what. Whatever it is he is upset by it and is blaming Tom. Tom swears he had nothing to do with it and doesn't know what Oliver is talking about. Anyway, the short version is you need to find out what has him so upset. Grandma doesn't want him to know you've been on his computer, though."

"Of course, she doesn't, which means a late-night job. And who's going to tell security and that German Shepherd that roams the inside of the building at night?"

"I'll make sure all that is taken care of, chicken." Guy ducked when a paperclip sailed past his head.

"He claims his computer was hacked, but is that the truth, or could there be something on there he doesn't want anyone to believe is his? He couldn't be our guilty guy, could he? Something is so dirty, I can smell it." Graham started tapping away on his laptop.

"There's one more thing, but I'm sure it's nothing." Bailey grabbed Guy's hand and held it in hers. "She said something about maybe it's time to sell the winery."

"What?" Guy sounded stunned.

"I don't think she meant it. Has she said anything to you?"

Graham was glad that neither Guy nor Bailey looked his way. He wondered if selling the winery had been behind her request to be driven to a hotel for a meeting.

"We'll head out there and—"

"She said, 'Don't come today, come tomorrow.' She wants to rest. I'll get Mom to check on her and make sure she's okay. You've found where you need to look. So now you can take a break. I know you're like bloodhounds; once you get a scent, you're gone. But not today." Bailey made them both log off and get up and then herded them out the door.

Graham chuckled as he climbed into his car, knowing Bailey wouldn't let Guy leave until he had. He also knew she'd be checking on him later to make sure he hadn't gone back to the office. And since he'd promised himself never to take work home, he sighed as he looked at the time. No work... no date... and no one to go home to. A glance at Bailey and Guy sitting in their car, their heads together talking, made him feel like a voyeur. There was something so intimate, so personal, and he felt like an intruder. He also felt a pang of jealousy and, surprisingly, he actually wondered what it would be like to have that kind of relationship.

Enough of this.

CHAPTER 42

FEELING OUT OF SORTS, Graham decided he'd go for a drive. What he wanted was someone to talk to. His sister, a good friend, sadly was on a date and told him he'd have to wait until the next day to tell her his woes.

Am I an idiot? Or is she guilty? Is she in danger?

It shouldn't have surprised him that he found himself on Barnhill Road but it did. Following a side street, he wound his way out of there. If Tarin found him this close to her house, she'd flip. Especially after what they'd put her through.

Seeing a park up ahead, he pulled over, figuring it would at least be a quiet place where he could unwind. He slouched in his seat and closed his eyes for a while. Exhaustion seemed to be his best friend these days, both physically and mentally. Everything that had been going on for the last six months was draining all his energy reserves.

His mind, of course, immediately brought up the conversation they'd had with Tarin. Everything was pointing at her, or at least so it seemed. His going off on her without having all the facts was a testament to his tiredness. He still didn't know where she fit into all this, but his gut was telling him whatever she was into, it wasn't to screw them over. At least he hoped not.

Laughter reached his ears and, like a button had been pressed, his eyes popped open. He turned his head to look over the playground to find the source of that musical, energized mirth. A mom and her son were playing on the slide. Both seemed to be having a lot of fun. It was so refreshing to see such joy. How long he sat there, he wasn't sure but he saw something that caught his attention. The woman was Tarin. He climbed out of his car and walked across the expansive lawn to the playground. The two people were laughing and having fund, unaware they had an audience.

"Mommy!" the little boy squealed.

Graham stopped, chilled by that comment. He shook his head, sure he'd misunderstood, but when he looked back, the little boy was giving her big sloppy kisses. The bond he was watching was unmistakably one between mother and son. Feeling like an intruder, he was about to leave when she turned toward him. Startled, she jerked back, her body tense as though ready to flee. He could tell the moment she recognized him, her lips pursed together and anger spit at him from the depths of her being. Like an idiot, he walked toward her.

Something about her did not add up. He needed to find out what she was hiding... besides a son.

"What do you want?" She set the child down. "Go play, sweetheart. I'm going to talk to this man for a few minutes."

He watched the boy run off with the vigor of the Energizer Bunny. "Does he ever wind down?"

She looked at him warily before turning back to watch her son, who was vrooming his truck through the sand. "Not too often."

"Let's sit, okay?" He indicated the bench a few feet behind them.

"I didn't do anything, I swear."

"We may have found a leak." Was she a part of it? He needed to find out why she'd hacked his system and how she played into all of this.

"Oh?"

"Yeah. Listen, I don't want to talk about work anymore. Please look at me." He waited until she complied. "I know I'm an ass. I've barely said five words to you outside of work, and then I grab you today like it was my right.

Sorry. For the grab, that is; not the kiss. That I'm okay with." He locked eyes with hers, hoping she would see the heat in his.

"Momm—" The muffled scream shot her to her feet. A man was holding her son and was running across the field.

"Chance!"

Acting purely on instinct, Graham grabbed a rock the size of a fist and chucked it as hard as he could at the man before following Tarin racing after her son. The stone bounced off the top of the man's head, causing him to stumble and loosen his grip on the child, who dropped to the ground.

"I've got you. I've got you, love."

Graham barely looked at Tarin hugging her son as he barreled past, trying to catch up to an assailant that kept on running as though nothing had happened. He was moving pretty fast. He took a sharp left beyond a row of bushes, and Graham grasped the opportunity to take a flying leap over them. As he soared over the chest-high hedge, he could see the man in dark clothes, a black ball cap pulled low. He was so close he reached out, planning on snagging him. It seemed like a smart move, but suddenly his feet were snagged by the branches, and he was going down.

"Uhhh." He slammed down hard, the late maneuver only managing to avoid crashing on his face. Dazed, he lay there trying to push away the pain and orient himself.

"Graham?"

The guy's getting away.

Struggling to his feet, he staggered a couple of steps as he looked in the direction the man had run, but he had disappeared. Graham limped around the bush that had taken him down. Tarin was holding her son tight but was slowly and carefully making her way toward him.

"You're hurt."

"Bruised. Nothing serious. Are you two okay?" The little guy was snuggled in tight, his eyes drooping. His thumb had been popped into his mouth. Graham didn't blame him; he felt like doing the same thing. He shifted slightly only to have a sharp pain zip through his shoulder.

"He got away?"

"Sorry. Yeah. I was so close. Do you know him?"

"No idea."

"His father?"

She shook her head adamantly. "No."

"Let's get out of here." He walked her back to her vehicle and was watching her settle her son in the car seat in the back.

"Good arm, by the way. Thank you for saving Chance." She straightened, emotions clogging her words.

"I've thrown a few baseballs." He didn't bother to tell her they had been imaginary ones in a Wii baseball game. His mom would be happy to know the hours he'd spent on there had finally been put to good use.

Tarin looked around as though expecting someone to jump out at her.

"Come on."

They discussed the safest way to leave, opting for him to follow at a short distance to spot anyone else following her. A few minutes later, after a meandering route, they pulled into her driveway.

"Come in."

He followed her around the side of a simple two-story house. She unlocked a side door, and they headed down a flight of stairs.

"I'm going to put him to bed. Then I'll be out." She indicated that he should make himself at home.

He walked to the long, narrow window. He surveyed the immediate area before pulling the curtains tight.

"I don't know what I would have done."

He turned to face her. She was trying to be brave, but her face was scrunching up as she struggled to dispel her emotions. He strode across the room and pulled her into his arms. Perhaps the fact that she didn't fight him was indicative of her fear weighed on her. She remained so still that at first; he wasn't aware she was crying. She sobbed like no one he'd ever witnessed. Her shoulders shook ever so slightly; her body trembled. But there were no deep, heartbreaking bawls or wails. There was quiet snuffling, yet he knew her anguish was bone deep. The vibrations shaking her core were so contained but so intense, like a seething vault of agony. She was imploding rather than exploding.

After a while she pulled away, head down, eyes avoiding his. "Thanks." She walked across the small open room to the kitchen. She opened the fridge and pulled out a jug and then opened a cupboard and got down some glasses.

Barely glancing at him, she asked, "Juice?"

So polite, so controlled. Silently, he crossed the room. "Please."

Juice spilled across the counter as she jerked back in reaction to his rapid approach. He hadn't meant to scare the crap out of her; he'd simply wanted to close the distance between them. She reached in the sink for a dishcloth, but he grasped her hand first.

"Forget all of that. Talk to me. Who was that, and what's going on? His dad? Is this connected to the man who shot at you the other day?"

She walked around him and across the room to sit on the couch. As he joined her, she delicately backed away so a full cushion remained between them.

"No. I don't know. That man wasn't Chance's father, but could he be behind it? Maybe. Probably. Not the shooting though." She looked away.

Not only could he feel her embarrassment, but her cheeks turned a bright crimson. In contrast, her hands were white, clasped tightly yet primly in her lap.

"Are you safe here? Does he know where you live?"

She shook her head, but he noticed the slight hesitation. She wasn't sharing much. Instinct told him something of significance was happening, something she was obviously reluctant to share.

"What are you going to do?"

"I don't know. I think it was the same man I saw at a service station earlier today. I can't be sure. I didn't get a good look at him." She stood, walking to the window, lightly touching the closed curtain.

"You should report it."

She nodded.

"That's all you've got? Your son was almost abducted, and you just nod, whimper a bit and act like everything is okay? *'Would you like some juice?'*" He mimicked in falsetto.

She whirled on him, eyes flashing. "Go to hell. Who do you think you are? You don't know a thing about me or how I'm feeling."

"You're right; I don't because you're about as emotionally real as a Barbie doll."

She strode up to him and slammed her fist into his chest. "I'm so damn sick of people thinking they know me. Be a nice young lady, Tarin. Sit quietly, Tarin. Be ruthless, Tarin. Be a woman, Tarin. You're my wife, Tarin; that should be enough for you. You all think you're so goddamn smart. I'm sick of it."

"Is that all you've got? You hit like a little girl." It was all the goading she needed. He allowed her to use him as a punching bag, but he wasn't even sure she knew how to do this. She was still so controlled, so ineffectual.

"Damn you." She slammed him once more before turning away.

He grabbed her wrist, preventing her from leaving. She glared at him. He snagged her gaze, refusing to let her go. A flood of emotions coursed through the depths of her eyes, but when he saw the slight widening, the flaring of her nostrils; she was attracted to him. But he was shocked when she nearly launched herself at him. He staggered back under the sudden weight but quickly wrapped his arms around her. Her lips found his, her hands tangled in his shaggy mop of curls.

Do I have enough brain cells firing to stop this?

CHAPTER 43

TARIN PUSHED AWAY SO suddenly she found herself stumbling over the couch behind her. Mortified, she stepped away, placing several feet between them. Heat like she'd never felt before scorched her cheeks. She pressed her hand to her lips as she looked at him and then away. It was too hard to force herself to put on a professional face. She felt stripped, raw. With barely a thread keeping herself together, she said, "I'm sorry. I don't have any excuses. That was—"

"Mind-blowing."

She did a quick head shake, something she used to do when she was a child and wanted to quickly change her reality. It still didn't work. "Thank you for your help tonight. I think it's time you left."

She held the door open. Staring at the wall opposite her, he finally approached. Her body tensed with each step that brought him closer. When he stopped right in front of her, she had nowhere to look but at him. Unable to meet his gaze, she locked her eyes on the V of his golf shirt. With each breath he took, his chest expanded, showing her the quiet, broad strength hidden beneath... the strength she so desperately wanted to lean against. Clutching the door with one hand, she clenched the other against her thigh. He reached out and gently touched her chin to raise it. She couldn't help but suck in a breath as though it was the last one she would ever take. With her eyes closed, it kept her from seeing the disappointment in his. His breath whispered over her face. The heat of his tender scrutiny was a gentle caress, an invisible thread pulling her forward. She was leaning toward him, but snapped out of whatever spell she was under. Raising her hand, she drew back, pushing hard against the wall behind her. With nowhere to go, she finally met the intensity in his eyes.

Shaking, she scrabbled deep to pull out the shield. "Don't."

And with that one simple word, she found she didn't have the strength or the will to resist. Vulnerability flooded through her, something she hadn't felt in years, ever since she vowed never to cry after disappointing her father again. Silent tremors shook her core.

"I'm going to go. I'm not sure what's going on here, but I don't think either of us is in a place to deal with it tonight. Get some sleep. You'll be safe. Someone will be watching all night. I have work to do."

"I—"

"You're not alone."

He pressed his index finger against her lips. And then he replaced it with his lips. The kiss was so soft, so quick, but the effect lasted long after he'd left. If he hadn't closed the door behind him, she wasn't sure whether that would have happened. How long she stood there after he was gone, she also didn't know.

Graham's words echoed in her mind long after, but their meaning failed to penetrate her defenses. She'd always been alone. Even Bobbie had only been with her for a short period of time. Somehow, she'd always known something would separate them. Everything and everyone always left her.

It was the shifting of shadows that finally pulled her back to the present. She couldn't say where she'd gone. No real thoughts coursed through her mind, only emotions that confused her, opening her to a longing she thought she'd shut off long ago. Shivering though the basement was warm, she grabbed her purse. The cell phone she'd thought many times of throwing away was right where it always was. Now she grasped it with trembling fingers. The acid in her stomach kicked into overdrive, eating away at her insides with such intensity it almost doubled her over.

Am I making a mistake? A colossal one?

Everything to do with her father was a gargantuan blunder, one constant line of them. She stared at the device in her hand. One simple press of a button and he would come running. He'd be there. All the mess she found herself in would be taken care of. But there would be a price to pay.

You always run to Daddy when things get tough. She was sixteen when she'd had that realization. She'd let him fix a perceived wrong she'd never committed. But he'd made it go away, and in return she'd given up her soul and become his dutiful daughter. She'd finished school at home with a tutor. Whatever she had wanted was one click away, from shopping to movies to gourmet meals. He'd built an in-home theatre, but she'd never had any company to watch with her. Never needing anything, if she wanted to shop, the store was brought to the house. If she wanted to watch a new movie, it was brought to the house because he'd built her a room with a full-size screen, with ten overstuffed recliners to watch it from. Not that she ever had any company to fill any of the others. Her dad was always too busy to sit and watch a 'stupid' movie. If she wanted a gourmet meal from a certain restaurant, the chef was brought to the house. If she wanted friends over, well she wasn't allowed any; definitely not Bobbie. She hadn't been allowed any contact with her.

He'd kept her busy with schoolwork, learning about the hotel business, being the submissive daughter. She was his hostess at parties held at their mansion and his assistant at meetings conducted in the stately home's conference room. Their conversations were always the same.

No, you're not a prisoner, Tarin. I'm trying to teach you how to do well in life.

You know I'm not guilty, right, Father?

It doesn't matter. You won't ever be put in that position again. You should never get caught, Tarin.

But, Father I didn't—

He'd already left. The thought of her being falsely accused of something that could have sent her to jail had she been charged hadn't been the issue. All that mattered was she'd been caught. Innocence wasn't the problem. Being blamed was.

Her spirit had withered up and died that day. The girl who had so desperately wanted a father's love had finally realized he didn't have it to give. All she would ever get from him was the impression she wasn't good enough to hug his ankles; only his rare, pursed smile, and the slightest of nods could ever be her reward.

Then there was the day she tried to tell him what had happened when she'd lost seven days of her life. He had ordered her to apologize to her boss for failing to give notice that she was going to be absent. It had shocked her to her core. He hadn't heard a word and hadn't cared to. If she lost her job, that was her problem; he'd done everything he could to make sure she was good at it.

Her boss, Ed, had always enjoyed screwing with her. He'd hated supervising the owner's daughter. Repeatedly she'd been accused of mishandling reservations or last-minute cancellations; anything that went wrong had been blamed on her, although none of it fit into her job description. When she'd disappeared for a week, Ed hadn't fired her because he had been intimidated by her father. But in his formal report, he accused her of nearly losing a significant contract with the annual Southern Giftware Exposition, an event that sold hundreds of rooms and meals as well as their entire conference center. Of course he'd managed to save it, so suspending her was perfectly okay with her father.

She should have been running the place, but in the end it hadn't mattered that she'd worked sixteen-hour days to prove her loyalty and dedication—or that she'd brought in million-dollar contracts. It didn't matter in the good old boys' club that her boss frequented strip joints and loved lap dances on his two to three-hour lunch breaks. She had shamed her father.

She had walked away. At the time, she had thought she'd been in hell, but she'd only been dancing at its edges.

What price would I have to pay this time?

Who would have wanted to abduct Chance? His father? Or hers? Had someone tried to kill her to take her son? Her knees buckled, and she dropped as if she'd been knocked out. Barely having the reflexes to stop her face from smacking the hardwood floor, she was able to turn at the last minute and take the brunt of it with her shoulder. Her cell phone popped out of her hand, shooting across the floor.

Everything that had happened came crashing back to her; everything since she'd discovered she was pregnant with Chance and since she'd left Stephen slammed into her with the force of a dam bursting. The weight of the world wrapped its mass around her, crushing her. She curled into a tight ball as the tears coursed down her face, but no sound escaped her lips.

CHAPTER 44

SLOWLY OPENING THE DOOR, Tarin peeked around it. When she saw the inner office was closed, she quickly entered, gently and quietly closing the door behind her before making her way to her desk. She hoped Bill had been truthful when he told her Graham wouldn't be in until later.

Graham had insisted she come into the office. He thought it was safer for her than to remain at the house. Reluctantly, she'd agreed, partly because she wasn't the type to sit around all day watching television. Besides, waiting to see what was going to happen next wasn't her style.

"Mommy. Pee."

She smiled at her son and quickly led him to the bathroom. She was quite sure she wouldn't get much done with him accompanying her, but there was no way she was going to be separated from him. When she first arrived in town, the urgency to get answers had been like a new puppy nipping at her heels. Now with everything that had happened, it felt as though she was risking attack by a fearsome animal that was not only going to bite her but rip her world apart.

After getting Chance settled with his toy cars and racetrack, she sat at her computer. She took a slow, steady breath. She could do this. Graham hadn't given her a choice. His message early this morning was that she should show up for work voluntarily or the man he had watching her would bring her in. Whoever had been there all night must have been very good at hiding as she never spotted him.

Graham had said when he arrived later, they were going to talk... about everything. The mere thought of his questions left a gaping hole in her chest. She was feeling beyond sick at the prospect of how he would react when he learned all about her and her predicament. Like everyone else in her life, she was certain he'd run far and fast.

Pushing away her thoughts, she quickly got to work. Her intent had been to log into Stephen's emails, but instead she went into her website. She scanned through several emails, not having the energy to deal with someone who might have gone through what she did.

The woman who'd met with her at the park responded to her email.

'Sorry. Had to run. My life is in danger. Whoever shot the arrow meant business. I think it was meant for me.'

Tarin immediately replied, *'But why? What do you know that someone else wants?'*

What could the woman possibly know that would make someone want to kill her? Had it been her ex? Or was it because she was meeting her? Tarin pressed her hand to her head as a headache threatened. Frustrated there were no answers, she logged out and hacked into Stephen's account. More than sure that he was behind the attempted abduction, she forwarded quite several emails to herself. Just to make sure he got it and knew she meant business, she set up a private webpage and posted all his pornographic pictures and then sent him the link. Wanting to ensure he'd read her note sooner than later, she pulled out her old cell and sent him a text.

'You threaten me or Chance again, you touch him again and I'll send your pretty little porn pictures to your boss, your father and all the staff. If you doubt me, check your emails. I have a copy of them. Here's a link where you can check them out on the internet.'

Anger and fear pushed and shoved as they warred within her like a volcano swelling and rumbling before it erupted.

To distract herself, she logged into her company email to find that Graham had sent her over two hundred more emails to check through. She wondered if Graham had forwarded them before the meeting the day before, and if so, she was quite sure he didn't want her to snoop through them anymore. The list was long, and she felt exhausted just looking at it. Something was way off. Why was someone doing this? What could they hope to achieve? Could she find her answers there?

Doubting it, she did something she was certain she'd regret. She pulled out the thumb drive with the information she'd stolen and started with the Knights Associates files. Scanning through several folders, something was off. There was no rhyme or reason in what and how Graham had labelled or stored files. She opened the first three files and found a jumble of special events they'd held, an employee list and some background information, types of wines, articles and more that she didn't have time to read. Glancing at the clock and then the door, if she was going to get any answers, she had to do some speed reading. She opened another two when it dawned on her that the one labelled CWA might be Caspian Winery account.

After opening it, she scanned it. Invoices to the company had begun about three years before, causing her to wonder why they'd needed private investigators.

After meeting Dorothea, it didn't surprise her that she would do anything to help her family succeed. Had Dorothea invented a reason to hire Knights Associates? Opening one from almost three years ago, she frowned as she read it.

Search for Cassidy LeFevre.

It made her wonder who that was. Closing that out, she opened a few more. After opening and closing a dozen bills, she realized what puzzled her about the receipts. For each paid invoice, a receipt upon payment had then been sent. It was the code that was included in the statement that caught her attention.

CW 08 14 2012

Jesus... that code. It's what he said to me. Someone at Caspian Winery is behind it. But who? And why dammit? Why?

****

"I quit, Dorothea. I've had it!" Oliver rushed through the door and stopped on the other side of her desk, startling her.

Before she could respond, Tom sailed in. "I don't know what he's told you but it isn't me. I don't even know what he's talking about. I quit. I've had it with his backstabbing games."

"Me? What the hell—?"

"Yeah, you've done noth—"

Dorothea brought her cane down hard on her desk. Both men's heads jerked around to look at her. Each man was breathing so hard they reminded her of bulls snorting before a fight.

"It's—"

"I didn't—"

She raised her hands, palms forward. "Stop. Both of you take a deep breath. I won't accept either resignation. Oliver was here first, so tell me what's going on."

At one point, she wanted to place her hands over her ears and bury her head. What they were telling her was unbelievable, yet she should have known something like this would be next. Each man said they'd been contacted by the media to ask what their part was in the wine hijacking, and of course, the reporter had indicated that the other one was the source. Someone was out to ruin her business and would use any dirty trick in the book, and she knew who was very good at that. It was time to have Graham and Guy to get to the bottom of this... and then it was time to retire.

Chapter 45

"WHERE IS SHE?"

"Who's this?"

"I think you know."

Bobbie swallowed. She'd been waiting for this call but had hoped it would never come. "She's not here."

"Your mother said you needed to tell me something, Bobbie."

Damn her. "I can't imagine why she told you that."

"Because she wants more money, as always. Need I remind you that you have one or two secrets you don't want getting out? One dates all the way back to when you were sixteen."

She inhaled slowly and steadily. Tears pricked her eyes as she fought to hold back the anger. It had been obvious that one day she'd have to deal with that lie, but she wasn't ready yet. "No."

"I don't like being lied to. You told me you haven't been in touch with her since you were sixteen."

"I hadn't. I swear to you. She contacted me recently. I've been trying to get close so I could find out what's going on."

"I want to know what's happened to her over the last three years. You'd better have answers. And soon. Keep her close. Do not let her out of your sight."

Bobbie clutched the phone long after the conversation had ended. What mess had her mother created now, and more than likely because she wanted something else she couldn't afford? Finally, she hit the speed dial on her phone and waited.

"Get over here now. What have you done?"

****

Tarin grabbed Chance and raced out of the building.

"Where are you going?"

"Bill." She took a deep breath and tried to still her thumping heart. She had no idea where she was going; she only knew she needed to do something. "I've got to get Chance home. He's tired. Time for his nap. Bye."

He nodded, so she took that as his consent. She was never sure what to expect from him. After strapping Chance into his car seat, she climbed into the driver's seat. Before starting the car, she had a strong urge to call Bobbie. She'd been concerned by her odd behavior, and taking Chance that morning was like waving a red flag in her face.

"Tarin, where are you?"

"Bobbie, you sound upset. What's going on?"

There was a muffled sound, as though she was trying to cover the mouthpiece while she talked with someone.

"Bobbie?"

"Yeah. Here. Sorry, just picking up some papers I dropped. Where are you?"

"Just taking Chance to the park or the zoo. Can't decide which."

"The park. It's supposed to rain."

Tarin looked out her window at the sunny, cloudless sky. *What's going on?* "Yeah. Or maybe we'll just go for an ice cream."

"Why don't I come with you?"

It was the desperation in her voice that grabbed Tarin's attention. Bobbie had always been the tough one at school, the one who wanted to be adventurous, to break the rules. Tarin had always been too timid. The only time she'd heard her voice so strained was when Tarin had been accused of something she hadn't committed.

"Why don't I come and get you?"

"That sounds great. You know you never did tell me where your office is?"

The hair on the back of her neck stood up. "No. I guess I never did. Hmm, I'm almost fifty minutes away, what with rush hour, maybe longer."

"Great, we'll see you in an hour."

She sat there for a long time, only becoming aware of the sweltering heat when Chance started whimpering and she saw how red his face was. The air conditioner wasn't great, but in ten minutes the car was cooled off to a manageable temperature, yet she still hadn't moved. Where could she go? She could go back to Bobbie's, but who had she been referring to as *we*? Intuition told her she wasn't referring to Kim. Bobbie had been hiding something. It left a cold, unsettled feeling like an icicle's constant, incessant drip.

Someone knocked on her window. She jumped in surprise, jamming her knee on the steering wheel as her foot kicked the gas pedal, revving the car. She whirled around, her heart thumping and her breathing rapid. Then with relief, she opened the door.

"What happened? What's going on?" Graham squatted so they were eye to eye and gently pulled her toward him.

She wanted to resist but couldn't find the strength. "Nothing," she whispered as she pressed her face into the V of his neck.

He held her tenderly, one hand cradling her head and the other rubbing her back in reassuring circles. The tension finally eased from her shoulders, but the chill that had invaded her core remained. She pushed away, leaning back against the seat.

"I don't know what's happening. I just know I'm scared."

"Talk to me."

"Bobbie's acting suspiciously. And someone's at my house. She tried to muffle the mouthpiece, but I heard her tell someone that she'd find me. Why would she say that? Who was she talking to? I thought I was safe there."

"Let's go inside and see what we can find out."

It took several minutes for him to convince her, but finally she acquiesced. She had no plans. For the first time, she felt completely lost.

After carrying Chance up the long stairway and settling him into the bed in his office for an overdue nap, Graham logged onto his computer. Tarin sat beside Chance and lovingly brushed back his fine, sandy blonde hair. The careful way Graham had carried him, like he was his own precious son, was something she'd never forget.

"What's Bobbie's last name?"

"Benson."

He asked her for more information about her friend. As she answered, she felt as though she was betraying a confidence, but the disconcerting call she'd had with her hung over her like a cloud. After the first few questions, she had no problem giving him all he needed.

"Did you know your friend doesn't work?"

"Yeah, I knew that. She looks after her mom, who lives in the same neighborhood."

"No, actually her address is in Leaside."

"Impossible; that's an expensive neighborhood. She can't afford that."

Graham was silent for so long that curiosity got the best of her. She made her way behind his desk where she peered over his shoulder. A recent picture of Bobbie was open on one screen, the address of an expensive house on another, and her bank account data on a third.

Tarin blinked a few times as she tried to make sense of what she was seeing. Graham showed her property ownership records; she had acquired two houses, one she was sharing with Tarin and a million-dollar property her mom was living in.

"It can't be true. Where'd she get that kind of money? Could her sister have had life insurance?"

"It appears she's getting a yearly salary."

"From whom? For what?"

"I'd have to do more digging."

"I'm going out there."

"Not without me you're not."

"Fine. Let's go." She stopped barely taking one step before stopping to observe Chance sleeping. To protect him, she couldn't drag him around town.

"I have a suggestion, but you might not like it."

Twenty minutes later they were on their way to check out Bobbie's other residence. She pressed her hand to her belly in an effort to quell the queasiness and focus on what they were doing. Every time she thought of leaving Chance behind, she wanted to heave. Graham squeezed her hand as though he knew what she was thinking. She had to trust someone, not that her judgment had been any good in that department.

"He'll be fine. He'll probably sleep the whole time we're gone. Bill won't let anyone near your son. He's a gentle soul. And the place has a good security system."

She nodded but thought she needed her head examined. She'd left her son with someone who reminded her of a homeless man. Nervous laughter bubbled inside her, but she tamped it down, concerned that if it escaped, Graham would think she was nuts. Her fingers pressed against the tender spot on her forehead. Maybe the incident had done more damage than she'd first thought. The memory brought back all that had happened in recent days. Her stomach convulsed, and her throat compacted. She tried to push away her thoughts and the gut-wrenching feeling that had taken hold of her.

They came to a stop across the street from a three-story Tudor-style house with expansive, immaculate gardens. Bobbie wasn't and never had been earning that kind of money. There was no way she owned it.

"I'll be right back," Graham said.

"Wait. Where are you going?"

"I'm just going to see if anyone is there. Stay here."

She watched as he walked down the block and disappeared around the corner. Tapping her fingers against her thighs, she was almost ready to follow him when she spotted him sticking his head out the front door, waving at her. She hurried toward him and followed him into the house.

"Are you nuts?"

"Yes. Now see if you can find some clues as to who owns this place."

The living room with closed French doors sat off to her right. Alongside a set of stairs leading upwards was a hallway that led to the back of the house, to what looked like the kitchen. To the left was a closed door. Graham turned the gilded knob, revealing an enormous oak desk.

Tarin moved toward it, pausing only when several family pictures arranged on a wall unit behind it caught her attention. She gasped as she picked up the first one within reach. It was a faded picture of her and Bobbie at school. She used to have the same one but had no idea where it had gone over the years. In the middle of the shelf was a recent picture of Bobbie, her mom and niece, obviously professionally photographed. They were all smiling and looked happy. The diamond teardrop necklace Bobbie was wearing caught her attention. Tarin hadn't seen it since her dad had given it to her for her sixteenth birthday. She'd been sure it had been lost.

Sitting behind the desk, she opened the laptop. A short time later she had figured out Bobbie's password; what she called her when they were twelve—y2ktarin. The name had come about because of her fascination with computers and the Y2K scare, where everyone was sure with the approaching millennium computers were going to crash. Tarin had been convinced they would die out after that. So Bobbie had dubbed her y2k Tarin.

"We've got to go. Come on."

"Just give me a sec."

"Now... Now... Now... Someone just pulled up."

"I'm hurrying."

"It's an older woman. She's out of the car and on her way to the door. She looks pissed."

Tarin slammed shut the laptop and followed Graham out the back door.

"Did you close the office door?"

"Yes."

"Everything's the way we found it, right?"

Tarin gave a barely perceptible nod. She pretended to be looking around cautiously to avoid the questioning look in his eyes. The small picture she'd taken probably wouldn't be noticed.

"I don't understand. Why would she lie to me?"

"Hey, don't think about it. I know it sucks. How do you know her?"

"We met in first grade and we became instant friends. We went through so much together. I don't know what I'd have done without her. Why?"

Graham pulled the car over.

"What are you doing?"

"Giving you a shoulder to cry on." He turned and took her into his arms.

She tried so hard not to let him in, but she was alone and didn't know who was trying to hurt her. Graham, a virtual stranger, had treated her better than her family and friends had. That alone opened the floodgates.

CHAPTER 46

GRAHAM TOOK A LONG, deep swallow of his beer as he stared out at the blackness. On one hand, he was relieved not to have a starry, moonlit night, but on the other, he didn't want any surprises. Guy was in place watching for anyone who didn't belong in the area; he'd offered, refusing to hire anyone else. Not many people knew Graham's home address, and he liked to keep it that way. According to Guy, he had the place fortified enough that Fort Knox had a thing or two to learn from him.

The softest of sounds made him turn his head. The light from the kitchen backlit Tarin, causing her to appear ethereal. As though being reeled in by an invisible thread, he walked toward her. At one point, she looked like she was going to bolt, but she didn't. The only sign that she was uncomfortable was the stiffening of her body, making her appear like a statue. As he came closer, he reached up and brushed the back of his fingers against her cheek. She held his gaze for a long time before she gently nuzzled his hand.

He cupped her face as he lowered his lips to hers. Her arms lifted and molded their way around him, pulling him in tight. He took that as a sign, a good one. He lifted her up and almost stopped to grin as she wrapped her legs around his waist. The hallway was short and wide and didn't hinder his movement at all. But the heat they were generating made him weak in the knees, and he had to stop to lean against the wall. Their lips remained fused as he finally stumbled into the bedroom, and although he'd planned on setting her down gently, they crashed onto the bed. He barely managed to flip out his arm to keep from landing heavily on her.

She was making the cutest mewling sound he'd ever heard. Pulling back slightly despite her protest, he watched her until her darkened, kittenish eyes opened and told him all he needed to know. Her hands caressed him under his t-shirt, raking her nails down over his hard abs one minute and clutching him to her the next. To make it easier for her, he pulled his top over his head. She bit her lip as her eyes drank in every last bit of his chest. That look alone damn near sent him over the top.

His lips brushed against hers just before he flipped over, placing her on top.

"Eeee."

He loved her little squeal. His hands reached under her blouse so he could stroke her skin.

"Ohhh." She placed her fingers on his forearms. He held still, watching her, letting her decide where this was going. She squeezed her eyes tight for the longest moment before she took a deep breath and sat up. He let his arms drop to his sides. Her gaze locked onto his as she slowly reached for the top button. It felt like forever before she managed to finally undo it. The teasing was almost sending him over the edge. She'd undo it, pull back her blouse a bit and then slide the button back through. When she finally got to the third one and was flashing him some pink lace, he wanted to rip the blouse from her body. But he didn't; he could tell how much she was enjoying the control she had. His fingers curled into the bedsheets. That's when she upped the torture.

Her hips started undulating against his raging erection. Unable to take anymore, he pulled her down to him. How they ever managed to get all their clothes off he wasn't sure, because neither one of them could keep their hands off the other's body.

When he finally had her naked, he took a moment to drink in her perfection. "You're so beautiful."

Her happy smile dimmed a bit, and she dropped her gaze down to look at his chest.

He tipped her chin up with his index finger. He searched her eyes. "I'm not sure why that bothers you because you are—inside and out. You're an amazing woman. And I don't have to tell you what you do to me." He arched his hips slightly, letting her feel the full length of him.

Her teeth nibbled at her lower lip as her eyes darkened.

"I don't sleep with a lot of women if that's what you're thinking. Or that it's a line. It's not. I've been fighting my attraction to you since day one." Realizing that talking never made a difference, he let his actions speak for him. He pulled her down to him and kissed her deeply and fully, letting her know she was the only woman he was interested in. And she was in charge.

There were times he wasn't sure if he was going to survive his decision to let her control their lovemaking. She was a natural-born tease. And he loved every minute of it.

****

Tarin lifted her head to look down at the man who might have stolen something from her. Only he didn't know it, and she had freely given it. She didn't believe in love, or at least she hadn't. Now she wasn't sure. She only knew that this man, who didn't trust her, might have every right to hate her. And now she'd complicated it by jumping into bed with him. She'd only wanted to feel something real for a change.

Slowly getting up, she tiptoed from his bedroom. Her jacket was tossed over the arm of the sofa. She picked it up and pulled out her cell phone and dialed.

"Hello." The groggy answer was almost enough to get her to hang up.

"Hi Bobbie."

"Tarin."

"I want answers. I've known you all my life."

"You know."

"I know. But I want to hear it from you. I need to hear you tell me that you screwed me over."

"I didn't, it's not—"

Unable to listen to the sobs that choked her voice, Tarin hung up, but that didn't stop the contact. Ten texts came in rapid succession, each one apologizing and begging to explain. She texted her back, a time and a place to meet, then shut off her phone.

CHAPTER 47

THE EARLY MORNING SKY was awakening beneath a sliver of sunlight, but phantoms still danced in the shadows. Though major objects—houses, trees, vehicles—were easy to make out, undulating silhouettes were not. It was beautiful and yet eerie, alluring, and mysterious.

Graham peered out the window, his eyes roaming as he pressed the cell phone to his ear.

"Nothing out of the ordinary out here."

"Go home. I've got it from here. Thanks Guy. Please apologize to Bailey."

"Who do you think kept me company?"

The guilt of having Guy sit out there all night tripled. "Hey, I'll make it up to you guys."

"No need. It's what I do for a living. Remember?"

"Yeah, but—"

"Graham, stop. You did a lot for me when I needed it. Now it's my—our turn. No payback ever," Bailey said.

He dropped his head against the wall and pressed his fingers against the bridge of his nose. Guy was damn lucky. A soft sound drew his attention across the room. Tarin was curled up in his bed watching him. Everything about the scene in front of him looked right, felt right.

"Graham, are you there?"

"Uh. Yeah sorry. Just got distracted."

"How's Tarin holding up?"

He grinned. "Just fine." It must have come out a lot deeper and sexier than he'd intended, because Bailey and Guy started laughing.

"Got it. Take care of her. We'll see you later. Watch your back; we're still not sure she doesn't have a role in all this."

Tarin climbed out of bed and began a slow, gentle stretch. He couldn't take his mind off her or concentrate on anything else.

"Uh-huh."

"We'll stick around for another half hour."

He heard Guy's words, but their meaning didn't register as he made a move to hang up. Their soft chuckling was brief as he clicked off his phone, setting it on the dresser beside him. He strode toward her, not stopping until he was mere inches away. She smiled, grabbed him by the shoulders and pushed him back onto the bed. Then she climbed over top of him, slowly sliding her way up his body.

There's something else I should be doing. It wasn't more than a fleeting thought that came and went so fast it hardly registered.

****

She awoke with a start. At first she was disoriented, unsure of where she was. But then she moved, and a slight ache permeated her body, reminding her of the previous night. It was so vivid in her mind that she couldn't help but blush—not only at the memory of what they'd done but the memory of what she'd done. Not wanting guilt or remorse to settle in, which brought back memories of the week she'd lost, she pushed herself upright.'

Chance giggled, reminding her of the sound that had awakened her. The warmth of his beautiful voice washed over her but also compelled her to investigate what had him so happy. She slipped on her lingerie and pulled on one of Graham's t-shirts that hid her to mid-thigh. Strolling into the kitchen, she couldn't help but laugh. Two happy but filthy faces turned to look at her. One expression quickly slid into guilty.

"What are you doing?"

"Momma, Momma." Chance reached out one hand toward her.

She walked over to him and touched his nose. "I don't think so, big guy. Not until we wash—" She looked at Graham for clarification.

"Breakfast. Superman style."

She shrugged, unsure what that meant. "Breakfast, Superman style, off your face." He seemed fine with that and settled back into Graham's arms.

To show her what they had been doing, Graham peeled another banana. Chance grabbed it in his tiny fist, squeezing it to mush and dropping half. Graham caught what he had lost. Chance then shoved what he could into his face. Then he reached for more and shoved his next fistful at Graham to eat, but most went on his face.

She giggled as she watched how seriously her son took his job of eating and sharing his banana. Then Graham squirted chocolate syrup on the next piece, and she watched in horror as they walked toward her.

"Mommy, eat." His tiny fist was outstretched toward her with a yellowy glob with chocolate drippings.

Her hand shot out to stop them as she stumbled backward to get away. Graham quickly grasped her wrist, stopping her retreat. Before she could react, Chance was shoving his mush onto her forehead. Laughing, she reached up to wipe it off, but the look in Graham's eyes stilled her. She watched mesmerized as he leaned forward and licked it off. A shiver of excitement shook her to her core.

"Eat."

It was Chance's insistence and giggle that brought her back to the present. Stepping back, she reached for him. "Let's go wash up."

"No." He leaned back against the strong chest she'd been cuddling a few hours before. He looked like he could take on the world. It was a good feeling.

"I, well, Guy and I have to go out and talk with Dorothea later, but you'll be safe here."

"Oh, is something up?"

Graham shoved his hand through his hair. "It would appear she might be thinking of selling."

It took all her willpower to force her knees not to buckle. "She's going to get rid of the winery?"

"I don't know. We're looking for answers."

"Do you know if she has a buyer?" Her mouth had gone dry. *James Madsen has purchased one winery and is looking to buy another.* The information she'd found the week before immediately popped into her head. *God no.* But she feared that somehow he knew.

"I don't know anything. She just dropped that little bomb yesterday."

Chance took that moment to squeal. Thankful for the distraction, she reached for him again. "Come on, love. We need to get you cleaned up."

"No." He wouldn't let her take him.

"I'll take him. You get the bath ready."

"I was going to shower with him."

"Do you think the three of us would fit?"

In lieu of a reply, she made her way to his bathroom. She pressed her hand to her thumping heart, trying to still its fluttering insistence that she take Graham up on his offer. Leaning over, she filled the tub a quarter full.

"Spoil sport." Graham lowered Chance into the tub and then climbed in right behind him. All long lean muscle of him. Her eyes were peeled so wide, it took a moment for her to realize the two of them were grinning up at her.

"I'll just—I'll just... go." She waved and slowly made her way out, closing the door behind her. Weak in the knees, she sank to the floor overwhelmed with emotion. Chance had never experienced a man who treated him as if he were precious or important. He was lapping it up like a starved puppy given a bowl of milk. And she'd never had anyone look at her the way Graham did. It was frightening to think with only a simple glance, she felt like the same little puppy wagging her tail, begging for more.

What the hell am I supposed to do with him? Many delicious ideas immediately popped into her mind, and she wondered when she'd become so amoral. It made her smile when she considered how horrified her father would be if he knew how sensuously unladylike she'd been the night before. And she had every intention of doing it again. But first, she needed to get her life in order and figure out who was intent on harming her... and why.

CHAPTER 48

"OKAY. WE'VE GOT A problem." Graham took in the view from the marble balcony. It didn't matter how often he went to Dorothea's mansion; the grandeur still put him in awe. He couldn't imagine Guy growing up in such a luxurious place, even though he also knew this child's playhouse was also a very lonely place. With a step-grandmother running an empire, battling the media's love of controversy, and overseeing the upkeep of the mansion and expansive grounds—complete with lawns, themed gardens, fishponds and swimming pools—there wasn't much time for a young child. Then there had been Geoff, the great-uncle who used to beat the pulp out of Guy when he could catch him.

Graham smiled. He wouldn't have traded his own upbringing for anyone else's. He grew up in a blended home of siblings, half-siblings and stepsiblings. It was chaotic and crowded with nine crazy kids, but there had always been love. There had always been someone to hang out with, get in trouble with.

"Why? What's going on? Do we have any answers yet? Tarin? Oliver?"

Pulled from his reverie, he looked at Guy. He'd left Tarin at the office that morning, thinking it was the safest place for her to be. Bill would keep a close eye on her.

"I don't know. How do you like them apples? Oops, I mean grapes. I wouldn't want your grandmother to think I disrespected her." He looked around surreptitiously, as though he was going to get in trouble.

Guy chuckled before sitting in one of the oversized, cushioned bamboo chairs. "I'm going to tell her what you said. That you forgot you were standing in the middle of wine country and had the audacity to mention apples."

Graham jerked back, his eyes wide, his right hand pressed against his chest. "Nooooo. Anything but that."

"Anything but what, Graham?"

He gave Guy a look of panic before he came to his feet as Dorothea joined them. He nodded in greeting and sat after she had taken her usual seat under the large umbrella.

"I was just telling Guy how much I admire the place. Emilio has outdone himself with the gardens. They look outstanding. And will be perfect for the wedding."

She smiled knowingly. "You're a real charmer, aren't you? All right, let's get to business. Do you have an answer? Who do you think is out to sabotage my business?"

"We're not sure, Gram. We're still looking into that. Sorry. What we need to know is anything about your employees that we won't find in a background check."

"I already told you, Guy, it can't be one of my staff. It can't be." The conviction with which she said it was sorely lacking. "On Oliver's computer, what did you find?"

Graham glanced at Guy, hoping they didn't have to say anything until they reached the end of the meeting. How did he tell her someone had been on his computer and had erased all the information? I've skimmed it; copied some information and I'm doing a deeper dive at the office. I've upgraded your security, so it'll be difficult for anyone to get into any of your information."

"Let me know what you find."

"I know it's tough, Mrs. L—" Her stern look stopped him. "Dorothea. Let's start with your frontline staff. You get new ones each year to help with the picking, right?"

"Yes. I used to meet each one but sadly I don't anymore. A few years ago, I could have told you each and every one's name, where they were from and their dreams."

Graham noticed the slight tremor in her hand as she sipped her iced tea. "And the staff who do the packaging? You've had quite a turnover?"

She stiffened before answering, "There have been some, yes."

Guy looked at him. It was enough to know they were thinking the same thing. Things had changed since her brother Geoffrey had caused such havoc for her, almost taking down Caspian Winery. She'd been fighting for its life over the past two years, trying to untangle Geoff's web of lies and deceit, including the fraudulent way he'd used the company's money. She'd brought it a long way, but Graham still felt the current situation was somehow connected. They'd exhausted every other sensible possibility.

"None of them would have the kind of access needed to swap out a bad bottle of wine with a good bottle. Yes, one of them could have stolen a bottle and a label, but it wouldn't have been easy."

"Okay, how about the more permanent staff?"

"Well, let's see. Oliver is my shipping and receiving manager, and until I hire someone else, he also oversees the wine tasting room. Tom is our vineyard manager. Martin is our senior winemaker. Cara is our account manager. Then there's my new assistant, LJ. There are several others on staff, but that's my senior team." She looked sternly at Guy.

Obviously, Graham thought, they'd had words about the new help—LJ. She had a checkered past. Guy and Bailey had tried to reason with her, but she was adamant the woman was right for the job. She had all the qualifications she'd been looking for—able to run a successful business, able to give as good as she got and with a keen eye for how to expand a business. It hadn't mattered to her that the woman had once run an escort service; something Guy and Graham considered half a step away from a brothel. Dorothea had been amused by that and impressed with the woman's gumption. She had, however, made it clear that none of them were to meet her, talk to her, interrogate her or do any more background checks on her until Dorothea had given them permission.

It didn't make sense to Graham, but to cover his tracks so any sleuthing wouldn't be discovered; he had to be careful. He certainly did not want to be on the receiving end of Dorothea's wrath.

"Oliver's been here a long time, right?" He changed the subject so he could possibly find out who had wiped his computer clean and where he might be at that moment.

"Oh my, yes." She sported a genuine, happy smile. She obviously had wonderful memories of him. "He's been here for fifteen years. He was the first man I hired. Oh, in the beginning we butted heads. He hadn't wanted to take orders from a woman. But he's a good man—married for thirty-five years, they have two married children, four grandchildren, and he's active in his church. He's very principled. His wife was a lovely lady."

"Was?"

"Sadly, she died of cancer three or so years ago."

"And how long has Tom been here?"

She frowned but quickly relaxed. "He's been here for about three years. He's the only good thing Geoff did for this company." She paused. "He's good with the grapes. Had us change our handling procedures and the watering. And he was right. His mother is in a retirement home. She has severe rheumatoid arthritis. She became too much for him to look after. It broke his heart to have to put her there. Thankfully, he found a place for her at Living Life on the Avenue. He's not married."

"That's a retirement place."

"Yes, Living Life on the Avenue is. He's hired a full-time nurse to look after his mom and said it was better than moving her into a nursing home. She's happy. He's normally an easy-going man, but he does have his moments when he's dealing with Oliver. Although that's all Geoffrey's—" She looked away as though ashamed of what she'd been about to say.

Guy took her hand in his. "I know you don't want to talk about him. But what do you mean it's all Geoffrey's—what, fault? What are you referring to?"

She squeezed his hand before waving her other hand in the air in dismissal. "There are some personality clashes at work."

"Grandma, if he created some issues at work, we need to know—especially if you're still dealing with problems two years after his death."

She gave him a chilling look. What was she hiding?

"He caused some trouble between the two men. He promised them things I couldn't deliver. Everything he did fueled the animosity between them. We're finally at the point, though, where I believe that's all in the past. Things have settled down."

Graham caught Guy's eye. If Geoff had stirred up something over two years ago and it was still an issue, then they had a problem.

"What's this about selling the business?"

"That's none of your business."

"Which means you're considering it."

"No. I think I've found someone to take over though."

"Who is it?"

"I'm perfectly capable of running this company, Guy. I've been doing it for most of my life. And I think I've done a pretty darn good job." With that, she got up, gave them each a nod and walked laboriously toward the house. At the door, she paused and slowly turned. "I hope you find out who's been doing this."

Graham and Guy took the five marbled flights of winding stairs to the front door. Once inside Graham's Hummer, Guy spoke up. "She doesn't look good, does she?"

"Considering she's thirteen years past normal retirement and she's still running an empire, she looks pretty damn good. But I know what you mean. She's clearly exhausted."

"And pale. Gray even."

"Yeah."

"Oliver appears to be a prime suspect. Tom is too, if for no other reason than because Geoff hired him. What do you think?"

"Same. She sees them all through rose-colored wine," he quipped. Growing serious, he continued, "She's still living in the '50s where loyalty was the norm. Nowadays, everyone is looking out for themselves. What are we missing? We did a background check on all of them." Graham contemplated their conversation with Dorothea, wondering about the usual conviction in her voice—somehow, it seemed lacking. "And then there's Geoff."

"She insisted we come out here because she wanted to tell us who has been responsible, yet she didn't share anything."

"No, but did you see her expression when you mentioned Geoff's death?"

"Yeah. She doesn't think he's dead either, does she? But there's no way she could come out and say she thinks her brother is responsible. Again."

"Dig again as deeply as you need to. Has any staff received large sums of money or spending more than they make? I'll check with Walters at the police station and see if he'll do some checking through their system. He owes us."

"And who's going to be the one to tell Dorothea if we find out one of her trusted employees is sabotaging her business? Or that Geoff might be behind it, dead or alive? He could have easily set something in motion to take her down. As feeble as she's getting, this might kill her."

CHAPTER 49

"Hi. You don't look too pleased. I'm assuming your meeting didn't go as planned?" Tarin struggled to tamp down the impulse to hug Graham as he came through the door and remained seated behind her desk instead.

Graham thrust his hand through his hair. There was still a hint of frustration in his manner; it was because of her and the step back she was trying to take from whatever it was they had. His blue eyes bore into her as if he were searching for answers. "No. It just led to more questions. And you? How's—?"

Tarin couldn't help but smile as Chance launched himself at Graham's leg. Graham swooped down and picked him up, tossing him into the air. His squeal of delight widened her smile into a grin. She'd never seen her son so happy with someone other than her, not that he'd ever had much opportunity to meet anyone else.

"Hey, big guy."

Seeing Chance so gleeful reminded her that she needed answers so she could end this crazy, unnerving life. Until she did, there was no chance for her son to have a normal life. There was only one way she was going to get answers.

"Hey, would you mind watching him for a bit? I need to get some supplies—pull-up diapers, snacks, that kind of thing."

"I'll go."

"No. I need to get out. I'm feeling claustrophobic. I'll be fine. There must be somewhere close I can shop?"

Graham gave her directions to a store a few blocks away. She leaned up to kiss Chance only to have Graham steal a kiss, leaving her breathless and feeling even more sleazy for lying to him. If anything was going to change, if she was truly going to learn anything, she had to do this. What choice did she have?

She walked out without looking back.

****

"Were you able to follow her?" Graham stared down at Chance as he lay sleeping. Though he'd felt privileged that she trusted him with her son and he hadn't questioned her intent, he'd asked Guy to follow her. Guy would protect her, and though he hated to admit it, he still didn't totally trust her.

"Yeah. Sorry it's taken me so long to get back to you, but her little jaunt down the street went a little farther than you imagined. You won't believe this. She's at Union Station, standing in front of Purdy's Chocolates."

"Any other time, I'd tell you to pick me up some. What the hell is she doing there?" Graham frowned.

"She's scanning the area. So, meeting someone?"

"I have to get a babysitter—"

"A what?"

Graham ground his teeth. *What the hell was she up to?* "Just keep an eye on her, and I'll be down as soon as I can."

"Don't. Get on your computer and do what you do best."

Graham scooped up Chance, raced out the door, and down the stairs., He walked around to Bill's place. His face lit up as soon as he saw the little guy.

"I need you to come upstairs and keep an eye on him, okay?" Bill didn't totally trust the cell phone they'd given him and often left it shut off, so Graham knew it would be faster to go and ask him.

Without question, Bill locked up his place and followed them upstairs. Since Chance was sleeping, he turned on the television for Bill to watch.

An hour later, Graham was reeling from all he'd learned—all he should have known before he'd hired Tarin. He had to give it to her; she was good. It had taken some major digging to discover the truth about her. He felt sick.Watching Bill and Chance with their heads together playing with a small truck, made him feel slightly better. It was a wonderful sight. Bill was a bit of an unorthodox babysitter but a good one.

Graham's phone rang. Picking it up, he wandered to the outer office. "What's happening?"

"A woman showed up dressed in a burqa. I only caught a glimpse of her face. I'm sending you a picture."

Graham studied the picture. "I think it's the friend she's been living with. They went to school together. Private school paid by Tarin's father. You'll never guess who he is?"

He went on to fill Guy in on all he'd discovered.

"So could dear old dad be involved in all this?" Guy asked.

"It looks like they may have had a falling out. She quit her job at his company. There are some murky reasons for it. I'm not sure her quitting would have gone over well with Pops." Graham shoved his hand through his hair. "I don't have a clue what's going on, but I want you to grab her and get out of there. The Blue Jays game will be ending soon, and that place will be zoo-city. Oh, and if she gives you trouble, tell her that Chance will be handed over to the authorities if she doesn't cooperate." He hung up and had to lean against the counter. The thought of giving her child to Social Services made him want to retch. But then so did the whole situation with Tarin.

CHAPTER 50

"I'M SORRY. I'M REALLY sorry. I didn't know how to tell you."

"Tell me what?"

"That Kim is your sister."

Tarin staggered against the building pillar. "What?"

"I wanted to tell you, but I was sworn to secrecy."

"The house."

"All part of it."

"Your sister. She died."

"Yes, but not Kim's mom."

"Your mom and my dad?" Tarin said. Her voice was barely above a whisper.

"When you begged for me to go to school with you, your dad made a deal with my mother. She was to be his on-call companion. They'd had the arrangement for years. But I guess somewhere along the way, they forgot the basic science of how to prevent a baby. And along came Kim."

"The year I left school?"

Bobbie nodded. "Your dad was furious. He didn't want any more kids, and he didn't want you to have anything more to do with me because he figured you'd find out about the baby."

Nausea burned inside her throat, and acid clutched her stomach as it rolled and churned. She pressed one hand against her belly while she clapped the other one over her mouth.

"And you just went along?"

"I never knew until my sister Tammy died. That's when I got suspicious. I was told that Tammy was Kim's mom. I

didn't know. She was so wild then. When Tammy died, I
stepped up and said that I'd raise Kim. I was already more
of a mother to her than Tammy was. After I got Kim, Mom
started making demands, telling me how to do things.
Letting some things slip. She finally told me everything.
Tammy wasn't Kim's mom; she was. And your father has
been paying her for years to keep her mouth shut and to
raise his child that he's never seen."

"And you couldn't tell me?"

Her sobs were so gut-wrenching it was hard to understand her. "Mom got cancer. I had to look after her. That's
when I learned the truth about Kim. I didn't even know
where you were. And how could I have told you anyway
after all that time? And I didn't tell you about your dad
and my mom because I got to go to a fancy school and
be with my best friend. It felt like a secret I could keep.
I didn't think it was hurting anyone. It's not like either of
our parents wanted us."

"And that theft of the school's finances that I got
blamed for?"

"It was me. I'd been told that if I didn't, I'd have to leave
school and my family would be financially ruined. I didn't
know it was to frame you. I swear. Your dad acted like he
was in dire financial straits, so I thought I was doing both
of us a favor. I tried to tell the principal it was me, but she
didn't believe me."

"But Kim—the paperwork?" As soon as the words
were out of her mouth, she swore softly. Her dad had
taken care of it. He had made it look like Tammy had been
her mom.

I have a half-sister.

"The money. The houses. My dad was paying you."

"Yes. I made a deal with the devil when I was sixteen.
And he had made one with my mom long before that.
When Kim came along, he agreed to pay child support.
And he was generous with it; however, my mother is not
good with money—or men for that matter. Anyway, I took
over the finances. And because I wouldn't let her buy her

latest boyfriend a car, she told your dad about you. I'm sorry. I swear I didn't."

"But he asked you to." Feeling light-headed, she turned away, unable to look at her friend anymore. Bobbie's body shook with her guilt and anguish. Several people gawked at them. Tarin was so numb that she wondered if she could even feel anymore, especially when it came to her father. Bobbie reached out to hug her, but she couldn't take anymore. Shaking her head, she stepped back. Bobbie's face crumpled as she fought to hold back the tears. Her misery was like a living, breathing thing, but Tarin couldn't go near it; couldn't believe the one person in the world she thought she could trust had lied to her... for a very long time. She wanted to walk away, but she didn't think her legs would carry her. And she couldn't leave Bobbie like this, even if she did bring it on herself.

As she scanned the surrounding crowd, she spotted a man wearing dark clothes, sunglasses and a baseball cap pushing his way impatiently through the throng. Rude behavior was nothing new at Union Station, but when he looked in her direction, she got an eerie feeling he was headed for her.

"Did you bring company?"

"What?" Her friend sniffled, blowing into tissues she pulled from her pocket.

"Who did you bring with you?"

"No one. I swear. I came by myself." Her head whipped around behind her. "Run. I don't know who that guy is, but I've seen him before. Get out of here."

Tarin didn't question her. Even with Bobbie's betrayal, she could see the fear in her eyes and knew she was being straight with her. Spinning on her heels, she hurried into the crowd headed in the opposite direction. It wasn't easy to move against the flow of traffic, but it was her only choice, especially if that man was after her. One of the subway doors opened; people poured out. She sprinted for all she was worth, now flowing with a movement that sandwiched her, pulling her forward. Commuters pushed and shoved their way onto the train. She was about to step aboard when she was grabbed from the side and jerked out of the swarm. Reflexively, she brought her elbow up and back. A quick glance showed her it was an older gentleman holding his jaw and calling her names that she didn't even think a man of his age would know.

"Sorry," spilled from her lips as she was yanked away from the angry passenger.

Stumbling, she was in danger of falling despite her assailant's firm hold on her.

She struggled with every ounce of energy she had left, but no one paid any attention as she was half-dragged, half-pulled through the crowd.

Since the assailant was moving too fast, she did the next best thing. She kicked out with her foot and shoved, and at the same time she reached out with her free hand and snagged the arm of a brawny man striding past her in the opposite direction. Without even glancing her way, he shook her off as if she were nothing more than a pesky flea. As he thrust her aside, she came solidly to her feet and slung her arm around a nearby railing. Without wasting another second, she lashed out and kicked her assailant. Hard.

"Damn you," he grunted.

Someone swung a fist at the guy. The two men were scuffling back and forth until the other man realized he was losing and disappeared into the crowd. She turned to run only to find herself face to face with Bailey.

"Come with me."

She hesitated only for the briefest of seconds before following a fast-moving Bailey through the crowds. Once they got on the subway to Eglington Avenue, which would drop them off near the office, Tarin turned to her. "What's going on?"

"I think that's my question."

"Why are you following me? Because there is no way I'm going to believe that was a chance occurrence. Was that Guy?"

Bailey stared at her hard before nodding. Now at least she knew who her knight in shining armor was. Sitting back, she closed her eyes, but the gentle swaying of the car was making her sick—or maybe it was the realization of what was happening to her settling in. She clasped her hands in her lap, trying to still their shaking. A warm hand clasped them.

"It's okay. Just take some deep, slow breaths. That's it. A few more. Okay, I can see some color coming back to your cheeks."

Tarin managed a smile of gratitude. "Thank you."

"Who wants to kidnap you?"

"I don't know."

"Who wants to take your son?"

"How—?" She should have known Graham wouldn't keep it to himself. "I don't know."'

"I think whoever grabbed you had a reason."

"Look, my life is boring. Nothing interesting has ever happened."

"You don't think your husband might have taken offense to you taking off with his son?"

Heat flooded her cheeks, but she refused to look away. "It's not—Stephen is many things, but I don't believe he's behind this."

"What about your father, Mr. Madsen, owner of C-Lite Hotels?"

"Is there anything you don't know about me?"

"That's it. That's all I've been filled in on so far. Is there more we should know?"

"You may have had a pristine life, growing up on a winery—"

Bailey snorted and then laughed. "My life was anything but."

"I know it's pathetic to complain about not having a great childhood when your father had nearly as much money as Bill Gates. But let me tell you, I haven't spoken to my father in—"

"Three years."

Tarin's mouth dropped open.

"And you got fired for—no, you quit for some reason."

"Christ. You guys don't leave any stone unturned, do you?"

"Hey, I'm not the private investigator; that's Guy and Graham."

At the mention of Graham, she was glad she was seated as all her remaining energy drained out of her. *Chance. I left him with Graham.*

"So now what?"

"Now we go to the office and figure out what's going on."

Though she wanted nothing more than to flee, the option was no longer open to her, or she'd never see her son again. A fleeting thought that maybe he'd be better without her crossed her mind. The gut-wrenching fear and anguish that shot through her system convinced her she couldn't live without him.

"Hey. If you want my honest opinion, I don't think you're the villain here. I've done pretty well on my gut instincts, and they're telling me you're not the guilty party."

Tarin didn't respond but stared out the window. The blur was exactly how she was feeling inside. Nothing made sense, nothing had any definition, and there didn't seem to be any end to this ride.

CHAPTER 51

"SHE'S TALKING TO SOMEONE about selling the winery. You need to stop that."

"What do you want me to do?"

"Watch her. Better yet—" It was time, way past time, to end this. "Do away with her."

"And how would you like me to do that? Poison? Shooting? Stabbing? Torture? A bomb?"

"All sound enticing, but I want to send a clear message. I want her to know the enemy she faces." He issued his orders with calm and cool resolve. Soon everything would be perfect. Dorothea would know who was trying to get her attention.

****

"What the hell were you thinking?" It was the last thing Graham had intended to say, so he was nearly as surprised as she was when he did.

"I'm trying to figure things out."

"And you couldn't tell me?"

"Right," she snorted before brushing her hand lightly over her son's sleeping head. "I'm not behind this crap that's happening to Knights Associates." Tarin marched to his desk and sat at his computer.

Bailey had brought her up a few minutes prior and then disappeared. Now he wished she hadn't. He wanted to shake Tarin until she understood the gravity of her situation. His hands curled into fists at his side. He was so tense he was almost vibrating. Stepping back he kept his eyes glued to her every movement. Figuring it would take her a while to break into his laptop, he glanced out the window at the darkened, deserted street.

"The truth? I believe you. I'm just not sure if that makes me an idiot," he said in his best Elmer Fudd voice, "or someone in—" Realizing what he'd been about to say, he clamped his mouth shut.

"Come here."

He strolled to his desk, intending to enter his password, but he found that not only had she already hacked into it but she'd accessed the company's emails. His jaw dropped as he wondered if he'd spoken too soon.

She was scrolling through his messages, pointing out source code as she went. Her fingers were nimble and her observations rapid-fire, obviously taking for granted that he was with her. Leaning in closer, he tried to follow the code.

"I don't see what you're seeing."

She turned to speak to him, only to draw in a quick breath. His gaze caught hers before he quickly looked away. Way too dangerous to go there, especially when he still had no idea if he could trust her. The next time he looked at the monitor, she had scrolled back to the beginning and had started her explanations again, more slowly.

"This, this, and this one are all sent from the same IP address."

Graham gave her his get-real expression. The smirk she wasn't hiding, was off-putting but woke him up. She was deliberately talking to him slowly as though he were dimwitted. The last vestiges of tension left his body. Later, he'd figure out where they stood; for now, they needed to identify who was scamming Knights Associates and, more importantly, who wanted Tarin dead or alive.

She opened the other emails he'd forwarded to her, explaining what she'd discovered and what she suspected. Patterns emerged; there was consistency in the source, the format, the similar design of some websites. He was about to say something, but she was staring straight ahead not focused on what was in front of her.

She started clicking on a dozen of the other twenty she had opened, skimming through them. That's when he understood things had progressed beyond similarities. Four had identical sites containing duplicate information. The names were almost the same as well.

John Templar
Don Templor
Sean Templur
Juan Templer

It didn't make any sense. Their culprit was getting lazy. Why?

"Graham."

He was standing so close behind her, peering into the screen, that when she turned, her nose came almost to rest against his chest. His body instantly responding to the sweet floral scent of her hair. Thankfully, she was doing better at controlling her urges than he was.

She quickly turned back to her computer and pointed at the screen. "These four sites are almost identical. Why would someone go to the trouble of developing fictitious sites without attempting to hide the fact that they're fake? Look at the names. They're ridiculous." She checked another business. "Same name, different extensions. It's so obvious."

His hand landed on hers, taking over the mouse as she casually slid hers out from under his. He was already clicking through multiple screens, aware of her every movement, yet he couldn't take his eyes off the monitor. The answer was there. It had to be.

"This is insane. Not only are these obvious, but I just discovered the IP address of this jerk. Is this a trap?"

Tarin turned around. "It could be. What could they gain by sending us on cat and mouse games?"

"When we started working for the feds, they made us jump through hoops to analyze how we handled information, what we could figure out and how good we were. It took us about four weeks to figure it all out. In fact, we got so good at it that we could anticipate what they were going to do. It drove them nuts, but they hired us. So if this is someone's ploy to hire us, why so much? Why make it almost impossible for us to keep up?"

"Are they trying to keep you away from something else?"

He scowled. That question had come up before, and yes, he was certain she was right, but he still didn't know who or why. The fact that Oliver's computer was a bust still frustrated him, and now the man had taken a long overdue holiday. It could be awhile before he got some answers.

"There's a code I need to ask you about." She pulled up the ones from Caspian Winery. "What does this mean—the number and letters?"

"I'm assuming it's their billing numbering system."

"Can you find out?"

"Sure. I'll ask Dorothea."

"This is no life for Chance. It's got to be someone good with computers. My dad's good on one. After all, he taught Bobbie. God, this has to end," she muttered to herself.

"What?" His cell phone rang.

"Graham. I managed to tackle him, but he got away. However, I did pilfer a business card from his pocket. C-Lite Hotels."

Tarin's dad.

"I should have known he'd be behind this." Tarin's shoulders slumped.

Graham wandered into the outer office; he didn't want her to overhear any more of the conversation than she had.

"Man, can this get any crazier?"

"Hang on; Bailey's calling me."

Graham stared into space, his mind grasping for answers. A moment later, Guy returned.

"Someone's trying to sandbag our wedding. We hadn't received RSVP's from a lot of the guests. Bailey's been

on the phone constantly about whether invitations had
been sent. Well, it turns out a mail sorter stored a bunch
of them in his garage. It's a total fluke they were found.
He'd reported a burglary two nights ago, and when the
police investigated, they found our invites. He confessed
to having been paid to steal them and says he doesn't know
who hired him—cash under the table—the money was
good, and he thought it harmless."

"This is crazy."

"I'll pick up Bailey and we'll be in. Anything new on
your end?"

"No. But we may need the big guns. We're in way over
our heads. Since Tarin has arrived, nothing has gone right."

"I understand. See you soon."

He returned to his office to be met by Tarin's dark and
disturbed expression.

"So, I'm guilty again." Tarin climbed to her feet, walked
over to her son and picked him up. He snuggled in close.

Graham stepped in her path to stop her. "Look, if you
heard what I said—"

"Do you mind?" She tried to sidestep him, but he
mimicked her movements, as though they were dancing
a waltz without touching.

"Get out of my way."

"No. Let me explain."

"Why? It's true. Things have gone to crap since I arrived. They aren't going to get any better until I get answers."

"Give Chance to me; he's heavy." He plucked her son
from her arms before she could protest. Then he strode
across the room and put him down. When he turned back,
he was shocked to discover she'd left. He raced to the
outer door just as the sound of her shoes tapping on the
stairs faded and she disappeared from view. Letting her go
was not an option, but he couldn't leave her son alone.

What the hell?

Fifteen minutes later when Guy and Bailey arrived, he had done so many laps of the office, pacing back and forth. He was ready to punch walls.

"She's gone," he said as soon as they entered.

"Where?"

"No idea. She raced out of here, and by the time I could get Bill up here to babysit, she was long gone."

"Let's look at what we do know. The wedding, the winery and our business are all being targeted. Unfortunately, we all have a common enemy—if he is still alive. The question is where Tarin fit into all of this?" Guy sat at Graham's desk and started tapping away at keys. "Have you looked at this?"

Both Bailey and Graham crowded in behind him. Tarin had left open all the emails, the websites, the things she'd googled. Guy rapidly flipped through them.

"Before you called, she was asking about a code on Caspian Winery bills. Why would she want to know that?"

"I should have looked at her emails. Dammit, that didn't even dawn on me."

"You're going to hack her account?"

"I don't have much choice." Graham didn't mention he'd done it before. He waved Bailey over. "She left this message on my laptop."

Keep Chance safe. I'll be back as soon as I have answers.

If I don't return, please follow this link.

I'm sorry. T

CHAPTER 52

TARIN KNEW TWO PLACES she had to try, though she wasn't ready to go near one of them. She drove for almost two hours before she pulled into a hotel's parkade. She headed for the spaces reserved for executives, knowing she shouldn't, but it didn't stop her from parking there, anyway. On impulse, she dug through her purse and pulled out a permit with similar colors but for another hotel chain and hung it from the mirror, hoping no one would look too closely.

The dim lights attempted to cut the shadows in the darkened garage, but they weren't enough to stop her from glancing over her shoulder. Her subconscious played games with her, turning silhouettes into assailants and the average passerby into someone who might ask her what the hell she was doing there after all this time. Her nerves were strung taut as she made her way into the hotel. The dark earth tones and buttery light cast a warm and inviting ambiance. She hoped that was the reception she was going to get.

Brushing her hand down her wrinkled skirt, she took a deep breath, tossed back her hair, pointed her chin in the air and made her way down the short hallway to the desk. "Hi. I'm here to see Mr. Cooper."

"I'm sorry, but he doesn't—"

"Please don't. Tell him that Tarin Roth—Madsen is here to see him."

She didn't have to wait long before she was ushered to a private back elevator and escorted to the top floor. Her hands were clamped together so tightly she wasn't sure she could pry them open to knock on the lone door.

"Hmhm."

The sound of the security guard behind her reminded her she wasn't alone. Closing her eyes, she rapped on the solid oak door. Even though no timepiece was present, she was certain she could hear the incessant ticking of the old Howard Millar grandfather clock that used to grace the foyer at home. The door swung inward, and it was only then that what she was doing hit her like a sledgehammer. She was going to ask someone she'd never met to help her. It was a shock when an old man opened the door, his full cap of snow-white hair crowning a relatively long, lean frame. Piercing hazel eyes, like hers, stared back at her. There was no sound. No air. No movement. Nothing but the man in front of her, who appeared as stunned as she.

"Oh, my beautiful girl." She was enveloped in two benevolent, solid arms.

She wrapped hers tentatively around him, but when he made no indication, he was going to let her go; she held him tighter. Eventually, he pulled back, and unashamed tears coursed down his face, getting lost in the wrinkles only to find their way to his chin and drip into his open collar. She reached up to brush them off his cheek before she recognized the motherly reflex. Before she could jerk her hand back, he clasped it in his, thwarting her intent to pull away. The most beautiful smile ever directed at her lit his face.

"Come in. I'm sorry for making you stand in the hallway."

Within minutes, an assistant served tea and muffins fresh from the oven. Not realizing how hungry she was, she'd downed two before she remembered her manners. She set down the little that was left, daintily wiped her face and hands with the lace napkin and folded it neatly beside her cup. She sat forward on the edge of the couch; one ankle crossed over the other, and her hands clasped in her lap.

He sighed heavily. Startled, she looked at him. He was watching her closely.

"I know I shouldn't have barged in here. I'm sorry. But I—"

"Don't. I know what you want. You need me to kick my son's butt; something I should have done a long time ago. I am so sorry to have been absent from your life."

"I didn't come here, Mr.—" The sorrow in the depths of his eyes was almost her undoing. "I—I don't know what to call you."

"Grandfather would make me happy."

"All right, Grandfather." The term stumbled on her tongue, a simple word with such a complex significance. With shaky fingers, she reached for her tea. "I need your help, but I don't know if you're the right person to grant my request."

"What has that son of mine done now?"

She'd carefully studied all she could about her grandfather over the years. Everything she'd read about him depicted him as an honorable, hardworking man, fair with his staff. Well-liked. But then the media sometimes portrayed her dad that way as well; all they published was not accurate.

"I haven't talked to Father in several years. I need you to know that upfront. We had a falling out, of sorts."

"Probably similar to the one we had thirty-some years ago. It was a few years before you were born. As soon as I learned about you, I tried to mend fences, but he used you as a pawn to control me. Ultimately, I knew it would hurt you, so I walked away. It was the toughest day of my life."

She had to blink back the tears in response to the devastated emotion in his voice.

"He was such a smart-mouthed kid, always wanting to best me. He didn't want to work with me; he wanted to crush me. I don't know why. His mother—your grandmother, God rest her soul, was such an enabler. I wasn't home much, so I suppose I became the target of his anger."

A sad smile curved his lips. "I tried to see you over the years, but he told me if I didn't stay away, he'd make certain I never saw you again. So, I waited, hoping he'd change his mind."

Someday, perhaps the two could compare stories about all the things her father had done, but right now she couldn't waste time going down that road. When he paused for breath, she said, "I need your help." Once she started, she couldn't seem to stop. She told him everything, including things she'd never told another living soul, including about Chance.

He listened without interruption. Nothing she said seemed to phase him, although her cheeks felt as if they would burst into flames born of embarrassment. When she'd finished, he stood and opened his arms wide. The years seemed to roll back as she rushed into them, the little girl who'd always dreamed of familial love. The minutes ticked past as they held each other. Then eventually, they sat side by side on the divan while he made a telephone call.

"Dorothea. We have a bit of a situation. You recall our discussion last week about the sale of your winery? Right. Okay. We'll be there first thing tomorrow morning. What? He's there. Okay. I'll tell her. Thank you. Bye."

Tarin tried not to eavesdrop, but since she was right beside him, it was impossible not to.

"I'm sure you heard Chance is at the estate with Dorothea. He'll be safe there."

"But I left him—" A sob ripped through her, preventing her from continuing.

"My dear, you made the most difficult decision a parent could make. But I think it was a smart one. You found someone you could trust."

"I don't know him. Them."

"Your indoctrination, no doubt, was unmitigated under my son's tutelage." He winked at her and smiled. "But it's good to know you overcame that to follow your gut instincts. I've known Dorothea for a very long time, and

I would trust her and her family with my life. She is the best of friends but she is certainly one lady that cannot be trifled with. You can call in an hour to speak with your son. Graham is tending to his bath at present."

Though she tried not to react when he mentioned Graham's name, his shrewd perusal made her realize he had seen right through her. Her cheeks felt so heated, she was certain they were crimson, but he only beamed in response.

"Our plan for this evening, my darling, is to have a warm, relaxing dinner followed by a full night's sleep, for tomorrow we have work to do."

"You knew Dad was trying to take over the winery?"

"Let's say it had come up recently."

"We can't let that happen."

****

"You were right. She arrived at Cooper-Lite Hotels to see her grandfather."

He clenched his fists. At least he finally knew her location. "Thank you. Good job. Keep an eye on her." He'd also just learned that Dorothea was meeting with Guy, Bailey and Graham. The timing couldn't be better to take out all of those who had tried to ruin him.

CHAPTER 53

SHE FELT LIKE A prisoner entering an interrogation room with all eyes upon her. Hers were locked onto only one pair. Graham stood, bringing her son, who was happily snuggled in his arms.

"Mommy."

She laughed as she pulled him to her chest and hugged him. It was the longest she'd ever been separated from him. She'd awakened her grandfather at 4:00 a.m., but he said he'd forgiven her because he understood a mother's instinct to reunite with her son. Chance wrapped his tiny arms around her neck and squeezed tight. The joy she felt reminded her that what she was doing was for him. For them.

"So this is my—"

Tarin spun around and shook her head at her grandfather before furtively glancing at the others. "Mr. Cooper, I'd like you to meet Chance."

"Calib. Please. Hello there, young man." The two of them beamed at each other like they were already the best of friends.

"I'll talk with you later," he said to the others but before they could respond, he left.

A fit, smiling woman who looked to be only slightly older than Tarin entered from a side room. She immediately started engaging with Chance, who clearly loved all the attention.

"I'm Amanda. I'm going to watch your son while you're in the meeting."

Tarin clutched Chance a little tighter. "I—"

"It's fine," Graham said. "The woman has her early childhood education, several years of experience and a black belt in karate. Besides, there's a window here that lets you watch everything they're doing. The only exit is through here." He opened a panel over a large window into the small but well-equipped playroom. It helped to ease her fears, especially when she noticed Chance was already leaning toward the woman. Reluctantly, Tarin let him go and watched as Amanda playfully chased him into the play area. He laughed and giggled as he ran as fast as his little legs could carry him.

Tarin pressed her hand to her heart, unable to tear her eyes away from them.

"He'll be fine."

Graham placed his hand in the center of her back. Though it helped to steady her, she stepped away from him when she discovered the others' questioning eyes upon them.

"Everyone will tell their story. What they know, what they think and who it might be." The authority in Dorothea's voice brooked no argument as she entered the room on Calib's arm.

Tarin's eyes met her grandfather's as he gave the slightest of nods. He trusted them implicitly, but she didn't and couldn't share her darkest moment with them. Not in that way. She shook her head with barely a hint of movement, but the widening of his eyes let her know he understood. There was deep empathy in his expression; he'd stand behind her either way.

Somehow, this entire chain of events was linked to her. How she'd brought it to these people she didn't understand, but there had to be some connection. Looking at her grandfather and then at Dorothea, she wondered if she was mistaken and it wasn't actually her father behind it. Fighting back a nervous wave of nausea, she moved to the center of the room.

Tarin sighed heavily. "Everything I've found appears to be tied to Caspian Winery. I don't know why. I don't know if I've brought this on—"

"You didn't," Graham's response was immediate.

The conviction in his voice nearly had her believing him. She glanced at him, thankful for his presence, but she didn't want to be distracted. She picked up a felt pen and turned to a large flip chart set up at the front of the room. She quickly divided the page into quarters. In one quadrant she wrote *Caspian Winery*, in another *Knights Associates*, in another her name, and she left the last one empty. Bailey walked up, took the felt from her and wrote her name in the fourth square. Tarin frowned as she watched her, but Bailey was busy writing bullet points.

Geoff
Abduction
Kidnapping
Explosion
Dead?

Tarin wasn't sure what to make of it, but everyone was nodding. Then she added,

Wedding
Sabotage???

Guy came up next. Under *Caspian Winery*, he wrote,

Vinegar wine
Hijacked loads
Staff issues
Geoff?

Graham filled in under *Knights Associates*.

Flood of requests
Tail chasing game
Someone has been hacked
Geoff?

Tarin wasn't sure what all of it meant, but she definitely wanted to learn more about Geoff. Under her name, she put.

Someone tried to take Chance
Someone after me

I left my husband
Poor relationship with my father

She was tempted to write Geoff to keep with the theme but didn't. She had no idea who he was or why they thought he'd be behind this.

"Could Geoff have survived that blast?" Dorothea spoke quietly, but it cast a silence over the entire room.

No one said anything for a very long time. Guy and Bailey looked at each other, obviously sharing similar thoughts but debating whether to voice them.

"Grandma," Guy said finally. "We don't think he died. We think he staged it. His garnet ring was the pinnacle because he never took it off. Wouldn't that be the perfect way to ensure everyone thought you were dead?" He looked at his grandmother apologetically.

Bailey sat beside Dorothea and clasped her hand.

"Who's Geoff?"

Dorothea whispered something to Bailey, who quickly rose and left the room.

"He's Dorothea's half-brother," Guy explained. "When Bailey was a baby, he abducted her to sell her on the black market."

Tarin couldn't hold back a gasp or prevent her mouth from hanging agape as she listened to Guy's story.

"We found her only two years ago and brought her home to meet her real family. Then Geoff tried to kill her. He wanted Caspian Winery and saw her as direct competition."

Tarin immediately looked at Bailey when she re-entered a minute later. Never would she have guessed this woman had been through something so devastating. She wondered what her life had been like. Sympathetic guilt must have shown on her face because Bailey gave her a slight nod and a warm look that she had no hard feelings. She was carrying a picture frame in her hands, and she handed it to Tarin. Frowning, she accepted it and turned it over. The sun was pouring in the picture windows behind her, so when it hit the framed photo, the glare made it difficult to decipher. She adjusted it a little.

The room darkened, and everything around her seemed to morph into an impressionist painting with no defined edges. Her fingers became numb as though they were completely disconnected from her. She couldn't feel the object slip from her hands but vaguely registered it shattering on the floor near her feet. Somewhere in the distance, someone called her name, but like a total eclipse, her world faded into blackness.

CHAPTER 54

"WHAT'S GOING ON?"

"I can't see much. You didn't tell me the place was locked down like Fort Knox."

"But they're there."

"Yes. All of them. Dorothea. The two you gave me pictures of and a few others."

"Who?"

"How am I supposed to know? You asked me to do away with her and her family, not get to know them. Just some people."

He laughed. Those who were trying to prevent him from executing his grand plan were going to pay and pay dearly. He didn't care who else was involved.

"You've got everything in place?"

"Working on it. You didn't give me much notice, you know. I need another half hour."

"Where are they?"

"In a room on the second floor."

"Perfect. Make sure you have time to get away; I don't want anyone discovering you by accident. Disappear. Your payment will be waiting in your bank account. Check your phone; I'm sending confirmation that it's been transferred. Don't screw up or you'll be joining them."

****

Voices floated in and out of Tarin's consciousness. They were near and then they were far. A gentle touch on her face had her turning her head to seek more of it. But then it was gone. She felt as if she were drifting on a cloud. There was no genuine connection to anything. No weight. No shape. Nothing. But then it would change. She could feel her body. Feel the headache tapping away at the inside of her skull. The one thing missing were thoughts. There was just awareness; fleeting images that danced elusively just out of her reach.

Something cool brushed her face before being placed across her forehead. This time she was instantly brought back.

"Hey. You okay?"

She didn't have to open her eyes to know it was Graham's low, soothing voice. Somehow, she'd known all along it was him there with her. Tempted to hide, but all that would accomplish was wasting time. Realizations of everything that had happened and everything she suspected came stampeding back and reminded her of why she'd blacked out in the first place.

"I'm all right. Sorry." She sat up. He instantly shifted some pillows behind her back. When she was upright, she glanced around the bedroom she found herself in. Everything was pristine white, from the bedcover she was resting on to the furniture, the walls and the curtains. Her eyes were drawn to Graham not only because he was the only color in the room but because she needed reassurance that she hadn't passed over to the other side. Although she was sure where she was going wouldn't be white. Fiery hot red maybe.

"I know it's a little overdone. Or underdone. I'm not sure what you call it but it's about as pure as you can find." He grinned at her.

That was the grounding she needed. It settled her insides like a shot of bourbon would do for others.

"What happened?"

"Too much stress. Not enough to eat. I don't know."

"Really? It seemed that picture had something to do with it."

"The sun was glaring off it. I could barely see it." She held his gaze and prayed the morsel of truth in the statement would hold up against all that she was withholding from him. "Where's Chance?"

"He's fine. I'll get him." He gave her a long look before getting up and disappearing.

He knows.

How could she tell him what she suspected; Dorothea's brother might be connected to her problem? It made her want to throw up. That nausea had been part of her life since the moment she woke up from that week she'd lost.

A few seconds later, the door was pushed wide and Chance came running through, chortling and babbling as he ran. Graham was right behind him, pretending to catch him. Tarin smiled as her son launched himself at her, only to scramble across the bed in a gleeful dash to get away from Graham. It was heartwarming and heartbreaking at the same time. She'd been the only one in his life for so long that she felt a rare pang of jealousy. But the joy on her son's face soon pulled her out of her angst.

"I hate to break this up, but something's come up."

Graham swung Chance up in his arms and put him on his shoulders before turning to Guy. "Be right there."

Tarin was on her feet and moving out the door when he grabbed her. His probing eyes were searching for more than reassurance she was okay.

"Go, horsey." Chance's demand was the excuse she needed to move aside so he could pass her.

They all met in the large sitting room with leather sofas, beautiful artwork and intricate vases, curios she had nightmares about Chance grabbing. The photo that had caused her grief was gone, the shattered glass cleaned away. Her son accompanied Amanda enthusiastically into the playroom.

Her grandfather, who still gave her a shiver of excitement in realizing that connection, put his hand on her arm as she passed. He looked at her questioningly. She smiled reassuringly in a mute effort to tell him she was okay. He nodded before taking her arm and sitting beside her on the couch.

"I think we need to clarify a few things. First, to those that don't know me, Dorothea and I have been friends for a very long time. I think she stuck gum in my hair in first grade to get my attention. See, I had a horse and rode to school while she had to walk. She convinced me I needed to give her a ride every day. We've been good friends ever since."

Dorothea laughed. "Oh Calib. Let's not get started on the stories of who did what."

He grinned. "You're quite right. Now, to introduce myself properly. I'm Charles Cooper. I own the Cooper-Lite Hotel chain. But please, my friends, call me Calib. My son is James Madsen-Cooper, although he dropped the Cooper to spite me and then named his business chain, C-Lite Hotels."

There was a quickly drawn breath. Tarin looked at Graham to find him studying her. He knew who she was. She pursed her lips and turned away. She had done the same background investigation on him. Part of a blended family, he had two natural siblings, two step-siblings and two half-siblings.

"And this is my granddaughter."

Tarin knew she should have seen that coming, but she hadn't, and she wasn't prepared to reveal her identity to others. All eyes were focused on her, and she wanted nothing more than to act like a bug and scurry away. Since she couldn't do that, she squared her shoulders and raised her chin. Her grandfather squeezed her hand.

"I bring that up so everyone is clear who I am. I do not believe my son is behind any of this but to be honest, I know he's capable of some underhanded things."

It was Tarin's turn to return the reassuring gesture. Everyone began talking at once but Tarin tuned them out as she thought back to the photograph. *It couldn't be? Could it?*

She'd barely been listening when she heard them mention the wedding.

"I think that's a great idea. We'll do it next weekend. Just family. Then we'll have the formal services later. That should throw a kink into our perp."

Tarin wasn't sure what they were talking about. Were they changing their wedding from four weeks away to next weekend?

The keening cry of a young child would grab anyone's attention, but when it was a mother's child, she could hear the slightest peep from a mile away. So when Chance first whimpered, Tarin was on her feet and through the door. Amanda was kneeling in front of him, checking out his leg. His lip was sticking out, and big, fat tears filled his eyes.

"He tripped over the dump truck and fell. He banged his knee."

She lifted him into her arms. "I'm going to take him outside." She needed some air and Chanced was a good reason to take a break. "What's the most efficient way to get there? Grab a few toys, please."

She turned to leave and found Graham standing at the door watching them. "Great idea. Come on."

He suggested everyone follow and join them on one of the expansive verandas, as the sunshine and fresh air would do them all good. Tarin kept walking, and Graham caught up with her, leading her down the stairs, down a meandering hallway and out through a pristine kitchen the size of a magnificent room. Penelope, the tiniest, happiest woman she'd ever met, winked at them as they passed and said she would bring out their refreshments shortly.

The veranda was a large, stone-covered area that overlooked a pond and a man-made waterfall. Tarin strolled toward it in an effort to show Chance all the brightly colored fish when she discovered that despite his injury, he was almost asleep. Graham pulled out a chair for her, placing it in the shade of the umbrella, and helped her get comfortable. Guy and Bailey joined them, sitting close by. Dorothea and Charles soon followed with their heads together, talking quietly. They were both smiling and happy. Then Dorothea looked in her direction and stopped. Her face was glazed with shock as she slowly walked toward Tarin and Chance.

"Geoffrey?"

The words were barely out of her mouth when an explosion rocked the ground, causing the rocks arranged around the pond to scatter as though an earthquake had occurred, and as chairs tumbled over, Tarin saw Dorothea clutch her chest before she stumbled and went down on rickety knees. Calib tried valiantly to hold on to her, but as the windows blew out of the mansion above them and debris hailed down upon them, he was forced to let go to prevent landing atop of her. Graham instantly took his place, catching her and shielding her with his body. As events played out before her as if in slow motion, Tarin simultaneously dove for cover under the patio table, her primal instinct to protect Chance as debris rained down upon the table with such a ferocity that she was terrified it would collapse upon them.

As the dust settled, and they took stock, everyone sprang into action. Guy phoned the police, and Bailey rushed to Graham's side to check on Dorothea.

"We need an ambulance," she said as Guy repeated her words to the police dispatcher. "She's sweaty. Pulse is rapid. She's conscious, complaining of an ache in her shoulder." Though her words were deceptively calm, Tarin could see the panic in her eyes.

Graham knelt in front of her; his face etched with deep concern as members of the household staff and groundskeepers rushed to their side.

She was clutching Chance so tight that he felt a part of her. It took a moment for her to realize that his whimpers might be because he was hurt. She eased him back, her hands roaming over him. He cried out, snuggling tight against her, hiding his face against her chest. His thumb jammed back into his mouth. He was scared but seemed fine.

Several people were talking over one another excitedly. The tiny woman she'd passed in the kitchen let out a keening wail when she spotted Dorothea on the ground. She rushed over to crouch beside her. Dorothea grasped her with a hand, even paler and more fragile than before.

"Tarin, are you okay?" Her grandfather assisted her and Chance in climbing out from beneath the table. He cleared debris from the chair she'd vacated and helped to situate them, looking them both over for injuries.

Confident they were physically uninjured, he sat in another chair, pulling it close to hers. He was watching her so intently that she wondered if she was in fact injured. She ran her palm along her face, relieved it was covered in dust but no blood. What he said next made her thankful she had been sitting.

"Do you think your dad could have done this?"

CHAPTER 55

HOURS LATER, GRAHAM STOOD at the window staring out over the darkened street. The only time he'd taken his eyes from the window was to glance over his shoulder at Tarin and Chance, who were sleeping on the cot in his office. Though he'd briefly considered taking them back to his place, he determined the office to be more secluded. Since they had no idea who was behind this, he wasn't taking chances. Geoff had found his home once before.

Bill was canvassing the neighborhood on the lookout for anyone who didn't belong. He hadn't wanted to ask Bill for help, for he feared that something like this might just send him mentally back to Vietnam. But he had been more than determined.

The events of the day, which had never truly left his mind, came flooding back like a movie on fast forward, disjointed scenes and thoughts pushing their way to the forefront. Dorothea had suffered a heart attack and a few abrasions, but her prognosis was good, as long as she received plenty of bedrest and remained relatively stress free. Graham closed his eyes as exhaustion pulled at him and the realization that the clock was ticking; they had to figure out who was behind this—and fast. Whoever had blown up the room where they had been had meant to kill them. All of them.

If Tarin hadn't wanted to take Chance outside—

He cut off that thought for fear of the fate that had almost awaited them. Glancing at the two of them sleeping in the corner, he was beyond grateful that nothing had happened to them. The gnawing question was, how did she play into all this? Someone seemed just as eager to do away with her as with them. But why? How could she be connected to them?

He no longer believed she was behind their business disruption; it just didn't ring true. He tamped down an inkling of doubt that threatened at the corners of his mind. With one last look at the deserted street, he turned and sat at his computer.

He was missing something. He quickly made a list.

Crazy number of emails.
Tarin came to work for them.
Bad wine situation.
Tarin meets a woman only to be injured—her fault?
Wine hijacked.
Someone tried to abduct Chance.
Part of Dorothea's mansion is blown up.

He added several minor occurrences.

As he was skimming the list, one thing stood out loud and clear—something Tarin had said a long time ago. What if someone was trying to distract them? But from what?

The reminder he'd written to himself to go to Jaspers Menswear caught his attention. First because he still hadn't made it there, but secondly it reminded him of Guy's and Bailey's wedding. Was that the target? Geoff was reaching out from his grave to continue to make Bailey's life hell? Could it be some minion of his? Or was he still alive?

Following a hunch, he keyed in some information. He studied it for a while. It convinced him of one thing; he needed to get Guy. They had work to do.

He glanced at Tarin and Chance, who were still sound asleep. Not wanting to leave them, he had no choice; not if he was going to put an end to this. He scribbled a note and taped it to the inside of the door, which he gently closed behind him.

Bill will watch over them.

He called Guy and told him his plan—they needed to get back into that house Geoff had blown up two years before.

****

Tarin kept her eyes tightly closed, listening to Graham tap away at his keyboard and murmur out loud. Just listening to his voice made her want to smile. But she didn't. Because then he'd know she was awake. Every now and then she could feel his eyes on her. She resisted the urge to open hers, just to make sure, because now she had but one option open to her. He would inevitably ask questions, and she'd have to give him half-truths or evade them altogether. She couldn't tell him everything. At least not yet. Not that she knew everything—but she had a feeling there might know someone who did.

As soon as he was out the door, she climbed out of bed, careful not to disturb Chance, and raced over to his computer. He'd left it on but asleep, so she quickly typed in his password. Before she performed her own online search, she checked to see what he had been looking up. Graphic pictures filled the screen of an area that looked like a bomb had been dropped on it. Curious as to why he'd been looking at something so gruesome, she checked for an address. She was shocked to discover it was on Dorothea's property.

Tucking away that information, she quickly logged onto her site to see if she'd ever gotten a response from the woman who'd agreed to meet her. There was a message.

I'm sorry. I have to vanish. He's sick.

That was all she was able to read before the site froze up. Not knowing what else to do, she shut it down. She tried to log in again, but it wouldn't let her in. As she sat there contemplating what to do, her father kept knocking at her thoughts. *He couldn't have done that today. Could he?*

Her mind spun with what that meant. As she looked for a media story about the detonation at Dorothea's home, a headline grabbed her attention. Leading the Way convention was in town, which meant so was her father. He'd never missed one. Would trying to kill his daughter change that? She didn't think so. Global business leaders attended, so it was an opportune venue to mingle with potential clients. Since his hotel hosted it, he had every right to be there to schmooze with the bigshots.

Stop playing defense, Tarin; start playing offense. Take charge. His words echoed in her head. She needed to see him. Confront him. She had to see for herself if he was behind any or all of this. She didn't want to believe it... but she had to know. If he were, she had to stop him.

The softest of sounds reminded her she would need someone to watch Chance; someone she could trust. Someone who would lay down his life for her son. Feeling sick at having to leave him again, but he was safer there than with her. She had to end this deadly game now, or they'd always be looking over their shoulders.

She gently kissed her son on the forehead, praying that he'd sleep until dawn. Before leaving, she opened the cupboards, looking for anything for him to eat if he awakened. A box of rice puffs, his favorite, was a big surprise.

Graham had to have bought these. But when?

And there was milk in the fridge. Not having the time to question his motives, she said a silent thank you and headed down the stairs. Convincing Bill she had to leave was not going to be an easy task.

Squaring her shoulders, she slowly unlocked the door but had barely opened it six inches before he was blocking her exit.

"I need to go, Bill. I think I can stop all this."

"Graham said you're to stay."

"I know, but that was before he knew my father had suffered a stroke. I need you to watch Chance. If anything happens, call me."

He stared her down for a long time.

"Please. This might be the last time I get to see him. Please. I promise I'll be back as soon as I can."

He stepped back, letting her step into the murky streetlight. Impulsively, she reached up and kissed his dirty cheek. He immediately ducked his face.

"Please look after my son. Only Graham or I can take him. Okay?"

He nodded before slipping inside, letting the door close behind him. A second later, she heard the deadbolt sliding into place.

Thankful he hadn't asked any questions; she sped to her car and drove the fifty minutes to the hotel.

CHAPTER 56

TARIN PEEKED AROUND THE corner. The preconference crowd was starting to gather. Now she just had to wait until the one person she wanted to confront showed up, but she wouldn't have to wait long. He wouldn't want his adoring public to be without his presence.

It took longer than she had expected. She had to pretend for ten minutes that she was doing something and not just stalking the guests of the hotel. As soon as she spotted James Madsen, she stepped behind some people and watched him. The gray at his temples surprised her; he'd always kept his hair a perfect black. She was about to step out when she noticed a young woman dressed in a hotel uniform approach him. He stepped to the side to speak with her. Though Tarin was too far away to decipher his words, his tone was neither pleasant nor conciliatory, and she noticed the woman's face changed from shocked white to brilliant red before she walked away with clenched fists.

He hadn't changed; he remained a bully. Why she thought he might have undergone a transformation, she didn't know, but she made her way toward him despite the revelation. She noticed that his dark gray Italian silk suit was as crisp and perfect as though it had just been pressed. But since it was already almost 8:00 in the morning, he'd already had it on for hours. At least that was one thing she always remembered about him—impeccably dressed, always.

He glanced her way a couple of times. Though there was no sign of recognition, it could simply mean he was masked with his professional persona, a facade that concealed his penchant for picking out only those faces in the crowd that were likely to slingshot him to the top of one pinnacle or another. Then she remembered her hair hadn't been blonde for many years. It had been a reminder of her mother he hadn't been able to stomach.

Squaring her shoulders, she stepped forward ready for the inevitable battle of wills.

"Hello, Dad."

His head swiveled so fast it brought to mind the iconic head spinning scene in *The Exorcist* when Regan was possessed by a demon. For whatever reason, he had always been engrossed and mesmerized by the gruesome scene.

"Tarin. What a surprise."

"It is, isn't it? We need to talk."

"In case you haven't noticed, I'm busy."

"I know. I'm willing to have our father-daughter chat right here. I don't have anything to hide but I think you do." She'd always thought of him as a giant, so it surprised her to realize that she only had to look up slightly into his blue-gray eyes.

"I'll arrange a more private setting."

She watched as he made his excuses to titans whose opinions mattered to him. Then he found his sidekick Cal, whose expression was pure hate, which he turned her way. If he could spit daggers through his suspiciously narrow eyes, she was sure she'd just been attacked. She glanced around to see if anyone else had seen it, but no one else appeared to have noticed. When she turned back, he had a neutral expression pasted on. Her father finally returned and gestured for her to come with him.

She'd been reluctant to follow him into the elevator and up to a suite permanently designated for his use, but she did. And at some point, the anxiety she experienced wasn't because she feared him. That fear had been present for a good part of her life, but now their relationship would change forever, and it was highly unlikely to be a positive outcome.

He stared out the window for a moment before turning to her.

"So you think you can take off and then come crawling back when things aren't good? You want me to fix your mess?"

The muscles in her back instantly tightened to the point of cramping. She felt like a little girl again, accidentally soiling her panties because he'd taken too long to get her to the bathroom. Of course, he'd claimed it hadn't been his fault because he'd never admit any weakness, whereas in his eyes, she was one long series of faults. At that moment, she saw his tactic for what it was, to put her on the defensive. He had almost succeeded. Almost.

"Did you try to have me killed?"

"Always the drama queen, weren't you?" He sat, crossing his legs while he scrutinized her with disdain.

"Who's my mother?"

He sighed. "She died—"

"Bullshit." She wasn't sure who was more surprised. An insistent buzzing began in the back of her brain; her mind was on overload.

"And I have a half-sister. When did you plan to tell me about her? Or was it meant to be a deathbed confession?"

His permanent tan appeared to have lost a bit of its color. But he still said nothing. It was the only time she ever remembered him speechless.

Sickened by all she'd learned, she relished the new-found feeling of having bested him. She'd gone there for precisely that reason—to knock him off his pedestal. He'd rally back and volley a ton of accusations and hurtful insults but she wouldn't remain for any of it. Glowering at him, she hoped never to lay eyes on him again.

"What makes me feel particularly sorry for you is you'll never get to know your grandson. He's amazing." She turned to leave.

"What do you mean, grandson?" Her father stood as the remaining color drained from his face.

"Oh please. I know you have Calvin spy on every last detail. I'm sure he knows about this one."

"How old?"

She frowned. *What game is he playing?* His stunned expression looked so authentic. And although he was a consummate actor forever playing to the crowd, she had the impression he wasn't pretending.

"Two. And if you have someone attempt to abduct him again, I'll air your dirty laundry in every news outlet in the world. I doubt you or your business could survive that. And last but not least, stay away from Caspian Winery or I swear I'll go to the police. I'm sure they can dig up something to charge you with. I'll give them a lot to search for."

Though her legs were trembling so badly she wasn't confident they'd carry her out, she made her way to the elevator at the end of the hallway. She tried not to think about all that she had said until she could process it alone, away from his scrutiny. One thing, however, stood out clearly; she was convinced he was more affected by the threat to his hotel chain than anything she'd shared about herself.

As quickly as the doors opened, she stepped in and hastily pressed the lobby button. Closing her eyes, she leaned her head against the wall.

"Tarin, I see you're still trying to make my life difficult."

CHAPTER 57

ALL THE DEBRIS HAD been removed, and the burnt trees chopped down, but there was no hiding the huge crater left by the explosion. Ironically, one wall of the old house still stood. Graham's thoughts returned to that time, an urgent push to arrive in time to save Bailey. To pull her out of the house before Geoff blew it sky high.

How could he have survived that? And who else would have done the same thing to Dorothea's house?

Graham and Guy had been searching for some time for an escape route, checking for any depressions that might lead to an underground tunnel. They had dug about fifteen holes in an attempt to uncover a shaft. Graham tossed a shovelful to the side before jabbing the blade in the ground and leaning on the handle grip. Guy was still working away like a demon after his quarry.

"Good job, 'ol boy."

Guy swore before chucking a mound of dirt at him. Graham grinned as he dodged it. Guy copied his stance.

"Who said you could stop? Get crackin' man, we have work to do."

Guy grimaced before glancing around the area. "Come over here."

Graham made his way over to him.

"Okay. So, assume you're Geoff—"

"That would be a stretch."

They both peered at the remaining wall. There wasn't much to look at. Geoff had cunningly built a fortified house inside of an existing ramshackle structure. Graham hadn't paid much attention to the remnants of the wall emerging from the ground. He moved toward it. It was blackened and charred. With his shovel, he whacked it in a few places, Guy following suit. It was when Guy reached the bottom left-hand corner that they heard a distinct hollow tone. Using their shovels, they pried away at the wall. When the sturdy bricks would not give, they dug down a few feet. And there, buried underneath it all was a latch. As Guy reached for it, Graham raised his shovel like a baseball bat. It was times like these that he wished he still carried a gun.

Guy slowly lifted the heavy trapdoor, dropping it onto the ground behind the hole. Both peered into what appeared to be a well-fortified tunnel. Guy reached inside with his shovel, the implement disappearing into the blackness after only a few meters.

"Son of a bitch. He did get away."

"It appears that way."

"Everything with our business—the wedding, the explosion at Dorothea's... it all makes sense now."

CHAPTER 58

"CALVIN. WHAT DO YOU want?" She looked at a man only slightly older than herself but whose face and demeanor bore the brunt of a life lived on the edge. Dressed now in a dark suit and tie, he looked more like he was with the Secret Service, and not her father's right-hand man. His dyed jet-black hair, so much like her father's, was slicked back like a character in a '60s Brylcreem commercial. When she'd arrived home at twelve to discover him living in the guest house and acting as her father's bodyguard, he'd put her through an hour-long interrogation. He'd demanded she not upset her father while she was home for her Easter-week holiday.

"Oh, I've got what I want. Or at least some of it." He pulled out his cell phone and flashed it at her.

She gasped when she saw a picture of Chance at the park. "You. You tried to steal my son?"

"You should be more careful with him."

"You bastard." She flew at him like a lioness attacking her prey. Her nails ripped into his cheek while her heel slammed down on his foot.

He staggered back momentarily with the surprise of the attack, but it didn't take long for him to react. He grabbed a handful of her short hair and yanked her head backward, arching it at an awkward angle so her neck felt as though it might snap. His other arm wrapped around her waist, clasping her so tightly that she struggled to breathe.

"Where's your son?"

"I'm not—" She groaned in pain.

"Yes, you will tell me. Where is he?"

She knew exactly where her son was, but there was no way she was going to let him know.

"Why do you want him, Cal?"

"I told you my name is Calvin."

He punched the third-floor button. He wrenched her arm unnaturally behind her, and when the doors opened a moment later, he shoved her into the parkade. She struggled, swinging her free arm back and kicking backward with her left foot. He slammed her into the side of the wall, and she crumpled against it, almost sliding to the concrete floor but for his rough hands holding her upright. It was as if someone was flipping overhead lights on and off as objects came into fuzzy focus only to fade again. Trying to clear her head, she was grabbed and shoved into his car. A seatbelt was put on her, and duct tape was wrapped around her wrists and ankles. She'd managed to wrench her legs from his grip, but her efforts were too little, too late. From within her confines, she tried to swing about and kick him, but he was too fast. He slammed and locked the door on her. But that didn't stop her. She was able to unlock it, but he quickly locked it again with the remote control.He opened his door and stood with one hand on it. That's when she acted. She hit the unlock button, grabbed the handle with her two hands as they were still taped together and dove out. But he was just as fast. He grabbed the back of her clothing and yanked her back inside. She fought and struggled, but he slammed a beefy fist into the side of her face. Pain exploded in her head. Her brain ricocheted against her skull, leaving her feeling woozy. Despite somewhere in that pain, her mind was still urging her to get out, but she had no strength. She slumped in her seat.

Simultaneously, time stood still, and time sped up until they pulled in front of Bobbie's house. Tarin's first instinct might have been relief except for the painful memories of all she'd discovered about her friend.

"So, are we going in together for your son?"

"'No."

"Well, let me—"

"He's not there."

He stared at her before turning around and pulling away. The split second of relief instantly gave way to alarm. Where the hell was he taking her? She didn't have long to wait. He parked in the office parking lot. Panic set in. He knew a lot.

It was late in the day, and traffic had died down; pedestrians had vanished. As soon as he climbed out, she began her struggle, desperately using her teeth to chew at the tape like an animal caught in a trap. Her efforts only tightened the tape, turning it into a twisted rope. She had only pulled a few strands out by the time her door was jerked open and she was pulled out. Unable to move quickly enough, she flung her arms out as she felt herself tumbling and sending Cal off balance. With a primal reaction, she snapped her legs straight, propelling herself out the door and driving her shoulder into his stomach. He jerked forward at the waist, and she wiggled her body reflexively like a fish violently catapulting through the water. It was enough to send him flying backward.

"Ooomph." The wind was knocked out of her as she landed hard on top of him. With superhuman effort, she forced herself to her feet and vaulted toward the car. With Cal still lying on the sidewalk, she grabbed her bag, emptying its contents onto the seat.

Reaching for her phone, she hit the speed dial for the office. "Bill, please answer. Bill, please answer."

"Hello. Leave your message."

Her words tumbled over one another. "Please help me. I'm in the parking lot. Cal has me. He wants Chance—"

The connection abruptly ended, and the groan behind her served as an urgent reminder that she needed to get moving. She bit into her ties with the ferocity of a starving coyote. Tiny strands tore into shreds, but the binding held.

"Here."

Her body nearly spasmed at the voice at her ear. She spun around to see Bill's scruffy beard and a knife he held out to her. She held out her arms and then her legs as he quickly sliced through the tape.

"Thank you." She jumped to her feet and gave him a quick hug. His cheeks turned ruddy. He ducked his head when she pulled back.

"Ooohhh." Cal moaned.

"Bill, we've got to get him into the office. I need to interrogate him before we turn him over to the police. Can you help me?" Before she could even move, Bill had hefted a still-dazed Cal and rushed into the building and up the stairs like a soldier carrying an injured comrade in the heat of battle.

Following, she quickly strapped Cal to a chair with the same duct tape he'd used on her. Once she ensured he was securely contained, she tossed a glass of cold water in his face.

"What the hell?" he spluttered as his chin came up.

"Glad to see you're awake, Cal. Now you're going to give me some answers."

"Like hell I am."

Tarin glanced at the closed door where Bill safely had Chance in her office, while she used Graham's. Though anytime Graham or Guy had a meeting in there, she'd never been able to hear them, she wondered how soundproof the walls were. As she turned back to Cal, her eyes rolled over the phone on the desk. She'd arranged with Bill to call the police as soon as she hit the intercom buzzer.

"Oh, but you are." She held up Bill's knife, raking it along Cal's cheek. "Did my father put you up to this?"

"Yes, it was his idea."

That sounded like BS.

"What was he hoping to gain?"

"Your child, of course. He had always wanted a son. You, if anyone, should know that."

"But I thought that's the role you were filling, his prodigal son?"

"I am, in every way that matters."

"And what did he want with my child?"

"Blood is always thicker," he spat. His lip curled, and his eyes flashed with rage. Spit hung at the corner of his mouth.

"Ah yes. And you're not related, are you? You're just some schmuck my father took off the streets. I guess you didn't realize you weren't of any lasting value to him?"

"That's bullshit!"

"Nope. True. Really? You think you hold a special place in my father's life?"

"You don't, you're a girl. He never wanted a girl. Said you were useless to him. He needed an heir. A man."

"Did he hire you to steal my child?"

But Cal was done. His face was now red and puffed up. She stepped back slowly until she was within arm's length of the computer keyboard. "Did he hire you? Or was it your idea, so you'd remain the prodigal son?" She clicked record on the laptop. His eyes were focused on the far wall.

"I did everything for him. I was going to save him from a leech he didn't even know existed."

Tarin stared at him. His meaning was clear, and she struggled with a mother's wrath at his reference to Chance.

"I'll make sure he knows the little bugger exists before I do away with the both of them."

She was tempted to hit the intercom buzzer but couldn't just yet. She just had to keep herself from strangling the lowlife who had dared threaten her son before she got answers.

CHAPTER 59

"OKAY, BAILEY IS LOOKING after Grandma at one of Calib's hotels. It seems to be the safest place for her right now. Detmier will keep an eye on them both. The police will keep them under surveillance."

Graham fired up the Hummer and pulled out of the parking lot. "No response from Tarin. Bill said she left because her dad had a stroke, which sounds awfully fishy to me. If that son of a bitch has her—"

"We'll find her. Don't worry. Where to first?"

"Let's head back to the office and get a plan together—and make sure Dorothea is safe. Now that we know Geoff could have survived the blast two years ago... we should have known he had it planned. He'd have arranged an escape route. What a sick bastard. Who kills someone else and plants them, so they'll be mistaken for you? He's got to be behind all this." Graham stomped on the gas pedal, squealing tires as he pulled away from the curb.

****

The door flew open, cracking against the wall with such a loud bang that Tarin dove for cover behind Graham's desk.

Chance!

She peeked around the side of the desk. There was no one there. Unsure where they had gone, she decided to make a run for it. She had to find her son. Staying crouched, she ran. She'd barely made it through the door when an arm snaked around her, halting her. Going on instinct, she brought the heel of her shoe down on his foot and her elbow upwards toward his jaw.

"Jesus, Tarin."

The hold loosened a tiny bit, but it was enough. She dropped downwards, sliding through his grip. She could feel his arm sliding past. Freedom. But he recovered just as quickly, managing to wrap both arms around her and scoop her off her feet.

"No. You son of a bitch. You low life. Let me go. I'll—"

A hand was soon clamped over mouth. She bit down hard.

"Tarin! Will you stop!"

She wasn't sure whether it was the fact that he'd been saying her name that got through to her, his masculine scent or the three pairs of eyes that were staring at her. Guy with a raised eyebrow. Bill, who was covering her son's ears as best he could. But her gaze immediately rested on Chance, who was snuggled up against Bill, watching her but very content with where he was. He was fine. She went limp as all the energy and the fight went out of her.

"Hey, you okay?"

Tarin barely nodded as she stepped into Graham's embrace, wrapping her arms around his waist and resting her head against his chest. The steady beat of his heart was the tonic she needed.

How long she stood there in the cradle of his arms, she wasn't sure, but it felt like time had stopped. She was safe. Chance was safe. And for that short period of time, nothing in the world was going to get to her. Pushing back, she looked up. Graham kissed her long and hard before gently setting her back from him. She reached for the doorframe as she watched him stride across the room and take a sleepy Chance from Bill. He brought him over to her.

She should have known Bill would call Graham.

Taking her child from Graham's arms, she held him for a minute, but he was ready to get down. Bill had set up some toys in the corner. As soon as she set him down, he toddled over to them. Bill squatted beside him. She watched for a moment, but then she heard the distinct scrape of a chair. Striding into the inner office, she glared at the man she was sure had been trying to destroy her life. Wanting to punch him, she chose instead to clench her fists and burn off some energy by walking back and forth a few feet in front of him. Cal's eyes tracked her every movement. And every now and then he'd jerk, making the chair grate along the floor.

"So, Cal. The men in the next room are ex-military. Ex-Navy SEALs who are good at torture techniques." She slowly circled him. Finally, she stopped and leaned in close. "What's it going to be, me or them?"

His expression became immobile, his eyes dark and hardened. She pushed back and made her way toward the door. He made a grunting sound, and she glanced over her shoulder to find him making head-tossing motions.

She stepped back and, without warning, ripped the tape off his lips. Tears immediately filled his eyes, which he blinked frantically to clear.

"My father never knew you were doing this, did he?"

He glared at her.

"It was all your idea. You're the one who wanted to take Chance?"

Defiant, he held her gaze.

"You're the one who wanted to abduct me? What were you hoping to gain? Kill me? And then what? My father might not like me, but I don't think he wants me dead. Might be bad for business." She doubted that. In fact, she was quite sure he'd use it to his advantage.

His sullen face never changed.

"So, I guess when the police get the arrow that would have killed me had I not dodged it, they won't have any problem lifting your fingerprints. I wonder how much fun jail is these days, for a young good—"

"Screw off. I never shot anything at you."

"Come on, Cal, I have it. I know you did it. I just want to know if my father knew what you were doing. You have to the count of five. One. Two. Three. Four—"

"He only had you to have an heir. And then you turned out to be a girl. All that money spent and he couldn't even get a son."

"What do you mean, all that money spent?"

"He hired a chick to have you. Once you were born, he paid her, and she split. Pissed of course, because he only paid her a quarter of what she'd have gotten had you been a boy."

The room spun ever so slowly. She reached behind her for something to hold onto but her hand vaguely waved in space. She closed her eyes for a second, but the scraping of the chair had them flying open again. He was trying to lunge at her. He'd managed to get one of his feet loose from where it had been bound to the leg of the chair. She sidestepped just in time, and he landed face first.

Graham, Guy and Bill rushed in. Graham didn't pause to ask questions. He immediately grabbed Cal and flipped him upright as though his weight was inconsequential and then got right in his face.

"I am going to enjoy dealing with you."

If her mind hadn't been in turmoil over Cal's words, she might have laughed at the look of horror that crossed his face.

"Are you working with Geoff?"

As Guy and Graham interrogated him, she went to her office and sat at her computer. Bill and Chance were playing cars in the corner, which seemed so out of place with what was going on. Shaking her head, she quickly logged into her site to find several messages. Six were new women sharing their stories, while only one had some similarity to hers. She skimmed the rest, several of which were spam. It was on the second page of messages that she spotted the one she was looking for. It was from the woman who had planned to meet with her at the restaurant but had never showed or responded to any emails. Fingers shaking, she clicked on it.

Sorry I didn't show, but someone doesn't want me to share my story. I feel like I've been followed since I had my daughter four years ago. She died two years ago, but that feeling won't go away. I have to disappear. I can't help. Good luck.

"Noooooo." Tarin propped her elbows on the desk and dropped her head into her hands. Frustrated yet feeling she was so close, she considered how she would ever find out the truth about what had happened to her three years before.

Her cell phone vibrated, and she reached for it. It was a text from Stephen, who had been surprisingly silent.

You've upset him. He wants his child.

Tarin almost heaved. Since she no longer had to worry about contact with her father, she flung the cell phone against the wall and watched it break into several pieces. Graham rushed from the inner office but stopped when he saw the pieces sprawled across the floor.

"Testing your pitching arm, I see." He gave her a slight nod before going back into his office.

That small gesture made her feel so much better, almost stunning her with the impact it had on her emotions. Feeling energized, she opened several more emails. There were about ten more to go through when she decided she'd open one more. Randomly, she picked one and clicked on it.

Next time I won't miss.

She stood and strode purposefully into the other office. Guy and Graham were sitting on their desks. She walked right up to Cal, who was sitting in the chair, his head hanging down. She slapped him hard.

"What the hell?" he said as his head reared back.

She grabbed his shirt in her hands. "You ever threaten me again or come near me or my son, I'll kick your ass, with my seven-inch spikes down Freeway 401. And then

I'll ram that arrow up your butt and drop you over Niagara Falls."

Graham and Guy laughed.

"I never threatened you. I didn't try to kill you either. I just tried to kidnap you."

Graham was at her shoulder in an instant, but she ignored him. "It's bad enough you shot an arrow at me, but you send me an email telling me you won't miss again?" She was breathing so hard, her hands so tightly clenched in his shirt, she wasn't sure she would be able to unclench them.

"I never shot at you!"

"Like hell—"

"I never did. I don't even know how to shoot a bow, let alone load an arrow into one. Check my history; the most active thing I've ever done was run from the cops."

She stared at him, trying to decide if she should believe him. She released him and stepped back, never taking her eyes off him.

"He's telling the truth about that. He's got a juvenile record a mile long." Graham had obviously taken him seriously.

"How did you get that information? It's supposed to be sealed."

Graham tore his attention away from her to smile wickedly at Cal.

"But if it's not you, then who?"

"I swear it's not me. I don't like you, and I don't like that your father would drop me in a snap but I never tried to kill you." The way he stared at her defiantly contradicted his words. Not only had he thought about it but he would do it. But this seemed too distant; he'd want to be up close and personal, so she'd have no doubt who was doing away with her.

"What do you do for my father? Besides beating the crap out of people?"

He sat up straight. "I'm his personal security. No one gets near him without going through me. I help negotiate deals. I keep his life simple. But I don't kill people."

As she looked at him, his tough outer shell seemed to fall away and she saw instead a young, frightened man, who had thought his life had changed because her father had taken him in, trained him, taught him how to be a shark in business. Only he never got past being his lackey, his muscle. Depressed at how many people her father had hurt, she gestured for Graham and Guy to follow her out.

"I'm sorry about all this. I swear I wasn't trying to hurt you or your business. But it would appear I have. My father is a ruthless man. And if Calvin isn't behind it, that doesn't mean he doesn't have someone else. I'm—I wish I had told you sooner."

She sat at her desk and showed them the email. She clicked on the source code in an effort to decipher where it had come from.

Graham grabbed her hand to stop her from clicking off the current message. "That son of a bitch. I don't think it's your father who's been creating havoc with our company. It's all been a little too personal. I'm quite sure I know who's responsible, though."

CHAPTER 60

"EVERYTHING IN PLACE?" GRAHAM looked around, making sure the undercover cops were where they were supposed to be.

"Yeah, unfortunately, I couldn't talk Dorothea into not attending. No matter how many times I told her this was a fake wedding, she said she wasn't missing out. Calib graciously gave us use of his hotel even though I warned him it might get damaged. He didn't care." Guy shrugged.

"Do you think Geoff will show up?"

"He seems to want Tarin badly. I don't get it. Since she's been getting threatening texts from the guy she married, it wasn't hard to convince Walters to check into it. He called a buddy in Calgary to lean on Stephen, and he gave up Geoff awfully fast. Not that he knows much about him, just that a man paid him well to keep her inline, keep track of her, keep her from contacting her father. Anyway, he told Geoff that Tarin and her son would be here for your wedding. Listening to the audio, they confirmed that it was definitely Geoff's voice."

"Are we sure he won't try anything?"

"He wants the boy. So I'm quite sure he'll be careful, so he doesn't get hurt."

"Do we have enough men?"

"We kept it small as we didn't want it to leak. Everyone who's here is either undercover or has been trained. This is crazy, but we had to call him out. We have to get him to show his face."

"I agree. I don't like that we've had to include the others."

"Me neither, but there's no other way to get close to him. We have to use Tarin as bait. Don't worry; we'll keep her safe."

Graham didn't respond but looked around at what they'd set up. He certainly hoped this worked. "You know Dorothea is still going to insist you have the big ceremony at her mansion?"

"I know, and if things work out well, Bailey and I will be married today. And then we'll get remarried on the day we were supposed to. It'll be a good day regardless because we'll catch Geoff."

"We have to stop him; he's abused enough people. This plan is our best chance at catching him. He must be livid that you, Bailey and Dorothea are still alive. I'm sure he'll want to handle this himself."

"Let's hope so."

"And let's hope we're prepared."

****

At seven, Graham knocked on the door. Her cell phone buzzed at the same time, but she ignored it as she rushed to open the door. Fluffing her hair with a last flick of her hand, to volumize the messy, sassy style she'd chosen, she opened the adjoining door. Her mouth dropped open when she saw Graham in a tux. It hugged his broad shoulders, following the lines of his long, lean body. She almost felt the need to fan herself. She grew warmer still as she felt his gaze travel the long length of her sleek gown, right down to where the slit in the side left her right leg bare.

Chance ran past her, which jerked her back to the present. He launched himself at Graham, who caught him and swung him high. He giggled.

"All right. I think we need to get going or we'll be late."

He led them out of the room and took the elevator up to the twenty-first floor.

They heard soft, romantic music emanating from Room 2121 even before they reached it. The door was opened ceremoniously by a man in a tux and white gloves. It was awash in flowers—roses, lilies, daisies, carnations. The scents were amazing. Several rows of chairs were arranged. Two men sat on the left, causing Tarin to wonder if they were Guy's brothers or friends. Two other men were standing at the back by the refreshment table.

Dorothea, who looked like nothing would stop her from attending, was sitting in a wheelchair with an oxygen tank, its hose wrapped around her head, the tubes up her nostrils and an IV in her arm. She was very pale. A young, nicely dressed lady sat on her left, attentively checking on her and the equipment.

"Okay, stop fussing. I'm fine. The worst that will happen is I'll die right here," Dorothea's voice was quiet but carried very well in the small banquet room.

Tarin gave the young woman, who'd turned red but was smart enough not to reply, a reassuring smile. She returned it before facing forward again, still slyly ensuring that everything was working fine.

Her grandfather, who was sitting on Dorothea's right, turned and, upon seeing them, gestured for them to join him. Before she made her way to him, she scanned the rest of the room. Bill was seated in the back, as close to the door as possible. He sat so stiffly, his feet flat on the floor, his back so ramrod straight that it didn't even touch the chair. He wore new khaki shirt and pants. She smiled at him, and Chance waved and grinned at him as she walked to the front. Bill gave her a slight nod as she passed. She sat and her grandfather grasped her hand in a reassuring squeeze. She held on to it. A few minutes later, Guy, who was decked out in a white tux, walked in with the minister.

"That's my cue." Graham, who had followed her and paused by her chair, touched her shoulder before taking his place beside Guy at the front of the room. A few minutes later, the doors opened again for Bailey, decked out in a classy Valencienne bridal gown, to enter.

As Tarin watched the beautiful ceremony, she saw them gaze at each other with love and trust. She tried to recall her own wedding and realized she didn't remember much about it. The whole thing was a blur. It was as though she had been in a fog. As she tried to concentrate, bits and pieces started to come back to her. There was no way she had looked at Stephen the way Bailey looked at Guy, nor had he looked back at her with that much loving emotion. Stephen had been too busy rushing to the justice of the peace. At the time, she'd thought it was endearing. Little had she known, she'd just become his prize possession.

He'd whisked her out of City Hall and had taken her back to a hotel room. It was his goal to get her into bed, quickly. She hadn't been able to. He'd been angry and decided that ordering a bottle of wine would help. It had. She'd downed most of it. They'd made love—or rather, they'd had sex; not that she remembered much about it in her inebriated state. But there was something else niggling her brain. Something she wasn't quite able to recall. Stephen had said something. She pressed her hands to her face, digging her fingers into her skull.

It's too bad you're pregnant...

She sat upright so fast, she almost dumped Chance onto the floor. He squealed, thinking it was a great game. She looked horrified as she gave him a toy to quiet him down, as everyone was now staring at them. He'd known. Stephen had known she was expecting, but she hadn't told him until a couple of months after they were married. In fact, she hadn't been sure herself.

The drone of the service was there, but she never heard a thing.

He'd known. Had he been in on it?

Her mind immediately conjured up the hell she'd gone through. A whole week of her life had vanished with only tidbits of memory—voices, whisper of air over her skin, trying to move, feeling odd sensations, her mind knowing something was wrong, her thoughts screaming at her to run, praying it was all a dream, a nightmare and being so scared she wouldn't come out of it alive.

Who's sick enough to do that? Could Stephen have been part of it?

She had to get out of there, and soon.

You may kiss the bride, pulled Tarin back to the present and to the realization of what she had to do. She glanced around to see if anyone had noticed her mental absence. Thankfully, people were already rising to congratulate the happy couple. Graham had taken Chance and was now busy bouncing him on his knee. He was giggling so much she couldn't help but smile.

"Congratulations, you guys. It was beautiful." Tarin kissed Bailey and then Guy on the cheek.

"And will be repeated as soon as we can have it at the estate with all the guests," Dorothea said very firmly. No one would have guessed the woman had just had a heart attack.

Guy rolled his eyes but laughed when Bailey mock-punched him. Guy, Graham and Bailey soon were standing in a huddle in the corner of the room. Whatever they were talking about had them baffled.

"Where is he?"

"I thought for sure he'd show up."

That was all that she managed to hear without knowing who they were referring to. Her new cell phone dinged, which surprised her as she had meant to leave it in her room.

'Come to your room. Bring the boy. Now. Or I'll make sure you and your new friends don't live to see your child grow up. Do anything to alert them, and you're dead.'

Her fingers curled around her phone. How the hell had he gotten her number? Trying to act casual, she looked around. The champagne had been opened, and Graham was handing her a glass. Reluctantly, she accepted it. She waited patiently while a few toasts were given. Being patient right then was difficult. She shifted from foot to foot, glanced at her watch, and gulped her drink as if it were water.

"What's going on?"

Startled, she looked up. Graham was gazing at her.

"I don't do well at weddings." She gave a half-hearted smile. "Actually, these new shoes are pinching my feet. Do you mind watching Chance for a bit? I just want to run down to the room for a minute."

"No. If you're going, so am I."

"I'm fine. Okay. I'll just go to the bathroom down the hall. I'll be right back. Keep Chance safe." She kissed Chance on the cheek, and he gave her a big zerbert in return before snuggling into Graham's arms as he watched her leave. Closing the door behind her, she leaned against it for a moment, wondering when her nightmare was going to end. The soft sounds from the wedding reminded her that she now had a lot to lose. It was no longer only about her and Chance.

After slipping into the bathroom, a flashing light signifying she'd received an email. Stephen must have grown tired of her nonresponse. Even though it was from him, she felt compelled to open it.

'It's time to end this game, Tarin. I know where you are, but so does he.'

Her body involuntarily shuddered. She'd been getting a pretty clear picture of who might be behind her missing week, but she still didn't understand it. She had to get out of there. Tucking her cell into her bra, she opened the door and peeked down the back hallway. Sending one of the men to find her personal supplies seemed to have worked. She made sure it was clear before making her way to the stairwell. Slipping through the door, she made her way down a few flights before taking the elevator. She made her way to her room.

She opened the door, and when she didn't see anyone; she made her way to the closet. Someone cleared their throat. She froze as though whoever was sitting in the chair behind her wouldn't be able to see her.

"At last, we meet, Tarin. Officially, I mean."

She turned slowly. The heavy curtains had been closed, casting the room in darkness. But his gray sideburns stood out in the darkness beneath a fedora. His hands were resting in his lap. He was casually aiming a gun at her.

Her eyes widened. "Who are you?" It had been his picture she'd seen when she'd fainted.

"Oh my dear, I'm hurt that you wouldn't know." He shook his head as though he were talking to a child that had disappointed him.

"Why me?"

"Why not you?" He smiled without warmth. "Let me see. Your father is rather ruthless in his business dealings, but certainly you don't think he's created all that success on his own, do you? Your father is slick. He took a lot from me in a deal, so it seemed quite logical to choose you."

Tarin glared as she let that sink in. She had her father to thank. Again.

"I feel now that I've got my heir, we're almost even. I still have a surprise or two, but nothing you need to worry about."

"Your heir?"

"Why, of course, my dear. Chance is my answer to the future. With him, I'll take back everything."

"You. You're his father."

"Yes."

She struggled to control the anger coursing through her so she could think logically. "But he's two."

"Yes. And it's time I started grooming him. You've done a decent enough job, although I question some of your decisions. Stephen was trying to look out for you, keep you safe."

"You were paying him?"

"That wouldn't be right, would it? But then, when have I ever done what's right? Let's say he was my insurance for the future. Obviously, I chose poorly in that area. So I guess we both picked the wrong man."

Tarin wanted to punch him until he bled but knew if she was going to get out of this alive, she had to keep a level head.

"Do you mind if I sit? My shoes are killing me." She edged to the side of the bed, well aware of the gun pointed at her heart. Gingerly, she sat and eased her feet partway out of her shoes. While she was making a big production of that, she reached into her bra where she'd tucked her cell phone and pressed the button on the side to record, hoping the audio would be decent. "Oooohhh, thank you."

"You do look lovely. That was also one reason why I chose you. I mean, I could have had my pick of women, just as your father did."

"How do you know so much about me?"

"Didn't I mention your father and I go way back? I found the woman who became your mother. Well, I guess I should say, gave birth to you. She didn't stick around after she got paid. And of course you were instrumental to me in conceiving my son."

She couldn't even go there; it made her so nauseated. "You sent me an email saying you knew my mother. I suppose you put Stephen up to it as well?"

"I needed to get your attention, and I needed to find you. You did very well in hiding yourself. Congratulations on that. I do admire someone who thinks outside the box."

Tarin didn't know how to respond. He was chatting with her as if they were talking about the weather.

He stood. "It's time I handled this situation. The idiots I've had to hire have almost set back all my life plans. But no more, I'll make sure things are done right. Get up."

She was so riveted by his demented plan, she couldn't move. With more force than she'd have expected from someone his age, he grabbed her arm and yanked her to her feet. She stumbled over her shoes, falling to her knees. It had pulled him off balance. Using that momentum, she dropped flat onto the floor before rolling away, only to come to her feet just as fast and race to the door. Her fingers scraped over the doorknob as an ear-piercing bang sounded simultaneously to something whizzing past her ear. She flattened herself against the wall.

"Damn you. You'll pay for that. Where's my son?"

She shuddered, hating the reference. "He's at my friend Bobbie's. I'm sure with all you know about me, you know about her. We have to go to her house." She stepped forward and brushed her hands down the silk dress, now horribly wrinkled. If she acted normal, maybe she had a chance. If there was one thing, she'd make sure of, it was that he'd never get near her son.

Since he didn't say anything and wasn't doing anything to stop her, she opened the door. When she turned left, he jammed the gun into her ribs.

"Good try. We're going in the opposite direction. I'm sure the wedding party has to be wondering where you are. And I'm sure Chance, it is Chance? Not sure I like the name you chose for my boy but then again, I can always change it. Anyway, I'm sure he's waiting for you with the others. Besides, I haven't seen all of those invited for a long time. I can't believe they didn't invite me. Rather rude not to have family there, isn't it? And it's probably driving them a little crazy that I didn't crash their party like they were expecting."

The whole time he was talking, he was prodding her to walk to the service elevators. He shoved her inside. "The twenty-first floor. You know this worked out so much better than I'd planned. I was just in your room, checking to make sure I hadn't missed anything. I don't like surprises. And besides, I just planned on taking my son, well, not before I made sure the others got what they deserved, of course."

"You'll never get my child, at least not while I'm alive."

"Don't make any promises I can keep."

"You. It was you who had someone shoot the arrow at me."

"Actually, it was supposed to kill the woman you met with. You were getting a little too close. And I couldn't have you learning all my secrets and then going to the police, could I?" He smiled at her.

Her world came crashing in on her as she saw what insanity looked like.

CHAPTER 61

"WHERE'S TARIN?"

"She said she was just running to the bathroom. We have guys everywhere, right?"

"Yeah, but we're talking about Geoff."

"Dammit!" Graham ran for the door and yanked it open. "Johnson, where's Tarin?"

"She went in there." He pointed to the women's bathroom.

Graham burst past him, pissed enough to punch him. He raced through the empty bathroom and into a second hallway.

"Where's Cooper?"

The young man turned tomato red. "Ms. Roth asked him to buy her a feminine product."

Graham was about to yell when he saw the staff elevator at the far end of the hall open. A glimpse of a sparkling blue dress was all he needed to see to know it was Tarin. He wasn't sure who the black suit next to her belonged to, but no doubt it wouldn't be good.

Geoff. Shit!

He shoved Johnson, despite his protest, back into the women's bathroom and waited several seconds until he heard her pass by and then eased open the door. He hustled across the bathroom and out the other side. There was no way he could make it into the ballroom without being seen. But it didn't matter; Geoff had already made his grand entrance.

"Hello, Bailey."

The noise in the room vanished faster than the speed of light. Graham could only imagine what was happening. Tarin was standing slightly in front of Geoff.

Graham sneaked back through the restroom and into the hallway, leaving Johnson at the other door. If he came at Geoff from behind, he had a chance that he wouldn't see him until it was too late.

"Bring me the boy."

"Geoff. What are you doing?"

"Uhhhh, Dorothea. I see I still haven't succeeded in making you die. Natural causes would have been so much more... dignified for you. I tried so hard to make that happen. But I see you still won't, you know, die. That option is now out. But you won't have to worry about it much longer."

"Why, Geoff? What the hell are you doing?"

"You mean besides destroying Caspian Winery?"

"You were behind all the sabotage. The vinegar—"

"Oh my, that was brilliant, wasn't it? You know Tom was easy to convince that if he helped me, I'd put him in charge. Like that would ever happen. And you all thought it might be Oliver. It was such a good plan. Tom hasn't wanted to be disloyal, but money will buy anything."

Graham wanted to punch him for the angry, hurt flush that filled Dorothea's face.

"The hijacked trucks?"

"I orchestrated that. Brilliant, wasn't it? The vinegar wine, oh, I wish I could have seen your face, dear sister, when they brought you that news. I guess it wasn't quite as devastating as I'd hoped because I was planning for your ultimate demise." He looked at her oxygen tank. "I guess not all was a loss; I managed to at least start your downhill spiral."

"Oh, Geoffrey."

The tears in her voice and the weakness alarmed Graham more than anything else. Geoff just might succeed in killing her without lifting a finger.

"Don't move, Guy. Bailey. Your henchmen. Not only can I take out one of you, but I can take out Tarin too. Maybe her young son? Back up. Send the child to his mother. He's mine."

"What have you done, Geoffrey?"

"I started my family, Dorothea. I know how important that is to you. Well, now I have mine—several girls and another boy—all are pretty much useless. This child is the only one I want. He's my heir. I will train him to be so brilliant and so powerful."

"No!" Tarin jerked her arm out of his grasp, only to grunt in pain as he jammed the gun into her back before she could even take a step.

Graham knew he was running out of time, but he also couldn't run the risk of alerting Geoff to his presence. Just then, he caught sight of Johnson, who'd made it across the other hallway and was standing right outside the doorway. Graham motioned for him to wait until he gave the order.

Geoff was continuing, "Oh, Dorothea, you always tried to be the mother I never had. Always tried to make up for the humiliation. Well actually, your real mother, my stepmom, and dear old dad, who couldn't keep his zipper zipped, just stood by. We had so much fun, didn't we? The whippings, the beatings, all the things that let a boy know he just wasn't good enough."

Dorothea was openly sobbing. A woman Graham hadn't noticed earlier stepped in front of Dorothea.

"Ah, Laura-Jane. Nice to see you again."

"You."

"Get out of the way; Dorothea gets to be first. Don't worry; you're going to get yours as well, for not doing as I asked."

"You're a sick man. I won't be part of your depraved world."

"And you won't be, and once I've done away with you, your child will be next."

"Nooooo."

"Enough, Geoff."

"Shut up, Bailey. You're still on my list too. And I don't mean Christmas list, either."

"You tried to blow us up!" Tarin cried.

"Slight miscalculation; you weren't supposed to be there. Thankfully, you were able to get out. But to be fair, I don't care about you but my son, that would have been unforgivable. That man who made that mistake is no longer in my employment."

"Meaning he's dead," Guy stated.

He shrugged and turned to Dorothea. "This will be the last breath you take."

His hand came up fast as Graham leapt forward at the precise moment as Tarin grabbed Geoff's arm. The gun fired; the roar was deafening. Then everything seemed to morph into slow motion. One of the officers had also jumped onto Geoff and was already taking him down with Graham. They all collapsed in a pile on the floor. Graham was dazed and winded, but he scrambled up to find blood splattered everywhere. His eyes scanned the others: Bailey, Guy, Dorothea—Tarin wasn't moving.

CHAPTER 62

TARIN KNEW SHE SHOULD move, but for once she felt safe and free. She shifted slightly in Graham's lap, his arms immediately tightening around her. She only hoped he'd still want to do that once he knew everything about her. It was one of the reasons she didn't want to get up; she didn't want to face that reality yet. When she'd first opened her eyes, she'd found herself held gently in his arms while he was sitting on the floor with his back to the wall. Her first thought had been of Chance. It hadn't taken long to find him. He was being held and rocked by Bill, laughing and giggling. Geoff had come to taking everything from her.

A moan escaped her lips as she shifted trying to get more comfortable. There was no question she was going to be black and blue from the dog pile that had happened when Bill and Graham had tackled Geoff. Thanks to Geoff's hard grip on her, she'd ended up somewhere on the bottom.

"You okay?" Graham's gentle concern and the warmth of his breath whispered across her cheek and straight to her heart.

"A bit of a headache and bumps and bruises. But I'm fine," she whispered, not wanting to break the warm, safe cocoon she was enveloped in.

"Hey guys. Everyone okay?"

Tarin lifted her head to look at Guy and Bailey, who had their arms around each other.

"Yeah. I don't think it's quite the wedding you'd planned, but it sure had a big bang—and the ending we wanted. Well, mostly, anyway." Graham smiled tiredly.

"A little more than we had wanted or hoped for, but we're married. And that son of a bitch is dead." Bailey gave Guy a deep kiss.

"Dorothea, I think you should go to the hospital."

"I'm fine, LJ, but thank you. I'd like you to meet my family." Dorothea introduced her new assistant to everyone.

"And since I know what you do for a living," LJ looked directly at Guy and Graham. "I know you're aware of my life prior to this job. Yes, I ran an escort service. And yes, I was interested in Caspian Winery for purely selfish reasons. I met with Dorothea a few weeks ago and shared my story with her. She knows everything, and she had me thoroughly vetted. You can as well, but I promise you, I'm not here to destroy her. Geoff had wanted me to do that, but I couldn't. I never thought he would want me to do something so sick."

She looked each and every one of them in the eye, but when she got to Tarin, she watched her carefully before walking toward her. Tarin pushed herself to her feet.

"I have so much to share with you, but I don't know where to start. I'm the one who's been sending you emails about finding my daughter."

"Did you?"

LJ took her hand. "Yes. And I'm slowly building a relationship with her."

"There's more. I think I went through what you did. Geoff, I think, is the father of my daughter. I never slept with him, but he had me drugged and artificially inseminated. I'm assuming it was the doctor who helped him that left me with the piece of paper with just a logo on it. It led me to Caspian, but I hadn't heard from anyone, and I wanted my life to go back to normal. Which it was for a long time. I thought the whole thing was some sick bastard who got off on drugging me and having his way with me for a few days. Especially since I couldn't identify him. When I found out I was pregnant, I almost had an abortion, but I couldn't. But I wasn't mother material either. I gave her up for adoption. But when Geoff threatened that he'd hurt her if I didn't do some damage to Caspian Winery, I had to do something. He watched everything I did. He knew every move I made. That's why I contacted Dorothea."

Tarin gasped. She'd been right. There was someone else who'd gone through what she had. "Do you know whether there were any more?"

LJ shook her head. "I think I found the doctor who might have helped Geoff, but he died in a freak accident. But I'm betting he kept some records."

"I had a piece of paper stuck to my back as well. He obviously was trying to do something to stop Geoff by giving us a clue. He also gave me a code; I've seen it on bills from Caspian. Maybe there's a paper trail." Tarin looked at Graham to gauge his reaction. He was watching her with a question in his eyes. Not feeling able to answer them just yet, she turned away. The ringing in her head, thanks to the gun that went off right next to it, intensified. She pressed her fingers to her temple as she watched Bill entertain Chance in the corner. She couldn't believe how much she owed that man. Not only did he treat Chance like a precious child, but he'd saved them all. The minute Geoff had raised the gun, he'd charged. She shuddered to think what would have happened if he hadn't been brave enough to make that move. Thankfully, this was over, and Geoff had been the only one shot.

It was Dorothea, though, who answered. "When you were cuddling Chance the day of the explosion, I knew he was Geoff's. I used to hold him like that when he was a baby. There is no question he's my nephew. I'm truly sorry for what my brother put you through, but I'm so very grateful for the beautiful boy you're raising."

Tarin simply nodded; she didn't know what to do. She couldn't look away from Graham, but she couldn't read his face either. There was no question he was stunned and hurt, but she didn't know if it meant he didn't want to hear her version.

At that point, the police returned to the room they'd all been ushered into after the shooting. They'd all been questioned. One officer called Graham and Guy to go outside into the hallway with him. They all seemed to know each other. It was twenty minutes before they came back and another half hour before they were all allowed to leave—but only after they'd confirmed where they could be reached. Everyone went their own way. Tarin, Graham and Chance, who was sleeping in his arms, made their way back down to their hotel room. They hadn't talked since Dorothea had shared her news.

Graham laid Chance down. While he was busy, she remembered her cell phone and pulled it out of her dress, unsure what shape it would be in. She clicked off the recorder. It was almost dead. She looked up just as Graham turned to face her. He caught and held her gaze.

"I want to find out if there are any other women whose children were fathered by Geoff. There might have some I've connected with on my site. I may need your help." She pursed her lips as she handed him her phone. "This has some information the police would want about Geoffrey."

Graham slipped it into his pocket. "I'll pass it on to Walters. Tomorrow." He remained still, with his hands in his pockets.

"I'm sorry. I should have told you, but I didn't know how. How do I say, by the way, I don't know who the father of my son is? Makes me sound like a bit of a loose woman, right? I had to find some answers first."

"So your interest in the job was because of the ties to Caspian Winery?"

She nodded.

"Hacking my computer, same thing?"

Again, she moved her head in acknowledgement. "Umm, I did something else you won't be happy about. I hacked into Caspian Winery and took some information off Oliver's computer. You were talking about him and said you couldn't find any files. I may have what you're looking for. It's pretty damning." She told him briefly what she'd found.

"That's classic Geoff. He probably had someone Photoshop Oliver's face onto them. He's that sick. It appears Tom might have been helping Geoff, but we're not sure of his motive. Money, maybe. His mom's in a very expensive nursing home. The police will have to sort that out."

She sat down wearily on the bed. "I truly am sorry."

Graham's lack of response was enough to compel her to look at him. He was staring at her bare legs, where her skirt had risen without her knowledge. She quickly stood.

"We're going to have to track down all those women and the kids that are Ge—that man's. I tried to find who might have helped him. LJ says she tracked the doctor, and he's dead, but maybe the code meant that Geoff was paying through Caspian?"

"It's possible. We'll look into it. Dorothea has already commissioned us to find everyone that pretty much has ever come into contact with Geoff. Every child that might be his. She wants to make sure all of them are all taken care of. That son of a bitch damn near killed her this time."

"He's sicker than anyone I've ever met, and he's destroyed so many lives."

"I know. Hopefully, we can help repair some of them." He smiled tenderly at her. "I have to tell you; I know about your internet group for abused women."

"I know, Janice. Cute name, by the way."

He walked toward her until he stood a foot away. "How'd you find out?"

"I check out everyone who joins or asks to join the inner circle. Do you think you're the first guy who's tried it?"

"Sorry. I was just—"

"I know. Making sure I was on the up and up. Don't worry; I'd have done the same thing."

"I couldn't get into much."

"Well, not through your name, but when you hacked mine, you could."

"Uh—"

"Yeah. I'm that good too."

"Well, it's better than Tari Lynn. Cute alias, by the way." She smiled and shrugged her shoulders.

He grinned. "Damn, this is gonna be fun."

"Is it?" She stared at him long and hard, trying to determine if he had forgiven her for all she hadn't shared with him.

He gently pulled her into his arms and lowered his lips to hers. She leaned into him and pressed her mouth firmly against his, while her arms looped around his neck. She smiled, but it soon turned into a frown when she thought about all she hadn't told him. "Uh, I haven't told you about my—well, everything."

"We have time."

"I know, but there have been so many secrets, so many things I've kept from you. My father's not a good man. Although he's not quite in the same category as Geoff, he's done his share of ruining lives as well. I have a half-sister I never knew about. My mother was a prostitute, if Cal is to be believed. So you can see," she added sardonically, "I come from fine stock. Stephen—"

He kissed her long and deeply. "—is an idiot who didn't know how to savor what he had. I'm not like him, but—"

"I didn't think that for a minute. He's—"

"Going to jail for a long time."

"What?"

"It appears he was selling secrets to rival oil companies. His father isn't too happy with him."

"Stephen's plenty of things, but I don't think he'd—"

"He probably didn't. Anyone who crosses Geoff, pays. So do you want to rescue him or let him pay for all of his other illegal and immoral activities?"

His raised eyebrows and expectant look let her know that her future clearly rested on her answer. She may not have been the perfect daughter or the perfect wife, but she wasn't an idiot. The man standing in front of her was far better than anyone she'd ever had in her life.

"He's not my problem. I just want my marriage over. Maybe he and Cal can share a cell together." She told Graham about the ten-thousand-dollar dress she'd left for Stephen tacked to the bed.

He whistled long and slow. "Hmm. Remind me never to piss you off."

"I want to help the women I've connected with. They've been through some awful things and may have no one else to turn to."

"Any ideas?"

"Some."

"K. We'll figure out something."

"Thank you. I am sorry about my father, about Stephen, about Cal, about—"

"Stop apologizing for them."

She jerked away. "Yeah, but—"

"It's a waste of your time and energy. They aren't your fault." He pulled her to him. "I guess we'll have to find something better for you to do, with all that pent-up anger. Any ideas?"

Tarin laughed. For the first time, she wasn't worried about her future because she'd found one of the good ones.

****

THANK YOU

Thank you for reading **Deceitful Truths.**
I hope you enjoyed it as much as I enjoyed writing it.
If you'd like to share your thoughts, a short online review is always appreciated.

~~~~

Continue reading for an excerpt from book 3,
Split Seconds

The twins are reuniting but thirty years of lies are unravelling. And someone will kill to keep the truth buried.

SPLIT SECONDS

Book Three
The Caspian Wine Series

———————◄○►———————

Excerpt

Walking across the street, she strolled a few blocks before cutting across to a park. She needed grass and the outdoors. Leaning against a tree, she pulled out her phone and dialed her mom. She needed to talk to the one person who could always ground her.

"Tijan. Where are you? I've been worried sick. Are you okay?"

Tijan took a deep breath, feeling a lot of the stress and pressure ease. "Hi, Mom. I'm fine. I sure miss you. The big city isn't like anything I've ever experienced before."

"You're still in Toronto, right?"

There was almost the sound of hope that she wasn't. If only her mom knew what was going on. Tijan tensed. "Uh. I'm kind of switching. I mean exploring. I'm currently in Montreal." She winced as the lie rolled off her tongue. The last time she'd fibbed to her mom, she'd been thirteen and had wanted to wear a certain short dress to the school dance. Her mom had said no, so she'd snuck it out.

That had been the last time she'd worn a dress. Kyle, her boy-crush, had laughed at her. It had all backfired.

She just hoped this wouldn't. Then she realized this whole trip was a lie.

"Oh. Tell me about some of the places you've been. Who have you met? Did you go to Niagara Falls? They're amazing. But it is a very touristy place. I bet it's crazy there."

Feeling deflated and not really chatty and having totally killed the good feeling she'd had from hearing her mom's voice, she looked around. What was she supposed to say?

'I met a man who's my father that you told me was dead. I found my sister that you told me was dead but I know you kept hope that she wasn't. But how did that come about? How come she wasn't in my life? What the hell, Mom.'

"Tijan?"

"Sorry, Mom. I just wanted to call and let you know I'm okay. I'll send an email soon. And tell you all about it. I've been putting in some long days. I'm exhausted."

"Oh, that's good to hear. I hope you've seen a lot and met a lot of people?"

"Yeah. I have. I really have to go."

"Is there anything you want to tell me, Tijan? I get a sense that things aren't good."

Tijan closed her eyes. At any other time, that would have been a welcome thing to hear. In fact, in the past they'd have stayed up late talking. Her mom really was her best friend. But right now, her best friend had a lot of questions to answer and Tijan didn't know quite how to ask them.

"I'm good, Mom. We'll talk soon. I miss you. Love you."

"Love you too. Don't ever forget that."

Tijan hung up as tears pricked her eyes. She clutched her phone in her hand, wondering again how life had gotten so crazy.

Kicking off her shoes, she walked barefoot, loving the bright green grass under her feet. For a few minutes, she let herself enjoy the beauty of it. But it didn't take long for the noise and general hum of city racket to infiltrate her senses and destroy any peace she'd been feeling.

The whole purpose for the walk had been to get rid of stress but that, too, had backfired.

Her phone rang. Glancing at the one in her hand, she frowned before remembering that she carried two phones. She pulled the one Tarin had given her out of her pocket.

"Hi, Tarin."

"Are you alright, Tijan? You sound down."

Tijan shrugged her shoulders a few times to ease the tension. "Yeah, just a bit overwhelmed."

"You don't have to stay. We can figure something else out."

"That would mean you'd have to come out of hiding and that might put you and Chance at risk. I'll survive. I am making a serious mess of everything. And I don't know that I've done one single, solitary thing for the business but it has been an eye-opener."

"Yeah, sorry for the crash course in being a shark. Anyway, the reason I called, wait... do you have a minute?"

"Yeah. I'm at the park, so we should be fine. No ears to hear me." She looked around to make sure.

"Great. Okay, we looked into all of the employees. There are a few who have had some interesting pasts, including several who lied on their applications. But the most interesting is what we found out about Chris Simmons."

"JT?"

"Yeah. He was an orphan who got adopted at the age of five. Interestingly, though, there are no records of who his parents are. Nothing."

"That's weird, right? How can there not be any record of that?"

"Someone obviously destroyed it. He does have papers mentioning his adoption, his name and a date of birth but no other information—at least not that we can find."

"Okay, this may sound odd. But are you guys any good?"

Tarin laughed. "Very. I'm quite good at hacking a lot of websites but Guy and Graham not only surpass me, but they also have some crazy mad skills when it comes to the Internet and cybersecurity. They also have some really good connections."

"So essentially, you hack for a living?" Tijan was sure that wasn't meant to be a good thing.

"I guess that's one way of putting it. We try to figure out what the bad hackers are doing so we can stop them. Really, the main focus of Knight's Associates is stopping cybercrime. Initially, it was finding the bad guys by following their digital footprint. Now the company has evolved into a major contender in preventing hackers from accessing personal data in big companies and the government."

"Someday, we really need to sit down and talk about that. I'm fascinated. For me, turning on the computer is an accomplishment. Hey, I'm getting a text. Hang on." Tijan looked at the message. "Well, it would appear that JT wants to meet with me. And Mary has texted me four times. I guess sneaking out on this job isn't a good thing."

"Be careful, Tijan."

Continue reading in **Split Seconds.**

Her twin didn't die. She was taken. Now they're switching places to take down the man who tore them apart, their very wealthy father.

ACKNOWLEDGEMENTS

TO MARY AT NORTHERN Computers for answering all my questions about computers. Any misinformation or errors are mine. To Shawn McCormick at UncorkOntario.com. Thank you for all the information to do with wines, wineries and specifically Ontario wines. Any misinformation or errors are mine.

To my sisters - my best friends and the strength I lean on. I am forever grateful for you.

To my critique group, thank you, I couldn't do this without your invaluable feedback.

To my family, your love and belief is what keeps me going. :)

To my readers - for your endless support, your honesty, your encouragement but most of all for your love of reading, is what keeps me going.

ABOUT THE AUTHOR

Whether her thrillers are set in a real town, city, countryside, or one pulled straight from her imagination, **Best-Selling and Award-Winning Author Maggie Thom** writes engaging suspense that dives deep into a family's lies, ties, and deceit. Her stories are rollercoasters, featuring strong women who know what's right but must navigate a maze of twists, turns, and dangerous secrets to get there.

Maggie believes in happily-ever-after, but she'll take you on one unforgettable adventure before you reach it.

Buckle up, you're in for quite a ride.

Growing up in a house full of books, Maggie made weekly trips to the library and often disappeared into stories when the weather was too cold to play outside. She started experimenting with writing at a young age, letting her imagination carry her away on countless adventures. As an adult, she's had just as many real ones: white-water rafting, sky diving, travelling, mountain hiking, kayaking (lakes, rivers, and ocean) and more.

Now, she writes so *you* can go on thrilling adventures too.

Become a member of Maggie's Readers' Group and get a free suspense thriller.

Her motto: *Read to escape... Escape to read.*
Take the adventure and enjoy the rollercoaster ride.

"Maggie Thom ... proves her strength as a master of words, plots and finely chiseled characters ... she weaves a brilliant cloth of the many colors of deceit." Dii – Tome Tender

Maggie

www.maggiethom.com

Connect with Maggie: Facebook / Goodreads / Bookbub / Pinterest / Amazon

Email: maggie@maggiethom.com

Books by Maggie Thom

The Caspian Wine Series

Captured Lies | Deceitful Truths | Split Seconds

The Twisted Deception Series *(read in order)*

Fostered Identity | Shadowed Footsteps | Exploited Innocence | Lost Tears | Last Betrayal

The Prairie Crime Thriller Series

Poisoned Promises | Toxic Attention | Collision Course | Breaking Free (TBA) | Shattered Dreams (TBA)

The Family Heir Looms Series

Concealed Inheritance | Saving Her | Unwavering Greed | Defying Death (TBA)

The Overton Files

Tainted Waters | Broken Trust (TBA) | Buried Sins (TBA)

Standalone Thrillers

Deadly Ties | Fractured Lines | Blurred Lines *(free at maggiethom.com)*

Join Maggie Thom's Reader's Group

Receive a **free exclusive suspense-thriller eBook**. Visit: **maggiethom.com**

Connect with Maggie

Facebook | Goodreads | BookBub | Pinterest | Amazon

maggiethom.com

www.ingramcontent.com/pod-product-compliance
Lightning Source LLC
Chambersburg PA
CBHW030656120726
47905CB00001B/239